MW01716311

Contrary to popular belief, I couldn't dodge a bullet, let alone the yard-wide beam of energy that lanced out from the other turret, no matter how fast my reflexes or keen my perception, both jacked to the human limit and maybe beyond.

I could read where a thug was aiming and get out of the way, same with the sweep of a turret barrel, but once the shot started, I was no different from anyone else.

The beam hit me dead center of mass, engulfing most of my upper body. What didn't hit me blasted past to make a light show across the Atlanta skyline.

If that weapon had been any kind of real, I'd have died instantly, but that turret was Pushtech. The energy was mostly phantasmal to me, no more intense than a heavy-duty flashlight.

Maybe it was because Pushtech had another degree of separation from the Whiteout than the Pushed themselves, but it honestly hurt even less than a Push Crook's blast.

As the beam ended, I blinked out the spots in my eyes, the skin on my face tingling as if I'd spent a smidge too long in the sun.

With my vision clear, I narrowed my gaze at the other turret operator. Understandably, he was gaping at me and my continued existence, and when I started marching across the roof of the train, panic flashed in his eyes.

Batman was right. Criminals really were a cowardly lot.

Also by J.B. Garner
From Ginger Blue Publishing

The Push Chronicles

Indomitable
Book One of the Push Chronicles

Infamous
Book Three of the Push Chronicles
coming April 2026

A Figment of My Imagination
Book One of the Carnivale Convenience Store Capers
coming September 2025

Injustice

Book Two of the Push Chronicles

J.B. Garner

GINGER BLUE

Injustice
Book Two of the Push Chronicles
Published by Ginger Blue Publishing

Editors: Lisa Dovichi, Jeanne Cook, Chrysta Stuckless
Cover Artist: Lisa Dovichi
Interior Design: Ginger Blue Publishing

ISBN: 979-8-88787-049-6

J.B. Garner
https://www.jbgarnerwrites.com/

Dedication

To Sam, whose love of superheroes matches my own.

Chapter 1

"I know you don't want to talk about it, Indy," Extinguisher began, his deep voice heavy with the same frustration I felt about the issue he was about to bring up. "But you can't keep putting this off. We need to talk about you and me."

For most normal people, there were only a few good places to have a serious relationship discussion. At the very least, it should be handled in private. The bedroom or on the couch, warm lighting, that would be preferable, at least in my mind.

Of course, we weren't normal people, and this wasn't a normal world, not any longer.

I was Dr. Irene Roman, former physiologist, now "Nationally Famous Superhero" Indomitable, considered by many to be the superheroic savior of the United States.

He was Extinguisher, real name unknown to me, former firefighter and current ice-flinging superhero, esteemed leader of the U.S.'s - perhaps the world's - first team of Push Heroes, the Atlanta Five.

And the world was changed by the Whiteout into the comic book reality of the Pushed - superheroes and villains made flesh.

"Can we do this literally anywhere or anywhen else, Ex?" I asked, trying to ignore the throbbing ache in my left shoulder. It was a reminder from a Push Battle earlier today, an impacted shoulder that had healed up to usable this evening. "The train we're here for is supposed to arrive literally any minute now."

Even Extinguisher, with his Whiteout-altered outlook, had to see that the top of a graffiti-marked wall overlooking

Hulsey Yard, one of the major train depots in Atlanta, was not the right place, especially with the trainyard lights making it as bright as if it was high noon.

Any more than "five minutes before busting a Pushtech arms deal" was not the right when.

The only positives to the locale were the faint breeze blowing through the crisp October air and the waxing moon casting a shimmer through the city's light pollution. It certainly wasn't the heavy smell of diesel fumes and burnt oil that wafted up from the train yard.

So, as much as we had feelings for each other and as much as I was hoping he'd spend the night in my bed at the Brooks-Choi Foundation, we were *not* having this conversation right now.

I glanced over at him idling on his physics-defying ice platform, which hovered just a few inches above the fence, and he shook his head, a faint smile on his square-jawed, damnably handsome face.

"How are you the by-the-books one tonight when that's my job? Besides, it's not like the crooks we're here to stop could challenge you, even if I wasn't here. You've literally gone toe-to-toe with the most powerful Push Hero *and* Push Crook in the world. A few ray guns or plasma cannons aren't going to stop you."

The frosty firefighter was both absolutely right and scarily wrong. I'd tangled with both Epic, my ex-boyfriend and progenitor of the Whiteout, and Reaper, more a victim in this than anything else. But I'd barely survived the experiences during the Battle of Washington.

Besides, it wasn't the Pushtech I was worried about – it was the conventional firepower the criminals might be packing.

Maybe it wasn't so bad for my Pushed colleagues with their reality-bending, superhuman abilities, but for me, whose only advantage was unrelenting stubbornness and a talent for ignoring the unreality that pervaded our world, it was a deadly risk.

My uniform might have upgraded protection these days, but even the best non-Pushtech armor was only bullet-resistant, not bulletproof.

"Look, when we started this whole thing between us, we agreed that it might always stay casual. Friends with benefits. I have needs, and so do you."

A cramp in my all-too-human calves forced me to shift on my fence perch, so I tried to turn it to my advantage with my best languid, seductive stretch. That usually did a good job at distracting Extinguisher from this line of questioning.

"Let's just focus on the moment, sugar," I said softly. "We'll talk tonight, I promise. But for now –"

"Lives are at stake." He'd picked up a scarily accurate habit of being able to finish my sentences for me in the past three months. At first it was cute, then it became a little tired, and now it was usually aggravating. "Right. Always the mission. I swear you use that as a convenient excuse these days, and I don't appreciate it."

I was about to fire back with a pinpoint retort of some kind when the distant roar of a train engine snapped us to attention. It was followed by the growing clackety-clack of the rails.

No matter the bit of friction between Extinguisher and me, when it came to our job – saving lives – we were deadly serious and utterly professional. The lovers' spat fell away immediately and, behind our masks, we had our game faces on.

The front lamps of a train not on the usual schedule shone in the distance as Extinguisher lowered his ice ramp down behind one of the parked boxcars.

As for myself, I relied on a few other benefits from the altered rules of the world as I leaped down the twenty-plus feet to the yard floor.

The physical constants of the universe had changed, and the limits of many human bodies along with it. But I also had something else, something only I and maybe one other had.

I let my mind and body slip into that gift, a harmonious state of focus that unlocked my full human potential.

It was the only side-effect of being a Natural – the term we coined for this rare state of being – that I enjoyed, even if the euphoria and calm it granted were temporary things, limited by my willpower and my endurance.

And all that athletic prowess, strength, and agility made a controlled fall that would break most normal people's bones into a simple task. As I hit the gravel, I broke my fall with a forward roll and came up neatly to my feet, back against the boxcar Extinguisher hovered behind.

With a quick mutual glance and nod, we followed our usual plan. Splitting apart, we moved to opposite sides of the boxcar to take a peek at the incoming train. I poked my head out and tapped the communicator in my ear to turn it on.

"Ah, there you two are," Rachel Choi, former FBI agent, now co-head of the Brooks-Choi Foundation and my esteemed sponsor, said crisply. "I take it the train's coming in now."

"You've got it," I whispered, knowing the sensitive mics would pick it up. "It's slowing now."

The screech of brakes heralded the train's arrival. The moment I got a clear look at the thing, it was obvious it wasn't your typical behind-schedule freight train. If the fact it was only three cars wasn't enough to raise suspicions. The fact that the cargo car was pure Pushtech was.

To 99% of the population, it was a massive, heavily reinforced boxcar. Just barely able to fit into normal rail tunnels, it was all some silvery space-age metal, rounded corners capped with extra plating and blast doors that would make Fort Knox feel inadequate.

Probably the biggest problem was the dome turrets replete with, well, some kind of crazy energy weapon. These gun smugglers were not taking any chances to protect their cargo, and honestly, outside of the most powerful Pushed, nothing was getting in there.

But I broke the rules of the Whiteout. While Pushed "super scientists" invented and built Pushtech, it was nothing more than random parts and junk cobbled together to me. So Pushtech didn't work for me at all, but it also wasn't "real" to me, with no more properties than the actual materials under the phantasmal shell.

And what was under the cargo car's shell was a rickety, rusty boxcar that had seen far better days, with random scrap welded and riveted on to it.

The "turrets" were cheap plastic domes with coils and rods arranged in a gun-like shape, each containing a gunner in a surprisingly nice-looking suit.

The side doors shook so badly in their frames, they only stayed on by the layer of unreality over it.

"Heavy duty Pushtech defenses," I noted over the comms. To my left, Extinguisher was peering at the last car as the train hit a full stop.

"Lights on in the caboose and moving shapes," he reported. "Our criminals waiting to be busted."

"Do you two need back-up?" Choi asked. "While we have many irons in the fire, I could pull Medusa and Hexagon in."

Normally, she wouldn't even ask. While the big Pushtech car was a small surprise, Extinguisher wasn't wrong when he said we could tackle it. Maybe Choi was astute enough to pick up little hints as to what he and I'd been up to and the tension it had caused, but we'd been very careful to keep our indiscretions discrete.

But whether we took her offer wasn't technically my call.

"What do think, Ex?" He *was* the leader, after all, no matter what most people thought.

"We're good, Rachel. Let them rest after that Valdosta investigation. Indy and I have this."

I glanced sidelong at him as the doors to the caboose car started to open. "Our usual play?"

He caught that glance and a bit of the spark we had when we first hooked up danced in his eyes. "Nothing wrong with the classics."

I couldn't help but smile as I broke cover from my end of the car, while Extinguisher surged out from his side on his ice slide.

For all the pain of struggling to try to fix the Whiteout, all the terrible responsibility I felt for the suffering and death that followed its wake, I always delighted in the surge of endorphins and adrenaline that came when I fell into focus. When time seemed to slow, my body and mind sang in harmony, and I felt fearless and invincible.

The turrets atop the cargo car swiveled sedately towards me, while a half dozen well-dressed goons started to draw weapons from their coats with all the grace of shaved apes, their eyes locked on Extinguisher.

"Freeze!" he shouted as blue-white energy collected in his hands. "Or I'll make you!"

I suppressed a groan at the weak joke, but I'd expected it. That was the nature of the comic book reality that had taken over our world. Ignoring that aside, and the twist in my gut at the growing unreality of the Pushtech, I turned my sprint into a tremendous leap.

In the early days after the Whiteout, this much Pushed stuff in one place would have me ready to curl up and vomit, but I'd gotten quite used to it. So used to it that I barely felt a twinge in my gut as I launched myself up through the air, touching down on the cab roof to the right of the closest turret.

My body weight was enough to make my boots sink through the phantasmal Pushtech shell. Not that the gunner noticed because he was staring up at me in shock. My speed had taken him completely by surprise, and I could see him desperately hit ghostly controls to reorient his aim.

If I'd been, say, Hexagon, our friendly six-armed powerhouse, I'd have taken the time to let out a quick quip or pithy saying before wrecking the turret.

But I wasn't him, or any of my Push Hero friends, so I just hauled off and punched.

After six months of constant Push Battles and general heroic work, I'd gotten down the perfect rhythm of a slow approach towards something "invulnerable" by letting my fist slip through the gelatinous outer skin, then throwing all my considerable focused strength behind it.

No more backlash, broken knuckles, and sprained muscles as my punch tore right through unreal metal and smashed the cheap plastic dome behind it, to land right across the turret goon's chin.

His head snapped back from the blow, his eyes rolled up in his head, and he went slack in his chair's harness. One down, one to go on my end.

Down below, a cacophony of gunfire erupted, followed by the distinct sounds of bullets hitting and chipping away at ice.

As expected, Extinguisher was having no trouble with his normal crooks. I'd just take out this last turret, then surprise any stragglers.

Rational Irene noted how much I'd changed over these past months, but I took Whiteout Irene's side on this one. Pushing Rational Irene aside, I focused on the second turret - just as it opened fire on me.

Chapter 2

Contrary to popular belief, I couldn't dodge a bullet, let alone the yard-wide beam of energy that lanced out from the other turret, no matter how fast my reflexes or keen my perception, both jacked to the human limit and maybe beyond.

I could read where a thug was aiming and get out of the way, same with the sweep of a turret barrel, but once the shot started, I was no different from anyone else.

The beam hit me dead center of mass, engulfing most of my upper body. What didn't hit me blasted past to make a light show across the Atlanta skyline.

If that weapon had been any kind of real, I'd have died instantly, but that turret was Pushtech. The energy was mostly phantasmal to me, no more intense than a heavy-duty flashlight.

Maybe it was because Pushtech had another degree of separation from the Whiteout than the Pushed themselves, but it honestly hurt even less than a Push Crook's blast.

As the beam ended, I blinked out the spots in my eyes, the skin on my face tingling as if I'd spent a smidge too long in the sun.

With my vision clear, I narrowed my gaze at the other turret operator. Understandably, he was gaping at me and my continued existence, and when I started marching across the roof of the train, panic flashed in his eyes.

Batman was right. Criminals really were a cowardly lot.

"See?" Extinguisher said in my earpiece. "You could've done this singlehanded."

As he spoke, the cries of Turret Boy's comrades rose up from below, only growing louder and more frenzied as cracking ice and a wave of unnatural cold filled the air.

"Maybe, but I don't want to get shot tonight," I groused as I picked up the pace from menacing walk to fast trot.

That let me build up just the right amount of speed that when I hauled off with a punt kick, my heavy biker boot had all the momentum it needed to shatter the junk weapon into a dozen disparate pieces.

Fear turned to abject terror in Turret Boy's eyes as his main weapon fell apart, and his gaze dropped to frantically scan over his controls. While he'd likely trigger some other Pushtech defense system that wouldn't do anything to me, if it was indiscriminate, it might hurt Extinguisher and his fellow crooks, if not more.

So I went for him.

It would have been easy if the goal was just to take him down, but that might accidentally hit whatever button he searched for.

Instead, I slammed my injured shoulder into the turret, a small sacrifice to crack through the plastic dome. That actually would've hurt if all my pain wasn't shunted off into a little mental box, one of the "gifts" of being a Natural.

Twisting as I broke through, I lunged with my good hand, snatched Turret Boy by his lapels, and hauled him clean out of his seat.

He let out a howl of pain as his harness snapped, and I held him aloft, clear off his feet. Six months since the Whiteout, and this strength still sent a thrill up my spine.

Turret Boy kicked his feet like a child, but he was a gun runner, so I didn't have much sympathy for him. That little bit evaporated when he pulled a pistol from his jacket instead of surrendering.

"Bad crook," I chided as I smacked the weapon out of his hand. No hesitation anymore, just an immediate reaction after having a hundred weapons pulled on me by a hundred criminals.

As the pistol went sailing across the rail yard, I glanced down at how Extinguisher was getting on.

Of the half-dozen suited goons, two were pinned to the caboose's wall by thick bands of ice. Another two were sprawled out, unconscious amidst broken chunks of ice that I guessed were remnants of whatever icy construct Extinguisher had blasted them with. That left a final pair of smugglers.

Ice encased the unlucky one of them from the ground up to his waist, and one of his arms had gotten caught in the block as well. I understood why he was in a panic as he hit the ice with the butt of his shotgun to free himself instead of blasting Extinguisher.

The last thug, Number Six, had lucked out so far as he ran for cover around the corner of the train, firing off wild shots that cracked off our fearless leader's ice wall.

"You're not going to get away with this, Indomitable," Turret Boy said fruitlessly, punctuating each word with ineffectual struggling. "Our boss is big news!"

The longer the Whiteout's influence reigned supreme, the more comic-booky even normal people acted.

This guy could be hitting my arm, kicking at me, or trying to pry my fingers. He had a dozen options to try to get away from me, but he was just happy spouting his own little monologue.

I was about to engage him anyway, see if I could get him to do the "reveal all his boss's plans in an effort to intimidate the heroes" bit, when the half-frozen guy stopped thrashing with his shotgun and turned the business end towards Extinguisher's back. Our fearless leader didn't see the new threat as he was still throwing ice after Number Six.

I didn't hesitate. In full focus, my mind raced like lightning, and my reflexes were almost as fast. Dropping Turret Boy, I took two steps to build speed and launched myself off the cargo car. I just had to hope I was fast enough to get down there before Ice Block pulled the trigger.

Speaking of Extinguisher, he managed to flash-freeze Number Six's gun just as I tackled Ice Block's side.

Ice Block let out a cry of pain as something cracked in his arm, followed immediately by the shattering of ice as the force of my impact ripped the block free from the gravel.

As we both started to teeter over, Ice Block tried to squeeze off a shot anyway, but I lunged one hand past, caught his wrist, and wrenched it wide.

The shotgun went off with a thunderous boom, spraying buckshot in a wild spread. Some tore through gravel as we fell together, while most cut through the evening air harmlessly. Extinguisher spun in surprise just as Ice Block hit the ground with me on top of him.

"Thanks for the save, Indy," Extinguisher called out with a smile I only caught out of the corner of my eye.

"Thank me by stopping the last goon." I shifted to straddle Ice Block's side. Just as he tried to thrust the butt of his gun at me, I threw a measured right hand down towards his jaw.

My fist hit, his jaw snapped downward, and his head bounced off the gravel. That nasty shotgun fumbled out of his now limp fingers to clatter to the ground.

Meanwhile, the air filled with one last hum of Extinguisher's ice manipulation powers and one last gasp.

By the time I looked up, Number Six had a band of solid ice wrapped clear around his chest and arms. He had the good sense to fall to his knees.

"I surrender!" Number Six groaned. "Ain't no payout worth being frozen alive."

"Sounds like you two have things just about wrapped up," Choi chimed in my ear. "Any idea what their cargo was?"

"Give us a moment," I said as I pushed off Ice Block to get back to my feet. "You okay, Ex?"

The frosty firefighter gave me a nod and a thumbs-up. "All good. Glad to know you still care."

I flipped off my mic as I rolled my aching shoulder to try to stretch it out. I didn't want to let go of my focus just yet, not until we'd checked out the cargo, but I did relax my control just a little. To conserve my energy and all that.

I wasn't one-hundred percent sure if it worked, but it made my voracious hunger after action less, which meant taking fewer appetite suppressants but more pain pills. It was a delicate balance.

"Oh, come on now. You know that I do, and I always will. Are you still sour about earlier?"

Extinguisher also flipped off his mic. "I'm not sour, but you can't put this off forever. The promises of 'we'll talk later' are wearing *really* thin."

"Hey!" a vaguely familiar voice called from atop the cargo car. "Did you two heroes forget about something?"

Oh crap. Turret Boy.

Extinguisher and I shared a "whoops" look, then turned our eyes up. Turret Boy had returned to his broken turret, as if it were his lifelong home. I just barely had the angle to see him raise his arm up high.

"The boss figured you'd wanna see the cargo, so here it is," he shouted as he slammed his hand down on what I imagined was his console.

Expecting some tremendous Pushtech weapon to blast outward or bomb to go off or something widely destructive, I threw myself in front of Extinguisher. He might be Pushed and thus quite tough, but against Pushtech, I was practically invulnerable.

No plasma barrage tore through us, and no sonic devastator exploded to liquify everything with focused sound.

But there *was* an explosion of sorts. A crackle ran across the Pushtech shell of the car, the reinforcing braces around the corners and loading door disengaged, then a split-second later, the door and a good chunk of the wall around it burst outward as if hit by some titanic force.

I didn't wait to see what caused it, even as my reflexes and senses hyped back to maximum speed, because that storm of metal shrapnel was coming right at us.

There was a chill as Extinguisher grabbed me, no doubt with the idea of saving me, but he was moving in molasses. Instead, I grabbed him and threw us both clear of the barrage.

We hit the gravel, me on top of him, as the terrain past us was shredded. The boxcar we'd initially hidden behind took the brunt of it, torn apart by high velocity metal chunks, with some hurtling past to put serious cracks in the concrete base of the yard's wall.

"You're going to let me save you one day, Indy," Extinguisher half-grumbled as I rolled off him.

"Now is *really* not the –"

A terrible roar cut off my pithy response, and my gut twisted with an upsurge of a familiar, unnatural presence. Why, of all nights, did it have to be *him*?

I got to my feet just in time to see a hulking, corpse-like figure garbed in tattered mining gear. A fine cloud of coal dust swirled around the undead monster as he hefted his all-too real pickaxe over his shoulder.

But the true horror was what lay within the monster's Pushed shell - a crazed man near death's door, a chunk of a mining machine pierced through his chest.

It was The '49er, my personal bugbear ever since we'd first fought at the Battle of Washington.

"Man said to make ya put me out of my misery, Indomitable," the coal-laced zombie roared, a wave of black dust and grave dirt blasting over us. "And if you don't, I'll kill the both of ya!"

Chapter 3

I didn't have time to worry about who The '49er's mystery man was, even with my accelerated thinking. That was for later, when we subdued the undead miner without killing him in the process. Or dying, for that matter, because the Push Crook wasn't waiting for us to work out the moral quandary at hand.

"Get the goons out of here," I yelled as I cut to the left through the billowing coal dust. Even though the coal cloud was only partly real to me, it still obscured everything in the area. "I'll keep the big guy busy."

"On it."

Extinguisher hadn't even needed to reply. Even if The '49er didn't have a laser focus on me, confirmed by his thunderous steps following me, Extinguisher could ice slide any survivors off the battlefield way faster than I could remove them.

Not that I was sure if any of them had survived The '49er's violent appearance, but if they did, well, lives were at stake.

"You can't run for long," the zombie miner bellowed. Which was totally wrong on his part. I was considerably faster than his quickest lumber and, though there were a few trains on the tracks, I had plenty of room to maneuver.

But Rational Irene *and* Whiteout Irene were quick to point out that any chase would increase both the damage to the area and the likelihood that innocents would stumble into the crossfire.

Besides, out in the open railyard was the best place to stand my ground, now that I'd gotten a good fifty yards away from the start of this.

But how was I going to stop The '49'er? That was the question I asked myself as I skidded to a halt, turning just in time to see the big lug hurl his pickaxe with all his superhuman might.

Accelerated reflexes and experience gained from months of fighting for my life every day kicked in, and I leaped to the side. The all-too-deadly weapon sliced through the air right where my head had been and rocketed off into the distance.

That strength was one reason why the '49er had been such a continual thorn in my side, because he was all too happy to use the real environment against me, something that could really hurt me.

He was nigh-invulnerable, too. While that wasn't usually an issue, my usual go-to in such a situation - pushing through a Pushed's phantasmal form to strike the squishy and vulnerable human underneath - was dangerous with the frail, near-death state of The '49er's true form.

I kept my eyes locked on him as I slowly circled. "Look, I can help you, but not by killing you. You know I can touch the real you, which means maybe we can save you, if you let us."

"Irene," Choi came in over the comms, "I appreciate the effort, but The Forty-Niner has never listened before, and he seems particularly incensed tonight."

The '49er himself answered my plea by ripping up a hunk of railroad track for a new weapon. Guess he couldn't see any other path to be "free" other than me killing him. Suicide by superhero, a sickening thought, especially as it sounded like whoever was behind this had manipulated The '49er into wanting to die.

"I'm not going to kill you, and I'm not going to let you hurt anyone else either." Bold words, especially facing down bargain-bin Solomon Grundy with six feet of steel in his hands.

"Fine. I'm through begging you to save me," he roared. "Now, I'm gonna make you." He turned away from me toward the north.

In this direction, past the yard and across Dekalb Avenue, there were businesses, restaurants, and plenty of innocent targets. And I knew he'd be powerful enough to get there easily.

I didn't need to see The '49er's powerful legs tense to know how he intended to make me kill him. My body moved on pure instinct, and I broke into a full sprint with everything I had behind it.

Time seemed to slow even more than it already had and, just as The '49er started his own mighty leap, I lunged, closing the last few feet between us.

My hands slipped through phantasmal flesh, and I barely secured a hold around the real man's waist underneath before the Push Crook launched himself skyward.

The sudden acceleration jolted me, but it was worse for the far frailer miner. I had to hold on tight to not get ripped away from The '49er, and two grunts of pain, one shriller than The '49er's gravely tones, cut the night air.

That didn't stop him from taking off though. The '49er's superhuman muscle sent us arcing up into the night sky. My only hopes were that I'd stay on for the ride so I could subdue him when we landed, and that the sudden pain would throw his aim off.

I had no idea if I'd succeeded in the second as we plowed into the side of a building. I was far too busy with trying to use The '49er's Pushed body as a shield from all the stone, wood, and metal crashing all around us.

My arms and half my head were safe inside his phantasmal form, but I felt things bounce violently off my body and legs.

Bruises from shattered concrete, scratches from broken glass, a shard of wood in my left thigh. Every new injury got cataloged before I shoved the mounting pain into a little box in the corner of my mind, a problem for Future Irene to deal with.

Future Irene didn't like me very much these days.

The landing was almost as jarring as going through the wall, but the fact there were no screams of pain or cries of agony around us was a plus.

Over the months since Washington, I'd gotten used to how hyperaware I was in my focused state, so it was no shock that I took in our new surroundings in a flash.

I had indeed knocked the big monster off-course. Instead of hitting some inhabited building full of innocents for him to use against me, we'd landed smack-dab in the center of some kind of machine shop.

Concrete block walls and a metal roof suspended by steel supports were lit dimly by the moon through the skylights and the dull glow of exit signs.

Shelves of parts and supplies lined the walls along with a few roller doors, and metal workbenches stood in rows. Tool chests of various sizes sat by the benches, though the fact The '49er had barreled through sent many of them across the room, along with their contents.

The insurance company would have a field day, but no one, save for me, was hurt. Thank God. I tried to climb up The '49er's real body without touching the terrible wound in his chest, which would've been easy if not for his thrashing, spinning, and swinging.

Yes, the natural laws had changed thanks to Epic's Whiteout, and I was running with all the hysterical strength my body could muster, but The '49er could toss a Buick like it was a softball.

While he was too angry at the moment to just reach behind his back, the sheer force of every movement threatened to tear me off, not to mention that chunk of track in his hands. Each wild swing crashed into more tables, more tool chests, more support pillars.

Despite every joint adding their protests to the growing box of cut-off pain signals, I managed to hold on.

However, by the time I managed to get my arms around his neck, The '49er had done enough damage that an ominous cracking hit my ears, mixed with the groan of stressed metal. My time was almost up to subdue him before the building collapsed.

Despite Whiteout Irene's urging, I didn't bother with a pithy quip as I locked in a chokehold around The '49er's real self.

Brooks and Choi had put me through a whole regimen of fight training, something at which I was a quick study. That was good right now, because this might be the only safe way to put The '49er down.

That got his attention, and his wild flailing ceased. There was a clang, then two massive undead hands reached over the zombie miner's head and down towards me.

I ignored him. If I had this choke applied right - and I hoped to God I did - The '49er's frail human self should pass out in seconds. And it'd take longer than that - hopefully - for him to reach me with his *real* hands.

The now-familiar sensation of phantasmal hands wrapped around my head before passing through my skin. That muffled the rest of the world, which was strangely soothing, as it blocked out the rapidly increasing sounds of building collapse.

I could focus on my job and modulate the pressure. Too much and I'd kill him despite all my best efforts. Too little and he'd take out another building or two before he went down.

It was just as I felt real human fingers brush my scalp that the world abruptly dropped. The slab floor cracked as The '49er dropped to his knees. Both his real and phantasmal hands dropped away, and he pitched forward, unconscious, before he faceplanted.

The sounds around me rushed back in. The sigh of relief about to escape my lips was overpowered by a terrible shriek of tortured steel, and my eyes shot up in time to see the last intact support pillar bend under the strain.

I might've stopped The '49er's rampage, but I didn't know what was going to stop me from being buried alive.

Chapter 4

I sprang up and rushed for the nearest door. Sure, the likelihood that, even with my bolstered speed, I'd make it out before the already buckling roof came down was a snowball's chance in Hell. But, as I'd witnessed a few miracles since the Whiteout, it was worth a shot.

At least The '49er would be okay, no matter what. His invulnerable Pushed shell would protect him just fine.

A quarter way to the door, the steel overhead caved in from the weight of the air conditioning unit that tore right through the ceiling.

This ripped through more infrastructure and conduits, which only accelerated the catastrophe. Debris rained down, and I put my arms over my head in a vain effort to protect it.

I'd only make it a few more steps before the industrial air conditioning unit would hit, and it brought enough of the roof with it that I had zero chance of making it out. Of course, I still tried.

"I've got it," Extinguisher shouted over the comms.

Before I could blink, the falling wreckage crashed down onto a triple-thick ice slide that formed under it.

Defying all sane physics, the debris didn't shatter through, but instead followed the winding curvature of the slide towards a rough but far less disastrous landing.

I glanced up to see my favorite Push Hero through the impressive hole The '49er had put in the building's side.

Extinguisher worked frantically, rapid waves of cold-blue energy firing off with every sweep of his arms. Impromptu ice sheets and pillars formed to brace the walls and deflect what still fell.

"Thanks, Ex." I didn't wait in the danger zone while I said my thanks. Instead, I crashed through the door I'd been aiming for, then kept going. Only when I got to the other side of the street did I stop to see just how bad things were going to turn out.

It shouldn't have surprised me that Extinguisher seemed to have a knack for structural engineering. How else could he have turned what should've been a pile of wreckage into an unstable but semi-intact building? Not that it would hold long, especially once the ice started to melt.

But that wasn't the worst of it. The shop was part of a larger block of tightly packed industrial buildings. Its uncontrolled collapse would likely start a chain reaction to take out a large portion of the block, if not all of it. Then the debris could fall outside of the block and spread the damage to the immediate area.

And *that* was before taking into account the possibility of electrical fires, gas lines rupturing, and industrial equipment exploding.

I glanced down the block both ways. Mostly industrial businesses, like this one, and they all seemed closed, so little chance of casualties.

But to my right, on the corner, was a coffee shop that already had a small group of people outside of it, staring at the Push Battle, and, to my left, across the street from the wrecked shop, was a rundown but still open hotel.

Before the Whiteout, this street would have been dark, that coffee shop would have closed no later than four in the afternoon, and the hotel would have been filled only with squatters.

But now, people, normal people, didn't act the same as before. They were drawn to the Push Battles, and tended to be in places they wouldn't have dreamed of a mere six months ago. Meaning I had far too many innocent bystanders to save.

"How long can you hold it?" I was already in motion, headed for the coffee shop, as I called into my comm. "We've got innocents gawking, and if that thing falls –"

"We've got no idea just how bad the debris field will impact everyone and everything nearby," Extinguisher finished for me. "I'll hold it as long as I need to. Lives are at stake."

I could already hear the strain in his voice, so I wasn't going to test his resolve if I could help it. "Okay. Rachel, I'm going to try to clear the area, but we'll need emergency services here pronto."

"Already called, and I'm talking to PART now."

The Pushed Action Response Team, the Atlanta Police Department's answer to Pushcrime, always tried to help, but they generally came up short, hence why we were always busy.

I reached the people by the coffee shop. "The building's about to fall. You need to get out of here," I shouted as authoritatively as I could manage. "At least a few blocks back, if not more."

Most of them started to flee. However, the manager, Jeff Q. as his nametag told me, looked back at the shop. "But the owner will fire me if I –"

"No stupid job is worth your life," I snapped. I had zero patience, especially as I could feel my focus slipping from all the action and injury. If it dropped now, well, we were all in trouble. "Now move it, so I can save all the other lives around here."

Maybe it was my tone, maybe it was the blood on my uniform, or maybe good sense actually permeated Jeff Q.'s thick skull. Whichever one it was, he finally complied with my command and rushed off after the others.

I turned on my heel and, as I sprinted toward the hotel, I willed myself to hold it together. The cracking of ice and concrete rang out through the night, and a sidelong glance showed that Extinguisher was barely keeping it together.

Erecting the partial ice dome around the National Mall had been one thing, but he'd had Medusa's power turning it into more stable stone to help. Without that, he was doing the same as me - pushing to hold on "long enough" and not a moment more.

"You can do it," I said, a mantra to myself as well as him, as I ate the distance to the hotel. In just the few moments it took, a few brave and/or stupid souls had ventured out to watch the oncoming catastrophe.

That couldn't be everyone inside, or maybe it could. The aging building was only four stories and flanked by shorter storefronts on both sides. The hotel hadn't been maintained well, and I doubted it attracted a large clientele.

I couldn't be that lucky, though. The only luck I'd had in some time was bad luck.

"Okay, show's over," I barked. "Get as far away from here as fast as you can."

As if I needed anything to back up my scowling demeanor, the tremendous sound of cracking of ice boomed out from the ravaged building.

I glanced back to see the top half start to list towards the hotel's side of the street, but a fresh spire of ice launched up from the pavement to shore it up.

"Better hurry, Indy," Extinguisher got out through a grunt of exertion.

Good sense broke through the Whiteout and most of the hotel guests scattered like rats from a sinking ship.

Once more, someone in more official clothes didn't immediately bolt, but this gentleman had a look of horror on his face instead of misplaced loyalty.

"Indomitable, ma'am, there's still somebody up there." The older gentleman, the night attendant, I guessed, shot a look up at the hotel. "A young lady and her baby, they just checked in a couple of hours ago."

"Room?" I wasn't trying to be brusque - this guy was actually doing some good here - but time was of the essence.

"Four-ten." Of course, the innocents in danger would be at the top floor. The Whiteout needed maximum drama, after all. "I can get you the key if -"

"No time and no need. Just get out of here and stay safe."

I didn't wait for an answer - I just hoped he'd get out of here in time. As for me, I did what heroes do.

I went right into the jaws of danger. I tossed open the front door and ran into the dilapidated lobby, spied the sign for the stairs, and beelined for them.

I hit the stairs. The floors flew by in a blur, and the growls in my stomach warned me I was pushing too far for too long. I ignored those, too, as I reached the fourth floor.

I pulled the door open. If I didn't know half a building was about to careen into the hotel, I'd have found it surprisingly cozy, despite the faded wallpaper and worn carpeting.

The hallway split right and left, but a quick glance at the posted room map had me going down the left toward room 410. There were windows on either end of the hallway, looking at a view that might have been nice decades ago.

To make things the absolute *best* they could be, 410 happened to be one facing the street, so among the first things to get plowed into by the oncoming debris.

"Indy…" Extinguisher's voice trailed off into strained growling. "I can't hold it."

"You can and you will."

The polished brass numbers of room 410 were on my left. All it took was a hard shoulder to crash through.

It was a small room. The window faced toward the oncoming disaster, but the curtains were drawn, a thin shield against what was coming. One battered suitcase sat unopened at the foot of the bed.

The only light was the dull red glow of an old LED alarm clock, but I didn't need it to find the woman or her child.

She was curled up in the bed, not even under the covers, and still in dirty, ill-kept clothing, with the baby clutched close to her. The child's swaddling was as worn as the mother's clothes, but cleaner.

Somehow, both had stayed sleep through the chaos outside, though my dramatic entrance managed to wake them.

There was a story here, but that was for later. The mother sat up, her mouth starting to open as the baby began to cry, but I raised a hand to cut her off.

"No time. We've got to go." I didn't stop moving as I spoke.

That was good, because just as I got to the side of the bed, the sound of a window-rattling crack of ice filled the room. On its heels was a cacophony of breaking stone, tearing metal, and more shattering ice.

As the first chunks of debris crashed into the hotel, I scooped up both mother and child in one motion, then charged for the open door. I went left, to the nearest window at the side of the building.

Before the oncoming debris buried us, I leaped, twisting so that I put myself between my charges and the glass I broke through.

Chapter 5

Glittering shards followed us like a trail of tears as we soared through the night air, safe for the moment from the wreckage.

I got a great view of the two buildings colliding in the few moments we were airborne. The industrial shop's roof split the front façade of the hotel as if it was The '49er's pickaxe.

It'd be a miracle if that was the only other building to come down.

I kept twisting in mid-fall so that I hit with my back on the roof of the adjacent building. Thankfully, it was just a story shorter than the hotel, so I didn't kill myself as I shielded the scared mother and wailing baby from the worst of the hit.

But we weren't out of the woods yet. There was no way to tell where the hotel would fall, especially as my doctorate was in physiology, not building demolition. Sound had become mostly useless as well, with the constant onslaught of crashes and smashes hitting my ears.

As I couldn't rest, I forced myself to roll both mother and child off me and get back to my feet.

"Indy, I've got eyes on you and the civvies," Extinguisher called over the comms. He sounded as beat as I was. "I'm doing what I can but –"

"I'll get us out of here," I replied, for his benefit as well as the mother's. She was rising slower than me, so I scooped her and her precious cargo up once more. That put my back to the unfolding disaster for just a moment, but the woman saw it all.

"No! It's going to fall on us," she screamed in abject terror.

"No, it's not." I didn't look back – I just took off in a full sprint for the side away from the hotel.

Before I even got three steps, the roof of this building shuddered. I held my charges as close as I could as shards of debris pinged off me.

This more protective uniform was working wonders on this small stuff, but I was still collecting nicks and scrapes here and there. Not for the first time, I cursed the lack of a helmet or a hood or *something*.

The mother muttered frantic prayers, the exact words drowned out by both the crying baby and the destruction behind us, and I kept running. There were no fancy tricks, no cheeky attempts at parkour. This was a flat-out race against the inevitable, and I had to win.

Another tremendous crash boomed behind us when we were halfway across the rooftop, and the impact almost made me stumble. I risked a glance back as I steadied myself – the hotel had just collapsed against the building we stood on.

The mother shrieked, but I wasn't going to let us fall into the sure death behind. I kept my footing, then started running again.

A cloud of dust and debris blasted past us. In the middle of the cloud, I couldn't see what was ahead, so I just kept running, focused on getting us to the other side.

Fully focused and one hundred percent rested and healthy, I was insanely fast. Not Quicksilver fast or Flash fast, but I'd give Spider-man or Captain America a run for their money.

But I wasn't rested and no longer felt healthy. I was hurt, tired, and riding the edge of my limits. Meaning this wasn't easy at all. But I refused to let the innocent lives in my arms die.

We reached the edge of this rooftop, and I could just make out that there was a small alley separating this building from the next.

I summoned my strength and pushed off hard, just as the roof collapsed. I wasn't sure that we'd make it, but we landed on the next roof rather easily, all things considered.

This time I didn't have to land on my back. I'd landed well and kept on running.

I risked another look behind me. The building we'd been on was now hit and starting to go down towards the one we were running on. Not a problem, I'd just get us to the next building. This domino effect couldn't last forever. There would be a point where we'd be safe.

I looked ahead. We had at least three more rooftops to go. Might as well head for the last building and figure out how to get down from there.

"We're almost out of this," I told the mother.

She nodded numbly and held on tighter to her sobbing baby.

Run, run, leap, repeat. The sounds of destruction were still far too close, but we reached the last roof unscathed.

I'd expected to find a fire escape we could climb down, but if there was one, we'd jumped over it.

I turned around to see if we should try to head toward the destruction in search of a way down, but that just meant I got to see the buildings continuing to fall. I figured we had less than a minute before this last building was hit.

"Ex, sugar, we're about to make an exit from the westmost building roof," I called over the comms. "The side facing away from the wreckage. Need a catch."

"Doing what I can to mitigate the damage, but I always have time to catch a pretty lady." Though his words were light, Extinguisher sounded as exhausted as me. He'd been straining his ice powers to their limit this entire time, after all.

"You're the best."

As I said this, the last building we'd been on hit the one we were standing on currently. I was going to have to jump down, with or without Extinguisher's help.

"Hold on, ma'am," I said in a hopefully reassuring tone. "One last jump, okay?"

The woman trembled but nodded. "One last jump."

I took two steps to get some speed and flung all of us off the roof.

If there was one thing I still trusted in this crazy world after Epic wrecked it, it was my friends, Extinguisher most of all. Our current squabbles aside, he was the closest thing I had to a pillar left.

That's why I didn't doubt for an instant that my fall to the street would be anything less than safe. My charges didn't know that, though, and while the mother had clearly put all her trust in me, she and her baby still screamed as we hurtled towards the ground.

Only to have our fall broken by a massive, fluffy snowbank. The cold was soothing on my aches and pains, and I savored the sensation of that and the feeling of safety.

"Thank you, Indomitable." I realized I was still holding on tight to the woman and her baby, so I let them go. "I'm Mary. Caleb and I, we'd have been dead if not for you."

I pushed myself to sit up. We were perched deep in the snow, but I could see up and out.

The industrial building and all the ones on this block were lost causes.

But a lattice of ice pillars, walls, and beams had contained the destruction to just that much. A miracle, to be sure.

"You're welcome." I almost let my focus slip, but then a sudden thought hit me like a thunderbolt. "Wait here, out of sight. I'll be back."

"What? Why? We're safe, aren't we?"

"Not if The Forty-Niner woke back up."

Chapter 6

The little aches and pains started to slip out of their mental box as I jogged over to the machine shop's wreckage.

I had to make sure The '49er was still out. If he was back up or about to wake up, this would start all over again, and I wasn't sure that I had anything left in the tank to stop him.

Finding out was easier said than done, though, because The '49er was buried under a quarter of a building's worth of wreckage.

The upside was that it was likely he was still unconscious. If he was up and about, The '49er could've smashed his way out. But that wasn't the only possible escape route. He could've gone down.

He was a former miner, after all.

As I tried to figure out a way to get deeper into the wreckage, wailing sirens grew louder, and multi-colored lights flashed down the streets. PART and emergency services were finally arriving. Too late to do anything more than clean up, which was the usual.

I scanned up and down the street then through the night sky, looking for my partner. "Ex, are things stable enough for you to come to me? I want to try to get to make sure The Forty-Niner is both alive and under control before the authorities get here."

"I'd advise that as well," Choi cut in. "There are some strange rumblings on the police band radios and other emergency service channels."

As if our words had summoned him, which they basically had, Extinguisher swept overhead on an ice slide before spiraling down beside me.

"The Department of Pushed Affairs, I'd guess." He looked me up and down, and I could see his jaw tighten. I must've looked especially rough.

"I'm fine," I lied as I turned to the job at hand. "The machine shop area was at the pivot point of the collapse, so we have a lot to get through." I moved to what looked to me like the least dense pile of rubble in our way, but a chilling hand on my shoulder stopped me.

"Indy, Rachel, there's no way we're getting through that rubble without Hexagon or a bulldozer. Trust me, as the rescue expert here. The skillsets we have on hand aren't going to cut it."

Give up on rescuing someone, even a villain? Whiteout Irene snapped from out of nowhere.

She was right. I shrugged off Extinguisher's hand and strode into the wreckage.

"Indy…" he called after me.

Or we could call it listening to the expert, Rational Irene countered, having found her voice again. *Or are you considering listening to my colleague simply because you're annoyed with your lover right now?*

My hands, which I realized were already clenched around a slab of concrete I was about to try to shove aside, relaxed. Taking a deep breath, I counted back from ten under my breath, then turned to Extinguisher.

"You're right. Sorry, I'm just…" My focus was fading hard, and as all-too-human feelings of exhaustion and pain broke through my resolve, I had to lean against the debris to stay standing.

"Fire and Rescue are just about here." Concern shone in his eyes. "Just get to the EMTs and I'll coordinate with them on getting the big lug out of there, okay?"

Frustration welled up inside me, aggravated by the blaring lights and sounds of the cavalry's arrival, such as it was.

But why was I frustrated? We'd stopped the arms shipment, cut off The '49er's rampage, and saved numerous lives. I just had to think about Mary cradling Baby Caleb to see the evidence.

Probably because this wasn't just some Push Crime. This had targeted me specifically. This damage and any casualties caused - there had to be some despite our best efforts - were an indirect result of that.

The best way to deal with something like this was to get to the bottom of it. Someone with the kind of resources needed for a job like this was dangerous, and they'd cause more harm when they invariably tried again. I needed to stop them from doing that, not get frustrated at the people trying to help, me included.

I mastered the frustration, like so many other things I'd dealt with. "Let me know if you need anything while I get patched up, okay? I know you can handle this."

"I *am* the team leader, after all." He flashed me a grin.

As I pushed off to head for the EMTs, he turned towards the PART team organizing the rescue workers.

I picked out Captain Joe Braxton. A tall, barrel-chested middle-aged man sporting a salt-and-pepper crew cut, he was PART's commanding officer and an old friend of Extinguisher's from before the Whiteout.

I fought off the curiosity to follow him. If anyone here had an inkling of what was going on at the law enforcement level, it was Braxton. But my last remaining shreds of good sense kept me on a straight course to medical attention. Best they get a look at me before my focus shattered, while I could still block the inevitable extra pain.

That was the plan, anyway, but I only made it a few steps before the twist of a fresh Pulse in my gut, the herald of another Pushed's arrival, snapped me back into full focus. I followed the Pulse to catch three figures streaking across the night sky, aiming straight for the street near me.

Fortunately, I recognized them, so I relaxed a little. But only a little, staying at full focus despite the strain. At the center of the V formation was a masked man garbed in a shiny red, white, and blue costume that oozed overdone patriotism.

Even if I hadn't had to shake this guy's hand at multiple photo ops and press conferences over the past months, the media was so inundated with him that he was immediately recognizable.

This was Colonel Liberty, the Push Hero poster boy for the U.S. military and the Department of Pushed Affairs.

Smash Superman and Captain America together, dial the power level down a smidge, and you'd get the Colonel.

His escort was a bit more troubling. Not for me personally, but for the broader implications they presented.

I'd heard that there were more than a few Push Heroes and Push Crooks who'd pulled a Tony Stark and built themselves knock-off Iron Man suits, but this was different.

Landing beside Colonel Liberty were two identical suits of Pushtech powered armor, but not the sleek superhero style.

They were bulky, with hard angles and weapon ports, painted in urban camouflage. United States Army rank insignia and identifiers adorned the heavy-duty shoulder plates.

Of course, under all the military razzle dazzle of the Pushed shell, they were really military body armor combined with sports pads, with various cobbled-together bits and bobs to form the weaponry.

It looked like the armed forces of the world were starting to invest in Pushtech arms, and that wouldn't end well for anyone.

"Sorry to pull rank here, Indomitable," Colonel Liberty began with surprisingly chumminess, "but my men and I were flying a test mission –"

"Let's skip the attempts at rationalization, Colonel." I was too tired to deal with a convoluted explanation as to why him and his two prototype power armor troops just happened to be in the area. "We've got a Push Battle catastrophe here to clean up and, if you're here to help, I'm not going to say no."

The grunts shuffled a little, something that would've passed my notice if not for the bulk of their armor, while Colonel Liberty nodded. "Well, that's not the only goal we hope to achieve here, but for now," he glanced at his two subordinates, "Hartman, DuBois, liaison with PART for rescue operations."

The two armored troops snapped crisp salutes, and maybe it was my imagination, but I swore they both seemed quite happy to have an out. They both marched off, heavy boots clanking as they went, and I narrowed my eyes at Colonel Liberty, trying to look tough despite how ragged I must've looked.

I didn't dislike Liberty. He really was a decent man who seemed to take his duty to the United States seriously, but when I kept getting dragged into political messes on the opposite side of him, well, it led to some lingering resentment.

"You're going to tell me about some special mission or top-secret orders, aren't you? And I won't like any of it, will I?"

Colonel Liberty kept his expression schooled into his usual calm, dutiful smile, but I caught the sigh of annoyance he caught in his throat. "I'm sorry, Indy, but your hunches are as right as they usually are. Yes, we're testing the new MS-X power armor before proper deployment, and yes, we're happy to help, but –"

I crossed my arms to enhance my tough girl credentials. "There's always a but with you."

"I have strict orders directly from the Pentagon to take the Push Crook known as The Forty-Niner into federal custody." Liberty put his fists on his hips. "Now, where is he?"

Chapter 7

I bit back the urge to snap at Colonel Liberty.

Yes, I was suspicious of what the government wanted with an extremely dangerous undead Push Crook, one who had a mad obsession with *me* in particular.

Whiteout Irene and Rational Irene also chimed in with their own suspicions but, at the end of the day, I needed Liberty's help to get The '49er out of the rubble and ensure he didn't cause more harm.

Even if I didn't, I was in no shape to pick a fight with Captain-Super-America here.

At least Choi could voice the snark I couldn't. "I don't like any of this, Irene," she said over comms.

I couldn't share my agreement. Instead, I sighed and pointed at the wreckage of the machine shop. "He's buried under there, hopefully still sleeping off what I did to him. I guess it's good, in a certain sense of the word, that you and your troops did show up."

I started toward the edge of the wreckage. "You can help get him out before he recovers and starts a fresh rampage."

"I don't want to sound like I'm giving you an order," Colonel Liberty put a hand on my shoulder to stop me, "but you need medical attention. My men and I can handle wrangling the target."

I almost elbowed him on reaction, but I was too banged up and worn out. That gave me time for my brain to catch up to my reflexes. Letting out a sigh, I stopped and turned back to him.

"I should argue with you, but I hate to say that I agree." I scowled at the fact I was relinquishing this bit of control to Liberty, of all people. "At least I'll be close if you need me." I poked a finger into the Colonel's chest, getting a little comfort at how my finger pushed into his phantasmal Pushed body. "But you're not taking him until we talk."

The honest truth was Extinguisher and I probably couldn't stop them if they did a runner with The '49er. But I had a pretty intimidating reputation after what I'd done, and a hard look and a reminder that a normally invulnerable Pushed wasn't so tough against me often did wonders in situations like this.

Liberty tried to do a bit of staring war with me, but backed down fast when I stared not at his outer shell's eyes, but the real man underneath. As if to mimic the Captain America story, Liberty was a rather sickly and thin young man under the powerhouse body.

"Fine." He turned on his heel. "Just get patched up, okay?"

"Glad to know you care, Colonel," I snarked back as I trudged towards the EMTs once more.

This time, I actually made it to the triage area. While our hard work had saved a lot of lives, people had still been hurt, some severely, and I knew deep down there'd be some dead found in the clean-up efforts.

Still, I took the solace I could, especially to see Mary and Baby Caleb giving a statement to Captain Braxton.

The paramedics went through the cycle I was now almost numb to after these past six months. Initial surprise to see I was even hurt at all - I blamed my outsized reputation for that - then frantic work to clean wounds, bandage cuts, and get some pain meds into me, finished off with another round of surprise at how I unflinchingly handled their work.

I had to peel myself out of my jacket, tank top, and gloves, basically down to my sports bra, so they could do their work.

What worried me was how I looked under the uniform. Usually, when I got undressed at the end of a night or day of superheroics, I was too exhausted or too injured to take a proper look at myself.

Then those nights I tumbled into bed with Extinguisher, well, I was too focused on the handsome man in front of me than my own condition.

But tonight, of all nights, I was lucid enough to take in what six months of constant strain and pain had done to me. To an untrained eye, I might've looked amazingly fit, muscular, and cut from all the continual exercise. While I was an athlete in high school and college, I'd never looked like this.

But my eyes weren't untrained. My doctorate in physiology told me that the radical definition of my abs and my arms was from dehydration as much as it was from working out.

The dry skin and rough nails were sure signs of the bouts of undernutrition I went through from pushing my focus too long, when my body ran out of fuel and started breaking down what it needed to keep going.

Then there were the scars I'd gained. I looked more like a grizzled action hero from the Eighties than the mid-thirties scientist I should be. The fact I'd gained almost all of them in just these few months said more about my long-term survival chances than anything else.

Tonight, I'd added some new ones, and who knew what would happen before I could drift off into fitful sleep? Assuming I'd get to sleep at all.

I tore my eyes away from me and over to the wreckage. While the EMTs did their work, I distracted myself with Colonel Liberty, rejoined by his two armored subordinates, as they tackled the rubble.

Extinguisher was headed my way, either worried about me or he'd just finished updating Captain Braxton. I waved him towards where the Colonel was at work. He nodded, no doubt wanting to keep an eye on the government Push Hero himself.

To the normal human bystanders, seeing a coordinated effort of superstrength, ice constructs, and super-advanced robots burrow through the collapsed building was enrapturing.

For me, it wasn't quite commonplace, but I'd seen similar things too many times to count. There was something I noted as disturbing, though, and that was in some of the fine details of the excavation.

In the reality I knew, the world before the Whiteout, physics and material science mattered as much as raw power when lifting or moving something.

A human-sized entity like Colonel Liberty lifting a large slab of concrete, for instance, wouldn't have gone well. Leverage, stress points in the slab, even the strength of the ground under his feet, all conspired to make it a challenge to attempt, no matter his physical might.

In the early months of the Whiteout, those pressures remained mostly intact.

Now, though, Liberty and his men were hefting debris and moving rubble with few considerations to the laws of reality I knew. In other words, it seemed like the comic book reality was imposing itself more and more as the months rolled by.

Epic, my crazed ex-boyfriend, the one who sparked the Whiteout into existence, and leader of the Crusaders, a vigilante mob of Pushed who dominated the southern United States, had to be pleased.

But I only felt the keen rise of anxiety. I was wasting time, and I wasn't doing enough to stop the Whiteout and bring back the real world underneath.

That anxiety actually made it a little easier to keep my focus for the EMTs. But after a few minutes, while I was still being worked on, the pair of power armor pilots flipped over a large slab of concrete while Extinguisher raised a U-shaped retaining wall of thick ice.

That kept the cleared debris from falling back in on whatever they'd just uncovered and, as Colonel Liberty stepped down into the clear area, I got the distinct feeling that they'd found their target.

Without thinking, I hopped up from where I sat on the back of an ambulance, pulling out of the lead EMT's grasp as he was about to check my impacted shoulder.

"Where do you think you're going, Indy?" he said. "We're not done."

I turned and grabbed my jacket. "Sorry, duty calls. I promise, I'll come back as soon as I've taken care of this."

"Right, I'm sure you believe that, but word gets around." He sighed and frowned. "I know better. Just try to get to a hospital or something tonight, will you? Atlanta needs you around."

I could hear the actual concern in the EMT's voice, but all I could do was lie. "Of course. Don't worry, I always get better. It's what I do."

Well, that was a half-lie, I supposed. I did heal far faster than I should, but it didn't hold a candle to an actual Pushed, especially those that had a healing factor. I could see the EMT didn't believe me at all, but all he could do was let me go.

A pang of guilt gnawed at me, along with the mounting hunger that heralded a crash, as I pulled on my jacket and headed over to the wreckage.

I tried to assuage my guilt by telling myself that I was the only one that could stop The '49er if he was rousing. Whether that was the truth or not, I didn't ask.

"The fact that there's no shouts of fury either means you guys haven't found him yet or he's still out," I said to announce my arrival.

"Number two," Extinguisher said, "but who knows how long that'll last."

I hit the top of the little ring of rubble. They'd cleared out a rough circle about three yards around and a yard deep, back down to the cracked and abused concrete floor of the shop.

True to my expectations, The '49er was there, a cloud of coal dust swirling around his sprawled form. Thankfully, I could still see the poor man inside breathing shallowly under his zombie shell.

Colonel Liberty was down there, too, kneeling beside the giant Push Crook to examine him. "Considering he's the living dead, I can't be sure what state he's actually in. He could be, well, inert for a century or a minute."

"A minute or less," I said as I hopped down to join him. "Trust me."

Liberty gave me an appraising look, but I didn't flinch. "I suppose I have to. We better get him contained then."

"I can ice cage him, but that won't hold him for long," Extinguisher offered, but one of the soldiers was already pulling something out of a compartment hidden in the armor's midsection.

I wasn't sure if it was practical to have anything useful held in the center of mass, where most people would shoot first, but the Whiteout didn't function on logic.

"Thanks, Extinguisher, but that won't be necessary." Colonel Liberty glanced up at his subordinate instead.

"Here, sir," the soldier tossed down what looked like some kind of metallic collar, "the sleep inducer."

I almost decided to be cheeky and snatch the collar instead, something I felt I could do with my still-hyped reflexes, but we were still playing nice with the government. Liberty caught the thing and took a moment to adjust some controls on the outside.

This close, I could see through the Pushtech to discover a dog shock collar. My idealistic reaction, without any prompting from Rational or Whiteout Irene, was that this was wrong and it made me nervous.

"So, I guess the sleep inducer does just what it says on the tin. Why do you think it'll work on an undead monster that doesn't have normal biological functions?"

While I knew better, everyone else was functioning on the laws of reality from the Whiteout, so best to attack it from that angle.

"It doesn't work on just biological principles," Liberty explained as the collar expanded in his hands. "The science guys told me it works on a psionic level too. So long as the prisoner has a brain, it keeps them napping until we take the collar off."

"You sound like you've been using these for a while." I was of a mixed mind about this thing – literally.

Rational Irene pointed out how elegant of a solution this was, considering I wasn't willing to put The '49er out of his misery.

Whiteout Irene, rebellious as always, noted that the government could rarely be trusted with a tool that could make its enemies disappear into an endless slumber.

As for me, the idea of being forced into an endless slumber - that total loss of agency - made me nauseous.

None of that stopped Colonel Liberty, of course, if he even had those thoughts. "Not so much me, but these have been pushed through prototyping fast to deal with the Push Crook epidemic."

He snapped the collar around The '49er's massive neck, and the undead miner spasmed once before going right back to sleep. "It's working on Reaper, which means it should work on anyone."

I wasn't the only one who tensed at the mention of the most dangerous Push Crook on the planet. At least Reaper was when his normal form, Gerald Schuller, was off his psychiatric meds.

Extinguisher's fists clenched as he was undoubtedly thinking about the Battle of Washington, where Reaper had almost killed, well, everyone that wasn't Epic.

We'd managed to revert him back to Gerald, then the Atlanta Five turned him over to the "care" of the Capital police force. Guess that meant a permanent sleep for Schuller. As much pain as his alter-ego caused, he himself had served his time.

Not for the first time lately, Whiteout Irene and I agreed that meant Schuller should get to live his life, just under the watchful eye of the authorities to make sure he kept on his medication.

Rational Irene shouted her opposition, of course, that Reaper was too big of a threat to the world to risk his awakening. And she wasn't wrong, either.

It was the typical comics dilemma, and I had no idea what to do about it.

"I suppose this is the part where you take him away," I motioned to The '49er, "and we're supposed to let you?"

"Irene," Choi warned in my ear, "this isn't a battle worth fighting."

As if on cue, perhaps because he might be hearing the same thing, Extinguisher focused on me. "I know what you're thinking, Indy, and I agree. But this isn't the time or place. PART can't hold The Forty-Niner, and we don't have the facilities either."

"I know this may seem fishy to you," Colonel Liberty chimed in, "but I'd listen to Extinguisher. For a Push Crook of this power, the sleep inducer and the new federal Pushmax holding facility is the only chance to keep him from doing more harm."

My fists clenched, and I took a deep breath. I counted back from ten, just as Mom always advised, even as Whiteout Irene was calculating our chances at decking Liberty and his soldiers.

Rational Irene, thankfully, had my back. My righteous indignation aside, I had to face facts. Extinguisher was right. Neither the Brooks-Choi Foundation, the city of Atlanta, or the Georgia Department of Corrections had the ability to hold The '49er.

Still, the inhumane idea of putting our problem asleep indefinitely stuck in my throat. All I could manage was a stiff, angry nod as I turned on my heel.

To give my lover credit, Extinguisher decided not to go after me immediately. It would've only led to us having another argument.

I hopped out of the pit and stalked back toward the ambulances. Probably would be best to let the EMTs finish what they could before I limped back to the Foundation and Brooks's tender ministrations. He might've had a gruff exterior, but he truly did have the gentle hands of a healer.

I didn't make it, though, because something else caught my attention. The mother I'd rescued, still clutching onto Baby Caleb, was pleading with Captain Braxton, and the head of PART looked equally concerned and frustrated.

"But you have to believe me," she said. "They took Rick. Sally, too. And they had powers."

"Miss Johnson, I'm sorry," Braxton replied. "I can't involve PART unless there's some hard evidence to go on."

He was about to dig himself deeper into a hole as he tried to explain the short arm of the law when I stepped into the conversation.

"But we can get involved." I looked Mary in the eyes. "Tell me what happened."

Chapter 8

"Irene, I don't normally stand in the way of things, but is this wise to pursue right now?" Choi chimed in my ear. Very rationally, I might add.

And yes, she was right. It wasn't particularly wise for me to latch onto this situation. Mary could be mistaken, wrong, or even malicious in what she was doing.

But I had my reasons for stepping in – it was a good distraction from my frustration with the Colonel Liberty situation and, for all my grumblings about my current lot in life, I *was* a hero now.

To turn a deaf ear to what Mary had said would deny who I was. Another innocent victim of the Whiteout would be left hanging, and I couldn't let that happen.

That's why I ignored Choi's question and focused on Mary. "Go on. I'm here to help."

Captain Braxton looked relieved that I'd stepped in, while Mary only stared at me for a long moment. "I know," she said. "And…thank you again."

"You're welcome again. It's a pleasure to talk to you outside of collapsing buildings. So, back to what you were telling Captain Braxton."

"Right." Mary adjusted Caleb on her hip. "A couple of folks I know, some strange folks swiped them right off the street. And Rick and Sally aren't the only ones, from what I've heard."

I looked over at Braxton questioningly. He was a good man, but he was also perpetually in over his head.

"There *have* been an uptick in missing persons reports, Indy, but this is the first I've heard of any Pushed involvement."

Captain Braxton sighed and gestured at the wreckage all around us. "PART's stretched thin, and this isn't going to help. Especially that." He nodded at where Colonel Liberty and his soldiers were pulling a still-sleeping '49er out of the debris. "The Mayor's going to see this as a PR disaster."

"Tell him to call me," I assured Braxton, "and I'll set him straight. Now, Mary…"

Turning back to her and Caleb, I took a moment to assess them, her especially, a bit closer. That was harder than it should've been, because it was maybe ten minutes tops before I was going to fall over, judging from the way my stomach wanted to chew through my abdomen in hunger.

The worn clothes they both had, the hollowness of Mary's cheeks, and the hardness in her eyes, I guessed they were destitute. Maybe homeless. The hotel clerk who'd told me about them mentioned they'd checked in late, just a bit before the Push Battle, and Mary had collapsed in her street clothes.

"You and Caleb need a place to stay, and this isn't the best place to go into the details." I reached out and put a gentle hand on her shoulder. "There's space at the Brooks-Choi Foundation. You two can spend the night in safety and, in the morning, we can see about looking into the string of kidnappings." I shot Braxton some side-eye. "We'll coordinate with you, of course."

"I already know that it's futile to argue about this," Choi said in my ear, "just as much as I know you're in no position to discuss it. But we will when you get back, assuming Duane doesn't recommend immediate bedrest."

I knew why Choi wasn't precisely happy with this situation. Our two big goals right now were finding Ian MacKenzie before his anti-Pushed terrorism exploded into a new situation worse than the Battle of Washington, and keeping Epic and his Crusaders in check until we found a real solution for the Whiteout. An unassociated kidnapping case wouldn't help those goals.

At the same time, I knew that if Choi and/or Brooks were here, they'd be doing the same thing. In fact, I had some added back-up over the comms while both Mary and Braxton chewed on my proposal.

"Come on, Rachel," Extinguisher chimed in. "We're Push Heroes. It may not be to our best tactical advantage, but helping is what we do." I saw him walking over, now that Liberty and his men had The '49er secured.

It looked like Liberty's team were just going to fly him off, a giant zombie baby cradled between the three of them. Not an image I wanted to look at, so I focused on Mary as she spoke up.

"Even if it wasn't you asking, I'd be a terrible mom if I turned down that offer." She looked past me, to the collapsed hotel. "What little we had is under all that rubble. Besides, it might help my friends."

Captain Braxton nodded. "You know my people and I will help in any way we legally can. I'm just sorry we can't do more."

"You can help us right away, Captain," I said, "and that's to give Mary and Caleb a ride to the Foundation building. There's only so much room on Ex's ice slide."

Extinguisher nodded. "That'd be a big help, Joe." He was the only one on the team who called Captain Braxton by his first name. Ironic, because he never called me anything other than Indy or Indomitable. "There's unfortunately not much else we can do here, now that Colonel Liberty is hauling off The Forty-Niner."

"I'm just glad you two stopped him, or else things would be a hell of a lot worse. We'll take things from here, don't worry." Braxton then turned to Mary and Caleb. "Right this way, Miss Johnson. I'll get a cruiser to get you there."

Mary glanced from Braxton to Extinguisher before settling on me, clearly a bit nervous. When I gave her a reassuring nod, she sighed a bit. "Okay, Captain. Thank you."

"Don't worry, we'll beat you there, I'm sure." I grinned at Extinguisher, though it was getting very hard to keep up the look. "As long as we get moving. Ready, Ex?"

"To give a pretty lady a ride?" He matched my grin. I won't lie, it felt nice. "Anytime." He flicked out a hand rimmed with ice, and he conjured up one of his ice slides. Stepping on, he offered me a hand.

"See you soon, Mary." I took Extinguisher's hand and let him pull me up onto the slide. As I grabbed hold around his waist, I allowed my focus to drop. I was finally away from the public. Couldn't afford to look weak or else Push Crooks and Crusaders would get the wrong idea.

Thank God I had a death grip on his waist, because the exhaustion and hunger hit me so hard, I would've collapsed without his support.

And the pain, of course, was let out of its carefully locked box in my mind, and what pain relievers the EMT had given me - none of the good stuff - was about useless.

It was only the fact I bit down on the shoulder of Extinguisher's fireman's coat that I didn't scream into the night.

While Extinguisher steered our flight with one hand, I felt the soothing cold of his touch where I clasped my own hands around his waist. "I've got you."

"I know," I murmured against his shoulder. One of the benefits of being this close was that his aura of cold, enough to induce frostbite in normal humans, was like a full-body ice pack to me. I tried to speak up after a moment of collecting myself. "We'll be home soon, Rachel."

"Understood," she said over the comms. "I'm already making arrangements for our guests, and Duane will be waiting for you two at the loading docks." I could almost hear a reproachful edge in her voice, but I pointedly ignored it.

"Great, thanks." I used to relish a ride with Extinguisher like this. To soar over the streets of Atlanta on his ice slides, thankfully real enough for me to make contact with them, was the closest I'd ever get to controlled flight. But now, all I could really do was focus on staying awake and aware.

"Any news from the rest of the team? Or from Facet and Ken, for that matter?" Talking was the only thing I could do to increase my chances of keeping upright, so I indulged. Besides, checking in on my old friends turned heroes was something I didn't do enough.

"I'll start processing the intel Medusa and Hexagon uncovered in Valdosta in the morning and, with any luck, Mind's Eye and the Human Tank will return from Athens by tomorrow evening."

I could hear Choi shuffling papers and moving around her office. "As for your friends, Kenneth gave me an update this afternoon that he and Facet had just about wrapped up the Stellar gang in LaGrange. With any luck, they'll be back home by week's end."

I should've known that myself, but it was getting harder and harder to keep all the threads straight when I had so much to do.

In the first few months post-Washington, I'd kept my fingers as deep in the pie as I could, running through the daily reports with Choi and Brooks, a silent third partner in their private investigation firm.

But, as more and more things came up that needed my special attention, from political rallies to public relations appearances to fighting the most dangerous Push Crooks that only my immunities as a Natural let me face down, I'd let that control slip.

I'd let go of my agency to the literal agency, so to speak.

"Thanks for the reports, Rachel," I said softly. "I literally don't know what I'd do without you."

"You're welcome, Irene," she replied. "Extinguisher, after you drop her off into Duane's care, can you meet me in my office before turning in?"

"Of course, though I'll want to check on Indy after Duane's done," Extinguisher answered, concern plain in his voice.

"I shouldn't hold you up long, though if I need you later, should I check in your room or hers?"

Extinguisher stiffened against me. Choi certainly caught my attention with that, too. "Why would you ask that?" he began, but I sighed to cut him off.

"Come on, Ex, we shouldn't be shocked that one of the FBI's finest minds couldn't cut through our high-school level tomfoolery."

"And we're all mature adults here," Choi added. "Supposedly. So as long as you two can keep that in the bedroom and stay professional in the field, I don't care, though I will advise you both that it's likely everyone save perhaps Tank has put the same clues together."

"Our teenage super-cyborg might be a bit naïve when it comes to some things, true, but he's just that – a teenaged boy," I pointed out. "He's probably got his suspicions."

"Look, we'll figure out how to discuss it all when we have a chance to talk about this particular wrinkle," Extinguisher said as he started to bank his ice slide down through the night sky. "Anyway, we're almost home. Talk to you soon in the flesh."

"Understood, over and out." With that, Choi clicked out of the comm channel, leaving the two of us alone.

Extinguisher took us on a spiraling descent around the Brooks-Choi Foundation building, an eight-story structure in the heart of downtown Atlanta. I had these last few moments of relative silence to think about the impending talk Extinguisher and I had to have. As much as I wanted to avoid it, it wasn't something I could manage any longer.

So what would I do? Was I really in the headspace to have a relationship, a *real* relationship, after what Epic had done to me? What about the fact that I was the walking antithesis to the very reality that made Extinguisher what he was today? Most of all, were these all just excuses so I didn't have to make any decision at all?

His voice broke me out of my thoughts. "Don't worry about it, Indy. We'll figure it out once Duane has you on the mend."

"I'll do my best, but I'm a worrier by nature." I looked over his shoulder as we made one last spiral.

Below, in the yellow pools cast by the back-alley lights, stood Brooks, his usual suit exchanged for a set of hospital scrubs. He was chewing on nicotine gum as he leaned on a wheelchair and, as he saw our approach, all he did was shake his head ruefully.

"Now I feel like I need to stick around as Duane works on you." But that didn't stop Extinguisher from pulling right up beside the wheelchair. "Hey, Duane."

"Hey, Ex." Brooks looked over at me, sighed, and patted the wheelchair. "Come on, Doc, let's see how bad you hurt yourself tonight."

Chapter 9

As it turned out, I'd hurt myself pretty badly, but it wasn't the worst night on record.

Not that the situation made Brooks happy. As the main person patching me and the Atlanta Five up - though it was mostly me - he saw almost every bump, bruise, scrape, cut, puncture, and break.

Not even Extinguisher knew exactly how much and how often I got hurt regularly saving the city/nation/world.

I was a mass of bruises, my impacted shoulder was upgraded to a full sprain, lots of shallow cuts on my face, but the worst was the splinter of concrete that'd gotten driven into my thigh. I cheated and used a little bit of focus to not scream when he pulled the thing out.

In the end, my shoulder was taped up, as were my ribs, little adhesive bandages dotted my face, and my thigh was thoroughly cleaned, dressed, and bandaged.

In between the painful parts, I brought Brooks up to speed on what happened with the Pushtech train, the faux arms shipment, Colonel Liberty, The '49er, and how Liberty was using a sleep collar on Reaper as well as the '49er.

Brooks responded with a litany of grunts and affirmative noises, until he got to the end of fixing me up.

"You can sit up, Doc," he said as he went to the wash station in the infirmary.

I'd never asked exactly what all concessions and support he and Choi had wrung out of the FBI and the US government, but it'd been enough to set up the Foundation with a trauma center as good as Grady Hospital's.

"As for the news, hate to say it, but it tracks with everything else."

I'd forgotten my tank top at the scene of the battle, so I pulled on my jacket and left it unzipped for now. "That's it? None of this worries or surprises you? Even the fact that someone had the resources and desire to plot my assassination via undead monster?"

"Of course it worries me." Brooks peeled off his gloves and scrubbed up. "But it doesn't surprise me. The government's scared, so putting Reaper and other Push Crooks they can't contain to sleep is probably the most humane thing we could hope for. Doesn't mean I like it."

He turned to face me, towel in hand. "As for the plot, I think you're as un-shocked by it as we are. How many Push Crooks have you put away? How many normal criminals have you disrupted? You've got a list of enemies a mile long, just like we all do, but you've got it worse. You're the big girl on campus." At least Brooks didn't take the glee he used to when he brought up my idolization.

"Yep, I'm the poster girl of a political movement and the publicly appointed savior of the United States, I'm aware." I sighed deeply. "You're right, I shouldn't be shocked, but I still am. At least a little."

Brooks chuckled as he finished drying his hands. "I sometimes forget you were a civilian before the Whiteout. Hate to say it, but you'll get used to people plotting your death soon enough." He tossed the towel over his shoulder. "What's more surprising than all this is you and Ex. But only marginally."

Was it the influence of the Whiteout that made Brooks focus not on the critical events that had played out, but the potential interpersonal drama of the superteam he worked with?

I couldn't be sure, because most people were focused on that kind of stuff beforehand. It only became worse because of the inherent nature of this new comic book reality. Either way, I knew when I was beat.

"Before you grill me, can I at least have food and water?"

The appetite suppressants I'd popped before the stake-out had lost all their efficacy during my treatment. Instead of the mere sensation that my stomach was twisting into knots, it felt like my stomach was about to chow down on the rest of my body.

In a way, it already was. Long bouts of focus and pushing my limits led to my body cannibalizing itself to function, just as it did with conventional starvation, and with all the injuries to heal, it didn't stop when I let the focus go.

Fortunately, Brooks was a doctor who cared for his patients. He was already wheeling a tray table laden with Styrofoam hot food containers, along with a liter-sized water bottle. "Already ahead of you. You eat and talk, I'll provide my usual sage advice."

With that, he pulled up a chair by the examination table. By the time he sat down, I was already tearing into my midnight dinner like a ravenous wolf.

Unlike the first few times I ate like this in front of him, Brooks didn't even bat an eye. He just waited patiently until I slowed to a more normal pace of consumption.

"So, what's your first question, detective?" I asked, trying not to sound *too* annoyed. While this was my private life, I also saw how this could affect the very public business of trying to save the world and reverse the Whiteout.

"I'll start with the big one - is this serious?" He gave me a knowing look and, for the first time, I had a feeling I couldn't dodge this particular question.

Sure, I could stall behind food and pain until I could make an exit, but Brooks didn't stand for my crap as much as Extinguisher did.

The only other person who didn't let me get away with this kind of thing was Medusa and, now that the cat was out of the bag, she'd be the next one to track me down for this very talk. Guess I should get some practice in.

"Do I sound like an asshole when I say that I don't know?" I sighed. "Ex and I clicked, sure, but after what happened with Epic, I'm not looking to declare my love for anyone."

Before Brooks could say anything, I raised my hands defensively. "But I was super clear about us being friends with benefits up front. There were no guarantees of anything more."

Brooks nodded slowly. "Wasn't going to question that, but you were sure quick to be defensive about it." I bit down the desire to make another defensive statement. "I get being reluctant about diving into anything after dating a megalomaniac with a messiah complex, but you've gotta know Ex isn't that kind of guy."

"Trauma doesn't always listen to rationality."

For a moment, I wondered if I should stop there, but Rational Irene stepped up to tell me that I needed this. I hadn't talked to anyone about this - not Medusa, not Facet, not even Mom. Another thing I thought I could handle on my own, but was I handling it or just avoiding it? Time to change that.

"But that's not all of it. What about the Whiteout?"

Brooks arched an eyebrow as he dug into his pocket. "What's the Whiteout got to do with this?"

"Everything." I waved around the room. "It's everywhere and changed almost everyone and everything.

Some of those changes are subtle, some are dramatic, but consider this - what happens when we succeed, and the world goes back to the way it was?"

Brooks was just popping another piece of nicotine gum into his mouth as I asked my question, and he took a few long moments to think about it as he chewed. I hoped I wouldn't have to spell it out for him, but with the Whiteout's influence, I couldn't be sure.

"Okay, I see what you're saying. We fix this, everything changes back, and Ex isn't the same man he is today." Brooks rubbed his stubbled chin. "Or maybe he's exactly the same guy. Yeah, you say we're all affected by the Whiteout, but think about it. Dude was a firefighter beforehand, and a decorated one. He's always been a hero, even before the powers."

I'd already thought about all that, of course. "I'm not saying he'd turn into a terrible human being or anything, but the Whiteout is subtle, insidious." I closed my eyes and hung my head in my hands. "He might not be a totally different person, but he *will* be a different person. You all will. Maybe even *I* will."

Those were things I'd thought about for months but, like my concerns about my relationship with Extinguisher, I'd kept them to myself. It wasn't important to the mission and honestly, I think every one of us who knew the truth had these same concerns deep down.

"I've only really got one thing to say about that, Doc - if we dwell on that kind of shit, we're going to go mad. You're worried about what happens in the future, so you're trying to control everything. Right now, that's manifesting in your relationship with Ex."

I opened my eyes, and I looked up to see Brooks rubbing his ring finger, right where a wedding band would be. "I used to do that, too. Tried to control the future, keep my wife insulated from my world, but that didn't work out so well."

"Oh God, I'm so sorry, Duane. Was it some Mafia hit or something?"

Brooks chuckled. "I appreciate the apology, but it's not *that* bad. Wendy's not dead, we're divorced. Not that it's much better." He sighed. "I loved her, you know? But I couldn't let go, couldn't trust that she could handle being an FBI agent's wife, and so it fell apart."

"Just like this could all fall apart if I don't get my head out of my ass."

"Pretty much." Brooks slapped his thighs and stood. "I don't know what choices you'll make about this. Hell, you've got a ton of baggage with Epic that's going to make this hard. But I trust you'll figure it out and do what's right for you and everyone else."

"I wish I had your faith." My own rise was slower, stiffer as the pain from my injuries hampered me. "Uh, Duane, before you let Ex know I'm good to go, I could really use more –"

He knew exactly what I was going to ask, and he didn't like my request. "Hell no, Irene. If you're out already, you're taking a hell of a lot more than what you're supposed to. You need to scale this shit back. It's not healthy. These kinds of painkillers are addictive."

"Sure, I'll do that." Pain and need turned into a frustration I didn't think I had. "I'll sit back, take a day or two off to rest, and let, who knows, a dozen people die. Maybe we'll be lucky, and it'll only be five."

"You keep this up, and you'll only be responsible for one death - your own. Even with how fast you heal, you're getting hurt faster than I patch you back together."

Brooks crossed his arms, a deep frown etched on his features. "Nobody here wants to see the day when someone brings you home in a body bag."

I wanted to shout something, to make a clever retort, to demand he give me the painkillers and muscle relaxers I swore I needed to keep doing my job. Staring into his eyes, though, I couldn't. I could almost see what I was turning into reflected there.

My stomach flipped, and I felt weak in the knees. Maybe it was all the injuries, maybe it was this psychic slap at the realization. Either way, my legs started to give out.

Brooks was there and caught me by my good arm before I crashed to the floor. The world lurched for a moment then stabilized. I was still in agony, but I could stand. Even so, I didn't push him away.

"What the hell am I doing, Duane?"

"Doc, let me get Ex to get you to your room. Just get some rest and shit will sort itself out."

I wanted to believe it'd be that simple, but I still lived in the real world, not the Whiteout. Deep down, I knew that none of this would sort itself out unless I took hold of the reins.

I only hoped it wasn't too late for me *and* the world.

Chapter 10

In the immediate aftermath of the Battle of Washington, my break-up with Epic, and every moment of my life now consumed by Indomitable and the Foundation, I'd moved from the spacious apartment I'd shared with Epic into a small set of rooms in the Foundation building itself.

Extinguisher and I had walked up the three flights of stairs from the infirmary to my apartment more than a few times, even those times when I probably should've taken the elevator.

I leaned on Extinguisher like a crutch to lessen the strain on my wounded leg. He seemed to be lost in thought, too, as we stepped out onto the fourth floor. It was only when we got to my apartment door that I broke the silence.

"Thanks, Ex, I really appreciate it." I almost slipped out of his grasp to go through the door, but I stopped myself. Maybe I couldn't solve this in one night, but it sure wouldn't get fixed if I kept avoiding it. "Do you want to come in?"

"Are you sure you should be considering *that* in your condition?" he replied, half-jokingly.

I gave him a serious look. "After the night we've had, I am absolutely not thinking about sex. But I still want you to come in. Both because it'll hurt less to have your help to get ready to sleep and because I want to talk."

He matched seriousness for seriousness. "Are you sure? As much as I've pushed for this kind of talk, well, the kind of talk I'm hoping you're talking about, I don't want you to feel pressured because of tonight."

"That right there is why we need to do this." I prodded him gently with my elbow. "You're too good a man for me to keep you dangling like I have." I reached over and opened the door. "So, you in?"

"Nowhere I'd rather be." With that, Extinguisher helped me into my rather plain apartment.

Really, it was more a guest suite or a hotel room than a real apartment. No kitchenette or dining area - just the main room with bed, dressers, and closet, a small office area that I barely used against the building wall with a view out onto the street, and a large bathroom.

He helped me to sit on the edge of the bed then grabbed a chair from the sitting area. While I carefully pulled off my dirty and abused jacket, Extinguisher pulled the chair over, took a seat, and started helping me with my boots.

I didn't even have the energy to get the jacket into my dirty clothes hamper. I just tossed it onto the ground beside the bed, then gave Extinguisher a thankful smile as he got my other boot off.

"Thanks." I smiled through the pain and exhaustion. "So, do you want me to start, or do you want to? I've got a lot I want to say, but you've been trying to have this conversation for months now." I couldn't even give a proper shrug with one shoulder taped up. "I figure you've got every right -"

"To say my piece first?" I gave him a chiding look, and he chuckled a little. "Sorry, Indy. I'll rein in the impulse to do that. Seriously, though, I don't know if I really have much to say that you can't already figure out."

Extinguisher sat back, gazing off out the window as nostalgia colored his voice. "From the first night we sat over there, watching the Independence Day fireworks as we decided to try this out," he pointed one frosty finger back and forth between us, "I've always thought about pursuing something more serious. Maybe that makes me sound a bit crazy or possessive, but it's not that."

I nodded slowly. "I believe you, but you can see why that might be a little worrisome for me. Considering that the trouble the world is in comes from my ex-boyfriend who turned out to be, well, *really* crazy and possessive."

"You've got to see that I'm not him, though, right?"

"I do, I really do." While I didn't want to rush ahead, I still wanted to show a sign I really meant this.

So I leaned forward just a bit so I could put a hand on his knee. "If I thought you were like Epic, we wouldn't be having this conversation, no matter how good the sex is."

"That's a relief on two fronts then. Glad to know I've been doing some things right."

I grinned. "Yeah, a few things." I grew serious then. "But a lot of my hesitance about taking things beyond a casual level stems from what happened with Epic. He betrayed me, stole from me, and thought I'd be okay with it."

Extinguisher locked gazes with me, and I could see past the icy blue of his Pushed form to the warm brown of his natural eyes. "I don't know how much weight what I'm about to say carries, Indy, but I'd never do that to you."

"A lot of weight, actually. You're a real hero, after all, and as I've been reminded very recently, you were a hero before the Whiteout. But that dovetails into another concern of mine."

I sighed and gathered myself. Time to dive into the heart of the issue. "Honestly, this is the big one, the real thing that's made me avoid having a serious discussion. Well, aside from the trauma of Epic's betrayal."

Extinguisher didn't say a word. He only straightened up in his chair, as if bracing himself for something horrible, and nodded.

"I'm –" I wanted to say "worried," but that was too weak a word. I took a deep breath and pushed myself forward. "I'm afraid. Afraid of what happens if – when – we stop all this madness and fix the Whiteout."

"Afraid of what happens to what? Or maybe it's better to ask to whom?"

He knew me well enough to finish my sentences. It shouldn't have surprised me that he was aware enough to probe beyond the obvious conclusions.

"You. Me. Hell, any and all of us. But for the purpose of this moment, you and me."

I shook my head slowly. "I know enough about you to realize you won't turn into a monster when the world's made right, but the Whiteout's insidious, subtle. It's probably changed you in dozens of subtle ways. I don't even know your real name, Ex."

As I moved to rub my eyes and cheeks to keep focused, I realized I still had my mask on.

"And look at me. I'm no better. I *choose* to live behind this mask now. Sure, maybe the Whiteout isn't succeeding in feeding me new thoughts and feelings, but it's changed me all the same. But unlike you, when we fix this, I won't change back."

Well, crap. I was tearing up. Maybe I shouldn't have been surprised. It'd been a long, terrible day, and between Brooks and Extinguisher, I was having to face some hard truths.

My eyes were blurry and my aching body tight with sobs, so I don't know what Extinguisher was doing while I continued rambling.

"You'll think I'm crazy, but I've had literal arguments with myself. Two of me, actually. We had a whole lecture hall and everything. And they're still in my head. Me, myself, and I."

My laugh probably sounded truly crazy. "So, maybe, I've kept you at arm's length just so you don't get too involved with a madwoman."

I snapped back to some degree of my senses as Extinguisher's unique chill came over me, his arm now around my shoulder.

I'd been so wrapped up in my emotions that I hadn't noticed him shifting to sit beside me on the bed, but I was very much was aware as he pulled me close. His presence was an emotional comfort even as the cold roiling off his body soothed my aches.

"You're not crazy." Extinguisher's voice was deep, and his tone serious. In that moment, it was a rock to which I could cling. "The fact you're still holding yourself together, still doing this frankly thankless job, speaks volumes."

I leaned into him - no, better to say I collapsed into him. For the first time since I put on the mask of Indomitable, I let everything go.

God, it felt so good to do that. I didn't need to be strong, invincible, unflinching. I could just be normal Irene Roman and grieve for what I'd lost.

"It's okay, Irene."

My eyes widened in surprise, my sob catching in throat as I pulled away enough to look at Extinguisher. He was looking back at me.

"What did you call me?" It was so hard to believe that I had to ask the obvious question.

"Irene. I - I should've called you that sooner." He took a deep breath and let it out slowly. "And, uh, my name - my secret identity - is Will. Will Washington." The way

Extinguisher's lips twisted and brows furrowed, it looked like it took him actual physical effort to say the words.

For all I knew, it did.

I sniffed back the lingering tears and smiled. "It's nice to meet you, Will."

Extinguisher smiled back and, in that moment, I gave him a bit of reward for the effort he'd put in.

Which is to say I kissed him, good and proper. For the first time, it felt like something more than a release for me.

He responded in kind, and I won't lie in saying that I lost a few moments in the bliss of the moment.

But all good things end. We pulled away from the kiss, both of us breathing heavily. That was the only sound in the room for a good few moments before I broke the silence.

"So, uh, yeah. Let's try to be more serious."

"Alright." It would've sounded flippant save for the tone of his voice, which was as serious as death and taxes. "But right now, for your own good, you need to sleep." He gave me a pointed look. "Alone."

"A small part of me wants to argue that point, but the vast majority of me agrees with you." I smiled a bit. "But I feel better getting this off my chest and starting to move past all this."

"Me too." Extinguisher stood, took a step toward the door, then turned back to me. "It's early days, but at least we know what we're tackling. Just don't go back into your shell, Irene. Do you need any more help getting ready for bed?"

I shook my head. "I think I've got it. Thanks, Will."

While it was still clearly foreign to him to think in terms of real names still, Extinguisher smiled and headed toward the door. "Good night, try to get some rest."

"You, too. We've still got a world to save."

"As always."

As he spoke, I chimed in with him. "Lives are at stake."

With that, Extinguisher went off to his own quarters down a floor. I was left with the faint butterflies of real affection in my stomach, mixed with the pain of my injuries, and the flutter of worry in my heart.

I was taking a chance, at least that's how I saw it. Opening my heart up again after what Epic had done wasn't easy, and it could explode in my face. It could ruin everything we'd worked and bled for these past six months.

But I couldn't argue with the fact that I had some actual happy thoughts in my head as I finally took my mask off for once in a long while.

Chapter 11

Maybe an hour before sunrise, I crawled out of bed and into the bathroom. The happy feelings of the night before had faded into a faint glow, which still helped with the dull, throbbing aches in my shoulder and thigh.

Despite the food I'd wolfed down, a gnawing hunger growled in my stomach. My body had eagerly gone about rebuilding itself, first using up all the nutrients and calories I'd refilled it with, then kept going with no mind as to whether there was anything in the tank to build with.

I tried to focus on the strides I'd made with Extinguisher, and that helped. Knowing his real name was a treasure I'd wanted, even if I hadn't fully grasped how much until I had it. That and the work that I knew was waiting kept me going through a vigorous shower, making sure to protect my wound dressings from the scalding water.

I almost kept myself from looking into the drug cabinet over the sink.

But almost only counts in horseshoes and hand grenades. Before I even realized what I was doing, I opened the cabinet and glanced through the cornucopia of medications sitting there.

If the "me" of six months ago had seen this, she never would've believed it.

Pills for muscle and nerve pain, antibiotics by the bucket, muscle relaxers, multivitamins of every shape and color, and let's not forget the hunger suppressants.

Most of the pain relievers and hunger managers were close to empty. I'd taken to some creative combinations to deal with my needs.

Maybe it was my talk with Extinguisher, but for the first time, I opened my eyes to all this. I couldn't believe the degree to which I'd fallen. I'd just kept doing what I thought needed to be done, damn the consequences.

I touched a bottle of oxycodone with my fingertip. I really could use help today - Mary's friends needed saving, and she had to be waiting to put us on their trail. As if on cue, the gouge in my thigh sent up a flare of pain so as not to be forgotten.

I flipped the bottle forward into my hand and brought it close. I read the label, as if I hadn't already memorized it. Who'd know? And if they did, what right did they have to judge?

I let out a cry of rage and turned, hurling the bottle with all my strength. The plastic cracked and splintered against the wall, sending the last few pills scattering across the tile floor.

I knew, and I had every right to judge myself. But that wasn't all. If Brooks didn't know, he was suspicious of my excesses. And Extinguisher. Did he know or suspect?

I needed help with this. But right now, there were other people that needed me. I could handle this for the moment. I told people my "power" was willpower. Maybe it was partly a lie to avoid people questioning my non-Pushed status, but it was also partly true. That meant I could beat this. I had to.

My body tried to rebel as I got myself ready. It was as if it acted on its own volitionand, since it wasn't getting what it felt it needed, it turned every pain, weakness, and twitch up to eleven. Somehow, though, I managed, to put on on a pristine uniform.

I stared in my dresser mirror for a few moments, strangely entranced by the bloodshot eyes, the early wrinkles, the dark circles around the eyes, and the wet, limp, brown hair.

I dug down deep, focused on the breakthrough I'd had with Extinguisher, and forced myself to reach for the mask and the spirit gum that ensured it stayed glued to my face. It was time to go to work.

So committed was I to the idea of doing things the "normal" way that I took the stairs down to the Foundation headquarters proper on the ground floor.

As I went downstairs, I assessed how badly I was still hurt after some time sleeping and healing. And I checked through my phone for news updates and messages on the encrypted Foundation message system.

As I had since the start of the Whiteout, I was healing far faster than I had any right to do. My thigh still ached fiercely, but it held my weight properly and moved well enough. My impacted shoulder was mostly fine, too. Some of my bruises were gnarly colors, but they were hidden under my uniform.

I guessed I was maybe at seventy or eighty percent, but it'd been so long since I was fully, properly healthy that I could've been wrong.

It didn't matter. It'd have to be enough to keep going.

Per my phone, Medusa was waiting for me at the cafeteria to grab breakfast before we headed to the meeting room for the morning briefing.

A note from Choi let everyone know about the situation with The '49er from the night before, and that the Foundation had two new guests. Mary and Caleb were given a room on the second floor, and Mary would explain all she knew about the kidnapping situation at the briefing.

The rest of the messages were general operations. The Human Tank and Mind's Eye had wrapped things up and were still on schedule to get back to Atlanta by late afternoon, while Facet and Ken had a solid lead on the Stellar gang's hideout. They'd be making a move that evening with a squad of PART officers. No suggestion they needed more backup, thankfully.

I was slipping my phone back into its belt pouch as I left the stairwell and went into the main lobby. As always, a small army of photographers and assorted paparazzi camped outside the double glass doors to the street. They, like so many other things, were a fact of life in our new reality. I ignored them.

The cafeteria was wisely situated close to the main meeting room, and I was thankful for that today more than any other. It was a small affair - calling it a cafeteria was a bit overblown - but there were enough tables to seat twenty people, and the Foundation staffers served up set meals three times a day.

The place was almost empty right now - save for Medusa, who waggled her scaled fingers at me in greeting as I headed for the counter - and the staff.

Fortunately, they knew me well enough to have a double serving of today's breakfast and a huge mug of coffee - with honey and extra cream - waiting for me.

With a genuine smile of thanks, I grabbed my breakfast and settled down across from Medusa. "Morning, Meds."

Now, if Extinguisher was my lover, Facet my kid sister, and the Human Tank my younger brother, Medusa was my best friend. Sure, she looked like she'd stepped right out of Greek mythology, snake hair, scaly skin, and petrifying gaze included, but she was perhaps the most human of all of us, me included.

"Good morning yourself, Irene," she hissed, a smile on her scaly lips. "I'm glad to see you up and around already, especially with the night you had."

"It wasn't what we were expecting, for sure," I said between bites of sausage and eggs. My body thanked me for the donation of new fuel for repairs. "I'm sure you read the reports. I'm only sorry we didn't call for reinforcements."

"To be fair, I don't think Hex and I would've gotten there before it was all over."

Medusa was already finished with her own plate. She just sipped at the last of her coffee while we caught up. "That's the nature of Push Battles. They're over almost as soon as they begin. All we can do is pray to come out on top and with as few people hurt as possible."

I nodded sadly. "Did the Valdosta investigation bear any fruit? I've only caught up on messages, no time yet to read reports."

"Yes, I heard from Rachel how badly you were hurt last night." Medusa's hiss always grew in intensity when she was hurt, upset, or angry, and it intensified now. "I know Brooks already said what I'm about to, and I'd hope Ex has as team leader, but you've got to slow down, *chica*. None of us want to lose you."

Whiteout Irene scoffed at the notion. Heroes didn't die, after all, and if they did, just wait for the next adventure - I'd be back, right as rain. Rational Irene objected to this nonsense, pointing out most astutely that even Epic didn't seem to have the power to bring the dead back to life.

I certainly sided with Rational Irene on this one, but there were nuances her starkly logical mind didn't take into account. I mulled it all over as I polished off breakfast.

Medusa, as always, was patient as she waited for me to finish. Maybe it was her experience as a social worker pre-

Whiteout, but she knew when to push, when to stop, and when to listen.

"Okay, I don't want to die, trust me, but there's too much to do. Too many lives hanging in the balance, lives I can save. I can't exactly sit on my hands, can I?"

"No, but the counterpoint is that you won't save anyone's lives if you're too hurt or too exhausted to help. Or worse." Medusa looked ready to go into a second chorus of reasons why I needed to take a vacation when our comms beeped.

"Medusa, Indy, I hate to rush you," Choi said over the comm, "but there's much to do today, and everyone else is already assembled for the briefing."

"Good morning to you too, Rachel." I grabbed my empty tray. "Be there in a minute."

"Taking the convenient escape, I see," Medusa teased as she followed me to the front of the cafeteria. "I'll allow it for now, I suppose."

"Don't blame me, Meds." I grinned, more than willing to dodge out of this conversation. "Duty calls."

Chapter 12

The adjacent meeting room was quiet when we stepped inside.

That didn't surprise me, especially as there was an invisible line separating the two sides of the conference table that dominated the room. It was a line that the Whiteout had created and, despite the months that'd passed or how closely we all worked together, it persisted.

On the left side of the table sat the Push Heroes of the Atlanta Five, those that were in town, anyway. Right now, that was Extinguisher and Hexagon, the team's resident six-armed powerhouse, though Medusa moved to sit next to him the moment we crossed the threshold.

On the right side of the table were the normal humans - Choi, Brooks, and a much more put-together Mary Johnson. I guessed baby Caleb was in the care of someone on Foundation staff.

What divided them was the Pulse. My Pushed friends tried to describe it to me a few times. To them, the Pulse was an instinctual sense of connection, a feeling in their hearts that others that had it were of their tribe, even if they were villains. Pushed could use the Pulse to pick their brothers and sisters out of a crowd of normal people, easy as pie.

Their interpretation of it was a lot nicer than how I felt the Pulse. It's what twisted my stomach and hurt my head the moment I got close to a Pushed, a signal that they were inherently unreal, at least to me.

From what I'd seen, while normal people didn't perceive the Pulse in a tangible sense, it seemed to influence their thoughts and feelings, engendering either awe and worship or fear and horror.

As for me, the Pushed knew I was something *different*, and that provoked either curiosity or concern. Normal people had a similar reaction, though they tended towards trust more than anything else.

In the first three months, I wondered often about why this complex interplay of reaction happened, but then the constant work wore most of that curiosity out of me.

At least these past six months had worn down the fight or flight reflex of normal people to a vague but constant tension. Choi and Brooks reacted to it even less, no doubt from the close proximity with which they worked with both the Five and Facet, but it never faded entirely.

"Sorry we're a little behind," I said to break the silence. "I had a very late, very rough night." I took my usual seat at the head of the table, in between the two sides.

"It's quite alright, Indy," Choi said as she tapped away on her tablet. The main screen at the opposite end of the room came on. "It's always to our advantage to have our best assets fed, rested, and ready. Now, let's get started."

A murmur of assents rippled around the table. Choi tapped at her tablet again to bring up a map of Atlanta. The trainyard was marked bright red, while a seemingly random array of blue dots sprang up across the city. At least a dozen places were marked with the dots, and no area of the city was left untouched.

"I'd originally planned on starting today by going over the Valdosta investigation Medusa and Hexagon led into the Humans for God terrorist group, but last night's unexpected Push Battle and the even more unexpected fallout must take precedence."

The Humans for God, or Hogs as everyone called them, accurately, were bigoted religious fanatics, domestic terrorists, and all-around bad guys.

The fact they'd tried to kill all of us on our train ride to Washington hadn't improved my opinion of them. We'd want to take them down no matter what, but there was a topper to the Hogs' crown of horror.

We suspected that they were pawns in Ian Mackenzie's anti-Pushed campaign. He was the mastermind who'd provoked the Battle of Washington, and the Hogs had been one of his tools then. We were sure he hadn't stopped now.

"I'm sure those of you who were there," Choi nodded to Extinguisher, Mary, and me, "know at least part of why it's our top priority now, and the rest of you have looked at the mission report."

Brooks, Hexagon, and Medusa all nodded. "Got an idea of how bad it was based on how much I needed to patch up our girl here last night," Brooks said.

I tried not to grumble at the combination of tease and warning, even as Extinguisher and Medusa added their own glances of concern. After all, I had to put on a strong front for Mary's sake.

"The Forty-Niner's attack and the detainment by Colonel Liberty aside," I said as I sat up straight and squared my shoulders as if I still wasn't aching like crazy, "I've got the bad feeling your real concern is the kidnappings Mary told me about."

"Astute as always, Indy." Choi gestured to Mary, who seemed to shrink a bit from the attention the room paid her, especially the Push Heroes – the Pulse in action.

"Mary Johnson and her infant son, Caleb, were caught up The Forty-Niner's rampage, but why she was in the area is the bigger story. Would you like to tell everyone what you told me this morning, Mary?"

Mary looked over at me, I gave her a nod, and received a small smile in return. "What happened to my friends was two days ago, but from what I've heard in the shelters, people have been disappearing off the streets for weeks now."

Medusa's expression shifted from curious to deep concern, so much so that her snake hair started to let out a low hiss. You could put the social worker into a mythological snake woman, but you couldn't take the social worker out of the mythological snake woman.

"That awfully concerning, Miss Johnson." For such a big man - his Pushed shell at least - Hexagon always had the soothing charm of a kindly Southern gentleman. "Rest assured, whatever happened, we'll get it sorted out and save your friends in the process."

"And until we crack the case, you're our guest at the Foundation," Medusa added. "You and Caleb will be safe and sound."

"I can't thank you enough. Trust me, I tried all this morning with Miss Choi and Mister Brooks. Let me get back to what happened, even if it's not going to be a lot of help."

"I'm sure it'll be more help than you think," I said.

"Okay, well, I've been down on my luck since Caleb was born and the father...no, that's not important. Let me focus." Mary took a deep breath and let it out slowly.

"The important part is I've had to bounce around the women's and homeless shelters in the city for the past few months. You get to know folks fast on the streets, especially folks to be wary of and those you can trust. Rick and Sally Greer were two folks I could trust, at least until they got nabbed."

I nodded. "Right off the street, I think you said last night. You hinted that Pushed had something to do with it, too."

"Yes. Not that the cops believed me, not until Captain Braxton, but his belief didn't do much. I'd still be lost if it wasn't for you."

Medusa's snake hair grew agitated again, but her tone was soft and kind. "Who or what took your friends, Mary?"

"I didn't get a clear look, it happened so fast. It was late, we'd just gotten done with some work and were headed to Harmony House."

I wasn't personally familiar, but I'd seen the ads and signs. Harmony House was a well-regarded homeless shelter and non-profit charity. No doubt Choi had already pulled up all the info on the place, even if it wasn't directly relevant to the case, and anything Choi didn't know, Medusa did.

"Cutting through the alley was our real mistake, I guess, but we'd done it a dozen times. And everything looked fine, even if it was dark. No one was loitering or anything. But there was something there all the same."

"What?" Medusa asked gently.

"It was fast. Like, Pushed fast. So fast I didn't really see it. Some kind of high-pitched whine hit my ears, then before we could do anything, it came out of the shadows on one side of the alley, right through us. Then I was alone."

Silence fell across the table as we all absorbed the story, brief as it was. But it didn't need to be long, not for something that happened in the blink of an eye.

Considering all the crazy powers in the post-Whiteout world, as many as in the comic books and superhero movies I used to love, there were dozens of possibilities for what happened.

"I take it the blue marks on the map are other mysterious disappearances from the last few weeks?" I asked Choi to break the silence.

"Correct, Indy."

Brooks spoke up. "I called my contacts in the police department this morning to ask about these events. Where they've got an actual witness statement, they all match up with Mary's story. Including the fact every incident took place at night."

I took note of that, but it was likely nothing too important. If I were going to kidnap people off the street and try to hide it, I'd do it at night, too.

"You'd think they would've taken these reports seriously," Medusa hissed, "considering everything that's happened since the Whiteout."

Mary gave a mirthless laugh. "They don't listen to people like me, like us, very much."

Medusa nodded knowingly, and I turned to study the map.

There was actually a bit of a pattern. Atlanta had had plenty of bad parts of town before, and the constant chaos of Push Battles had aggravated that problem. The locations of the blue dots all looked like they were in or adjacent to those worse-off areas.

Time to speculate. "I'm going to ask, but I'm pretty sure I already know the answer - all of the victims were poor and homeless, weren't they?"

Choi and Brooks both nodded.

Extinguisher scowled. "So, we've got a rash of - let's call them what they are - kidnappings affecting the worst-off people in the city." That familiar flame of righteous indignation was in his voice. "And the police are sitting on their hands."

"Not that they could do much to a Push Crook," Hexagon countered. "And there's certainly at least one behind this, for sure."

Mary sighed. "I wish I had more to tell you, some clue or something that'd help you find my friends and the rest of them. It was over so fast, though..."

"You've told us more than you probably think," I assured her. "Right now, all you need to worry about is staying safe here in the Foundation and taking care of Caleb. We'll get right on the rest."

I realized I'd overstepped and, considering Extinguisher and I were going to try to make this work, I looked down at our fearless leader. "Uhm, assuming that's the plan, Ex?"

"Absolutely." He smiled at Mary. "Why don't you go see your son and try to take it easy? You've been through a lot in the past couple of days."

Mary went to the door, stopped, and looked back at me. "I'm sure you hear this a lot, but thank *you* especially. For last night and, well, all this."

I smiled as, for a few moments, the aches, pains, and burdens all felt a little lighter. "My pleasure, but you can really thank me when we save your friends."

Mary nodded and left the room.

"So," I turned back to the others, "what *is* the plan?" I focused on Choi in particular. Extinguisher was the leader of the Atlanta Five, but Choi was our master planner. "And don't say we don't have one. I know you too well."

Despite her usual poker face, Choi couldn't keep a knowing little grin off her lips. "Of course I do."

Chapter 13

Choi didn't leave us hanging. She never did, always one to get to the point with surgical directness.

Tapping away at her tablet, Choi shifted one of the blue pinned locations to green. I recognized it immediately as the site of the attack Mary had just described to us.

"There's something else about the locations beyond what you've already noted, Indy."

Choi continued to work, and the rest of the markers lit up in green. "If I overlay the locations of the attacks with these schematics of the out-of-service portions of Underground Atlanta plus the sewer system…"

My shoulder and leg were both starting to throb again, and the wound in my thigh started that terrible itch only a healing cut can produce.

I tried to ignore all that - plus the needling thought that I could take a few of the oxycodone pills I had on the floor upstairs to make it all go away - and focus.

While much of Underground, a historic Atlanta landmark, had been refurbished to form a new retail and entertainment district, parts of the subterranean areas remained unused, save for the desperate and the homeless.

The sewers were deeper, of course, but the commonalities they shared with Underground was obvious.

Both schematics linked up to most - though not all - of the reported disappearances through nearby entrances and access points.

"I think the connection is obvious," Choi concluded.

"It makes sense," Extinguisher mused. "Our Pushed must be insanely fast, almost invisible, but their victims aren't. They've got to get them off the streets fast."

Medusa's snakes shuddered and hissed. "And while Atlanta isn't known for its winters, people in need who can't get help at the shelters are going to use both old Underground and the sewers. Whatever monster is behind this, they'll have their prey come to them as the nights grow colder."

"That does make for a large collective area to search, and we're still down on people." Rational Irene had supplied that. While she was sympathetic, she also noted that this was a huge mission that would be one more obstacle towards stopping the Whiteout entirely.

I sided with Whiteout Irene this time, though. "But it doesn't matter. We have to stop whoever's behind this and save these people, and the sooner we start, the sooner they're safe."

Choi nodded. "I assumed you'd all be eager to tackle this, but there's more. We have a likely suspect."

Choi switched the display from the city map to show several images and a looped video.

One image was a selfie pulled from social media, and the other was of a graffiti adorned brick wall. The video was pulled from a bank's security system mid-robbery and replayed on a ten-second loop.

The selfie and the video caught my eye immediately, because they starred the same individual.

Unsurprisingly, they were Pushed, something anyone could tell immediately because their form was blurred. Not shrouded in mist or obscured in some trick of photography, but like they were continually shaking or vibrating at some rapid frequency.

It looked like when the Flash would vibrate through something at superspeed in the comics, especially in the video, and the constant shaking made it almost impossible to pick out more than the most basic details.

That's when I realized the video was playing at one-quarter speed. At full, I wasn't even sure what we'd be able to pick out.

I focused on what I *could* see. What I figured was blurred skin was dusky, but I couldn't tell what ethnicity.

Black and red formed the predominant streaks of color that I guessed were clothing, with the occasional smear of chrome. Assuming the streaks at the top of the "head" was hair, our Pushed was a brunette.

While the details were indistinct, what they could do was clear. They didn't just vibrate with startling speed, they flashed across the camera's view just as fast.

But that wasn't all. Our Pushed zoomed past a bank guard with an upraised pistol, and the Pushed lashed out with what I guessed was a swipe of their arm.

It didn't just pass through the firearm's barrel - it sliced right through.

The graffiti wall was easier to process. Over the older works of art and gang signs was a new mark - a stylized piece depicting the letter B stretched into a smear of red and black, much like our Pushed's appearance.

"I'm guessing there's a high-pitched buzz reported at this bank robbery?" I asked.

"Correct," Choi confirmed. "All of which matches the situation Mary found herself in."

"That's not the only robbery with this same Push Crook behind it," Brooks said. "And that graffiti is their tag, or better to say their gang's tag. Word on the street calls them the Buzzkillers and that little untouched space is the heart of their territory."

"Seems cut and dried to me," Extinguisher said. Hexagon nodded.

But I was quick to interrupt. "Too cut and dried, if you ask me. Unless there's been an uptick in human trafficking or something, which I'd think we'd know about, how do you jump from bank robbery to mass kidnapping?"

"Indy's right," Medusa agreed, "but at the same time, I don't think we can ignore these clues."

"Especially," Choi said, "as bank robbery isn't the only crime our Push Crook, who we're calling Buzzkill, has committed."

"What else has this varmint done?" Hexagon asked, sounding ready to use all six arms to pummel Buzzkill into a splat.

"Assault with a deadly weapon, of course," Choi replied, "but also a variety of industrial thefts. Chemicals, lab equipment, and some surprisingly mundane supplies. No one act that'd get our attention, especially with us focused on McKenzie and Epic, but it's added up."

"A drug operation, then." I might've been a rookie at this whole crimefighting thing compared to the two ex-FBI agents, but I'd been connected to the medical world throughout college and my research career. "So, you suspect these kidnappings could be for what? Slave labor or something?"

"Or this Buzzkill character could be running a trafficking racket on their own," Hexagon growled. "This criminal is so fast, it looks like they can vibrate through walls. They could run a victim to auction, drop them off, and get back to the Buzzkiller lair or whatever before anyone would know."

"Hex is right," Extinguisher said in his firm, no-nonsense, I'm the leader voice. "Buzzkill could be up to anything, and they've been smart enough to go under our radar."

Something felt off about this situation. Not that we didn't need to deal with Buzzkill sooner or later. They were a Push Crook causing real harm, and that kind of superspeed would get someone killed, if it hadn't already. But this didn't feel like it fully lined up with the kidnappings.

Still, there wasn't a concrete fact I could point at, just a gut feeling.

"Okay, I agree, but we shouldn't put all our eggs in one basket." I looked to Choi. "You said you had a plan?"

"Yes, I've put together a general search pattern to make this as efficient as possible."

On the main screen, Choi highlighted a search route through all the possible entrances underground.

"Your team will split into pairs. The first will be Indy and Medusa, while the second is Extinguisher and Hexagon. Those pairs are going to pursue different approaches."

She nodded to Medusa and me. "I want you two to handle surface investigations. The old walk and talk, as we say in law enforcement."

That made sense to me. We didn't have superhuman movement powers, so we had to go by the streets.

"Medusa's skills and knowledge from her social work combined with Indy's 'America's Savior' status should give you both the best chance to get information from the people."

I did my best not to react to the title Choi gave me, but I failed, if the others' chuckles were any indication.

"You two also have senses you can access beyond the norm," Choi continued, "making you best suited for crime scene investigation."

She turned to Extinguisher. "You and Hexagon will head directly to the underground access points to investigate.

Don't go deep – I think any evidence of passage or tampering should be evident."

Extinguisher nodded. "I get it. Our speed will let us get down there and out quickly, plus if we find any victims, Hex and I are better equipped to evac them."

"Six arms and two shoulders means eight people out at a time," Hex added with a grin.

"That still leaves a lot of ground to cover," Brooks said as he looked over the map. "If Tank and Mind's Eye are still fresh when they get in, Rachel will add them to the search."

He turned back to the rest of us. "Meanwhile, I'll see about raising hell with the Atlanta PD and PART. Maybe if I drop all this actual detective work in their laps, I can rustle up some more boots on the ground."

"Joe seemed swayed last night," Extinguisher noted. "But PART might still be too tangled up in the aftermath of The Forty-Niner's rampage to be much help."

"Still, we'll take what we can get," I said.

Choi nodded. "I urge caution. The only thing we know is that this Pushed can move fast enough to be unseen by the normal human eye. The fact that half the team will be going underground may make calling in reinforcements difficult. There's no telling how badly being underground will affect comms."

"What Rachel's saying is play it safe for once." Brooks wasn't looking at me directly but, after last night's talk, I knew I was his primary target. "If you get a positive lead and there's no immediate threat to a victim, pull back and call for help, alright?"

It shouldn't have shocked me that Medusa was also looking at me through her snake hair, even as she seemed to be focused on Brooks and Choi. "Yes, we'll all be careful."

She swiveled in her chair to face me with *all* her eyes then. "Won't we, Indy?"

"Sure, but here's the unanswered question - who's looking into Buzzkill?" I crossed my arms and tried to look strong, ready, and with it. "My team is the obvious choice, but it's not my call to make."

It wasn't arrogance talking. In addition to my Natural status, the only person on the team whose reflexes might match my own when I was in focus was Medusa, and reflexes were one of the best assets to have when dealing with a speedster.

Extinguisher opened his mouth to speak, but Medusa showed off those serpentine reflexes by cutting him off. "No way, *chica*. You're not going into gang territory, with an unknown threat, in your condition."

Part of me, part of the real me, wanted to lie. But I was tired and hurt and maybe even feverish and, God, I just wanted to take some painkillers to help me function correctly.

"We all want to watch out for each other, Meds," Extinguisher began, "but Indy isn't made of glass, either. You two are the best equipped of the team to deal with a Push Battle with a speedster, if it comes to that."

"More importantly," Choi cut in, "the search route runs along Buzzkiller territory, but doesn't directly cross into it. If our other investigations come up empty, I'll have you regroup and head on in."

That seemed to appease Medusa. "Sounds perfect, then."

"So when do we get going?" I asked.

"The sooner, the better." Extinguisher stood. "Let's all hit the streets."

Choi nodded. "Good luck, everyone, and good hunting."

Medusa and I headed off to the garage. We'd take our motorcycles for speed and maneuverability.

A brief memory of when I used to bike for fun, to release the stress of a day of research, flashed through my mind before my leg twinged in agony and brought me back to reality.

We were walking by the elevators, and I almost stopped there. Almost begged for Medusa to wait a moment while I grabbed some pills from my apartment.

I didn't, but Medusa caught something. "Something wrong, Indy?"

"No." I forced myself to not think about the pain, the itching in my palms, or the beads of sweat on my forehead. "I'm all good. Let's go save some lives."

Chapter 14

The drive from the Foundation building to the site of the kidnappings Mary witnessed, our first stop on the search route, was a brief moment of peace.

Or it should have, but I couldn't lose myself in the ride. My mind was racing with all the things slipping through my fingers.

I hadn't looked into the Valdosta reports. I hadn't talked to Tank or Mind's Eye in days, Facet and Ken for almost as long. If not for the briefing, I'd have only exchanged a few brief words with Hexagon and Medusa. Hell, I hadn't even talked to Mom for a month.

And what had I gained from all the extra time on the streets or giving speeches?

Yes, I'd saved a lot of lives, but I was no closer to finding Mackenzie before he struck again or turning public sentiment against Epic and his Crusaders.

My musings were interrupted as we pulled into the alley where Mary's friends had been taken. We agreed it'd be the best place to stow the bikes while we walked and talked. Besides, the best chance we'd have to find physical evidence was here.

We were in one of the rougher parts of town, not that it worried me. Muggers were something I wasn't afraid of anymore.

"Should we start with the locals, or search the alley?" Medusa asked as she pulled off her helmet. Her snake hair writhed and stretched, freed from its enclosure. "I don't know if it's even worth the time to do a physical search. It's been days. Any evidence is probably gone."

"Don't be so sure." I took my helmet off, too, and we both dismounted. "There was never an official investigation. No one's been poking around, and it's not a main street. A clue could still be here tucked into a corner or under some debris."

"Fair point. A sweep can't hurt, then we can get to talking with the locals. I'll take one for the team and sniff for anything out of the ordinary. The girls and I have a good sense of smell."

"I'll take care of the rest." While I wasn't a trained detective like Choi and Brooks, years of being a scientist had trained me to have a knack for observation.

Plus, I could cheat.

I closed my eyes, took a deep breath, and focused my will. That sweet surge of adrenaline, endorphins, and so much more flushed the aches of my injuries, the itch of need for a few pills, and the worries distracting me away. When I opened my eyes, I was in full focus, and my mind and body were back in harmony.

While my focused state was incredibly helpful in a fight or doing rescues, basically anything physical, it wasn't just a way to be stronger and faster. It sped up my thoughts and sharpened my senses.

No way to know if it made them superhuman but, in the context of the altered reality of the Whiteout, it made my senses as keen as humanly possible.

The cracks in the pavement, the chill of the faint breeze running down the alley, the footsteps down the surrounding streets, the stink of rotting trash from the dumpsters lining the walls, all that snapped into sharp relief.

Since I knew Medusa's snakes had even stronger senses of smell than my focused self, I turned my attention primarily towards my sight and hearing.

One thing I picked out immediately were several Buzzkiller graffiti marks along the buildings to the right. No surprise there, but it was good to know our assumptions about the gang's boundaries were correct.

While Medusa walked down the alley away from where we'd parked our bikes, I headed to the mouth of the alley, intent on following the shortcut Mary and her friends took.

Advancing slowly, I scanned the alleyway. Despite my hyped-up senses, I didn't really expect to find anything, but again, thoroughness was important in an investigation like this.

For the first few yards, nothing in particular caught my eye. This was exactly as it appeared - a grungy alley in the bad part of town.

Sure, I could pick out a smattering of minute details that could connect to crimes and wrongdoing. A broken glass pipe under a dumpster, the bowl still blackened with drug residue, scuffles in the alley muck that might match the motions of a fight, scratches and dents around the lock of a deli's backdoor signaling a poor lockpick's work.

But nothing seemed tied to the sudden, superfast snatch-and-grab of Mary's friends.

Medusa had ranged halfway down the other end of the alley, and I was about to step around our parked vehicles to follow in her wake when I saw something of real interest out of the corner of my eye.

It was a scuffed canvas wallet, half covered by a grimy fast-food wrapper and half stuffed in the grate of a rusty storm drain.

Maybe it was nothing, but maybe it was everything. I kneeled beside it and carefully brushed the wrapper aside. The wallet itself was blue with black trim, but a rusty red splotch stained the edge. Maybe blood, but the stink of day-old grease and even older sewer water gave my focused but untrained sense of smell problems.

As I opened the wallet, I heard Medusa's soft footfalls coming back my way. "Find something useful?"

I let out a non-committal grunt as I wiped away the grime that had seeped through the sides and clouded the plastic window over the ID.

Richard P. Greer.

"I found something very useful. At least I hope it is."

We'd check the rest of the wallet in a moment but, for now, I held the rusty red stained edge out towards her. "Apologies for the stench, but I'm hoping you and the girls might be able to confirm if this is what I fear it is."

Her scaled nose wrinkled while her snakes let out little hisses. "I get all the best jobs."

Still, Medusa swallowed and stepped close. Though she had a human-like nose, for this kind of careful sniffing she mimed what her snakes did - she flicked out her forked tongue. Individual snakes moved close to the wallet, too, and after a few moments, Medusa pulled back.

"It's dried blood, alright." Her tongue flicked out a few more times, either to sample the air a bit more or get the stink out of her mouth - I wasn't sure and never felt right asking. "There's something else that isn't sewer funk or burger grease. My snake brain says carrion, but that seems strange."

I turned the wallet over in my hands. No signs of organic matter or rotting meat, but there could be bits too tiny for my enhanced vision to see. I was still curtailed by human limitations, even if they were far greater under the Whiteout's rules.

"That's odd, I don't see anything that looks like carrion." I thumbed through the wallet. There were a few bills, a MARTA card, a few pictures of a man matching the driver's license picture and a young woman with black hair, but nothing else out of the ordinary. "Inside's normal, too."

"That carrion scent is odd enough that I might be able to track it, if you want me to give it a shot?"

I snapped the wallet closed, then dug into my utility bag. It was a part of my uniform now more than ever and held all manner of useful things for fieldwork. In this case, some plastic evidence bags.

"Let's do it." I dropped the wallet into the bag and sealed it. "Worst case scenario, we lose the trail and go to questioning locals." As I tucked the evidence away in my utility bag, I pinged Choi over the comms.

"Hey, checking in. We found Rick Greer's wallet with a dried bloodstain and another unusual scent Medusa thinks is rotting flesh."

"Strange," Choi replied over my earbud. "I take it there was no obvious samples?"

"Nope, but Meds thinks she might be able to track that scent." I glanced over to where Medusa was already in the act, crouch-walking with all her snakes flicking at the air. "I'll keep the mics open so you can stay up to date."

"Understood. Extinguisher and Hexagon haven't found anything yet and are moving on to their second search location."

"Gotcha." I let go of my focus – no need to burn energy unnecessarily – and bit back the wince as all the aches crashed down on me.

Medusa didn't notice, all her focus turned toward sniffing out a trail, and I took a moment to get a hold on myself.

I didn't get more than that moment before Medusa's snakes let out a chorus of hisses.

"It's frustrating, because that rot scent seems to scatter and diffuse about..." She rose, her gaze locked on a narrow gap between two buildings on the Buzzkiller side of the alley. "Here."

"Through the gap?" No normal human could squeeze through this pale imitation of an alley, an artifact of cramped urban construction where buildings were literally built against each other. Of course, we weren't dealing with normal humans.

"Yes and...no?" Medusa sighed. "It's too indistinct. As near as I can describe, it went down the crack *and* up over the walls. Like something exploded and left little bits everywhere."

"But there's no little bits, no physical evidence we can see." My first thought was Nitro, a Marvel villain whose whole shtick was blowing up and reforming himself, but Mary hadn't mentioned an explosion. "Let's take the bikes around to the opposite end of this row of buildings and see if we can pick up the trail there."

Medusa nodded and, as she turned towards me, her snakes stood up like a spike crown, focused past me to where we'd entered the alley. "Indy, we've got company."

I heard the crunch of boots on the gritty asphalt right after she gave her warning, and I spun on my heel. Reflexes ingrained from six months of daily superheroing snapped me right into full focus. By the time I caught sight of our new friends, my brain was singing as my mind and body snapped into perfect harmony.

Our new friends were a baker's dozen of people dressed in stereotypical gang chic, that style exaggerated by the Whiteout to an almost ridiculous degree. It was all leather, spikes, denim, chains, with variations of the Buzzkiller tag on their clothes.

They were armed, too, because of course they were.

"You masks are sniffing around the wrong part of town," the guy at the head of the pack growled, probably trying to sound intimidating.

He was tall, lanky, with a sharply angular face. He'd stand out, even if he hadn't gone for maximum Mad Max by styling his hair into a blindingly orange mohawk. "We got no problems with the Five, and we don't want none."

While Mad Max here was technically right in that we were sniffing around, we'd barely gotten started. Maybe the Buzzkillers had lookouts all around the streets that saw us drive in, or maybe the Whiteout was playing its usual games, eager to get heroes and villains of any stripe fighting for any reason.

Medusa moved forward to stand side by side with me, and I purposefully relaxed, just to let Mad Max know we weren't the least bit afraid. "Then maybe you lovely people would like to help us out. We're looking for a lot of missing folks, and two of them were snatched from this very spot."

That got a reaction out of the gang. Some of them seemed unnerved, others flinched, but a good half of them bristled with anger.

"You or your boss wouldn't happen to know anything about that, would you?" I asked sweetly. "If you do, we'd sure appreciate it if you told us."

Mad Max let out a guttural growl before glancing back at his retinue. "Shut it, y'all!" Then his narrowed gaze snapped back to Medusa and me. "We ain't telling you shit. Now get out of here before we hurt you."

I took a deep breath and let it out slowly. Whiteout Irene was eager to punch some crooks in the face and, while

Rational Irene didn't see the point of a scrap, she acknowledged this was a highly suspicious response. I had to agree, the only path towards answers was through these goons.

I glanced over at Medusa. "What do you think, Meds?"

"I don't think our new friends are being very hospitable." Her snake hair danced and hissed. "We're not going to leave until we have answers."

"You heard her, folks." I took a step forward and cracked my knuckles. "For your sakes, don't make us do this the hard way."

Chapter 15

Mad Max's answer was to let out an incoherent battle cry and lead the charge against us.

But either he wasn't as good of a leader as he thought or some of his friends had more common sense, because thirteen turned into eight as some of them broke and ran out of the alley.

I couldn't blame them. They were normal humans facing two of the Push Heroes who stood up to the most powerful beings on the planet and didn't die. I could even make a case that we'd won.

Of the remaining goons, they had a collection of pipes, knives, and chains, but one of them hung back and drew a pistol. Normally, he'd be my first target, but with Medusa at my side, I didn't worry.

Like when I worked with Extinguisher, neither of us had to say a word. We knew how to handle this situation.

I moved right for the pack of melee fighters, while Medusa hung back for the moment.

I didn't need to see her to feel the sickening surge of energy as Medusa summoned her power to petrify.

Like many Pushed powers, it had its own strange rules. If she met the gaze of a human, she could turn them into stone - dead stone. She and her snakes also carried a petrifying venom in their bites. Needless to say, it was a power she only used in the most critical of situations.

But she could also turn any inanimate object to stone if she could focus her gaze on it. No eye contact required.

So, as I crossed the distance between us and Mad Max, Mr. Pistol raised his gun to shoot me right in the face. Only for that intricate implement of death to glow a sickly green before turning into a solid hunk of stone.

Mad Max wasn't much more prepared. He might've been used to dealing with a speedster like his assumed boss, but he hadn't been expecting *me* to be so fast. He'd just raised his weapon, a crowbar, which left himself wide open for a sharp jab right in the nose.

By the crunch of cartilage, I'd hit him just right - enough force to break his nose but not so hard as to break the rest of his face.

That was one of the two difficulties of fighting normal crooks I faced, making sure to pull punches and measure my boosted strength to not kill anyone.

The other, of course, was avoid getting killed by their usually mundane arsenal, which was what I dealt with right after Mad Max fell back, his nose bleeding profusely. Goons came up on my right and left, one swinging a chain and the other thrusting a knife towards my guts.

Mass combat was all about assessing what was the greatest threat and what I was willing to risk. With my mind running as fast as it was, the calculations were easy.

As I could take a hit from a chain much better than a stab wound, I stepped into Knife Guy, grabbed his wrist, and guided his blade safely past my right side.

That also took me outside of Chain Gang's ideal range, but did allow me to give him a good back kick in the stomach that staggered him.

Only the very end of the chain managed to clip my good shoulder. My reinforced leather motorcycle jacket absorbed the impact.

"I'm guessing you don't need the boys to come back you up yet," Choi chimed in my ear, "or you would've asked."

"We're fine, *chica,*" Medusa answered for me. "Just some normal gang members, but thank you for asking."

"I'll call the police for clean-up and arrests. I'll adjust if the situation changes."

I took the wrist Knife Guy had so politely offered me, squeezed hard, and twisted. He howled in pain as I came within an inch of breaking his wrist, and his blade clattered to the pavement.

Mad Max had fallen back, clutching his broken nose, Chain Gang was coming back for another swing, and two more goons came around the flanks. While I was holding my own, I was about to become surrounded.

Medusa intervened, grabbing one new goon by the collar of his jacket as she shoved the other one hard enough to throw him into the alley wall. My hyped-up senses caught the crack of a broken arm as that goon slid down the wall and out of the fight.

Sure, she wouldn't petrify these goons, but she was still inhumanly strong, quick as a cobra, covered in tough scales, and her claws weren't venomous if she needed a weapon.

Considering we each had a goon by the arm, what we should do with them felt obvious. Medusa and I exchanged the briefest of glances before we swung our respective opponents into each other. There was the meaty thwack of flesh on flesh before the two dropped.

While that cut the numbers swarming us, it also left us both open for the rest of the Buzzkillers.

Chain Gang lashed his chain across the broad part of my back, just a few inches off from the back of my head. Yay for armor, because once again, my jacket absorbed the impact.

Meanwhile, the last two goons that were unhurt and still armed managed to get behind us. Medusa slipped with serpentine fluidity out of the path of a collapsible baton, but the last one managed to get a glancing blow in with his switchblade. It cut through her red jumpsuit and skidded across her scales, but I didn't see it draw blood.

Medusa and I moved back-to-back as if we'd be fighting together all our lives. It only took a split-second for us to focus on the new threats and lash out with blinding speed.

It really was a toss-up which one of us was faster, and that question remained unanswered. Switchblade's cry of pain from behind me as Medusa lashed out against him seemed to happen at almost the exact moment I slammed a kick with my heavy biker boot right into the side of Chain Gang's knee.

He let out a howl as his leg buckled, leaving him open for a knock-out punch. As Chain Gang fell, I turned back to Mad Max. He seemed to be working up the courage to get back into the fight even as his nose kept bleeding. "This is your chance to back down, and maybe we can just –"

Something hard and pistol-shaped clipped me in the side of the head hard enough to draw blood. The ringing in my head cut off immediately as my focus shut off the pain, and I immediately snapped my angry gaze at the source.

The guy with the petrified gun had thrown his useless rock at me.

Big on guts and shockingly close to a smart move, but he'd flubbed his shot. I think he realized that when he saw the look in my eyes because, instead of pressing his attack, he raised his hands and dropped to his knees.

While that goon might've given up, it took the pressure off Mad Max. Maybe it was the fact he saw me bleed or maybe he thought I was distracted enough that he, too, could get a cheap shot in.

Whatever the reason, Mad Max rallied himself enough to take another crack at me. He swung his crowbar toward my side, claw-end first.

Too bad for him that I *was* still paying attention, and I was through playing around. While the last goon Medusa was fighting let out a shrieking scream, I caught Mad Max's crowbar in the flat middle, stopping the swing.

I pulled Mad Max in by his weapon before he realized he could just let go. His eyes went wide for a moment, then rolled up in his head as I drove my knee hard between his thighs. A strained groan escaped Mad Max's lips as he collapsed to the pavement, cradling his groin.

"You should've backed down," I growled as I turned around, looking for more opponents.

No more of the Buzzkilers left were willing to continue fighting. My own dance partners were either down or in full surrender mode, while Medusa stood alone. Mr. Stiletto was bleeding from claw wounds in his knife arm, while the guy who'd had the pipe now lay in a crumpled heap clear past our parked motorcycles.

"You okay, Meds?"

It was an unnecessary question. She looked okay, especially her real body beneath her Pushed form. Truth was that as long as an attack didn't breach that outer shell of unreality, any Pushed would recover insanely fast, far faster than my own accelerated healing.

"I'm fine, Indy, but we need to take a look at –"

"I'm good." I didn't mean to cut her off, I really didn't, but we were still in front of the Buzzkillers, and the last thing I needed was for the local thugs to start swapping stories that

I was scarily vulnerable. "And, if you Buzzkillers want to stay as good as you are, you'll answer our questions."

The gun-thrower was the only one completely unhurt save for his pride, and he was the one that was the quickest to answer. "Yeah, we surrender. Whatever you want, we'll tell you."

"Good. Now, let's go back to those missing people –"

A high-pitched buzzing hit my ears, distant but approaching at superhuman speed, as the familiar stomach twist of an incoming Pushed hit.

I didn't think, I just reacted. I spun, grabbed Medusa, and threw us both to the side of the alley.

If I'd been any slower, we would've both been right in the path of the red, black, and chrome blur that ripped right through the center of the alley. That blur knocked the Buzzkillers and our motorcycles aside like yesterday's newspaper, leaving a gouge cut into the pavement behind it.

Groans of pain and the crash of steel mingled with the now-oppressive buzz in the air.

It was obvious where the gang got their name, because it sounded like we were in the company of a thousand angry buzzsaws, all revving in terrible harmony.

The source had stopped, though that wasn't the right term. The constantly vibrating smear of colors had only stopped in the sense that they weren't rushing in any direction. The street underneath their feet smoked and cracked, probably from the constant high-frequency vibrations running up and down their form.

While I could usually see clear through to the normal human at the core of a Pushed at this range, the constant shifting of the outer shell of unreality hurt my eyes and made it difficult to focus past it.

"You mess with my people, heroes, you mess with Buzzkill," they shouted, their voice distorted by the vibrations. Then Buzzkill charged right at us.

Chapter 16

Only because Buzzkill had stopped to make a threat like a good little Push Crook did we get out of the way in time.

Medusa split along the wall one way, I dodged away from the wall, and I felt the all-too real rush of wind as Buzzkill shot forward into the place we'd just been.

In some ways, dodging Buzzkill presented the same problem as dodging a bullet. They – I still couldn't tell their gender through the blurring and the voice distortion – moved slower than a speeding bullet, if only barely. But if we could keep a step ahead and read Buzzkill's intentions, we both had a chance to get out of the way.

Good thing we did, because Buzzkill's hands, vibrating faster than an electric carving knife, had plunged right through the brick. That might seriously hurt Medusa, and I had no idea how it'd interact with my Pushed immunity.

Best not to find out, which meant we needed to end this fight fast. That meant I'd have to risk myself, but *that* wasn't anything new.

"Madre de Dios," Medusa hissed in alarm, but she didn't stop for a monologue, thank God. She clearly shared my idea of ending this quickly, but wasn't aware of the crazy plan brewing in my head, so she lashed out with a swipe of her claws.

But even the speed of a striking cobra wasn't enough to catch Buzzkill. They blurred back out Medusa's reach – and out of mine, too – before I could even blink.

Then, in that same motion, Buzzkill spun in place, turning my assessment of them from the Flash to the Human Top, and rocketed off in a straight line down the alley.

And right past Medusa.

Thanks to that serpentine speed of hers and the benefit of dozens of pairs of eyes, she twisted away from Buzzkill just before their outstretched arm tore her in half.

But that didn't save Medusa entirely. She let out a pained cry as the blurred tips of Buzzkill's fingers barely brushed her shoulder. Where they passed, her scaled skin opened up like it had a zipper, and blood from the wound streaked a trail in the air behind the Push Crook.

"I won't miss the next time," Buzzkill growled as they stopped abruptly at the far end of the alley and spun once more. I was inclined to believe them, but I was going to use that to end this fight.

I glanced over at Medusa. "Stay back, Meds. I've got this." Before she could protest, I stepped into the center of the alley and planted myself in a wide stance. "Okay, Buzzy, let's make this easy for you. You're already a thief, I wouldn't want to make you a liar, too."

"Indy, what are you doing?" Medusa protested, even as she did what I asked. She pressed flat against the wall, one hand clamped over her bleeding shoulder. At least the wound hadn't gotten all the way to the real woman underneath.

"Yes, what's going on?" Choi echoed.

I didn't answer - Choi would figure it out from all the noise and call the boys in. I need all my focus on Buzzkill revving up in front of me.

"Come on, Buzzy," I taunted. "I don't have all day. Take your shot like so many others have. You'll fail, just like they did."

My plan relied on a few things. Some of those things relied on how it seemed Buzzkill's powers worked. While they certainly had enhanced reflexes, they still seemed to need some time to react. That meant it was possible to surprise them.

It also seemed they moved in precise, straight lines. Yes, I was working on a very limited sample size, but the fact was, if Buzzkill could maneuver as well as a normal human, they could've sawed us in half on that initial charge. The neat lines torn in their path formed precise angles that added more evidence to my theory.

But the biggest thing was what was going on right now. If I were right, Buzzkill would respond to my challenge in only one way. A Push Crook couldn't refuse a call-out combined with the implication that they could be the one to take down Indomitable, World-Saving Superheroine.

Brooks would laugh when I told him about all this. Assuming this worked and I lived through it.

True to the Whiteout, Buzzkill let out a discordant battle cry and spun forward in a straight line towards me. The moment they yelled, I started moving. Just a step to the left was all it would take - if I was correct - and I brought my right arm up in what would be - again, if I was correct - a perfect clothesline across Buzzkill's blurry throat.

It was over before anyone could process it. Buzzkill zipped forward in the exact straight line I'd predicted and right into my waiting arm.

That arm felt like I'd plunged it into the cushions of a massage chair, the vibrations running up and down my nerves. But then my arm plunged through the thin layer of unreality around Buzzkill before hitting the real person underneath.

Buzzkill's body wanted to keep going, but they couldn't without their head.

Thank God for their Pushed nature and my own peculiar immunities, because Buzzkill stayed in one piece even as they flipped a full three-hundred-and-sixty degrees before hitting the pavement and my arm stayed attached and unshredded.

It still hurt like hell. The fact it did, even for a moment before my focus shunted the pain off, surprised me, but I still tried to look nonchalant as I turned to the rising Buzzkillers around us. Couldn't let the thugs think I wasn't invincible, after all.

"I'll take that surrender now," I said loudly.

"We ain't fighting no more, don't worry," Mad Max said as best he could through his broken nose. "You win."

With that settled, I took in the scene.

Buzzkill turned out to be a young man. He was sprawled out on the pavement and looked to be barely out of his twenties, dressed in punk rock chic. Black and red leather, spikes, chains, the whole nine yards, which meant he fit right in with his gang.

Considering how lethal his vibrational aura was, he hadn't shredded a single one of his men when he made his entrance. He hadn't even sliced our motorcycles apart.

Maybe Buzzkill hadn't been as careful as he could have been, but he *chose* not to hurt his men.

I must've knocked Buzzkill clean out, because he were no longer a constantly vibrating smear of color.

In fact, if he hadn't been vibrating the whole time, I couldn't have picked Buzzkill out from this particular crowd. It probably lent him tremendous anonymity. The boy under the Pushed shell wasn't much different, but perhaps even younger than he appeared in Pushed form.

I wondered what in Epic's screwed-up Whiteout had picked Buzzkill to be a villain in the grand drama my ex-boyfriend had envisioned.

Medusa still had a hand clamped over her bleeding shoulder as she moved towards the downed Buzzkill.

"The situation is under control now, Rachel," she said over the comms. "I'll handle triaging the injured, Indy, if you want to get answers. Rachel, we need PART and emergency services here ASAP. We have wounded and a downed Push Crook."

"As you two certainly expected, Extinguisher and Hexagon are also on their way."

For once, I was glad for the backup.

"Understood," Medusa and I answered in unison.

I resisted the urge to tend to Medusa personally. She'd be okay, I knew that, so I focused on why we were here. Marching over to Mad Max, I loomed into his personal space as he leaned against a battered dumpster.

"This won't save you from getting tossed in jail, but if you answer our questions, we'll put in a good word for you." I didn't even have to put a hand on him to insinuate what would happen if he didn't spill the beans.

"Let me reiterate the bullet points. Missing people across town, but none in your territory. A couple snatched from this very alley. What do you Buzzkillers know about it?"

"We didn't take them," Mad Max stammered out. "And we've lost people, too. But Buzzkillers got a code - we don't go begging for help from the cops."

He tried to clench his jaw and look all tough, but he didn't pull it off at all. "They come in the night, faster than our boss even, snatch folks, and take 'em into the old Underground."

"I don't know if we can believe him," Choi chimed in my ear, "but it's worth pushing him."

But I knew I didn't need to push. Mad Max didn't have anything else to lose, so better to go with mercy now instead of a hard push. "Well, whoever is behind this, we're trying to stop them, and we're going to get all those people back, including your own."

Distant sirens started to scream closer, and I wondered who'd get here first, the police, the EMTs, or Hexagon and Extinguisher. Maybe the sirens prompted Mad Max to spill as much as my assurances, but spill he did.

"Fine, then I'll say this much - there's some old maintenance tunnels off Lower Alabama. Buzzkill and me tracked one of our snatched people down there, but lost the trail." Mad Max shook his head. "Lots of sealed-off areas down there. Maybe they took 'em there, where no one's gonna look."

"That's a start." I dug into my bag and pulled out a bundle of zip-cuffs. "Better if I do this before the cops get here. They'll be rougher."

Was I being too nice to these gangsters? Probably. But the knowledge there was something far worse than them behind these kidnappings put things in a different perspective.

Besides they were normal humans, under the sway of the Pulse of a Push Crook meaning, ultimately, that they were more victims of the Whiteout. If I wasn't going to show them a little kindness, no one else was.

I'd barely gotten the cuffs on Mad Max, while Medusa had done the same for Buzzkill - not that it'd help when he woke up - when we had more visitors. I felt their Pulses a moment before they appeared, but I was standing with a smile to greet them.

"Hex! Ex!" I called as Hexagon landed from the skies above, hard enough to crack the street. Extinguisher was right behind, arcing down on an ice ramp from the opposite direction. "Sorry you missed the Push Battle, boys, but you're just in time for the clean-up."

Hexagon didn't even give me a nod before rushing up to Medusa's side. "You should've called the moment things went south," he argued as he fussed over her shoulder wound. "Is that the only place you're hurt, Meds?"

"We had the comms open the whole time," I countered, "and Rachel called you as soon as Buzzkill showed."

Hexagon ignored me, focused purely on Medusa.

"Yes, yes, I'm fine, Hex," she answered and, if I trusted my read on the woman underneath the scaly facade, she was flattered despite the protest in her voice.

Maybe I wasn't the only one pursuing an office romance. Speaking of that, Extinguisher came right up to me, his hand frosting over. Without a need to ask, he placed his icy hand over the wound on the side of my head.

"Oh, that's nice." I sighed softly, then forced myself to be serious. "But we don't have time for much comforting. Our friends here gave us a lead, and I think we should follow it as soon as possible."

Chapter 17

Fortunately, the fallout from the Buzzkill Push Battle was dealt with swiftly.

No one had died, the injuries were fairly light, and there was only one Push Crook to wrangle. Mad Max was more than happy to keep spilling the beans, to the joy of both the Atlanta PD and PART.

The worst injury turned out to be Medusa's arm. Not because it was super deep, but because the EMTs didn't have a sharp enough needle to pierce her scales and stitch up the slash.

All that meant was she needed Duane's superior tools and experience with Pushed medicine. Hexagon gently scooped Medusa up in a princess carry, snagged her motorcycle with a free arm, and Hulk Jumped to HQ.

He'd catch back up when he could, assuming some other emergency didn't spring up. There were a lot of Push Crooks in this town, and more cropped up by the moment.

That left Extinguisher and me to oversee Buzzkill until PART got him ready for transit, just in case he woke up from his nap early. Most of it was the usual cuffs and restraints, but then a PART officer pulled out the medical kit.

A strong sedative had become standard operating procedure on Push Crooks that couldn't be physically restrained by conventional means. As the officer administered a dose of that sedative to Buzzkill, I thought about Colonel Liberty's sleep inducer again.

That, in turn, brought Rational Irene and Whiteout Irene up in force. It seemed as if all three of me had something to say about this now.

I know this is upsetting to you, Rational Irene began, *but this is only marginally different from the situations with Reaper and The '49er. Buzzkill's power is simply too dangerous to be left unchecked.*

Bullshit, Whiteout Irene shot back. *Even if you assume every other Push Crook is guilty enough or dangerous enough to deserve an endless sleep, look at this kid. He could be saved.*

I agree, I joined in. Honestly, it was the first time I'd joined into this mental chorus directly outside of a lucid dream, which probably said terrible things about the state of my psyche.

Buzzkill could've killed everyone in this alley except me, most of them in his first attack, but he didn't. If he had the right support, he could be a Push Hero, like Facet.

Extinguisher was glancing over at me, concern on his face, but I ignored him for the moment.

Rational Irene wasn't done yet. *I feel for the boy, yes. I may be rational, but I'm not heartless. But I'm trying to balance your boundless idealism with reality.*

Ultimately, if we focus on fixing the Whiteout, we will fix all these problems. So why not mitigate the harm in the most efficient way possible until then?

You're also the same bitch that thinks we should mercy-kill The '49er, Whiteout Irene shouted in my head. *It doesn't matter how much more efficient things are. What matters is doing what's right, and that's almost never the "efficient" way to do things.*

They were both correct, and I still had no idea of what, exactly, was the right thing to do.

Extinguisher leaned close. "Irene," he whispered, "are you okay?"

I snapped back to the world around me. PART was finishing their load-up, while the conventional police were rallying forces to go after the Buzzkillers' drug lab.

"I'm..." No, I couldn't lie. Besides, Extinguisher might have some insights of his own. "No, not really, Will. But we need to move. Can we talk on a private channel while we get back on the kidnapper's trail?"

"I'm always here for you." The casual but sure way he said those words helped calm the argument in my head. Both Rational and Whiteout Irene had come on board with our feelings towards Extinguisher, and they wanted to hear his thoughts on it as much as I did.

"Then let's ride."

It wasn't a long ride ahead, but it was almost noon when we got moving - me on my battered motorcycle and Extinguisher soaring above on his ice slide. Plenty of time before nightfall, when Mad Max said the kidnapper came out to hunt for new prey, but that didn't bring me much comfort.

I focused on the road and talking to Extinguisher via our now-private commlink. "Okay, here's what's been worrying me - the sleep inducer. But more broadly, how we deal with Push Crooks."

"That's a sticky moral question, isn't it? I can see how that could cause you to put on your Distant Irene face."

I shouldn't have been surprised that I had such a face. "Remind me never to play poker with you. Seriously, though, I don't think I need to go over all the questions and quandaries. It's bugged me since last night, but Buzzkill really made me question myself."

Extinguisher was quiet for a moment. "I think my time before the Whiteout, working with law enforcement like Joe, makes it a little easier to accept, but the way that sedatives and sleep inducers are turning into a universal answer to Push Crooks doesn't sit right with me."

"Why?" I had my own reasons, but Rational Irene, in particular, wanted to know Extinguisher's.

"Crime deserves justice, not punishment." His voice was sure and confident. "Painting all Push Crooks with the same brush and doling out equal penalties isn't very just, not to me."

Rational Irene noted her point on efficiency, but couldn't help but concede that Extinguisher was correct. I guess even my most rational fragment still had a moral center, no matter what Whiteout Irene thought.

"On that, we totally agree. All of me."

"More arguments with yourself, huh?"

"Yep."

"I can't say I fully understand it, but I guess it's good that enough for me. Probably best for you, too." He went silent for a moment. "Are you *sure* you're okay, Irene? I'm not a therapist or psychologist, but I'm worried about you."

"I can't blame you. I am, too, but I'm okay for now." I figured he needed a bit more reassurance, so I tried to sound as confident as I could. That was easier than I thought, as the other parts of me were satisfied enough to quiet down for now. "Seriously, you helped a lot."

We were close to the topside entrance to Underground Atlanta now. I went to park and he came with me.

"Okay, Irene. Just remember, you can tell me anything."

"Thanks, Will. I won't forget that."

"You're welcome, Irene. Just glad I could help."

As I dismounted, Extinguisher landed beside me, and we both took a good look at the old Georgia Railway depot, the oldest building in downtown Atlanta and the main entrance to Underground Atlanta.

The entire district was considered a historical landmark and had a wild and checkered past. Buried by viaduct construction in the early Nineteenth Century, used for speakeasies and other illicit activity in the Roaring Twenties, then forgotten for decades.

In the 1960's, Underground Atlanta was uncovered, turned into an entertainment district, boarded up again, turned into a shopping mall, and so on. The cycle continued up to the present, where it was currently "open."

I'd never call Underground Atlanta safe. The layout constantly shifted with every new renovation, with some roads losing surface access or being blocked off entirely.

With so many closed-off tunnels and hidden access points to the street, it remained a hotbed for petty crime and theft, as well as a good spot for murder and mayhem.

After the Whiteout, Push Crooks moved in, too. What better place to hide an evil underground lair than the bowels of Underground Atlanta, where the construction was already done for you?

During this current configuration of Underground Atlanta, we couldn't access Lower Alabama Street, our goal thanks to Mad Max, by just driving in. We'd have to go through the newly renovated mall itself.

"Ready, Irene?"

I took his hand and gave it a squeeze. "With you by my side? I'm ready for anything." And, like this, we headed underground to see just what was waiting for us.

Chapter 18

Extinguisher and I headed down into the modern, renovated part of Underground Atlanta. We caused a bit of a stir and did have to stop to sign a few autographs, but it was no real difficulty.

The maintenance tunnels weren't hard to find either, and we didn't worry about the "No Unauthorized Personnel" or "Danger! Off-Limits!" signs. It was only once we'd gotten into the older sections, unused since the 1920s, that we slowed down.

"Do we have access to any old blueprints or schematics of these old parts?" I asked Choi over the comms, my voice low. I squinted in the dim light, looking for clues that Buzzkill and Mad Max might've missed.

"I'm looking over what we have now." I knew that voice. It was the "Choi was in intense study" voice.

"Most of this section is well-documented, and I can't imagine that the Buzzkillers didn't already search them. However, at the end of this corridor, there should be a sealed door on the left-hand side. That's supposed to lead to an even older set of tunnels that was condemned decades ago."

She sighed. "Unfortunately, we don't have any schematics for that system, but I'll keep digging."

"It's not like we haven't had to improvise in the dark before," Extinguisher noted. "We'll keep you updated."

Finding the door Choi told us about was easy, especially as it was the only boarded-over door here.

Rational Irene wondered why the Buzzkillers hadn't already breached this and searched deeper, but Whiteout Irene was only focused on finding the kidnapping victims.

For now, I focused on Whiteout Irene's desires. "Ex, you can do the honors."

Normally, I'd have healed up from all the action, but the niggling injuries from the brawl with The '49er last night and the Buzzkillers today lingered. No need to strain myself any more than was necessary by dealing with a door Extinguisher could handle just as easily.

Maybe everyone was right. Maybe I did need to rest. But how could I? Certainly not now.

"Your wish is my command." Extinguisher focused pure cold in his hands but, instead of something loud and direct like an ice hammer, he carefully touched the rusty nails attaching the boards one by one.

Much as he'd used intense cold to shatter my restraints right before the Battle of Washington, he froze the nails to such a degree that they broke apart with just a little bit of effort.

He tugged open the door. It took a good yank to break the rusty hinges, but the creak was still minimal. A stale, rank stench permeated the air beyond.

Extinguisher stepped aside from the rusty metal door. "After you, Indy."

"Such a gentleman." But I didn't mind - if we had Pushtech heading for us, I needed to be the barrier between it and Extinguisher. "Okay, we're about to go in," I whispered over the comms. "Any word on Hex?"

"Unfortunately, Dischordia just crashed a charity concert at Chastain Park," Choi reported, "so I sent him to deal with it, while Duane stitches Medusa up."

"Alright, we're going to keep moving ahead, then. There's no telling when our kidnappers will strike again or what state the victims are in."

Extinguisher nodded. "We can't risk waiting. If things look hairy and we can delay acting, we'll pull back and call for help."

"Understood," Choi said. "Keep in contact."

Grunting an acknowledgment, I stepped through the open doorway.

This construction was old, lacking the refurbishments of the other parts of Underground. It was moist, dank, and the walls dripped with condensation. I could only guess that a forgotten sewer pipe or some natural steam vent had broken into these tunnels.

Even though the door had been sealed, I noticed two things. First, there were a few partial footprints in the deeper grime. Second, someone had strung some open bulb lights and wired them up to some power source deeper in.

That gave us some dim light, but it also confirmed that someone had been through this way in the recent past.

Forward was our only option, so we crept further along. I led the way while Extinguisher hung back a few paces so he could best use his powers at range if we ran into trouble.

We weren't ten yards into the tunnel when the familiar sensations of the Pulse hit me. Someone Pushed was nearby, confirming our suspicions about the kidnappers.

But there was something off about this Pulse. A shiver ran up my spine along with the usual sense of nausea, but the nausea itself was less intense than usual.

Maybe my senses were off. "Do you feel that, Ex?"

"I do, and I don't like it." Extinguisher conjured cold energy to his fingertips. "We better be ready."

I nodded, took a deep breath, and dropped into my full state of focus.

That moment of preparation and focus saved our lives. I took a step forward, and my enhanced hearing heard the faintest of clicks.

A rumble shook the ceiling overhead and, while there was no way to know what the hidden switch was attached to, I had a good guess. This was going to come down on our heads, more specifically mine.

Extinguisher, still hanging back, hadn't even noticed. Even with my accelerated thoughts and reflexes, there were only moments to decide on a course of action to save us both.

Without hesitation, I hopped back and shoved Extinguisher towards the entrance with all my focused strength. That'd ensure he was safe, which was my first priority.

The first rocks started dropping then - mixed with an explosion blooming overhead - and they were dropping to block me from Extinguisher. The world seemed to slow as I turned and made a wild leap further down the tunnel.

To say I was a stranger to explosions at this point in my life would be a lie. The Battle of Washington had plenty of explosions, ones I'd been too intimate with for my liking, then there were six months of Push Battles to make me quite familiar with things that went boom.

That experience, though, was not nearly as personal as the bomb that exploded around me. The claustrophobic tunnels channeled the explosion. A concussive wave caught me from behind and a series of stinging punctures tore into my back.

Most of the fragments seemed to have been caught in my armored uniform, but one nasty one punched through and into my shoulder blade.

The upside was between my leap and the shockwave, I was flung clear of the collapse. I landed flat on my stomach on the wet stone floor, rattled but alive.

Masonry continued to crumble behind me as I shakily stood and glanced behind me.

Darkness shrouded me. It looked like the explosion had brought on a tunnel collapse, and either one of those must've cut the circuit on the lights.

I'd have to find another way out.

"Ex?" I called out.

No answer, either from the comms or through the collapsed debris. I tapped my earbud and tried again.

"Ex? Rachel? Duane? Anyone?"

Only the sound of the collapsed stones settling answered me. The tunnel collapse must've been thick enough to keep Ex from hearing me. As for the comms, either the shockwave from the blast had damaged something in my uniform or the added stone from the debris was just enough to block the signal.

I was on my own, and there was no guarantee how fast help would come. Just like the building collapses from the night before, Extinguisher's ice powers weren't well suited to clearing the blockage, so he'd no doubt hunt from an alternate way in. With our lack of schematics, that could take a long time.

While I could sit around and wait for a rescue, that seemed foolish. Whatever had come down this way had to know I was here now, which meant I wasn't the hunter anymore – I was the prey.

Sometimes, the best defense was a good offense. Time to move ahead.

I felt through my utility bag for my headlamp. As much as it lacked style, I needed the ability to see. I had to assume that whatever was down here wasn't affected by the dark like I was.

I took a moment to get my headlamp in place and flicked it on. My vision adjusted to the new light, still sharpened by my focused state. There was nothing I could do about the shrapnel in my back - I was just thankful it was in deep enough to keep the bleeding to a minimum.

The casualness of that thought made me pause for a moment, but there wasn't anything to do for it.

Instead, I began to move forward.

The dust was still settling from the explosion, but I could see the tunnel continued with a slight descent. The humidity was getting worse, the walls slick and the exposed pipes dripping.

Maybe it was some kind of maintenance tunnel? It hardly mattered now.

I pressed on at a jog, still moving slowly enough to react to danger.

It was another two dozen yards before the tunnel made a sharp right turn. Even if my light was giving me away, I had to be cautious of the blind corner. The last thing I needed was to dash into a waiting bullet, a fireball, or some other esoteric insanity.

I plastered myself to the right wall and carefully edged to the corner. My gut was clenched - I was very close to the source of the strange Pulse now.

I looked around the corner to see what lay ahead.

There was only a short corridor before it opened into a round chamber with several other tunnels connecting to it. A junction of some kind, maybe even an abandoned storage area, as I also saw some old furniture and tools about, though an ominous mist obscured the ground ahead.

I saw no person or movement, so I started slowly down corridor.

A few things stood out clearly above the mist. A large steamer trunk sat the center of the chamber, more intact than the rest of the artifacts. Dirt was scattered all around the trunk in clumps, with more seeping out of the weakening boards.

I had no clue what that could mean other than it might be large enough to hide the Push Crook I was hunting.

Far more importantly, though, there was a human form lying in a pile of what I figured to be old clothing. I couldn't tell if he or she was alive, but I didn't feel the Pulse coming off of them.

This could be an ambush or trap. In fact, it most likely was, but I had to find out if that person was alive or dead and I couldn't do that standing here. I took a centering breath and moved into the room.

To my surprise, I was not immediately impaled, shot, stabbed, or otherwise subjected to bodily harm. My senses, though, were still screaming at the presence of the Pulse, not just close, but literally all around me.

I willed myself to keep calm and not lose concentration as I ran to the still figure.

I didn't even need to check for vitals - it was obvious she was dead. The corpse was that of a woman, skin chalk-white, though there wasn't quite the stench of decay I was expecting. Long black hair shrouded her face. I brushed it aside to be sure - she matched the picture in Rick Greer's wallet.

This was Sally Greer. I swore under my breath at another life lost to the curse of the Whiteout. That's when I saw the two deep puncture wounds right on the artery.

I barely had time to jump to the obvious conclusion as the air pressure abruptly shifted behind me. Something solid had coalesced out of the mists.

Accelerated reflexes took over as I tried to push up and off, to gain a little space from whatever was behind me, but it moved far faster. It grabbed me by the shoulders before hurling me through the air with inhuman force.

Careening straight into the far wall, I twisted as best I could to minimize the impact, but the collision sent a heavy shock down my spine.

I slid back down to the ground, the wind knocked out of me. Forcing the pain into its box, I struggled to get a clear view of my assailant.

What I saw was what anyone with even the faintest knowledge of literature or movies would call a vampire.

Male, once human, and dressed in blood-stained clothes, the combination of the pearly white skin, powerful physique, glowing red eyes, and knife-like fangs was frightful, even to me.

What was far more shocking was what lay beneath the facade of unreality.

Unlike the normal human at the heart of other Pushed, there was a corpse – a dead, pungently rotting man puppeted by the unnatural shell surrounding it.

Not that I had much time to think about this. The vampiric thing was already moving. With no real options, I did the only thing I could do.

I pushed to my feet and met the monstrosity head on.

Chapter 19

I accepted that it was nigh-impossible to prepare for anything in a world where everything was possible.

Still, I'd never thought that I'd be struggling with a dead body that was trying to kill me. One part of my swiftly moving mind tried to formulate some plan of attack or observe some insight on how to not get myself killed.

Normal Pushed had something universal I could exploit - there was a living human inside. I could get at the vulnerable thing in the superhuman shell and there were many ways to hurt a human for a trained physiologist.

But how did I hurt a corpse?

Worse, compared to this vampiric thing, I was moving in molasses, despite my bolstered speed. I'd only moved three steps before he lunged across the dank chamber, grime-encrusted nails curled like claws.

At least I seemed to be competitive in terms of pure reflexes, much like I'd been with Buzzkill. I slipped to one side of the vampire's attack before throwing a Hail Mary haymaker at his head.

The vampire seemed to have no conception of self-preservation and moved into the blow in his efforts to snatch me. As with all the "invulnerable" Pushed I'd faced so far, I felt the slight resistance of his outer shell before my fist carried through, powered by all the strength my body could put behind it.

Punching the partially rotten corpse was the most disgusting thing I'd done in my life.

My full strength tore into dead skin and flesh, knocking the jawbone completely free on one side. The air filled with an explosion of new, fetid aromas as coagulated fluids and decomposing tissue flew in a spray away from the impact.

Any living creature would've been instantly incapacitated from shock before dying a short time later from such an injury.

Unfortunately, I wasn't fighting a living creature. The outer vampiric form matched the inner corpse – his phantom jaw was knocked off his hinges with a tearing of alabaster flesh – but it didn't fall.

Instead, the vampire let out a guttural howl as he turned back to me. Some unnatural force was forcing the jaw back into place, just as the vampire's form seemed to regenerate in mere moments.

The distraction of watching the bizarre double-action was a stupid mistake.

The vampire seemed to feel no pain and, in his animalistic rage, he barreled into me. It was only a few steps before my back slammed once more into the dripping brickwork.

This time, though, there was a supernaturally strong corpse jamming me into it and driving the shrapnel in my shoulder blade deeper.

The vampire pinned me to the wall by virtue of his rotting forearm across my chest. As my collarbones creaked, a blood-stained hand snaked up to grab my head, hoping to pry it aside and get to the blood vessels in my neck.

Classic movie monster move.

This vampire was far stronger than I was, but I got some relief by pushing against his elbow with one hand. My other hand intercepted his groping claw. I didn't try to match his grip. Instead, I deflected the arm to one side, sending the corpse's fingertips burrowing into the bricks behind me.

My accelerated thoughts cycled through my options. Any physical damage I did to the vampire would be temporary, I assumed. The Pushed shell would simply force the broken bits back into position and carry on. He felt no pain, no shock. Frankly, he had no conventional vulnerabilities, so I'd have to get unconventional.

What I needed to remember was every popular myth about vampires. The Whiteout stole its template for the universe not just from Epic's mind, but also bits from every mind it touched. Whatever the myths said were the methods to kill a vampire were most likely true - it was all a matter of which beliefs were the strongest.

I ruled out sunlight immediately - no access to it - as I brought my free hand down with a hammer punch on the vampire's shoulder. The power of my blow was enough to crush his entire shoulder socket, giving me a momentary respite as the arm had to regenerate.

Using that opening, I released my grip on the vampire's pinning forearm and delivered a short, sharp blow to the ribcage. My hand dug into the viscous mass of the vampire's torso, and I was infinitely grateful for my leather gloves and full-body uniform.

With the vampire's equilibrium disrupted by the two structural breaches, I was free enough to bring my legs up to my chest and thrust outward violently. That sent him flying across the room into the steamer trunk.

The swollen wood burst from its bands and sent a torrent of earth spilling out to the ground. The vampire was already stirring, white flesh knitting together and corpse parts being shoved back into place.

I needed real options, and I needed them now. My brain delivered as I slid down the wall again, this time landing in a crouch.

I pushed off into a smooth pounce, crashing on top of the vampire while it was still off balance. Another spray of moist earth blasted up into the air as I tried to pin him with my knees. I frantically dug through the mounds of earth and debris for something long, wooden, and pointy.

A moment later, I had something suitable in my hands. It was time for a classic vampire staking. I raised the broken plank up high and brought it down, letting my scientific knowledge guide my hand towards the heart.

If it had gone according to plan, my strike would've been true. My aim was impeccable. Unfortunately, I'd failed to account for all the supernatural abilities vampires could possess.

Just as the makeshift stake began to part the perfect outer flesh, the creature shrieked and exploded. Not into inert dust like in a *Buffy* episode, but a sickly cloud of fog.

I held my breath as the mist burst past me on an unnatural wind, just in case it was poisonous, then there was another slight pop as the air pressure shifted behind me.

I threw myself from my kneeling position to spin onto my back, just in time to see a pair of massive fangs descend towards me.

There was no room to maneuver in the wreckage of the trunk. All I could do was throw up a forearm in defense.

My immunity to the Pushed saved me from the worst-case scenario. Those knife-like teeth were immaterial to me.

Still, the inhuman strength behind the corpse's jaws mashed hard into my reinforced sleeve. I could feel my forearm muscles get torn and mangled as my mind suppressed the pain.

My eyes locked with the double gaze of my attacker, who continued its attempt to gnaw through my sleeve, and I stabbed upward with the sharpened slat.

A shudder that ran through my arm as wood pierced inhuman flesh. The vampire's glowing red eyes went wide and, in a fraction of a second, I was free as the beast recoiled to howl in rage.

Though nowhere near the heart, the wood itself seemed an anathema to the beast, able to wound it better than my fists or feet. The vampire turned away from me, clutching at the board that impaled it through the guts.

I was sickened to see not only bits of dead matter drip out of the wound, but fresh blood as well. Willing myself to hold it together, I rolled to my feet.

For all the vampire's feral qualities, he seemed to realize that leaving splinters of wood inside it was bad, but it was having trouble extracting them all. I took the apparent opening to surge forward with the intent to drive the vampire chest-first into the wall, hopefully impaling it further and buying me time to find another sharpened piece of wood.

Either I underestimated the vampire's sensory powers or his primal instincts, because he met my rush with an immediate backhand. There wasn't even a muscle twitch to read in the animated corpse – I had no chance to divert.

At least I managed to roll with the impact as it sent me sprawling backwards. I wound up landing face-down on the slick stones.

Having been hit by the most powerful Pushed on the planet already, I certainly wasn't out of action, but I was left spitting up blood from my busted lip. The bruise would be impressive if I lived through this.

At least the impact had shattered the vampire's hand into fragments that even the Pushed aura couldn't form a proper hand out of again. While he struggled to regenerate, I pushed myself up.

That's when I caught a glint of silver on the ground.

It was a dirty but intact crucifix. It must've belonged to the victim, lost in the struggle before she could bring it to bear. I wondered if it would work at all, especially for an avowed skeptic.

That didn't stop me from crawling to it. It was just within my grasp when I felt a vice-like grip on my ankle. I immediately lashed out with my free leg. The sickening sound of biker boot squishing into dead flesh filled the air.

Unfortunately, there was no recoil of pain or shock, only that relentless corpse grip. The world whirled about as the vampire yanked me through the air by one leg. My muscles and tendons screamed before he let me go.

I sailed through the air before I had one more violent impact on cold, hard stone. It was only a miracle that kept my head from being brained open on jutting stones.

Still, my ability to shut down pain and push my body had its limits. After all I'd been through in these past two days, I'd come right to the edge, so I was slow to get my bearings or mount a defense.

The world was still a gray blur when the vampire hoisted me into the air again, this time by the scruff of my jacket. A cold, corpse hand pressed against my forehead, driving it back and to the side.

I had no protection there. It couldn't drink my blood with his phantom fangs, but he could easily chew open a deadly wound.

Two things happened nearly simultaneously to stop that.

First, I opened my clenched hand to reveal the glittering necklace with its smudged but intact cross. I'd managed to grab it right as the vampire threw me through the air.

Second, a pure, white flash, the same color as the Whiteout itself, radiated from behind the vampire, followed by a loud twang, like the release of a bowstring magnified tenfold.

The vampire dropped me, averting his eyes from the crucifix, as a large metal arrow pierced through his upper right chest. I couldn't be sure if that shaft was meant for me or the vampire.

After all, the white flash could only have been caused by one thing - Epic's teleportation portal. That meant the Crusaders - probably Epic himself - had sent someone here.

Whether they were here to help me or kill me was the question.

I felt the Pulse of our new combatant immediately but, more importantly, he was using Pushtech and a lot of it.

What to me was a suit of random looking armor bits with a crossbow strapped to one gauntlet had the outer appearance of a magnificent suit of powered armor with an advanced, mechanized crossbow, complete with a motorized ammo pack attached.

Because he had a real motorcycle helmet on, I couldn't see his features or read his expression, much to my annoyance.

"Monster!" he cried out, showing his intent for the moment, with an accent straight out of an Arthurian movie. "Stand down or I shall smite thee again!"

Great. It'd be a race to see if the vampire's teeth or this guys' horrid dialogue would kill me first.

Ultimately, I decided beggars couldn't be choosers as the vampire tore the arrow harmlessly from its chest. "Let's get him," I called to Arrow Guy.

I hated Crusaders, but I decided I hated vampires way more.

Chapter 20

If I could say one nice thing about the yelling and posturing mentally ingrained into the Pushed, it made for an excellent distraction.

The vampire snarled and leaped at Arrow Guy, who responded with another volley of metal-shafted arrows.

Though the projectiles didn't seem to harm the creature, the tremendous force they carried sent the vampire flying towards the far wall.

Tumbling out of the line of fire, my goal was the only obvious way to stop this - the shattered remains of the steamer trunk.

As I rose into a crouch just past Arrow Guy, he glanced sidelong at me.

"I'm most pleased to see milady isn't too badly hurt," he boomed, apparently lacking any sense of volume control or practical sense. "Lord Epic made no mention that -"

The vampire barreled into Arrow Guy during his commentary, and the pair hit the ground hard. The vampire had Arrow Guy's bow in his uninjured hand, pushing with all his unnatural strength.

The vampire could recognize a threat, obviously.

I could already hear the creak of Arrow Guy's armor as I gave up my search for another stake - there was nothing here that would work.

There was plenty in the room, but getting the right piece of wood quickly was going to be the issue. I knew the vampire was far too strong to pry off and Arrow Guy was in a bad position to get free on his own.

As much as I had my problems with the Crusaders, I certainly didn't want to see any of them as item one on the vampire buffet.

That's when the solution hit me.

I hopped off the pile of broken wood and rusted metal bands and I let the necklace chain wrap around my fingers until I felt the crucifix settle on the outside of my knuckles.

The vampire clearly considered me a minimal threat, ignoring me as I stepped up to it with my fist clenched. He didn't even flinch as my punch came in, the glittering cross at the front of the blow.

Instead of the usual feeling of striking a Pushed, there was a solidity I'd never experienced before. It was accompanied by a strangely comforting warmth from the crucifix itself.

The effect on the vampire, though, was far different.

Smoke billowed from where I'd hit, and the fetid smell of burning, rotten meat filled the air. His head recoiled to the side as if I'd fired a cannon in his face, then his entire body flew through the air.

I caught a glimpse of a cross-shaped melted hole in its flesh, giving a full view of the teeth in the beast's mouth.

In a strange reversal, what burnt the vampire had no effect on the corpse inside. The vampire retreated further, leaving Arrow Guy safe for the moment.

Holding my crucifix-wrapped fist out as a ward, I extended my other hand to the downed Crusader. "A little less conversation, a little more action, please," I said, channeling Elvis, one eye on the vampire, who scurried and scuttled, trying to find a way around the cross.

The melted hole in the vampire's face still smoked and refused to heal as his other injuries had.

"Yes, milady, well said," Arrow Guy replied as he took my hand to help right himself.

Unlike some Pushtech suits I'd seen in the past few months, his suit was lighter. Its primary purpose didn't seem to be making him stronger or more powerful - it was all built around the crossbow.

As Arrow Guy stood, he lined up a shot. "Have at you!"

I would've covered my face from the pure cringe had I not been fighting for my life.

As the overpowered twang of his crossbow echoed in the tiny chamber, the vampire, alerted to the danger to his vital organ, put on a burst of unnatural speed, almost disappearing from sight for a moment.

The steel arrow sunk deep into the brick wall as I tried to keep the crucifix facing the vampire. I really wanted to cuff Arrow Guy right upside the head, but I was far more concerned with keeping us alive.

The bad thing was that I didn't see the vampire any longer. Instead, the sickly mist had returned.

I grabbed Arrow Guy and pulled us both hard towards the shattered crate as the cloud of mist formed into a pouncing vampire.

While Arrow Guy was initially surprised, I was relieved that my would-be savior had enough sense to roll through our mutual tumble and come up in a crouch.

The vampire's pounce missed us. He landed on the other side of the crate and seemed unbalanced. Unlike before, he didn't blur out of the way immediately, seeming intent on regaining his footing.

There was a click and whir from Arrow Guy's bow as he fired. The head of this arrow was different and exploded above the vampire's head into a weighted net that wrapped around the target.

The force of the net yanked the vampire off his feet, and the weights on the net's edge bound the it together into a neat package, vampire firmly in the center.

Of course, this could only hold a creature that could turn to mist for mere moments.

I ran at the struggling vampire, the cross held outward in front of me. He hadn't turned to mist when confronted with the crucifix before. Hopefully, this time would be no different.

"It's just like the stories say!" Arrow Guy expounded. "Methinks I would've loaded wooden bolts had I known."

"Christ," I shouted over my shoulder, "there's wood all around you. Just grab something pokey and stake this bastard."

I held the little cross out of the vampire's struggling reach, honestly trying to believe in what it represented.

Concentrating so hard on it drained something out of me, but I shook my head and held off the fatigue mounting in my body. I heard rummaging behind me, then the sound of rubberized soles on stone.

"Make room, milady," Arrow Guy's voice came from behind.

I took a step to the side as the horribly loud sound of his crossbow loading echoed once more. I didn't even see the projectile's flight, only the huge splinter of wood crudely but powerfully ripping through the vampire's chest.

The vampire let out a final, soul-wrenching shriek as he slowly shriveled to a corpse-like state. For me, the phantom shell simply dissipated, leaving behind only the sad reality of the situation - a rotting corpse with a big sliver of wood impaling him.

"God, what a vile beast! 'Twas most well that –"

The moment the corpse returned to its natural state, the strange fatigue left me instantly, giving me plenty of strength to grab Arrow Guy by the plastic sport pads underneath his Pushtech armor and shove him roughly into the nearest wall. He let out a cry of surprise as I glared holes into his visor.

"Atlanta is *not* a Crusader town," I growled, anger welling up unbidden inside me. "Your beloved demigod knows that." I reared back a fist. "You've got ten seconds to tell me why you're here and, if 'because Epic wanted me to be safe' is the only one, I swear by all I hold dear I'll –"

"Please, milady, still your rage," Arrow Guy begged as he raised his hands either defensively or diplomatically. "It would be folly of me to lie and say that Lord Epic's concern for your safety does not often weigh upon his glorious brow, but it's not why he bid me to come here."

I didn't lower my fist, but I loosened my grip on his mock armor. Where my grip had cracked the plastic shell, the phantom armor was deformed and twisted.

"Verily, milord tracked vile scoundrels from the Humans for God group to this very chamber. He suspected some new treachery when his omnipresence failed him whilst trying to pinpoint what exactly had happened."

I so badly wanted an excuse to send Arrow Guy packing back to Epic – beaten, bruised, with his tail between his legs – as a message to keep his nose out of Atlanta. I mulled it over for a long moment as I held the archer to the wall.

Whiteout Irene thought my idea was a good one, and I should feel totally justified to do it.

Rational Irene pointed out that my personal war with Epic didn't mean that I should hurt a man who came here to fight something worse than either of us. What was more important? Taking a cheap shot at Epic or saving lives?

I unclenched my fist and settled Arrow Guy on his feet.

"So, the Hogs have vampires? Not very evangelical of them." I knelt beside the staked corpse for a closer look. "Did you or Epic have any idea he was, you know, like this?"

"Yes to the first and no to the second, milady. At least, if it was so, milord did not see fit to inform me as such." He cleared his throat. "Allow me to formally introduce myself. They call me the Argent Archer. 'Tis an honor to –"

"Please, no." I didn't even look up. The fading adrenaline as my mind and body down-shifted combined with the horrid stench of death made me feel sick enough. The way he was treating me wasn't helping. "No more of this 'milady' crap. Let's focus on the task at hand, okay?"

"Oh." There was a distinct hint of disappointment in Archer's voice. "As you wish." I heard an electronic whine. "While mi – you investigate the vampire's body, I'll employ my visual sensors and search for more clues as to what transpired here."

His booted footfalls began to move around behind me as I steeled myself to investigate the dead terrorist further.

I felt along the discolored flesh of the ex-vampire's neck and, just as with the girl's body across the room, there were two distinct circular wounds.

His wounds were larger than hers, which brought a chill to my bones. This wasn't the end of the nightmare ahead – this was only the beginning.

Forcing my nerves to quiet, I continued to search the body. There were still tatters of an olive-green wife-beater T-shirt tucked into the pants, black with a military cut and plenty of pockets. I rifled through them and pulled out a small pile of personal belongings to examine.

A battered leather wallet with identification and some cash, a half-empty matchbook, three filterless cigarettes, a roll of fishing line, a multi-tool, and a few spare bullets were the last possessions of our former vampire. It wasn't much to go on, but other, less tired eyes might find more.

I was brought out of my thoughts when Archer spoke up from across the room. "Mi - Indomitable," he corrected himself quickly, "I think you should look at this."

I rose from my crouch and turned towards him. Archer kneeled over the first victim's body, having laid it out respectfully on a relatively clean patch of floor. More specifically, he was looking at her teeth.

My stomach started to twist at what I swore was a growing Pulse in the room, the same strange version the vampire had given off, distinctly different from Archer's.

"Oh," Arched added offhandedly, "and bring another stake of wood from the rubble. And please, do so quickly."

Chapter 21

Sally Greer was turning into a vampire right before our eyes. And that meant there was only one thing we could do, as grotesque as it seemed.

With a heavy heart, I drove a large piece of wood through her chest. To his credit, Archer seemed equally disturbed by both the prospect and the deed itself. I was sure I caught his whispered prayer as I finished the grim task.

"My most sincere apologies. If I'd a wooden bolt, I would've spared you the need to do such a grim task yourself, but I dared not leave the body unattended, even for a moment."

I nodded slowly. Archer was right, and I was sure he was being honest.

"A brighter spot of news -- I finished my scan of the scene here, and I believe I've found a fair bit of useful physical and chemical evidence. Perhaps enough that we can deduce how some of this tragedy played out."

"All right, lay it on me, then you can head on back to Epic with your mission done, right? No more terrorist, after all."

"What? No, I couldn't leave this fair city in such peril. Not only must there be more than one of these 'Hogs,' I most certainly believe there are more of these vile, infectious monsters, as well."

I contemplated arguing with him, but there was a raw passion in his voice. Whatever insanity the Whiteout had pumped into Archer's brain, the words he was saying right now and his dedication to them came from some place deeper. Maybe Archer was like Extinguisher or Medusa, both heroes in their own ways even before the Whiteout.

Whatever the reason, I decided to take Archer at face value.

"Fine, but this isn't Crusader-land." I raised a warning finger. "We follow the rules and the law as best we can, got it?"

"Understood, Indomitable." Archer gestured towards the crate with a gauntleted hand. "As you may have guessed, that wasn't part of the original furnishings of this dank chamber. The earth within doesn't match the composition of the mud either in this chamber or in the surrounding area."

He then pointed at what seemed to be drag marks, still visible through the chaos of battle. "That was where they dragged it in."

"They?" I wasn't surprised that the vampire wasn't alone – the Hogs were rarely solo acts – but I wanted as much information as I could get while Archer was feeling informative.

"Oh yes. Most obviously, the weight of a steamer trunk with that much soil would be unwieldy for one normal man, no matter how strong, but there's more. Performing a digital reconstruction of the trunk, I discovered a false bottom in which the soil sat. There are trace residues of gun oil, metal shavings, and explosive chemicals in some of the wood. To conclude –"

"We had terrorists with a crate of arms, explosives, and something hidden," I finished for him. "Do you think that something was the vampire?"

"I do, I'm afraid. The quibble remains though. Did the Hogs know what they had, or was it a surprise set for them by another?"

I started to pace. "The Hogs obviously didn't live down here, even before…that." I gestured at the corpses. "They also had the sense to booby trap the entrance, which that vampire probably couldn't do with as feral as he was acting. So where are the rest of them?"

"Perhaps I could pick the trail back up on the surface?"

"Maybe, but I didn't see anything when I came down here. Besides, the booby trap collapsed the tunnel."

I wandered over to the pile of personal effects. While I hurt like hell, the adrenaline shakes had passed, and I was thinking more clearly.

A matchbook caught my eye - it was from someplace called Paul's Pub. There was no address, map, or phone number anywhere, just the boring name in a boring font. "Maybe we can retrace this guy's steps to see what he was doing before he died."

"It makes good sense to me." Archer came over, and I tossed him the matchbook. He shrugged. "It's a start. Perhaps the other clues I've found and this 'Paul's Pub' establishment will converge."

I nodded. "I can get the rest of this evidence to the Foundation - see what they can dig up. First, though…" I'd been trying to stay tough after my focus faded, but the pain in my forearm and my back was turning into agony. I held my arm protectively to my stomach. "We go topside and get some medical attention."

"Of course, Indomitable," Archer agreed. "Now, I'm sure my sensors can find a path out of here."

As if on some cue, there was a distant rumble and the distinct sound of cracking ice from one of the side tunnels.

"Looks like there won't be a need," I said with a sigh of relief. "The cavalry's here."

A blast of refreshingly chilly air flooded the room as Extinguisher appeared alone, coming into the room on his ice slide. Worry flooded his handsome face as he pulled to a halt.

"Indy," Extinguisher shouted as he slid into the room on a sheet of ice. "Are you okay? We –"

His fireman's jacket flared dramatically as he interrupted himself. "Crusader!" He raised a glowing blue hand at Archer.

Of course, Archer reacted in the way that Pushed tend to react to anything even remotely hostile – he aggressively raised his massive crossbow.

It was the classic comic book trope where heroes had to battle the instant they meet for the edification of their readers before teaming up afterward. In our twisted reality, it was just stupid and led to horrible injuries and multiple fatalities.

I'd almost run into it both with Facet and the Atlanta Five, but I'd defused it then, and I was going to do so again.

I stepped between the two of them. Archer was closer, so I shoved his bow away with my shoulder before raising my arms to my sides, legs set apart and braced.

I gave Extinguisher a hard look. He didn't deserve it – the Whiteout was to blame, not him – but if I wasn't firm, this gambit wouldn't work.

"Hold it," I yelled before quieting myself. "Both of you. No fighting." Despite the pain I was in and the hunger my focus had already induced, I forced myself to look as strong as ever.

"Are you sure?" Extinguisher asked. His fingers flexed nervously, and I could see the struggle against the influence of the Whiteout in his eyes.

Archer felt obliged to add to the conversation. "Do you know this brute, Indomitable? If he doesn't lower his hands, I'll be forced to attack."

I didn't hear the sounds of his bow unloading. That would've been nice, but I was certain that I would forever be denied nice things. A small part of me wanted to chalk this up to typical male posturing, but I knew it was reality itself twisting normally rational minds.

"Let's try this again. Ex, it's me talking. Trust me, if Archer here was trouble, I'd have already taken him apart." I turned to Archer next, doing nothing to mask my frustration with this nonsense. "As for you, lower your crossbow, shut up, and listen to me. Don't even speak, just nod if you understand me."

I looked back and forth for a tense moment before Extinguisher nodded and lowered his guard, followed by Archer. Letting out a sigh, I stepped out from between the two Push Heroes.

I favored Extinguisher with a smile, "Cool, let's get you caught up. My comms got knocked out when the tunnel collapsed." I pointed at the vampire Hog's corpse. "The Argent Archer here got sent to Atlanta to find a cell of Hogs. I know he's a Crusader, but we've already had a nice chat about that."

I glanced at Archer. "Archer, this is Extinguisher, who you *should've* known already from your divine muckity-muck's stories." Archer nodded slowly but wisely kept silent. "He's the leader of the Atlanta Five and a good friend."

I almost gave away the game and called it like it was, just so Archer would bring back the good news to Epic, but that would be sharing too much.

"Considering who you are," I continued, "Ex's concern was pretty justified, so stow the crap. You're in our city, so be respectful to its defenders." I folded my arms over my stomach, keeping my mangled forearm out of sight. "Now, questions. Ex?"

"Right, going to stick to the important stuff. I see two dead people with wooden stakes in them, so vampires are a real thing?"

"Yes."

"Right. So this isn't just a kidnapping case anymore."

"Exactly."

"What about the Hogs?"

"Well, my good man, it seems that these nasty lads brought a cache of weapons down here with a hidden vampire inside," Archer answered for me.

Extinguisher seemed to bristle a little at the Crusader's interruption, but I gave them both a warning look before continuing myself.

"Yes, though we don't know if they had any idea what they were carrying. It could've been a set-up of some kind. Either way, the only real leads we have are related to the dead Hog's personal effects. Considering there had to be more than one of those jerks and we have only one accounted for –"

"There's at least one more vampire terrorist, and at least one vampire who started it all," Extinguisher finished for me, right on cue.

"Right." I looked at Archer. "Any questions?"

"Do you wish for me to explain the scientific evidence in depth?"

"Later." I glanced at the tunnel Ex had come through, hoping it led to the surface. "Like I said, first priority is to get out of here and get medical attention."

Extinguisher shot me a concerned look. "Indy, for Christ's sake, why didn't you say so when I first got down here?" From the slight tensing of his muscles, I could tell he now saw the hole in my jacket and the blood dripping down, not to mention the funny way I was holding my forearm. "We're getting you back to the Foundation, double-time."

"Why the concern, Sir Extinguisher?" Archer asked. He sounded genuinely puzzled. "Is this not the woman who not only faced down my Lord Epic, but also Reaper, the most foul and powerful villain on the planet? In comparison, these must simply be flea bites."

Extinguisher lost his cool and gave Archer a hard shove. I couldn't say I blamed him.

Archer, unfazed by the shove, squared his shoulders and pulled himself up to his full height. "How dare you, sir? Have you no manners? Are you a mere ruffian?"

"Look, Robin Hood," Extinguisher said, "you have no idea what you're talking about. You weren't there in Washington, and you haven't been here. She's hurt so we're going, pronto."

"Sir, if not for the lady being present, I would –"

"Would what? I'm really curious to find out."

"Can it!" The two men ceased their arguing to look at me. "As much as I appreciate you defending me, Ex, and I really do, this isn't the time or the place. And you," I turned on Archer in a flash, "Ex is right. You don't know *anything* about this situation, about me, or about your so-called Lord Epic."

Extinguisher backed down immediately, and Archer, though clearly a bit upset still, took a step away. "Apologies, Indomitable. I'll try to rectify my ignorance."

"Good. Now, let's move. Archer, get the evidence. Ex is going to be ice-sliding both of us, so he needs both hands to navigate, while I'll be busy holding on."

Archer nodded and, as he gathered what evidence we had, I put my good arm around Extinguisher's waist, relishing the strange, icy tingle that permeated even my Push resistance.

"Okay, I'm ready when you are, Ex."

"Okay, Robin Hood." Extinguisher glanced behind him at Archer. "I hope that tin suit of yours can keep up."

"Is that a challenge, my frost-laden friend?" Archer asked. "Challenge accepted."

Flaunting itself in the face of conventional physics, what I assumed had just been the motorized ammo and power pack for the crossbow unfolded into some kind of jet-propulsion system.

"All right, let's go." Extinguisher gestured in front of him to conjure his ice slide, and we picked up speed rapidly. Archer kept up alongside, suspended by his jet thrusters.

Moments later, we burst into Underground proper, causing heads to turn and people to point and gape. I ignored the onlookers and simply held on as everything that'd happened over today hit home.

Terrorists were one thing. Terrorists dancing on the strings of a genius mastermind with all my same abilities was another. But vampire terrorists under the same madman took the cake.

I only hoped we'd figure out what Mackenzie's game was, before Atlanta turned from A-Town to V-Town.

Chapter 22

It was the spiraling descent toward the Foundation building that broke me out of my thoughts.

Archer stayed as our wingman the whole time and, as much as I'd love to say Extinguisher was faster, jet thrusters would beat an ice slide in an actual race.

Fortunately, the boys decided not to have a superpower-measuring contest and played nice the whole way home.

Sadly, we aimed for the most common way I entered the building - via the back loading dock, where someone was waiting to haul me off to the infirmary.

Who was waiting was the surprise - the Human Tank. The eager cyborg teen had worn a groove in the loading dock entrance with his treads. He was clearly there for me, too, judging by the cushion set on his tank-like lower body.

"What are you doing back from Athens already?" were the first words out of my mouth when Extinguisher and Archer landed on the deck next to Tank.

I didn't voice a complaint as Extinguisher helped me to flop down on the cushion, stomach first.

"Heya, Indy! Heya, Ex! Heya, armored dude!" I could hear the ever-present eagerness in Tank's voice.

Then he was really off in his usual thousand words a minute rush. "I'm really glad to see you, too, because I was with Eye and we were tracking clues on that Mackenzie dude, then Rachel called so I tore treads back here! How bad are you banged up, not too bad I hope, and anyway who's the new guy, I don't recognize him, so is he a new local or an out-of-towner?"

Extinguisher managed to get a word in when the excitable cyborg paused for breath. "Okay, good. Now, take Indy to the infirmary. I'll show our 'guest' to where he needs to go."

Extinguisher was very unhappy with the situation, and I couldn't blame him. Just because I was willing to put up with a Crusader for the moment didn't mean I was jumping for joy about it.

Fortunately, Archer kept his lips sealed in what had to be a rare burst of common sense.

"Okay, here we go!" Tank called out.

I gave him a clap on the back with my good arm as we rolled up through the loading dock doors. The Foundation didn't often need the dock for conventional purposes but how else would a kid with tank treads for legs get into the place?

"You've gotta stop getting beat up so much, Indy," Tank said as we rapidly rolled towards the infirmary. "I get all worried about you because you're not a Pushed even if you're a Natural but you're like my best bud!"

"You're my bestie, too, and I'll try to be more careful."

"Here we are," Tank announced. Even facedown, I could tell by the antiseptic white light that we were in the infirmary, so I pushed myself onto my feet.

Brooks was already there, snapping rubber gloves over his meaty hands. "Good afternoon, Doc. Glad to see you're still in one piece."

"Not for lack of trying. I need you to work on me as fast as you can. Ex is keeping an eye on our new Crusader friend –"

"Crusader?!" Tank's engines revved and energy started to crackle down his forearms. "Why didn't you say that guy was a Crusader because I would've whomped him right -?"

"Tank, chill," I shouted to get his attention. "The Argent Archer's helping out. This whole mess is something bigger than our two sides squabbling. For now, he's cool, got it?"

"If you say so," Tank replied, "but I still better go find Ex and everybody else then help watch the dude because you can't trust those Crusaders but at least they aren't Hogs or Push Crooks so there's that but still...those guys!"

"And get Ex *and* Archer to update you guys and Rachel about everything going."

Though if Mind's Eye was back, me saying that was unnecessary. With blind Indian psychic's return, she'd re-establish the constant mental link the others had.

While I didn't really want someone else in my mind, not with Rational and Whiteout Irenes crowding the place up, the fact I was a blank wall to her psychic powers stood as another little barrier between me and everyone else at the Foundation.

"Right, get on out of here and stop agitating my patient, kiddo," Brooks said to back me up. "Shit, who knows what injuries you have her opening up every time you make her shout like that?"

"I'm not a delicate, wilting flower, you know." Both of them patently ignored me.

"Okie dokie, Duane, I'm gone!" Tank left a gouge in the floor behind him as he roared off to find Extinguisher.

Brooks shook his head and slapped the examination table. "Now, get up here and let's see what you've mangled today. While you're at it, you can bring me up to speed."

I pulled off my gloves and peeled my jacket off. That hurt *a lot*. I couldn't tell what was worse, my crushed forearm or the shrapnel in my back. God, I wanted a handful of pills so badly.

Without a care for the mess, I dropped the clothing onto the infirmary floor and pulled myself up on the examination table.

Brooks let out a low whistle. "And I thought last night was bad."

"My injuries or the situation?" Brooks quirked his head at the question. "If Tank's back from Athens, so's Mind's Eye, which means you probably already know what's up."

Brooks nodded as he began his examination. "I'm getting the mental four-one-one, but I always prefer hearing it from your point of view, Doc. You notice shit others don't."

"The situation then. I'll give you my point of view on everything if it won't distract you from working. I meant it about wanting to get back out there as soon as possible."

Brooks gave me a hard look. "We talked about this. But we'll argue that after I'm done." He gestured to the examination table. "Lie on your belly and talk, while I pluck that metal out of your back."

It took a few minutes for me to run things down. The fact he was digging around the hole in my shoulder blade didn't help. But I didn't dare ask for either painkillers or enter my focused state to fight off the pain. Both felt too risky for my condition at the moment.

"Real vampires, huh?" Brooks said after I'd concluded. He was still fishing around for the last grenade fragments, much to my misfortune.

"As real as anything else these days," I said, chin propped up by my good forearm. "It was like Reaper, in a way - the Pushed shell was controlling the corpse. Really gruesome. What worries me is not knowing what spawned him."

There was a pulling feeling and a sickening sound in my back, and with it came blessed relief. I let out a gasp of a sigh and sank onto the barely padded table.

"There you go, you little bastard," Brooks shouted triumphantly. "You're lucky. Small bugger managed to wriggle deep, but it got stuck in the scapula so it didn't get to anything vital." There was a small clink of metal as he continued. "I think it's best to assume that every Hog is a bloodsucker now. What's your take on this Archer dude?"

"I almost punched him out," I confessed. "Just the gall of Epic teleporting his goons here almost made me lose my cool, but this vampire thing is new *and* bad. If he's willing to follow the rules, we shouldn't turn down the help."

I felt the spray of liquid as Brooks cleaned the wound to pack and dress it.

"I feel you. Hogs are one thing, but vampire terrorists? That kind of shit will give me nightmares." There was the tearing of medical tape as Brooks secured my dressing and, a few moments later, he tapped my shoulder. "You can get up, all done there."

I sat up, and Brooks looked at my forearm. "That does not look good." He shook his head, removed his bloody gloves, washed his hands, and put a new pair of gloves on.

"Feels worse." I told him what had happened in detail.

"This needs an x-ray." He rolled the machine over and carefully put my arm on it. The usual procedures done, he pulled the film out and we both looked at it.

"Well, I thought the bone was crushed but…"

"Yeah, your healing remains impressive. However, this is going to easily take as long as the injury in your back to heal. Soft cast coming up, and you'll be in a sling, too, and I don't want to hear one word about it."

I chose discretion as the better part of valor, and didn't complain as he did all of this. Instead, we talked about what had happened in general, as opposed to me specifically.

"I know it'll sound crazy, but the thing I'm least looking forward to is telling Mary what happened to her friends." I sighed. "Technically, there's a chance Rick is alive, but the woman was definitely Sally Greer."

"Always the hardest part of the job. Wish I had some advice for you there, but there's nothing to do for it."

"I know, but don't worry. I won't fob it off on you or Rachel. Speaking of bad things, how's Medusa's shoulder doing?" I didn't bother trying to hide my concern. "I've never seen anything rip through her like that."

"I sewed her up, just needed the diamond-tipped titanium needle and spider silk thread. She's going to be fine. Already healing up in that crazy fast way the Pushed do."

His eyes narrowed at me. "Speaking of, I don't want to redo the rest portion of last night's lecture, but my point stands."

I nodded even though I wanted to argue. Time to let my arm heal wasn't something we had a lot of, not with this vampire thing. We were looking at a mobile, cunning disease on two feet, directed by rabidly fanatical terrorists, manipulated by a madman who wanted to see the Pushed eradicated from the planet.

"Look, is there anything you can do for me in the short term? Just to get me through this." I glanced toward the supply shelves, and my palms itched oddly. "I promise, I'll rest when we're past the whole vampire plague. You've got to understand the implications of this."

"I can do the damn math, Irene." Brooks gave me a hard look. "But you're still cut off from the heavy stuff. Take a mix of Tylenol and Advil, that's the best I can offer until you've got yourself together." He helped me get into a chair. "Now sit."

I sighed, nodded, and stayed sitting.

"Good, let me get you a sling for that arm. Doctor's orders are to get at least a few hours downtime while we do some research and legwork on the evidence you and this Archer guy dug up."

Brooks headed over to the supply shelves to find that sling. "To make sure you comply with my orders, I had Mind's Eye send a mental ping to Medusa. She's going to make sure you actually go to your apartment and lie down."

I tried to find a position that didn't aggravate the wound in my back. I had to concede one thing - I was in no condition to go back out in the field. But there was one thing I'd ask Medusa to let me do before this whole rest thing.

As Brooks helped me get dressed and my arm into the sling, I swore I was going to talk to Mary. She deserved to know what was going on, and she deserved to hear it from me.

After all, I was the one that promised to help her and to save her friends, and I'd failed her.

Chapter 23

I was able to chow down on a protein bar and an electrolyte drink, which also allowed me to take the not-really-effective-for-this-level-of-pain over the counter meds.

It helped that it was Medusa playing assistant. I was glad to see her looking hale and hearty again after the Buzzkill fight. Other than the clean dressing over her shoulder stitches, I'd never have known we'd been in a big brawl at all.

She and I were at the elevators, and before Medusa could hit the up button, I stopped her. "I promise I'll go rest, but I need to talk to Mary first."

Medusa shot me an unblinking glance, then nodded. "Okay. You can't rest without your heart being at peace." Her finger drifted from the up button to press the down. "I believe she's spending some time with Caleb in the cafeteria, so we can kill two birds with one stone and get you some more food."

As we headed for the cafeteria I noted two things – the sun was still out and it looked like it was about noon, and the paparazzi outside were even more rabid than ever. I made sure not to lean on Medusa while we walked, not that it mattered. Our passage gave them a good show, especially with my arm in a sling.

Nothing to do for it, though. I had bigger problems than my public image right now.

As we stepped into the cafeteria, I saw Mary immediately, sitting at a table with Caleb in a clean jumper and a brand-new stroller. She didn't notice us, focused on playing with her son.

I took a deep breath to center myself as we walked up to them. Considering how empty the place was, Mary must've heard us - or felt the Pulse from Medusa - and looked up. "Oh, hello. You know, I can't -"

She cut herself off as she took us in, her eyes widening a bit. "Are you two going to be okay? What happened?"

"We're going to be alright," Medusa assured Mary as I sat down. "We're superheroes, after all. A few cuts and scrapes are just part of the job."

Mary nodded as she gave Caleb a pacifier, which the baby eagerly chewed on. Her eyes stuck to me, and I had a feeling Medusa's assurances didn't hold up in the face of the reality before Mary's eyes.

"Exactly," I agreed. "And we all heal fast. One of the fringe benefits of being what we are. As for what happened..."

It took a moment's pause to collect my thoughts and speak through the pangs of guilt. "With your information and some other digging, we found evidence of your two friend's kidnapping - Rick's wallet. Then we followed the clues it gave us to take us further on the trail of the kidnappers."

Her eyes widened. "Something bad happened, didn't it?"

"Yes. I'm sorry." I took a not-inconsiderable amount of willpower to stay calm, or at least a reasonable facsimile. "I found Sally's body. She was dead before I arrived. As for Rick, every bit of evidence points towards him being dead, as well." Unable to look Mary in the eye any longer, I lowered my head. "I made you a promise, and I failed."

I heard her sob. It drove a spike into my heart. Sure, this wasn't the first time sharing bad news but, if there was one hurt Choi and Brooks had tried to insulate me from, it was having to have this direct a talk with victims of the Whiteout.

Considering how busy I always was, it was easy for them, but they couldn't stop me this time, nor would I let them. I needed to see a therapist or something, because I had to be developing a martyr complex.

"I guess I should've expected that," Mary said between her tears. "It's just - with superheroes being real now, I was hoping I was wrong. That you could save them."

Medusa stepped around the table to sit next to Mary and put a comforting hand on her shoulder. "You have our sympathy and whatever help we can give you."

I forced myself to look up. "We'll do all that, Mary, but there's something else." Mary's tearful eyes met mine. "We failed to save your friends, but we're going to find those responsible and make sure they don't hurt you or anyone like you ever again."

Our gazes stayed locked for a good few moments before she nodded and wiped at her eyes. "I know you're a hero and all, that you're supposed to try not to hurt the bad guys too much, so what I'm going to ask is wrong. I know it is."

She sniffed back another sob as her eyes hardened. "But make the people behind this hurt as much as they hurt me, Rick, Sally, and all those others Miss Choi told me about, okay?"

Medusa glanced at me, unsure of what to say. I couldn't be sure if her hesitance came from the Whiteout's intrusive thoughts that laid a black-and-white morality on its Push Heroes or her own feelings.

But as much as Whiteout Irene warned me away from the idea of vengeance, I didn't have to do what she said, or what this twisted reality wanted.

"It's not wrong," I said with utmost certainty. "These people are monsters, and I'll make them feel your pain before we take them down. I swear it."

Either this was the start of my Batman arc or my villain arc, I wasn't sure which. But Mary's visible relief made that vow worth it, no matter the concerned look that flashed across Medusa's eyes.

"Thank you, Indomitable." She turned away to fuss over Caleb, so she didn't have to continue to face these tragic events head-on. "We'll be okay. Miss Choi said we could stay safe here as long as we needed, so you two should get back to finding the monsters behind this."

"I'll check in when we get them, Mary." I'm proud to say I didn't grit my teeth much to stand. "Come on, Meds."

Medusa nodded, gave Mary one last pat on the back, and rose. We didn't speak while I picked up a to-go carton of food, and we didn't speak on the way up to my apartment.

I wasn't sure if Medusa was just upset, angry at me for stepping outside the usual bounds of Push Hero morality, or something else entirely.

As for me, I was lost in my own thoughts and feelings. Today felt like a turning point in the ongoing push and pull of the Whiteout, but I couldn't put my finger on why exactly. Tragedy had been a constant since Epic had betrayed me and flipped reality on its head, and this was no different.

But there was an inherent, alien darkness to this vampire thing that made me shiver in my bones. Something so different from the four-color comic book nightmare Epic had unleashed. Maybe it was just my own anger and pain coloring things but, in my gut, I knew I was right.

Only when we'd gotten into my apartment, I'd taken off my jacket, and Medusa had guided me to sit down on my bed, did we start talking again.

"Thanks, Meds," I said, my meal forgotten on the dresser for the moment. "I'm sorry you had to do that with me. It really was only my responsibility."

"We're all on the same team, no matter the distance you make between you and the Five, or you and Facet." Medusa flipped a chair around, sitting down with that sinewy grace that couldn't be duplicated by a mere mortal. "But I need you to be honest with me, Irene."

I was just starting to relax when Medusa's serious tone snapped me right back to tense again. Medusa's reptilian eyes remained impassive, but I could see the eyes of the actual woman underneath grow concerned.

"There's been something eating at you, and I want you to tell me what it is."

"There's nothing wrong that putting Epic and Mackenzie behind bars won't fix. Or are you talking about what happened with Mary?"

"None of that is going to happen overnight or we would've already done it. But yes, I'm worried about what you said. We're heroes, Irene, a fact you've reiterated more times than I can count. We're about justice, not vengeance."

I let out a sigh. I'd thought the same thing earlier today, when PART dragged off Buzzkill.

"I know, and normally, I'd say those exact words. Meds, it's easy for us to talk about justice. We have power, you Pushed most of all. Think about what it was like pre-Whiteout. You worked with the poor, the disaffected, the oppressed, so you saw what people with power could do, and what people without power couldn't."

Medusa raised a clawed finger to interrupt, but I stopped her. "Sorry. Let me finish, then you can let me have it. I'm not saying we should throw the ideas of justice aside, because we *do* have power. But the normal people aren't always going to find comfort in that. They've been lied to about justice before. So maybe, this once, we avenge them instead of talking about justice, especially in the face of a threat unlike any we've faced."

"To start down that path is a slippery slope," Medusa said, her hissing voice filled with concern. "When do you stop once you've taken a step over the edge?"

"Meds, I understand what you're saying, but let's take a realistic look at this situation. We're not fighting people. We're not fighting Push Crooks, even. We're fighting *literal* walking corpses."

An involuntary shiver ran down my spine. "Be thankful you can't actually see that, but there's no one to save, no humanity to reason with. This is a plague, and we need to deal with it like one. So, yeah, if there's ever a time to be an avenger of the downtrodden, to bring holy vengeance and make someone like Mary feel safe for once, this is that time."

Medusa sat back in her chair, her snakes dancing as she seemed lost in thought. If anyone had a chance to get through to her, it was me. After a long moment, she let out a sigh as her snakes all blew along with her.

"Okay, Irene. I see what you're saying. I'm just worried about you. You've pushed yourself too far, too fast, too hard, and there's one thing I *do* know for certain." She reached out and put her hand on my shoulder. "We can't stop Epic without you."

I smiled and nodded. "Thank you. For worrying about me. Now, you'd better get downstairs. Someone's got to help Rachel herd the cats and keep Ex and Archer from fighting."

"You'd be better at it, especially with Ex." She gave me a wink as she pulled back. "But I'll do my best."

"I'm sure you can recruit Hex to help you out." I returned that wink.

Medusa let out a hissing little laugh and nodded. "Of course. Now, get some rest."

I relented and tried to relax. Maybe everyone was right, and the stress of bearing all this responsibility was starting to make me crack.

I rubbed my good hand over my face and realized I'd yet to take the mask off. I was beginning to wonder if, one day, it wouldn't come off, that it would be a permanent part of my face.

A gentle, scaled hand pulled my hand away. In the time I'd been lost in those thoughts, Medusa had gotten the acetone solution from my dresser and come back. She dabbed at the edges of my mask with a soaked cotton ball and peeled away at the loosened spirit gum.

"Meds, I'm sorry." Taking off that mask was like taking a thousand-pound weight off my shoulders. "I've really been stressed."

Her snake hair collectively hissed for silence. "Shut it, *amiga*." She shook her head slightly. "Apology accepted." She laughed, and her snakes hissed happily.

"I know. Just promise that someone will get me up before sunset."

"Even now, you're thinking about the mission." She threw up her hands, her snakes writhing in concert. "Fine, Irene, you win. I'll make sure."

"Thanks, Meds, I owe you."

"You do." She helped me get my boots off, as well as the rest of my clothing, and got me into a comfortable t-shirt nightgown.

Once I was ready for bed, she helped me eat my dinner. I wanted to argue, but the fatigue of using my abilities was beating out the pain now.

I didn't make a mess only because Medusa was helping me. Once done, she managed to help me find a semi-comfortable position and got me lying down. Then she closed the blinds and turned out the lights.

"Sleep well, *chica,*" she said softly as she left my apartment.

I wound up sleeping far less than I needed to. The nightmare prospect of what was now breeding in my hometown seemed to creep into every dream I had.

Though I wasn't an expert on pathogens or diseases, I had more than enough medical training to do the basic math.

Unchecked, a vampiric plague could spread quickly, especially if the vampires didn't need to kill to breed. The specifics of their breeding process depended on the mythology you drew them from - almost every culture had a vampire equivalent.

Still, I got a few hours of rest. When I rose, I felt marginally better, and the sun still shone in the afternoon sky.

My back and arm still hurt, but I was no longer in agony, and I could tell they were both healing. In fact, my arm felt well enough for me to remove the sling.

Even so, I realized that what I wanted to do - take a shower, brush my hair, and get dressed in a clean uniform - wasn't easily done by myself.

So, despite not wanting to, I texted Medusa to come back and help me. It was only then that I saw the time and date - I'd slept a full twenty-eight hours.

Medusa arrived and refused to let me complain about the loss of a day. "You needed it, *chica,* because we need you, and you weren't up to anything. Besides, we had to find the place, which was much harder than you'd expect for a business that presumably wants customers."

Once I was showered and dressed, we headed downstairs. I tried to relax, but that was impossible once we arrived, because the conference room was filled with tension.

There was clear animosity between Extinguisher and Archer, though Hexagon seemed to have no issues with the Crusader.

Nor did Medusa, who took a seat next to Hexagon after she helped me to my seat at the foot of the table. However Mind's Eye and Tank were obviously backing Extinguisher.

Brooks and Choi appeared to be going for neutral arbitrators, with limited success.

It was also clear that our arrival had interrupted conversation, and no one seemed willing to start that back up again.

Meaning it was up to me. "So, who's up for vampire hunting?"

Chapter 24

"You should still be resting," Extinguisher said firmly. "We still have three hours before sundown."

"It'd be best if we stormed the terrorists' lair before then," Archer said.

Extinguisher rolled his eyes. "We've been over this a thousand times, Robin Hood. We don't even know if there are any Hogs or vampires there, and we don't break down doors and bust heads without reason."

"I, for one, am quite happy to see you, Indomitable, even if it's through another's eyes," Mind's Eye said in clear, precise tones. "Someone may finally be able to take control of this circular dispute and refocus the investigation."

I nodded in thanks, and Mind's Eye smiled just a bit. Of the Five, we'd had the most contentious relationship at the start, caused by my invisibility to the blind woman's psychic senses.

We'd built on that in the months after, between my friendship with her ward, Tank, and the proof of my ability to think through situations as much as punch through them.

"To help bring you up to speed," Mind's Eye continued, "I must start with a warning. These vampires are no longer living creatures, and that's made them immune to my precognitive powers. As if they muddle the threads of destiny around them."

Mind's Eye gave me a wry grin. "Much like a certain Natural I know. That is to say, I can offer no psychic insights on this situation, and my advice is much the same as Extinguisher's - it's a fool's errand to barge in with no plan or no information."

That set off another round of back-and-forths that Choi and Brooks tried to moderate.

I wiped at my brow. Someone really needed to adjust the AC in here.

Hexagon looked at me, concern palpable. "Irene, even though you've slept for a day, you really don't look so good. You should listen to Ex and get some more rest."

"Considering what's going on, I don't think I can."

Amazingly, this earned me everyone's attention, which I took advantage of. "Let me address the elephants in the room. First, you've all spent the day and night, apparently, with the Argent Archer, our 'loaner' from Epic's Crusaders." I gestured to Archer, who felt the need to make a flourishing bow.

"He's here because I decided to let him stay. It doesn't matter what side of the debate he's on right now. We're facing what I'm sure you've been told is a walking plague. Let me say, though, that you all have my personal permission to dog pile him if he goes out of line."

I nodded to the Five. "But don't use that as a reason to keep him out of the loop. This is serious business, not just your typical Push Crook crime spree."

Then I glanced over at Archer. "Just think of the dog pile threat as an incentive to play by the rules."

Laying things out plainly seemed to settle the room's discontent. "Now, I'm sure Rachel and Duane have some actual useful information that isn't 'let's get, 'em, guys' or 'let's sit on our hands, y'all' to tell us." I nodded to Choi. "You've got the floor."

"Finally," Brooks growled. "This is the exact same shit we've been trying to get through to you guys this whole time, and by whole time I mean all the hours Indy was out."

"Not that I didn't need the time," Choi said. "The business was quite difficult to find, almost as if they wanted to be very hidden."

"Mackenzie," I said immediately.

Choi nodded. "But, ultimately, my tablet and I won out. Once found, Duane and I did some research and basic reconnaissance of the area while the others were 'discussing' our options."

"That must have been a nice break," I said pointedly.

Choi chuckled. "In a way, yes. Paul's Pub is a local dive with a colorful reputation. It's part of a block of older businesses in the heart of Downtown. The owner, Paul Blanchard, has a history of being a sympathizer to various 'White Power' hate groups."

"In other words, the guy's a classic profile for a Hog, either a member or an ally," Brooks noted with a look of disgust. "That's not ironclad proof of a crime, though."

"The curious thing is that, last week sometime, Paul's hours of operation changed. The old sign said they opened at one in the afternoon and close at two in the morning."

"But," Brooks said, "the new sign, taped over the old one, now says they open at seven in the evening and don't close until five in the morning - in direct violation of Atlanta's laws."

"I see they're committed to be as nefarious as possible," I said. "And those new hours align with what a sunlight-avoiding vampire would prefer."

"Isn't that sufficient cause to swoop in like the hawks of justice that we are?" Archer asked.

It was no surprise that Extinguisher was the first to answer that. "No, it's not. In this town, law and order are still important concepts."

"Shush, the both of you." I looked to Choi and Brooks. "You passed this along to PART, right?"

"The boys in blue are setting up observation on the place," Brooks answered, "but I don't think we can expect any real back-up on this. That'd just be turning cops into vampire chow if we're correct."

"Well, boys and girls, if Mind's Eye's third eye can't get a clear look inside and our intel is limited, someone has to go in, right?" Medusa asked. "In that case, we don't have that many choices as to who plays that role."

Choi nodded. "The five of you are obviously out. Even if you weren't locally famous, you're still quite obviously Pushed."

"I could remove my armor and infiltrate into this den of iniquity, Dame Choi." Archer tapped the side of his helmet. "No one outside my compatriots in the Crusaders knows my actual face."

"Assuming you could tone down on the Renn Faire speech for a bit," Extinguisher couldn't help but point out.

Before Archer could take affront, I jumped in. "That's not even the issue. The Pulse would mark you before anything else. Even outside of your Pushtech, you yourself are Pushed, Archer."

"Indy's absolutely correct, Mister Archer," Choi said. "As we've seen many times in the past few months, the impact of the Pulse can't be hidden or controlled."

Archer let out a brief sigh of disappointment and settled in his chair. "Very well. I'll remain content keeping watch from the skies. My armor's sensors will alert me to any brewing danger from within the pub."

Brooks looked at Choi and she nodded at him, which caused him to frown. He turned back to the room in general.

"Hate to say it, but there are only three possible candidates - me, Rachel, and Indy."

"How is that any better than sending PART in?" I asked. "I know you aren't glass sculptures but -"

"We're better trained, for one thing," Choi reminded me. "More importantly, this is meant as an information-gathering assignment. The more trained eyes in the building, the better."

"Don't worry," Brooks said. "We'll make an exit stage right the moment things seem fishy. The FBI didn't train us to be heroes - it trained us to be investigators."

The unspoken vibe they gave off, though, was that they were both worried about me being on my own. When did I ever give anyone in this room reason to doubt me? I wasn't sure, but maybe I just looked worse than I thought I did. No one had argued with Hexagon, after all.

"Okay, you're right." I wiped at my brow again. I had to get myself together and focus. I reminded myself that lives were at stake.

Irrationally, it helped.

"That settles it," Extinguisher agreed. "What's the ETA on Facet and Ken for reinforcements?"

That was something else that'd slipped through my mind. I should've checked on them myself.

I dimly remembered from yesterday something about a raid in LaGrange, but so much had happened since then and I'd slept a day away. And I should call Mom, especially after the other night with Extinguisher.

"I've sent them updates with all the info we have," Brooks replied, "but we can't count on them for back-up. They're primed to take down Stellar and her gang of human traffickers, and that's still priority."

I held in the sigh. How could I forget that? I really did need more rest, but I'd worry about that later. I just needed to concentrate and get through tonight.

"Alright. That leaves us to figure out the observation assignments. Huddle up, people." Extinguisher paused a moment, then looked at Archer, who seemed hesitant, as if we weren't going to deal him in on the action.

"Yes, you, too, Robin Hood. Indy's right, we're all in this together."

Chapter 25

"When you said this was a dive, you weren't kidding, Rachel," I whispered as I walked through the well-populated bar.

I was starting to feel better than I had, and Brooks had removed the cast on my arm before we'd left the Foundation, but the pain was still there, coming in fits and flare-ups and making me really wish I had some kind of decent painkillers in my system.

Like me, Paul's Pub had certainly seen better days. A few generations ago, it might've been a respectable, neighborhood watering hole.

You could see glimpses of old glories everywhere - framed photographs of Atlanta luminaries yellowed with age, the battered but still exquisite carving on the wooden bar, and the lingering, rich smell of hard woods and fragrant liquors.

It was the more recent decorations that brought the atmosphere down. Cheap electronic gambling machines lined one wall where a second bar had once been, blocking the window to the street. Blue aluminum box fans had been jammed into what few free windows remained, a cheap substitute for an actual air conditioning system.

To top it all off, there was the more discreet but patently obvious neo-Nazi and Ku Klux Klan logos, photos, and memorabilia. The South will rise again? In the post-Whiteout world? Seriously?

"I wasn't," Choi replied in my earpiece. "Just remember our code phrase to call back-up - 'something in my drink.' Now, Duane astutely noted that his appearance will cause the most stir, so I'll enter next in about five minutes."

It was another little reminder that everyone was worried I was off my game. I tried to ignore that and concentrate on the moment.

I'd gotten some attention myself. While I was a fairly attractive White woman, most of the attention was the gross kind, but it was, in a sense of the word, "friendly."

"Your entrance will, too," I reminded her. "You're not White, so you're not welcome."

"We work with what we've got," Brooks said. "I'll be in thirty minutes after that. That should give you guys time to scope things out before the drunks start to throw bottles at the Black man."

Extinguisher added a grunt of sympathy to Brooks' statement over the comms.

"Understood," I answered, then focused on trying not to draw any more attention than possible as I made for the bar.

I settled on a barstool and flashed a smile at the bartender. From the description, that certainly wasn't Paul. Paul was old, wiry, and on the short side. This guy was tall, young, and sported a waterfall mullet straight out of the Eighties.

"Can I get a pint of Bud please?"

He smiled toothily. "Anything for a pretty lady like you."

As the bartender grabbed a pint mug and got to pouring, I felt a growing twist in my gut coming from below the pub. It hadn't been there a moment ago, but it was like the slightly twisted ripple of the same Pulse I'd felt from the vampire before, only stronger.

That increased strength highlighted the difference between this and the Pulse of normal Pushed – this energy felt darker, cruder, the shiver up my spine unmistakable and strong. But while the vampire Pulse grew, it wasn't moving yet.

The bartender set the glass of beer in front of me with a loud clank. That snapped me out of my thoughts as it sent froth splattering on the bar. There was a faint reddish tint to the amber liquid.

"Hey," I said, pointing at the glass, "I think there's something in the beer." Strange coincidence that the codeword was something I'd be saying, anyway.

The bartender, who hadn't moved, kept the same smile plastered on his face. "Don't know what you mean, darling."

I glanced sidelong at what little window wasn't covered in poster or blocked by furniture. The sunlight was now gone, which confirmed my suspicions. Best for me to step out and regroup with the cavalry that was going to crash in any moment.

"You know, on second thought," I smiled disarmingly, "I forgot I was supposed to meet a friend uptown so let me just –"

The bartender moved to grab me by both wrists before I could stand. I thought he was about to bring out the old hackneyed "you're not going anywhere" line when I slipped into focus.

Fear, worry, and pain disappeared as the biochemical rush hit. Instead of lunging at my arms, the bartender now lazily reached at them. I could even pick out the swirl of red in the beer, refusing to mix no matter how hard it tried.

I slapped both the bartender's hands away, grabbed him by the lapel, and dragged him easily over the bar top. By the time the few other patrons could protest, I'd already slammed him against the opposite wall.

I wanted to question him, ask him to confirm what I thought was in the beer, but there was no time. The door that led downstairs into the cellar exploded off its hinges. Through the cloud of splinters and dust, malignant shapes moved in the darkness.

"You shoulda drank the beer," the barkeep cackled.

As much as I would've loved to beat him down then and there, I had more important problems as the shapes blurred out of the cloud of dust.

They were vampires, all right, and more than just two or three. There were enough that I didn't even bother to make a rough count.

Everyone was shouting on the comm, as were all the patrons in the bar, as I turned towards the swarm bearing down on me. I couldn't parse it all, especially as a high-pitched whine hovered at the edge of my boosted hearing.

I couldn't figure out what it was, because the first vampire was on me in a split second. Even in that moment, as time lazily crept into my perception, I saw notable differences between these creatures and the one Archer and I'd already laid to rest.

The corpse itself was somewhat better preserved, though if that was intentional or a matter of life outside the sewer, I couldn't say.

A red haze still shone in his eyes, but there was something akin to humanity in the gaze and the movement of the head. These could think, a fact that spelled nothing but trouble for us and the city.

Case in point - instead of trying to grab me and drain my blood, this vampire, dressed in military gear, led off with a quick double shot from the pistol he drew in a flash.

While I had on a light bulletproof vest under my clothes, I was thankful that, due to my amplified reflexes, I was already ducked down, so the shots hit the bar, over my head.

The bartender let out a scream of alarm, then started to make a break for it. I ignored him - I had far bigger problems.

As I stood up, the vampire ditched the sidearm and lunged at me. I grabbed the nearest barstool.

I was thankful for the pub's rich history and real wood decor - no cheap pressboard here - as I brought the stool around in a baseball swing. The stool splintered to pieces along the vampire's left side.

Though it didn't seem as effective as impaling it with wood, the undead thing howled in pain as the force of the hit sent it crashing through another table. The stool was no more, save for the two jagged legs in my hand.

I slammed one right into the first vampire's heart, leaving me with one stake left.

As I turned to face the onrush of undead, and the panicking patrons, something else odd hovered at the tip of my mind, but it would have to wait.

There was no time for deep analysis as vampires streamed up into the bar, some surrounding the patrons, the others going out into the Atlanta night, even as Hexagon made a brand new, plus-size entrance in the side of the bar facing the street.

What pleased me even more than the sight of my favorite six-armed mangling machine was that a dome of frosty stone made a solid barrier outside. Ever since the Battle of Washington, Extinguisher and Medusa had practiced to perfect this team combo favorite, and it always served us well.

"Containment is our top priority, team," Extinguisher said over the comms. "We're sealed in until we have a pile of staked bodies."

"Land's sake, there's a ton of 'em!" Hexagon's exclamation echoed through the bar as so many vampires swarmed over him, he had to fall back outside in a vain attempt to hold them off.

I was alone again, and the few vampires still in the bar turned toward the patrons who hadn't managed to escape in the initial rush. Even if I didn't have an innate sense of the value of human life, I really didn't want the vampires multiplying more.

"Hex is busy, and we have normals in danger inside," I called as I hopped over the pool table to intercept one of the vampires.

As if to emphasize my point, a vampire had already snatched a middle-aged woman from where she'd been cowering behind the pool table and pinned her to the wall.

Like the one I'd just dealt with, this vampire moved with swift deliberation instead of feral anger and wore well-maintained military gear. I was ready to stake him from behind when, out of the corner of my eye, I caught another bar patron about to be snack food.

I had to make a split-second decision and decided I could still stop the vampire close to me before he chowed down on the woman. Without hesitation, I twisted and hurled the jagged stool leg like a javelin.

There was no way I could manage a heart shot at this range with the vamp's partial side profile, but the leg plunged into his arm. He let out a loud, inhuman screech and dropped the drunk in his grip.

I hoped it would be enough of a distraction to buy me time, and it certainly distracted my initial target from his meal.

Expecting I might get a reprisal, I managed to duck the vampire's initial backhand. I swung a hard right hand into the creature's ribs as I reached for the pool cue still sitting on the table.

Though these corpses were in better shape, they were still corpses. My hand messily crushed into rotting flesh, sending the vampire staggering back a step in surprise - or was it recognition? A part of my accelerated mind thought about that as I brought the cue to bear.

The vampire trumped my stake with a machine pistol. The thought that I was going to die by a vampire terrorist shooting me in a White Power bar was so absurd I almost laughed as he pulled the trigger.

Despite my bulletproof vest, I was most certainly going to die.

Chapter 26

It was quite the surprise when I didn't die or even get any holes blasted through my body.

That didn't mean the focused burst of rubber bullets hurt with a pain I couldn't put into words as they smashed into my chest and abdomen. It hurt so bad that it punched straight through the wall of willpower that normally shunted pain away.

The sheer impact knocked me off my feet and into a cheap table, collapsing it under the impact. I was wheezing for breath, flat on my back and struggling to regain my focus, when another hole exploded in the front of the building.

As I weakly turned my head toward the new sound, I saw the source of the crash – Tank roaring through as the next wave of cavalry, with an angry Medusa riding on his back.

She pounced off Tank and onto a vampire that'd bitten a teenager who'd picked the wrong bar to flash his fake ID. Her halo of snakes hissed evilly as she drove the vampire to the ground.

Tank saw me, and I couldn't blame him for the conclusion that must've run through his head. I couldn't even gasp out a correction.

The poor kid didn't even say anything coherent. He just yelled, a yell fueled by the raging cauldron of emotion called puberty and the anger at seeing his friend dead, and tore a direct path to my shooter. Tank ground the flooring, furniture, and everything else under his treads, and debris flew everywhere.

I somehow mustered the strength to roll off the collapsed table, providing me with a little cover from the impending impact.

The vampire spun and fired a quick burst of rubber bullets, which had about zero effect on the rampaging cyborg. A split-second later, Tank impacted dead-on with the vampire.

Messy didn't begin to describe the after-effects of the impact. An arm went one way, a foot and part of the shin that way, and most of the rest flew straight back from the hit. Every piece sent a spray of blood and rotting tissue in its wake.

I considered and denied the request from my body to roll over and vomit continuously. Instead, I managed one complete, gasping breath and sat up.

Tank hadn't noticed my miraculous recovery as he ground his treads back and forth over the vampire's body. It was still trying to regenerate from the horrific injuries, a disgusting display that caused my stomach to flip once again.

Medusa seemed to have better luck as she goaded her vampire into a bite which she blocked with her arm. The fangs dug through her tough scales deep enough to draw blood, but that put the vampire's eyes right up to Medusa's supernatural gaze with bizarre results.

I could only watch for a moment as I tried to pick myself back up, but it was a dance of unreal forces. Medusa's gaze turned tissue to stone while the vampire's nature tried to return it to undead flesh. It didn't matter that neither seemed to win - the constant state of flux effectively incapacitated the monster.

"Alive," was all I could croak into the swirling mass of com chatter. I was hurting too badly to parse the rest, though I managed to pull the frayed threads of my focus together. I staggered to my feet, grabbing the pool cue I'd dropped before.

Tank's roaring rampage of revenge stopped, and he spun to look at me, eyes watering with tears. "Indy, Indy, Indy!"

The big kid would've grabbed me in a bear hug if the telltale sound of an assault rifle's charging handle didn't cut through the cacophony around us.

Instincts kicked into overdrive as I dove for the only hard cover around - Tank. In addition to being a super-cyborg, his chassis produced a protective force field. Thank God for that, too, as Mr. Skewered-With-A-Table-Leg unleashed a full clip of ammunition in our direction.

The air was filled with the sparks of bullets impacting air and deflecting aside, then a brief silence.

I took a glance over Tank's shoulder as the vampire threw his gun down. I could read his body language. He was about to take a hostage. There was no way I was going to let that happen, at least that's what I told myself. The truth was that what I tried to do was nigh-impossible, but damn if I didn't go for it.

For the brief moment the vampire still faced forward, as his rifle hit the ground, I hopped up on Tank's back and hurled the pool cue I had in hand like a javelin.

Yes, I knew exactly where the heart was and no, it was highly unlikely, even with my unleashed potential, that I could hit that mark. However, maybe to make up for all the bad luck today, Lady Luck cut me a break.

The pool cue hit dead on, slipping through that one gap in the ribs and sternum where it could hit the heart without obstruction. The vampire clawed at it and, with a final look of disbelief, fell backwards. The phantom vampiric shell faded away, and the vampire returned to its natural corpse state.

The older gentleman about to be eaten fainted dead away. That was probably the safest thing he could do.

"I'm so happy to see you," Tank began, but interrupted himself as his entire front end pitched up and back. "Holy crab cakes!"

I fell off, barely rolling clear as Tank toppled back awkwardly, hitting his head on a table first, then crashing sideways.

The vampire he'd smashed apart and ground under his treads had managed to reassemble himself in just a few moments, and he'd been the one to turn Tank over with a triumphant snarl.

Tank furiously tried to right himself with all the success of a flipped turtle. The vampire pounced at me, either to bite me or just snap me like a twig.

I vetoed both of those proposals, kicking up with both feet. My boots hit him right in the chest, and I kept pushing with enough strength to launch the corpse against the rafters.

I spun sideways towards the rack of pool cues on the wall, hoping to find a fresh weapon, but I only found empty air. As the vampire crashed back to the floor with barely any damage, I reached down for the nearest smashed table, the one I'd fallen through, but it'd been ground on by Tank's treads.

All I could come up with ragged splinters. I tucked the largest sharp shard I could find between my knuckles, hoping that Tank would get up, even if I knew that was probably not going to happen.

"Boss wants you, but I'm too hungry, sorry," the vampire hissed as he blurred towards me. I could barely understand it with how fast it spoke.

As I twisted away from its initial grab, I delivered a sharp scratch with my wooden shard in return.

More importantly, the niggling thought at the back of my head blossomed into full realization.

Though I'd lost it in the chaos of battle and near-death experiences, that constant high-pitched whine had only ceased when this vampire, the last one in the bar, spoke, but it was still super-fast and high-pitched.

To me, that meant the vampires had been talking and coordinating this entire time. The speech had just been so fast, so high-frequency, normal human ears couldn't hear it.

Hopefully, I'd live long enough to share and use that fact. Fortunately, even with my stakes broken, I had an ace in the hole as I reached for my neck.

Or I was supposed to have. I'd forgotten the crucifix from Underground on my apartment dresser.

I cursed my human weakness as the vampire's hand grasped my throat. I instantly responded by driving the sharp nub of wood deep into its forearm, but the creature didn't relent despite the pain etched on its face. Just like a human could try to ignore his instincts, these rational vampires could do the same.

"Indomitable is *not* on the menu, monster!"

The distinct twang of the Argent Archer's mechanized crossbow thundered across the pub, and the vampire grew a wooden arrow through the chest. The choking grasp around my neck abated as the corpse fell to the floor.

Archer was standing in the hole Tank made. He'd fired a bolt with pinpoint accuracy through the chaos of the melee with just enough force to punch through the beast but not impale me in the process.

It wasn't a bad shot, not at all.

Unlike most Push Heroes, I didn't make time for chatter, so I simply nodded to Archer before I helped Tank get himself upright again.

Medusa drove a bar stool leg-first into her half-stone/half-flesh opponent, and that disrupted the vampire's regeneration enough for him to turn into very bizarre lawn sculpture.

"The party is still going on strong out here, if you lovely people could come help?" Extinguisher spoke in his harried, "the-plan-is-falling-apart" voice.

Yes, we had been in enough bad situations that I could pick that voice out.

Medusa and I hopped on Tank's back. "You okay, Meds?"

"Just some scrapes on my arm, *chica,* which is more than I can say for you."

I nodded. "Hold on tight." With that, I clapped Tank's shoulder. "Let's ride."

As Tank charged for the hole he'd made coming in, I took my own advice and tightened my grip. "We're coming, guys," I called over the comm. And I don't know if it'll help, but these vampires communicate with high-speed, high frequency sound."

With that, we rode out of the hole and into a land of obscuring mists.

The largest part of the vampire pack had moved outside in an attempt to escape. There had to be some sort of limitation to their ability to turn to fog, as it was obvious that several had done so but couldn't escape the dome, despite the lack of an air-tight seal.

Still, some of them maintained their unnatural mist form, and that didn't help with the raging battle. The shadowy figures of the vampires seemed to vanish and reappear at will to make attacks in the billowing fog.

Hexagon and Extinguisher stood back-to-back, while Mind's Eye hovered above their heads with an honor guard of several telekinetically controlled shafts of wood.

None of my friends were unscathed. Even Hexagon's nigh-invulnerable skin had bloody scratches and holes from fangs in it. There was a messy circle of at least six corpses around them. Four of them were staked, but two were simply flash-frozen blocks of meat.

"The cavalry has arrived, and we're ready to stake vampire tails," Tank shouted as we roared to assist.

That attracted attention as vampires on either side emerged from the mists. The first ate one of Tank's plasma blasts and charred nicely as Medusa drove a stake into his chest. One of Archer's wooden arrows lanced through the side of the other, shooting it right into the ice-stone wall, down but still mobile.

"We need to see," I found myself saying pointlessly. Whiteout Irene occasionally got something through my mental defenses.

But Rational Irene had a more useful nugget as Tank rolled out to join the defensive formation. "These fogged ones aren't actual gas, or they would seep out the cracks in the shell. They're not like Nitro at all. They've got to be dispersing their physical matter but not so much as an actual gas."

"This is going somewhere right, Indy?" Extinguisher threw up an ice wall right in the face of a charging vampire before impaling it to said wall with the sudden growth of crystalline spikes.

"When do her musings not?" Mind's Eye asked as she speared the trapped vampire with a levitating stake.

"Mind's Eye, can you push out omni-directionally with some low-power telekinesis?" I said, focusing on the plan instead of the vampires swirling around.

I only hoped we could contain this before one of them thought to bring heavy ordnance into play. Archer had said that weapons crate had explosives in it, after all.

"I believe I see what your plan is." Mind's Eye nodded sharply. "I'll make it happen."

"Ah, the science seems obvious now." Archer fired off another wooden arrow. "Good show, Indomitable."

"Everyone, huddle up," I ordered. I hoped Extinguisher didn't think I was stepping on his toes. He was the leader of the Atlanta Five, and I had no problem delegating that authority. "Mind's Eye, the second we're together, do it."

"I'm ready when the others are."

It was only a moment before we were together in a defensive circle, ready for anything. It had to be obvious to the vampires that something was up.

Now that I knew what to listen for, I could hear the faintest edge of their high-pitched speech, even if I couldn't understand it.

If this didn't work, we'd be in trouble.

The moment we were together but before the vampires could swarm, Mind's Eye unleashed her power. A radiating pulse of invisible force radiated out from her. To me, it was only a very faint breeze, but I could see the others waver slightly against the psionic field.

As the telekinetic sphere slipped past us like a soap bubble and radiated outward, it steadily pushed the fog back. I could see through the lens of my heightened senses that the field wasn't pushing the mist away like a normal cloud.

Instead, I could barely make out how each "cloud" seemed to move as a unit.

There were four distinct clouds I could see, each one no doubt being one gaseous vampire. When the wave pushed against the solid vampires, it wavered a moment, then slipped around them, as it did with us.

A moment later, the mists were shoved against the edges of the stone shield, leaving five suddenly unprotected vampire Hogs out in the open. They had been in the middle of preparing some kind of rocket or missile launcher.

"Get 'em," was all Extinguisher had to say.

Though Mind's Eye was busy sequestering the fog vampires, there wasn't much that five unprepared beings, even vampires, could do under the coordinated attack of our team.

I even got to get in one last staking. The rubber bullet thing and the fact they wanted to take me alive weren't sitting well with me.

The fogged vampires didn't fare any better. When our attack began, they shifted back to solid form to try to help, which only led them to being locked down in the tighter, stronger grip of Mind's fully focused telekinesis.

They were the last four to get staked.

Chapter 27

"Everyone okay?" Extinguisher asked as we stood over the carnage. The stink of decay mixed with raw, fresh blood was stomach-turning for us all, I was sure. "Indy?"

Any previous annoyance at how everyone seemed to be overly concerned about my safety had evaporated with the rubber bullets.

I managed a smile for Extinguisher and nodded. I tried to convincingly look like I wasn't having any trouble whatsoever, despite the pain I was suppressing. I had no idea if it worked.

"We're all the worse for wear, Ex," Medusa replied as she inspected the bleeding punctures in her forearm, "but I don't think anyone is too badly hurt."

Tank flashed a look at me, which I answered with another sharp nod. We weren't finished here, and I wasn't going to let anyone fuss over me with work yet to do.

"If the bad guys are down, can you bring down the wall?" Choi relayed over the com. "We have PART ready to move in and EMTs are in route. They can't do their jobs with the current state of affairs."

"Roger that," Extinguisher answered. "Hex and Tank, give me a hand with the wall. Mind's Eye, get any survivors together and render aid. Everybody else, let's try to get some answers."

There was a general assent, and we split into our separate teams to get to work.

"Indomitable, what angle did those vile creatures attack from?" Archer asked as our team stepped back through the ruined storefront. Glass crunched under my boot as the smell of decay and spilled liquor mixed in the air.

"They came up from the basement." There was definitely a bit of tightness to my breath. My expert opinion was a cracked rib, at the absolute least very bad bruising.

Rubber bullets were intended to be non-lethal like tasers, but both could seriously injure or kill someone under the wrong circumstances. Why the hell did the Hogs want to take me alive, anyway?

Medusa gave me a concerned glance. "Got it. What about upstairs? Mind's Eye says there's one last human mind up there."

"Really?" Archer beat me to the question. "How could a mere mortal mind resist such awesome mental might?"

I wouldn't have phrased it that way. Also, it seemed that I wasn't the only one not connected to the Psychic Friends Network. At least in my case it was a technical issue, not purposeful exclusion.

"It's been done before." I walked towards the stairs. "We better get whoever it is out. No telling what traps or fail-safes the Hogs put downstairs."

That was the one thing we were all certain of at this point, based on the paramilitary gear and military-grade weaponry. And if there was one thing Hogs loved, as I'd already seen that day, it was bombs, like any terrorist, domestic or foreign. Maximum carnage and maximum terror in one neat package.

"Smart thinking." Medusa followed me, with Archer on our heels.

"Still, everyone needs to keep their eyes open," I said as we started upward. "There's no guarantee the Hogs don't have traps upstairs, too."

"Please, ladies. Allow me to focus my sensors on the stairs for a brief moment."

We stayed at the first few stairs and let Archer work his Pushtech magic. His armor hummed for a few moments then fell silent again. "The stairs ahead are clear, and I can confirm the heat signature of a human beyond the door above."

I nodded. "Then up we go."

When we got to the top of the stairs, we discovered why the vampires didn't make their escape attempt up through the roof. Someone had nailed three mismatched crosses to the door, as well as a string of whole garlic cloves tied from one railing to the other.

We'd considered garlic before our investigation-turned-battle here at the bar, but that much whole garlic would be obvious – both in the visual and aromatic sense – so we'd decided to save that for protecting entrances to the Foundation. Glad to see that it appeared to work.

"Someone knew about the evil that bred below," Archer observed. "Mister Blanchard, perhaps?"

"Possible," Medusa hissed. "He wasn't with the corpses or the survivors."

"Let's find out." I moved the string of garlic out of the way and knocked gently at the door.

"Go away, you bloodsucking freaks," came the hysterical reply. It sounded like a man with a smoker's voice, raw from either screaming or crying. Maybe both.

"Sir, I can't be one of those vampires," I explained. "The crosses and garlic would stop me."

"I don't give a rat's ass!"

"It's safe, they're all dead." Maybe that would work. I gave my compatriots a hopeful look.

"Prove you ain't a vamp," the man replied semi-coherently. "Take one of them crosses and put yer hand in the door holding it and not burning. No gloves or shit, or I swear –"

"Right, no problem, hold on," I assured him.

"I can't fault him," Medusa noted. "And his test actually makes sense."

Fortunately, the nails had been hammered in haphazardly and, with the help of the prybar from my utility bag, I pulled a cross off.

I gripped the crucifix, opened the door – which was unlocked – and put my bare hand through the door. I fully expected, with how my day had been, to have my hand shot off with a double-barreled shotgun.

That didn't happen.

"Okay, you can come in," the voice said instead.

I held my free hand up to Archer and Medusa, to tell them to wait here. We didn't know who exactly this man was, but there was a good chance he was a Hog affiliate. He wouldn't take kindly to seeing two Pushed.

Of course, he might not take kindly to me, but I was willing to take the chance.

I recognized Paul Blanchard immediately as I opened the door wide. He sat in a rocking chair in the center of the room, and he did, indeed, have a double-barreled shotgun in his lap.

Far more concerning was that he had a dead-man's switch gripped tightly in his hand. The connecting wire ran to the timer of a rather large and dangerous looking explosive device.

The first thought in my mind was an absurd one – why would anyone include a timer on a bomb attached to a dead-man's switch?

"Right, now lemme get a look at you," Blanchard said.

I held up my hands. "See? I'm not a vampire. Nothing to fear."

"But you're that Indomitable lady." Blanchard's tone turned suspicious as he raised the shotgun slowly. "Don't know if that's better than those vamps."

I really felt I could talk Blanchard down. If he knew he was safe from the vampires, I figured he'd be willing to come into custody.

But before I could say another word, Archer barreled into the room. "Stand behind me, Indomitable. I'll protect you."

"Archer?!" I gasped out. "What are you doing?"

"Liars!" Blanchard cried in despair. "You're not humans either!"

There was no time to see what decision he'd make. I guessed he was a Hog, and Hogs were fanatics.

I sprinted at Blanchard in an attempt to get that switch, surprising the others, who were still getting their bearings. I should've gotten to him, beaten him to the punch, but I was too hurt, too drained. My focus snapped into place heartbeats too late.

That gave Blanchar time to raise the shotgun, and I got a good look at both of the cavernous twelve-gauge barrels as he pulled the trigger.

Medusa must have followed on Archer's heels, though, and she reacted quicker than Blanchard and me. In a terrible way, the question of who was faster was finally settled.

With snake-like swiftness, she grabbed me and threw me to the side as both barrels exploded with sound and fury.

I still caught a few stray pellets in my arm. Medusa, though, took the brunt of the blast, peppering her with buckshot in the side, arm, and face.

Worst of all, Blanchard threw down the dead-man's switch as he fired.

There was a click audible even through the roar of the shotgun as the LED timer started to count rapidly through numbers.

I dove over Medusa's falling body towards the discarded switch. I had no idea how to disarm a bomb and, even if I did, I couldn't do it in seconds. I hit the floor at the same time as the dead-man's switch and caught it before it even bounced once.

Jamming the thumb switch down, my eyes locked on the LED clock.

It stopped at three seconds before detonation. A sigh of relief escaped my lips as I pushed up on my elbows and knees.

Then it hit me. Well, the butt end of a twelve-gauge shotgun hit me.

I'd forgotten about the old bastard. My world lurched a second, but I refused to let myself pass out, and gripped the switch hard.

Archer bellowed angrily, and the floor shook a little as his armored boots pounded the hardwood. I tried to clear my head and get my bearings, dropping onto one side to look up.

Blanchard's feet were dangling in the air as Archer held the old man aloft by the neck. Blanchard's feet were still kicking, so he was thankfully alive, though I doubted he would be for long.

Why did I care whether one old terrorist lived or died? This was a man who was going to blow up not only us but who knows how many others. This was a man who had just shot my best friend.

I had no real reason to tell Archer to stop as I glanced at Medusa clutching her side, blood seeping onto the floor.

But I'd be my own worst judge. I'd argued for vengeance against the vampires, sure, but they weren't living creatures anymore. Blanchard was a normal human. He could reform, repent. Even the most justifiable murder was still a murder.

"Archer, put him down."

"This madman deserves to die before he takes more innocent lives," Archer growled. I couldn't see though his visor, but his tone said all I needed to know.

"First off, he only spooked because *you* couldn't follow my orders. Second, his fate isn't for you to decide."

I shot another glance at Medusa. She was alive, which didn't surprise me much. Even those Pushed that weren't bulletproof were notoriously hard to kill, but she needed help.

"You swore to me you'd do things our way in this town. Are you telling me your word means so little?"

"I - He - No." Archer slowly lowered the panicked Blanchard to his feet, but Archer didn't let the man go. "I'm sorry, Indomitable. Forgive me for my impulsiveness and thank you for not letting me lose myself."

Crisis one averted. Two to go.

"If you disobey one more order, from me *or* from Extinguisher, I'll deal with you personally." I took a deep breath. I could dress Archer down more later.

"Now, show me your thanks by getting Blanchard and Medusa out of here. She needs a doctor, and he needs handcuffs." I shuffled until I sat cross-legged on the floor, thumb still pressed down on the switch.

"God! Where did my mind go?" Without a word of warning, he tossed Blanchard over his shoulder like a sack of potatoes and cradled Medusa in his free arm.

Medusa yelped in pain, and her snakes hissed defensively. "It's okay, girls," she assured her snakes, calming their writhing. "What about Indy?"

"Yes, what about you, Indomitable?" Archer paused at the doorway.

"We'll brainstorm over the comms. Just get them out of here, okay?"

Reluctantly, Archer disappeared down the stairs with his charges, leaving me alone with my silent, deadly companion.

"So, who knows how to disarm a bomb?"

Chapter 28

I tried to make the situation sound as happy and joyful as possible. My throbbing headache and the growing welts from the rubber bullets informed me it was all right to be sarcastic in a crisis.

As the comms understandably exploded, I took a closer look at the bomb for which I was the caretaker.

It was homemade but compact. I identified the timer and the plastic explosives before realizing there were far more wires and electronics than a standard "boom-you-die" bomb would need. Were they redundancies? Booby-traps? Or, worse, was there also a transmitter that would set off multiple bombs?

Ultimately, it meant I had no clue what to do other than hold on to the dead-man's switch for dear life.

The cacophony of concern over my earpiece that persisted until Extinguisher managed to be heard over the channel and bring about some order.

"Shut it, people," he ordered. "We're on the clock. If you have any experience with this sort of thing, say 'aye.' If you don't, coordinate with PART and evacuate the block, starting with the bar survivors."

"I've invented many an explosive weapon in the past few months," Archer volunteered. "Perhaps I can be of service?"

"I'm more than capable, and I've got all my tools here," Choi said. I thought I caught some objection from Brooks for the moment the line was open, but I lost it when her channel closed.

"Let Rachel see what she can do, Robin Hood," Extinguisher decided. "Not that I don't trust your skills, but we need our most mobile people focused on evac. No matter what, we can't let any innocents get harmed."

"Very well, Sir Extinguisher."

"Don't worry, Indy," Extinguisher added. "You know we'll get you out of there in one piece." I could tell from his tone that he wanted to say more, something personal, but we couldn't let that slip, not on open comms.

"Don't worry, I trust all of you," I said, trying to sound absolutely calm as I stared at the unblinking LED timer. I wanted this to be Pushtech, something I could laugh at. But it wasn't. This was a real bomb.

The timer was an electronic reminder of my looming mortality. Yes, most likely I'd walk away from this moment. The team would get the bomb disarmed, and we'd all celebrate back home.

However, all that kept my last three seconds of life from slipping away was my thumb on the button. And my thumb, like the rest of me, was getting tired.

I rubbed my eyes with my free hand. I was tired, hurt, and stressed to the breaking point. I was still kicking myself for letting my personal life fall apart these past six months, for not being serious with Extinguisher sooner, or not keeping up with my friends and family.

I was doing exactly what everyone else said I was doing - working myself to collapse.

"Are you conducting a private brooding session?" Choi asked from the door. "Or can I join you?" She tried to sound jovial, but I heard the justified undercurrent of nerves in her tone. "I promise I'll just observe while you spout Gothic poetry to the bomb."

I gave her a brief smile as she ever-so-gently set a hard-shell tool case on the floor. "You can join the fun, but the brooding is over for now."

I looked back at the weapon of destruction I was holding. "I suppose being forced to stay next to this thing with only a hair trigger and three seconds between me and death was making me morose."

"That's understandable." Choi opened the case and began to pick and choose her tools, laying them out with the utmost care. The closest things I could associate them with were surgical instruments - delicate and precise.

She put on a headband laden with a variety of magnifying eyepieces, then gestured for me to move to one side.

"If it won't break your concentration too much," I said as I scooted in place, "can I chat?"

Choi made a vague nod of assent as she started to examine the device carefully, gingerly moving aside wires and components using a non-conductive probe that looked like a sleek pen.

"Am I really pushing myself too hard?"

Choi paused for a moment. "Are you being serious, Irene?" Her eyes never left the dangerous work she was doing. "Or are you compensating for your fear of this situation with funny commentary?"

"I'll take that as a yes." I wiped my brow. I was certainly sweating a lot today but, considering the stress and my injuries, it made a certain sense now. I really wanted a whole bottle of painkillers right then and there.

"What can I do about it? Seriously, every day there seems to be another Push Crook or terrorist plot or public appearance that comes up. I've got responsibilities."

"We all do. Perhaps yours are larger than, say, mine. You could reasonably argue that, and I'd agree." I could see the sweat beading on her brow. "But all that means is you should delegate more of the responsibility to the people you trust instead of shouldering it all yourself."

"It's not their burden, though. It's mine." I didn't know if that was Whiteout Irene, Rational Irene, or me talking. Maybe it was all of us. The one thing we agreed on was our culpability. "I invented the last bit of science Epic needed to start the Whiteout. None of you are at fault. You're all victims in this."

"Most of them would disagree - I know I do. I'd go so far as to argue that we, as affected by the change of the status quo as you are, have as much a right to that burden as you do."

She retracted the probe and reached for some cutting tools. "I won't be surprised if you wind up being personally instrumental to fixing this - you're one of the few people that has any idea how - but you won't be there alone. You need to accept that."

"You're probably right."

My reply prompted a faint smirk from Choi. "I suppose I should be happy for a partial acknowledgment. Now, be very still and pray, if you think it'll help."

I wasn't religious, but Epic had shown me the power of belief with his God particle and the Whiteout. So I did, in fact, pray as Choi leaned in and started clipping.

A faint beeping came from the device, but Choi stopped me from panicking with a raised hand. We both sat in utter stillness for a full four seconds of beeping before it stopped, followed by the LED timer fading to dark.

"You can let off the switch now, Irene."

I nodded silently, then ever so slowly let off the deadman's switch.

The bomb didn't explode. Then, and only then, did Choi and I breathe easily.

From there, things proceeded quickly and smoothly. Within a few minutes, I was sitting in what was fast becoming my favorite nightspot – the back of an ambulance.

This time, I wasn't alone, as Medusa was being treated further back, while I sat on the back bumper, an EMT fussing over my wounds.

Captain Braxton, personally overseeing this PART operation, joined us, as well as Extinguisher and Choi. Between the three of us, we caught Braxton up on what all had gone down inside and out.

"This is only the start of it, isn't it?" Braxton asked as he scratched the back of his head.

"Correct, Captain," Choi answered. "This is not only a massive break from the Hog's anti-Pushed fanaticism, but they've been building this operation up undercover for some time. We have to assume Mackenzie is the one pulling the strings, and he meticulously plans operations with multiple redundancies."

Braxton let out the deep sigh of the tragically overworked. I knew it well. "Jesus. Well, PART will do what it can." He glanced at the bar. "But I'm not exactly kosher with you guys digging through evidence at the same time we are."

"Joe, it's okay." Extinguisher smiled and put an arm around Braxton's shoulder. "You know how committed we are to working with PART and the city. Honestly, have we ever kept any evidence from your team?"

"Well, no," Braxton admitted. "My only worry is – well, there are a lot of people starting to wonder if we are even doing our jobs or just relying on Push Heroes all the time."

"That's not true, Cap," I chimed in. "What about the Firebug gang? We caught Firebug, but his gang would've torched City Hall if PART hadn't tracked them down during the big fight and busted them. And there are plenty of other cases like that."

"Indy is correct as usual, Captain," Choi soothed. "As a former law officer myself, I certainly understand your concerns. When you give your press conference about tonight, just make sure to remind people of PART's involvement in the case and our close partnership. Whatever you do, though, please don't limit our access."

Extinguisher gestured at the pile of staked corpses. "The situation is just too dangerous, Joe, and all we know for sure is that this isn't where the plague started." He crossed his arms. "These were all locals and either recently reported missing or suspected missing. That meant they were made here in Atlanta."

Braxton nodded after a moment. "You're right, Ex. We've got Blanchard through processing, so I'm going to head down to the station for interrogation. The moment he coughs up something, I'll be in touch."

"Thanks, Joe." Extinguisher nodded and shook Braxton's hand before he left.

We sat there in silence for a few moments until Brooks finished working on Medusa and joined us at the bumper, pulling off his bloodied rubber gloves which he tossed into the trash.

"Good news is that Medusa is healing right up once I got the pellets out. With that crazy Pushed regeneration, she should be back to normal in a day, tops."

"The way you put that makes me ask what the bad news is," I glumly observed.

"The bad news is that everyone who got a bite taken out of them gets to swallow a horse's load of antibiotics for a while," he answered, a big grin on his face. "The average human mouth is a nasty enough place, but corpses who have been feasting on who-knows-what, including raw blood? We'll be lucky if no one winds up in the hospital with some crazy kind of infection."

"Ever the bright spot of my life," Choi chided. "Shall we go investigate the crime scene and let our casualties get transported back to the Foundation?"

"I think that's a prime idea." Brooks hopped out of the back of the ambulance. "Indy, tuck those legs up. I'm going to button this up."

"Wait, I want to –"

All three of them answered in chorus. "No!"

"You're going home and resting, Indy," Extinguisher added. "Your doctor, your landlord, and your team leader are all ordering the same thing."

Choi and Brooks nodded in agreement.

"Okay, okay. I'll go along with it, but that will leave us alone without any powered backup on site, unless Facet and Ken are back, which is highly unlikely. It's not like we'd be in a condition to stop anyone from doing anything and, considering how this went down, we just made ourselves a big target."

"Indy's got a point," Brooks muttered. "The garlic might stop the vampires if they try to come in, but we can't be sure they won't find an access that's unprotected."

Extinguisher rubbed his chin. "Fortunately, I've got an idea." He tapped his earbud.

"Robin Hood, we need someone up for escorting our injured and guarding them until the rest of the team is done investigating here. Considering you're in the doghouse after the bit with Blanchard, I'm making you do this. Can I count on you?"

While I wasn't looking forward to more one-on-one time with Archer right now, Extinguisher was doing the smart thing here. Maybe Archer could use this as a chance to turn things around.

"Yes, of course. I'll be right there," Archer said eagerly over the comms.

"Fear not, Indomitable," Archer assured me from his perch in the back of our ambulance, taking up most of the space that wasn't filled by my and Medusa's stretchers. "I won't let you down again. I'll be ever vigilant in my duty to protect you and Dame Medusa."

I didn't reply. My chest and side were throbbing in pain and, as if not to be outdone, the shrapnel wound from earlier today sang in shrill notes of agony. At least Medusa was managing to sleep peacefully through this.

"Never fear," he gushed on. "I forever strive to improve so that Lord Epic will be proud of me."

But perhaps this wasn't *all* bad. I hadn't considered it before, but this was an unexpected opportunity to gather intelligence about Epic's operations. Crusaders usually didn't share friendly words with those Push Heroes who stood against them.

For all his foibles, Archer was clearly different, and he'd earned some measure of my trust when he saved my life back in the bar. Of course, he'd lost it immediately after by ruining my parlay with Blanchard and causing all the fuss around the bomb.

The question really was - could he be trusted, or was he a fox in our henhouse?

Chapter 29

To be completely fair to Archer, everything started off smoothly. We arrived at headquarters safe and sound, then together we got Medusa moved to the infirmary.

She seemed to be resting peacefully. A quick look at her wounds showed me that nothing had actually penetrated to the real woman inside.

"I agree with Sir Brooks," Archer said. "She'll recover quickly. Now, would milady wish to rest here in the infirmary or retire to her apartment?"

I glared at him a moment before I spoke. "I thought we talked about the 'milady' nonsense. You were doing so well, too. Why do you even call me that, anyway? You don't do that with anyone else but –" That's when my brain finally caught up. "Oh."

"It's obvious you've made the connection." He started to undo the clasps on his helmet. "It's Lord Epic's firm conviction that you two will once again be together. A romantic thought, don't you think?"

"He's crazy. To be blunt, we will never, never, ever be getting back together."

There was a hiss of air as Archer took off his helmet, letting me finally get a good look at the man on the other side of the visor.

As with many Pushed, the outer shell was a handsome, idealized figure. There was more than a dash of Errol Flynn, topped with a perfect coif of copper hair. Under the shell was a middle-aged man who, while certainly not ugly, looked ridden hard and put away wet.

There were elements of the two faces shared, but they were night and day next to each other.

"Perhaps." Archer tucked his helmet under his arm. "But I think milord would be crazy to not keep trying. It could be said that all women are truly unique, but I can say with authority that you rival all the others."

I rolled my eyes despite my initial plan to be cordial. "Really?"

I was in too much pain to be polite. As that thought rolled through my mind, I wandered over to the supply shelves and started to finger through the pill bottles.

"I think it's probably a case of people wanting what they know they can't have. I've seen a thousand more beautiful women than me. Just glance though *Pushed Illustrated.*"

"Not to discount your physical appearance, but you're correct. However, there are more important things in judging the worth of a potential lover than that. I've seen enough today to identify qualities in your worth far more than mere looks. In that way, I can appreciate milord's interest."

Where did Brooks keep the narcotics? I was almost through the shelves and nothing. I wondered if Brooks anticipated a situation like this and locked up those drugs somewhere else. It felt like something he'd do.

"You can tell 'milord' to shove it up his ass, to be blunt."

"I'm curious why you'd say that, Indomitable," the Crusader mused. "In fact, to be honest, I don't quite understand the divide between our two orders. Don't we have the same noble goals?"

"The devil is in the details. Epic would level a village to save a city." Thwarted, I relented to my body's jabs of pain and crawled on top of the second infirmary bed.

"You exaggerate a tad," Archer said, but his tone had an undercurrent of uncertainty. "Sometimes, the greater good requires sacrifice but –"

"If we hadn't intervened in Washington, he would've leveled the city fighting Reaper. If that doesn't tell you something, what will?"

Archer stroked his thin, swashbuckler mustache thoughtfully. "I certainly don't know – I wasn't there. Even if what you say is true, that was an extreme situation. Months have passed, and there's been nothing like that since."

I let out a derisive snort. "How can someone smart enough to make that suit be so stupid? History repeats itself."

Our eyes locked, and I held his gaze. "You can't tell me that your group's tactics haven't been a bit excessive. I'm sure you've killed a Push Crook or two with that crossbow of yours."

"I, well…yes." He broke away from my stare and glanced at the folded bow on his gauntlet. "It was necessary. Innocents would've died if I hadn't acted."

"I find it hard to imagine a situation where someone absolutely had to die. What problem did you have to solve by killing when you couldn't subdue the bad guy instead? Unless you've been fighting the undead before now."

"Well, no, we haven't, but, in the heat of battle, we don't always have the time to think. Sometimes, we just act."

"Instincts don't absolve a person of responsibility for a crime."

Archer bristled. "Instincts aren't always wrong. As you seem to want to analyze my moral fiber, let us turn the light around to look at yours, shall we?"

"Sure, fire away." I leaned my head back to stare at the ceiling. I was getting monstrously hungry, but I was too drawn into this argument to say anything about it. "Do your worst."

Really, what could a Crusader who'd already admitted to killing a few people bring to bear on the morality front?

"Very well then." He seemed full of certainty as he stood next to the bed. "Let's start with the easy question – why do you hate the Pushed?"

I opened my eyes to glance at him. "Where'd you get that idea from?" Rationally, I denied the accusation, but there was something about it that made me uneasy. "It seems all I've been doing since the Whiteout is fight for Pushed rights. It's been Pushed, Pushed, and more Pushed."

"Don't you hear the resentment in your voice? What I find the most curious is that you have this ill-will in your heart towards something that you yourself are."

"To start with, I don't resent the Pushed. I resent Epic for bringing so much harm in the world." I forced myself up on my elbows. "Next, I'm not Pushed." Then I had to sigh. "But you're right, in a way. I'm not just a normal human. I'm what we're calling a Natural, and I'm not alone."

"Indeed, Indomitable." He gave a surprisingly derisive laugh. "Would a normal woman hold any appeal for Lord Epic? What of your own leader? I can't mistake the looks he gives you to be anything but adoration. Even I, despite the dishonor it would bring, can't deny that you stir something in my knightly soul."

"Hold it right there." I sat up straight, pain be damned. "You say I hate the Pushed, and here you are, looking down on the normal humans. Not six months ago, you were like every other person on this planet. Hell, your life was easier. It's not like you had to worry about a Push

Battle destroying your house or blowing up your car or straight out killing you in the crossfire."

"We don't look down upon the mortals like that!"

"Of course you do. You literally just laughed with your nose in the air thinking about them." I could tell Archer was the uncomfortable one now. "I'm sure 'Lord' Epic has talked about the need to 'wrest control' from the 'corrupt' government plenty of times. How 'mortals' need to be coddled and protected. How only the Pushed can save the world."

I shrugged. "That sounds like he's looking down on them to me, which means, by extension, you are, too."

His face went through several contortions in rapid succession. I recognized them because I saw them often in my own mirror. First there was denial, then anger, then realization, then defeat. Archer let out a long sigh.

"Well, it seems we share one thing, at least."

"What's that?"

"Our fair share of flaws."

That made me smile. "We wouldn't be human if we were perfect. Maybe we should both remember that."

"Indeed. We're all quite flawed, even Lord Epic."

"Especially Epic." I settled back onto the bed again.

"It'd be wrong of me to speak ill of milord, so we'll leave it at that."

"Fair enough." Since things seemed to have settled in our current episode of Morality Wars, maybe I could finally get some useful information from him.

"What is it like being a Crusader?" I said, trying to ignore the raging hunger. My secret wish was that we were having this talk in the cafeteria.

"I suppose it's not much different from the life you heroes in Atlanta live. Regular patrols for criminal activity, speaking with the press and media, recruitment of like-minded Pushed to our cause, that sort of thing."

I thought he was done, but then he looked up with a smile. "Oh, how I could forget! There are the parties, of course."

"Parties?" I wasn't shocked by the idea that our opposite number kicked back once in a while, no matter how much I denied that luxury to myself. I was surprised by the plurality of his statement.

"Oh yes!" He smiled wistfully. "We'd fall apart from stress if we didn't take the time to relieve the tension. Lord Epic encourages recreation time with formal balls at least once a week, sometimes more."

I couldn't help but think about our Fourth of July party. Extinguisher and I first got together in the aftermath, our first kiss under the glow of fireworks. It seemed an eternity ago, and I had the acute desire for him to be here with me instead of Archer.

I forced that desire out of my head. "That seems pretty risky. What if something goes wrong during those balls and no one is out there to notice?"

"One advantage of a large, organized force is the ability to delegate roles and rotate who's on active duty. There are always more of us to keep a sharp vigil when others rest. Seeing the arrangements here, I mean no offense when I say you're rather undisciplined and short-staffed."

"Yeah, funny how we like our freedom."

"Freedom is a blessed thing that bears little weight when you're dead."

I was about to sit back up again, but I took a deep breath and counted back from ten instead.

"It seems I must apologize. I can tell that I've offended you once again." He smiled brightly. "It pains my noble heart to see a frown on a woman's face."

It was almost like he wanted to run face-first into my fist or something. Did he really believe his act?

But I knew the answer to that – of course he did. The Argent Archer was Pushed. Who knew what crazy beliefs danced in his head, or what the Whiteout did to his perception of reality? Maybe this was a chance to find out.

"Apology accepted. Of course, maybe I'm just uncomfortable around the Pushed because I don't know as much as I'd like." It wasn't technically a lie. If I knew Archer better, I'd likely be more comfortable around him.

It just might be a comfort brough on by better understanding an enemy as opposed to a friend. "Would you mind if I asked a few questions?"

"Your wish is my command."

"Have you always been an engineer? Maybe a mechanic or a scientist?"

The sudden silence told me more than if I'd been staring at his face.

"Of course not," he finally said, his tone subdued. The faux-British accent was mostly gone as well. "See, that's what you don't get. We know all too well who we were before and how much better we are now."

"Here comes the superiority thing again."

"No, Indomitable." Archer's accent returned. "It's not superiority or arrogance or what have you when it's the truth. Who makes more of a difference to his fellow man – the genius inventor who uses his marvels to protect mankind or the pizza delivery driver?"

"You were a –" I interrupted my own thoughts. "Never mind. So how did you know how to build that suit?"

"The Whiteout," Archer intoned with a strange reverence. "It changed everything. It opened my mind and infused it with genius and knowledge. Not only did I suddenly know engineering, robotics, metallurgy, and so much more, it struck me with a flash of an idea, a true eureka moment!"

He snapped his gauntleted fingers, creating a spark. "I spent the next week feverishly creating this suit. Well, the first iteration, at any rate. It was just like the vision in my mind."

"What about your friends and family?"

Amongst the Five, only Medusa had family I knew of for certain, though she was guarded about it, even to me. Mind's Eye and Tank had each other. Facet, Ken, and I did, likewise. It was still a small sample size of how being Pushed affected the normal people in our lives, so I wanted to know more.

"Only a few friends," Archer admitted. "My parents couldn't be prouder, but it's dangerous to visit them any more than necessary. They understand the need, so I don't let it worry me."

"So, let me get this straight. It doesn't bug you that you've mostly left your old life behind? Is the man you are now are more important than the man you were?"

"Undoubtedly." His words were firm with unshakeable conviction. "The man I was before wasn't even half the man I am now. This isn't coming from some sense of machismo. It's the vital qualities I'm talking about."

Archer's lips twisted into a frown of disgust. "He was a man who was dull-witted and never applied himself. Content with great dreams, he never worked to make them come true." He clapped his breastplate with a gauntleted fist. "This man strives to live up to those dreams."

I didn't think the Whiteout was talking through Archer, not anymore. This man had been so elementally affected by what he'd become that taking it away would probably destroy him.

That left a terrible series of questions in my mind. Was the Whiteout really so bad, when it gave good people like this a better life? Would it, as Epic so often claimed, stabilize over time as the good outweighed the evil?

More than that, did I have the right to try to turn everything back or did the mere thought make me just like *him*?

"That is food for thought," I finally admitted.

"Speaking of food," Archer said, brightening up, "Sir Brooks gave me some instructions to make sure you eat. Something about calories and malnutrition, though I didn't totally follow. My specialty is machines, not biology." He put his helmet back on. "I shall return."

He left while I thought. I had a lot of new variables to consider and, no matter how fantastical the Whiteout seemed, it was still science.

Not to mention I had a lot to ponder about the vampire-terrorist plague and whatever Mackenzie's grand scheme was.

I considered all this for thirty whole seconds before the infirmary door opened back up, and Extinguisher stepped in, a plastic take-out bag in one hand.

"Irene, we need to talk."

Chapter 30

"Will, how are you back so soon?" I forced myself to sit up, despite the pain. "I mean, I'm glad to see you, but you guys couldn't have wrapped up the investigation so fast."

That's when the amazing smell of my favorite deep dish pizza joint hit my nose. "Is that what I think it is?"

He chuckled as he stopped bedside and dragged a side table in front of me. "I'll take that last to first." He put the bag on the table. "Yes, this is two personal pies with your favorite toppings. No, the investigation isn't finished, but yes, I'm back so soon because I'm worried about tonight, and that distracted me so much I left Rachel in charge of things so I could come back here."

Halfway through Extinguisher's explanation, I'd torn into the bag and, by the end, I'd laid out both pizza boxes, popped the first open, and downed a slice covered in peperoni, mushroom, onions, green peppers, and extra cheese. The travel time, likely by ice slide, had cooled the pizza down to just below the "melt the roof of your mouth" level, i.e. perfection.

"Oh God, I needed that." I glanced past Extinguisher at the door. "But we don't have too long to talk. Archer should be back with more food soon."

"I ran into him. Told him not to worry about it and do a round of security patrol through the building." He grabbed a chair and set it down by me. "Meds looks like she's sleeping peacefully and, even if she wakes up during our conversation, there's not much we have to hide from her."

"Not in my current condition, at any rate." Mom always said that a man who put you above his work was a keeper. She also said to pay attention if a guy bothers to learn your favorite foods. Extinguisher was winning on both points. "So, hit me with it. What specifically has you worried? Because, frankly, the entire situation has me concerned."

"I agree, but..." Anger flashed across his features. "I want to know why they wanted to take you alive, Irene. That's what worries me above everything else."

That was something of an elephant in the room that I'd been ignoring until I could analyze it more. I hadn't been sure if anyone else had picked up on it, so why start the engine of the worry train?

"I honestly don't know." I polished off the first pizza and started on the second. My body needed every calorie it could get. "But you're right. Mackenzie is behind this, I'm certain, so every step has a purpose. What we need to do is try to think about this from Mackenzie's point of view."

Extinguisher nodded, his brow furrowed. "There's the obvious, which I hate to say." And he must've, because that hate showed plain on his face. "If the Hogs captured you, they could execute you live. As the face of the Pushed Rights movement, your public death would be a massive blow to morale."

I shivered a bit at the thought of that but shook my head. "I don't think so. While it'd hurt morale, it'd also coalesce public sentiment against the Hogs and anti-Pushed causes, in general. If there's one thing the American public agrees on, it's that they like me."

"There's a lot to like."

I smiled at that, and I realized that even smiling hurt a bit, as Extinguisher continued.

"You're probably right. Mackenzie wants to get rid of the Pushed, that's obvious, and that reaction would hurt his chances, not help them."

"Not to change the subject, but that's what really bugs me about the vampire thing. Mackenzie hates the Pushed, but he's using something Pushed or Pushed-adjacent as his primary foot soldier against us? It doesn't make sense. Worse, there's no way the Hogs could've or would've voluntarily signed up for that. Most of them are religious nuts, after all."

Extinguisher sighed. "That'd only make it easier for Mackenzie to convince them to turn. If he sold it the right way, he could make them think this was some holy thing. Fanatics are easy to sway if you feed them a line that makes sense within their own beliefs."

That was a sobering observation and a correct one. "Good point, Will. Which leaves us back at square one."

"Maybe we're overthinking this. Maybe he just wants to try to turn you to his side."

I gave Extinguisher the most skeptical look I could muster. "Mackenzie's brilliant, at least that's what Rachel and Duane think. There's no way he'd think he'd ever convince me to join him, not after all the times I've been instrumental in stopping his plans."

He pursed his lips together as his jaw tightened. I knew this look well - Extinguisher had something on his mind that he thought I didn't want to hear.

"Whatever it is, it won't offend me, okay?"

"I'll hold you to that, Irene." He relaxed a little. "Here goes. The fact of the matter is that you're a Natural. You're a walking contradiction to the Whiteout and everything in it. We all know it, and we all feel it deep down. And Mackenzie is the only other person on the planet that we know of that's like you. He's certain to think there's a kinship there."

His tone grew regretful. "And he might be right. This might hurt you to hear, but I'll be honest - it doesn't just affect you physically, but emotionally and mentally, too. You know that everything's changed in the world but you and him. And I think, whether you realize it or not, that makes you lash out. Push people away."

I could feel a frown creep onto my face, and I looked away. "Like I did with you. I'm sorry, Will, you're right. I can't deny I've felt this space between me and the rest of the team. I feel it with normal people now, too."

Strong, familiar hands took mine, and Extinguisher's soothing coldness numbed some of the pain away.

"But you can fight it, Irene. You've been doing it this whole time, because if you hadn't, we wouldn't have had the talk we did last night. Heck, you wouldn't even be a part of the team. You'd have already broken away, either making solo desperate attempts to reverse the Whiteout or joining up with Mackenzie."

"I'll never join him." I bit back the tears threatening to form and looked back to him. As I squeezed his hands, all the way down to the real man underneath, through the layer of cold to the warm flesh underneath. "And I'm going to keep fighting. For you. For Meds, Facet, and everyone else."

"I know you are. You're Indomitable, after all." He lifted my hands gently, which was good because my forearm still hurt, and kissed my knuckles. "We'll always be able to count on you. Just count on us, too, okay?"

I really wished I wasn't a full body wreck right now, but a woman had to know her limitations. Still, I smiled and nodded. "I'm learning my lesson, so I'll do my best."

"Now, you should take Medusa's example and sleep." Extinguisher took his time letting go of me. "We'll take it from here."

"Right. I will." I yawned stiffly, and even that hurt. "Stay safe, okay?"

"As safe as you stay," he said with a chuckle.

"I guess that's all I can ask." I shifted to lay back on the table. "Good night, Will."

"Good night, Irene."

I fell asleep before he even stepped out of the infirmary. I must've barely been holding on, even if I hadn't realized. With my hunger quelled and my heart put somewhat ease, there was no reason to keep pushing to stay awake.

My sleep was fitful and plagued by flashes of shapeless nightmares. Considering I'd been in hand-to-hand combat with walking corpses, this shouldn't have been a surprise.

What was unusual was that there was a sense of anticipation in these dreams, an overwhelming sense of foreboding that sent shivers up my spine the same way the twisted vampire Pulse did.

A gentle shake woke me. I struggled against an imagined attacker only to be held down with an iron grip. As consciousness kicked in, I opened my eyes to Hexagon hulking over the bed, his two real arms holding me down with as much gentleness as he could manage.

"Indy," he said softly, "you're fine. Just a bad dream, I reckon." He flashed a big smile.

I mumbled something incomprehensible, even to me.

"Most of the others are working in the lab," he answered, as if my unintelligible mutter had been a question, "but, you know me, I'm not exactly cut out for that kind of work. Balance your budget, sure, but forensics, nah." He released his grip. "I thought you'd probably want to get all cleaned up and such."

"Yeah, right," I mumbled as the fuzz started to clear out of my head. "Did we get all the vampires from the bar?"

"Yes." Hexagon crossed his arms with a frown. "But we're all as sure as you are that there's got to be more of 'em out there."

I nodded, swinging my legs off the bed. Medusa was already gone. "God, what time is it?"

"Eight thirty-three on the button. Everyone took a nap once we got back in from getting things under control, then hit it hard and fast about a half an hour ago."

"Right, thanks, Hex."

I slid off the bed and onto my feet. I still hurt all over, but it had turned into a dull, burning ache. I wanted to swallow a handful of oxycodone and wash it down with a pot of coffee. First, though, I needed to wash the inch-thick stink off me.

"Anything else I can do for you? If there ain't, I'm going to stop on down by PART HQ and see if they got anything out of Mister Blanchard yet."

I nodded. "Good move. Hopefully they have and, if not, we'll figure something out. It's what heroes do."

Hexagon smiled at that, then suddenly gave me a very careful hug. "It is, Indy, and we do it together."

Without a second thought, I returned that hug. All the annoyance and frustration that'd built up from what I'd thought was excessive concern over me had already started to break down after talking to Choi and Extinguisher.

But this impromptu gesture from a member of the team I wasn't as close to shattered the rest of those feelings in one fell swoop.

"Thanks, Hex." We pulled apart, and I matched his smile. Hey, smiling didn't hurt today. "You're right. Now, let's get to saving the city."

Hexagon smiled that big good-old-boy smile of his. "You got it. See you soon, Indy."

With that, we went our separate ways. While that terrible foreboding from my dreams followed me up the stairs to my apartment, my heart still carried some of this light and hope with me.

I only wished that the light and hope could overcome my desire for painkillers.

Chapter 31

I stood staring in the bathroom mirror. I'd wiped away the condensation created by the blisteringly hot shower I'd been in for an hour.

Now, I was mulling over a vital choice.

The choice, on the surface, was a simple one. I could take a drug cocktail made out of the remnants of my pain pills and be feeling in tip-top shape for what was sure to be a critical day. Or I could stay clean and be at less than a hundred percent.

With so much at stake it seemed like a cut and dried thing.

The reality was far more complex. Brooks hadn't had to tell me how addictive these drugs were - I knew all too well. There were more important considerations than just "pain or no pain."

The simple fact that I'd felt entitled to rifle through the infirmary's dispensary last night was more than enough evidence that I had a problem.

The unusual sweats, the itches, the desire for painkillers at the drop of a hat, those all formed more symptoms of a proto-addiction, if I wasn't already addicted.

I looked down at the small glass filled with a shallow bed of pills ranging in size, shape, and color. A few remaining oxycodone, some prescription ibuprofen, a fair number of cyclobenzaprine, even a couple of hydromorphone pills I'd managed to save from those broken ribs two months ago.

Who the hell was the woman who could throw this back like it was nothing? I knew who - an addict, that's who.

My hand was shaking as I put the glass away, knocking a few empty pill bottles down into the sink. I couldn't let myself be this broken anymore.

There was more risk to myself and everyone else by my remaining addicted than by my going cold turkey.

My friends, my family, the man I had to admit I was truly falling in love with, they all deserved the Irene Roman that'd stared down Epic at the Battle of Washington.

I took a deep breath, focused on everything I'd felt last night with Extinguisher, this morning with Hexagon, the heart-to-heart I'd shared with Medusa, and all the other moments I'd had with the team.

With that in mind, I stepped away from the sink and suited up.

On the way downstairs, I had another realization. Just like so many other things these past months, I was trying to tackle my addiction solo.

By the time I was walking into the Foundation offices, that realization led to a decision - I needed help, and the sooner the better.

Hexagon had said the rest of the crew was working in the forensics lab, and that's where I'd find Brooks. Heading that way, I made only one stop, breakfast at the cafeteria to keep my body healing.

As I made it through the decontamination process to enter the lab proper, I saw the team hard at work. After a few quiet good mornings, I moved past the others to where Brooks was taking notes about a hair sample. I tapped him on the shoulder.

"Hey, Duane."

He put down his pen and looked up at me. "Morning, Indy. Looking better for the most part."

"Feeling a bit better, too. Can I speak with you for a few minutes?" I lowered my voice. "In private?"

"Of course. My office, then."

The only one who noticed our little exchange was Extinguisher. He gave me a questioning glance, and I replied with a reassuring nod.

He'd be the next person I'd tell about my addiction, but, as my doctor, Duane needed to know first.

Brooks and Choi each had private offices close by. Both of them maintained a certain immaculate order to their areas that I envied.

Brooks gestured for me to sit in one of the plush chairs in front of his desk. As I sat, he leaned against his desk, concern plain on his face. "So, what's up?"

I thought it'd be easy to say the words, now that I'd admitted it to myself, but they caught in my throat. Taking a deep breath, I tried again, and this time, my words came out.

"Duane, I'm an addict."

There was a long moment of silence. I started to worry that Brooks was going to judge me harshly for my clear personal weakness.

"Irene, I'm proud of you."

"You…are?"

"Of course I am. An addiction isn't easy to admit to anyone. Most addicts find ways to lie to themselves and the people around them, usually until it's too late."

Tears pricked at the corners of my eyes and my palms started to itch again. "I don't know. I've lied to everyone here, including myself, about this for at least a month. Maybe longer."

"You have, but I've known, probably for longer than you have."

I looked up at him, shocked. "What?"

He grinned. "Why do you think I locked up all the drugs in the infirmary?" Then his expression went stern. "But me knowing and you knowing - and admitting - are very different things. You can't save an addict until the addict wants to be saved."

"I do want to be saved. And I thought I could do that by myself. And I realize that I can't."

"And that is the proof that you're really ready to change and get well."

"I know I need to tell the others. But I wanted, and needed, to start with you."

"I appreciate that, as your doctor and your friend. I'll put together an actual medical plan to get you off the pain meds in a controlled fashion, because I'm guessing you've been going cold turkey, haven't you?"

I sighed and nodded. "Yes, Duane."

"Sometimes, I swear you just like to do everything the hard way." He chuckled. "No more of that, okay?"

"I promise. I'm going to let you turn my stubbornness into a weapon to beat this."

"Damn straight. We'll go over specifics a little later. You and Medusa need a full medical examination before I clear you two for action, anyway."

I bit back the desire to complain. Yes, I wanted to get out there and stop Mackenzie's scheme, but I trusted Brooks with my life.

"Of course. Speaking of action, Hex told me you guys have been hard at work since eight. Have you and Rachel worked your investigatory magic and figured out anything?"

Brooks shook his head. "Right back to the mission, as usual. Can't blame you this time, though, as this is getting more serious every day."

I didn't lie to myself. All of us – Rational, Whiteout, and Original Irenes – were eager to pounce on work as a distraction. "That sounds like you *have* figured something out."

"A few things, none of them good. First up, we've confirmed that Mackenzie was at Paul's Pub in person within the past few days. We found a few hair samples that matched, and Mind's Eye detected the same blurs and holes you make for her when she tried to psychically scan the place."

My fists clenched eagerly. "I don't know why you don't think that's good. It means we're finally closing in on him as opposed to feeling like we're a dozen steps behind."

"That's what worries me. Rachel and I told you how smart he is. If it looks like we're close, I bet it's because he wants us to be."

"Maybe he's just getting desperate?" It was a vain hope, but I had to ask.

"Don't know. I think that might be worse. I don't want to consider what Mackenzie is capable of when he's cornered." Duane looked genuinely concerned.

"I won't rush in, I promise."

That helped him shake off the worry. "The other big thing is that there's records of another Hog den hidden down in the sewer system."

That sparked my memory, something I'd almost forgotten with all the fighting and near-death experiences. "Wait a minute. The beer!"

"The beer?"

"In the bar, the barkeep poured me a beer, and there was a reddish taint in it, some liquid that wasn't mixing with the beer. It was blood."

Duane paled. "Bet it was vampire blood. If you're going to go with a lot of vampire mythology, that's a way to turn people into vampires."

"And, if that's true for these vamps, what better way could there be to spread the plague than contaminate the city's water supply?"

"I want to say that Atlanta's water treatment system is more than good enough to filter out that kind of contamination, but I can't be sure. Not when it comes to freaky Pushed vampire blood."

"Even if that's not the case, we still need to investigate it. Unless there's something else?"

"That's it." Duane pushed off the desk. "Maybe there's something else hidden in all the documents we recovered, but I don't think there's anything else we're going to learn any time soon."

"Then let's get this ball rolling. We still need to prepare, after all. You need to make sure Meds and I are ready for action."

"Absolutely. Rachel can coordinate with PART and Atlanta Public Works while we do that."

I raised a finger. "And there's one other thing we need to do."

"What's that?"

"We need to restock on a vital weapon - stakes. Lots and lots of stakes."

Chapter 32

"Do we really have time for this?" Medusa hissed with annoyance.

It was one of the few times I didn't agree with her. Considering this could be a "fate-of-the-city" kind of encounter, having Brooks' final medical okay was wise.

"This'll go faster if you stop squirming and let me do my damn job," Brooks grumbled. He looked over Medusa's scaled-over buckshot wounds and nodded slowly. "Now was that so bad?"

"So?"

"The new scales aren't hardened yet, so you're vulnerable on that side. Don't lead with your left for another day or two. Otherwise, you're good. Must be great to be Pushed."

She stuck a forked tongue out at him as she pulled her shirt back on. "I'm going to go suit up then. See you soon, Irene." With a waggle of fingers, she was gone.

I remained, sitting in a flimsy examination gown, and looked at Brooks.

"Irene," Brooks started before stopping with a sigh. "You don't need to be doing this. Shit, in the past forty-eight hours, you've been hit with grenade shrapnel, thrown into stone walls, had your forearm crushed, been shot with rubber bullets, and strangled. Let's not inventory the rest of the week."

"I respect your medical opinion, I do."

He didn't look like he believed me, but I pressed on.

"Normally, I'd sit this one out, Duane, but what if Mackenzie *is* there? We all know what he could do to the team if I'm not there to counter him."

"Look, Archer might get his ass handed to him, but the others have worked and trained with you since the start. They've probably all thought about what they'd have to do to fight a Natural."

He rubbed his eyes. "I know there isn't shit I can do to talk you out of anything, so I'm just wasting my breath."

"You're not. I'm..." I took a deep breath. "I'm trying, okay? I came clean about my addiction, right? Look, I promise, if this were any other mission, I'd go back to bed."

"But?"

"You know the but. I'm sorry, Duane."

He shook his head, then grabbed a manilla folder off his desk. "Here's your rehab plan. When you make it through a week, we'll talk."

I took the folder as he handed it to me. "Does that mean you're giving me the all-clear to go?"

"Only if you promise me that you're going to keep your dumb ass alive through today, all right?"

"I'll do my best, I swear."

Duane nodded. "If you die, just know I'm going to find some Pushed with necromantic powers to bring you back so I can kill you personally."

"That's totally fair." I started to change back into my uniform. "Hey, as I've lost at least a day somewhere in here, I'm completely out of the loop with Facet and Ken. What's their status? The more firepower we could bring to bear, the better."

Brooks frowned. "Stellar's cleverer than we thought. Worse, PART thought she was strictly street-level, but she's got some kind of big money backer."

I tried not to jump to the worst conclusion. "Is Facet okay? Ken? He's got to be, he's the man in the chair."

"Hey, calm down." Brooks put his hands on my shoulders. "Everyone's fine. Yes, the raid was an elaborate trap sprung on our people, and Stellar's gang was way better kitted out than anyone expected. But Facet got herself and most of the PART officers out of there before things fell apart."

"What about the ones Facet didn't save?"

"Dead or injured. The nature of the game against a Push Crook."

I knew he was right, but I didn't have to like it. However, I had to focus on the situation at hand.

"This means Stellar and her crew got away, confirming she's smarter than we've assumed and has a benefactor that might or might not be Mackenzie. And that means she could be coming to cause extra trouble for us." I was the one sighing this time as I massaged my temples.

"Which is a problem for another day, because it's going to take Stellar time to regroup, whether she's coming to back up the vampires for some reason or not. We have to focus on the immediate threat."

I nodded. "You're right."

"So, the real question is if we want Facet and Ken coming back to Atlanta to help now, or keep them in the field?"

During the Battle of Washington, I'd kept Facet and Ken, my two remaining friends from before the Whiteout, out of it, because that meant they'd kept Atlanta safe during the most chaotic period post-Whiteout alone. I'd hurt my relationship with them over this, then reforged it by bringing them into the Brooks-Choi Foundation's fold.

"Facet's ability to channel and concentrate electromagnetic energy means she could be a daylight laser for us. The downside is that she needs sunlight to channel. If only we had someone like Epic who could open portals. We could bring the sunlight with us, and Facet could nuke all the vampires easily."

"That doesn't answer my question, Irene."

"Sorry, thinking aloud. We should still call them in. Ken can give you and Rachel an extra set of investigative eyes, and Facet can still help us in the field. Not all our fights are going to be underground. We just can't afford to wait for them to get here."

Brooks nodded. "They won't get here until late afternoon, between wrapping up essential things in LaGrange then the travel time back home. Still, good on you for trying to spread some of the burden."

"Thanks. It had to happen eventually."

Brooks chuckled. "Now, get out of here, before I change my mind and tell you to rest, anyway."

It was after ten in the morning before everything was ready. There was the usual back-and-forth involved with bringing both Public Works and PART into this sewer expedition.

Then there was the physical prep. Even with a cutting-edge workshop, there's only so fast enough stakes to kill an army of vampires can be sharpened up.

Our cadre met with Captain Braxton in an innocent-looking Public Works enclosure erected for "emergency sewer maintenance" above our chosen entrance point.

The entire side street had been closed off from the public, and some undercover PART officers tried to look useful playing with some of Water & Sewers' equipment.

"Here's the deal, folks." Braxton showed us a sewer map with several highlighted routes. "There are a lot of ways in and out of this area." He pointed at the section that was marked as the Hogs' hideout.

"So they have plenty of escape routes but, at the same time, we have plenty of entry choices," Extinguisher said. "There are four main tunnels that aren't flooded. We could split up and hit them from all sides."

Hexagon shook his head. "That sounds risky. No offense to no one, but we ain't exactly at one hundred percent, boss."

He was right. The entire team, other than Mind's Eye, had suffered injuries last night and, while we all healed fast, no one was fresh today.

"Good point, Hex. Mind's Eye, no luck with your psychic senses, I'm guessing?"

"Correct. Mackenzie's presence is obscuring everything."

"I don't see much other choice than a single-entry, group effort," I said. "Between the vampires and Mackenzie, we can't afford to split our forces."

Captain Braxon sighed. "Unfortunately, heroes, I can't promise much in the way of support. I've got a unit of SWAT on standby, but I'm not sure they would be any good against these bloodsuckers."

"Thanks, Joe. I know you get your hands tied a lot. Best to keep them in reserve for clean-up." Extinguisher looked over at me. "I can't think of any other options either, Indy. I don't like it, though. It seems too simple."

"Maybe we just got lucky and finally got a jump on him even though we haven't had any luck for three months straight, and now, suddenly, we're on Mackenzie's doorstep, but I hear you can get lucky breaks all the time in police work, right, Captain?" Tank asked.

Captain Braxton just nodded. I doubted he entirely understood the question.

I agreed with Extinguisher. But what choice did we have? "Even if we didn't have a chance to catch Mackenzie, we have to act. We can't risk the Hogs contaminating the water supply with vampire blood."

Extinguisher looked to each of us. "Okay, team. You too, Robin Hood. Let's get to it."

Chapter 33

Navigating an active sewer system was one of many horrible things I'd only gotten to experience because of the Whiteout.

I didn't appreciate the stench of decaying sewage, the claustrophobic environment, or the moments of having to wade through wastewater.

Considering the nature of our new comic book reality, I fully expected that, with every turn, the Morlocks, the Lizard, or even an incursion of Mole Man's minions would pop out to accost us.

None of that happened, though. Our trip wasn't dangerous, just slower than I would've liked. It was the ticking time bomb of the sun's descent that worried me, even though we had hours before sundown.

Even if we made it while the sun was up, it might not matter. I thought about my first encounter in the bowels of Underground Atlanta - that vampire was certainly up for a fight during daytime hours - and tightened my bandolier of wooden stakes. At least I'd made sure to have that crucifix around my neck this time.

It was around two in the afternoon when we came to the home stretch.

The sewer tunnel opened a bit, letting even the mammoth Hexagon stand to his full height. Not a hundred yards ahead, we could see dim lights coming from the target chamber.

By now, we'd done assaults on an unknown enemy group a few times. There wasn't any need for words - we fell into our assigned roles easily, even Archer.

Hexagon, Medusa, and I ranged forward in a front arc, while Extinguisher and Archer stayed back to use their superior ranged powers. Mind's Eye kept with Tank in the middle, so Tank could keep her safe and mobile.

As we got closer, there was a sound outside the dripping water, our own footsteps, and - I strained my ears - was that classical music?

I could faintly hear Holtz's "Mars, the Bringer of War" as we got to the edge of the chamber. I thought I heard something else under the music, but I couldn't be sure.

Per the briefing Choi had given us prior to departure, this area was an old pumping station that had fallen into disuse and forgotten about with orders for renovation shuffled a dozen times. Numerous small tunnels and pipes led off to sub-chambers for pumping and storing water.

Someone had apparently decided to do their own work to bring things up to speed, as most of the equipment looked new and well-kept.

Of course, the new owners felt the need to do some redecorating as well. The thirty neatly arranged steel boxes, all about coffin-sized, really brought out the color of the sewer slime in the walls.

The music grew louder as we approached. It came from a CD player and speakers sitting on a folding card table, smack dab in the center of the room.

That's when we all felt it - the twisted Pulse the vampires emitted. It was low and weak, though. Nothing stirred and no booby traps exploded as we entered the chamber.

"My audio system is detecting numerous high-frequency sound sources," Archer said as Hexagon walked right up to the table. "My friends, I think -"

The air erupted with screeching. Vampire Hogs burst out of the water, formed out of rolling mists from connecting pipes, and suddenly sprang from the concealment of their coffins. A sudden, almost crippling wave of their Pulse washed over us.

The music was just a cover to make it harder to detect the super-speed squeals of their coordination. I didn't know how they managed to diffuse their Pulse, but they could. I wouldn't have been shocked if a misted vampire had been following us ever since we got within a half mile of this place.

We'd expected that this might be a big trap, so nothing in our planning changed. We'd prepared for a fight, so we all sprang into action.

"Circle the wagons, people!" Extinguisher shouted out as he conjured up a semi-circle of solid ice to shield our rear.

I snapped immediately into the sublime clarity of focus as the first four vampires rushed our front line.

Hexagon grabbed the first two and began to pummel them with his mighty fists. Medusa caught one with her gaze before being tackled by another.

Before the vampires could dogpile her, I slammed into one of her attackers and threw him hard to the sewer floor. I followed up with a stake to the heart in one swift, sure motion.

Hexagon dashed one of his opponents into the stone floor, a delaying tactic at best, and staked the other.

Behind us, the chaos of open battle was making it hard to tell just what was going on, but it was clear some of the vampires were trying to separate us.

"Thanks, Indy," Medusa shouted as she drove a stake into the vampire caught in stony half-life from her gaze. "We need to get back to the others."

I nodded then blanched as I saw a vampire deeper into the room aim an assault rifle at us. "Hex!"

"On it, ladies!" Hexagon hurled the now-inert corpse in his hands like a grotesque boulder.

It crashed into the gunman with extreme force and smashed both of them into messy chunks. The gunman would regenerate, but it'd take time.

It was hard for me to track twenty-five opponents, no matter how fast my brain and reflexes are. The gloom of the sewers made it worse.

That's why I didn't see where the grenade came from. I only heard the splash and metallic clang as it landed in the middle of the three of us.

"Grenade!" I warned as I dove away.

There was a tremendous clap of thunder and a bright flash from behind as I hit the deck.

Not lethal ordinance, but a stun grenade. My dive saved my vision, but it didn't save my hearing from the deafening boom.

I forced myself to stand, no matter how messed up my equilibrium was. Just as I stood, I felt cold, dead arms grab me from behind, around my waist.

I threw a hard elbow backward as something lifted me off my feet. I must've hit my attacker, because the sensation of bone and flesh caving in from the strike shuddered through my arm.

My attacker's grip loosened, and I twisted free. My balance was starting to return, even if my hearing wasn't, as I landed on my feet.

I spun around to see my attacker was another vampire, and his skull snapped back into place with a sickening crunch. He lunged at me with a hiss.

I managed to sidestep him but, in doing so, I was getting further away from my colleagues. While they seemed to be holding their own, I couldn't afford to be separated from them and swarmed by vampires.

I flung a stake at my current attacker, right into his heart, and sprinted for the team.

The first sign my hearing was returning was the sound of an incomprehensible vampire cry. A good dozen of the vampire Hogs turned to mist in unison, enough to flood the room.

I couldn't see my hand in front of my face, and my ears were still ringing from the stun grenade. I backed slowly towards the last wall I'd seen as I pulled the cross from my neck. The wall would cover my back, the cross my front.

The first vampire that appeared through the mists came straight at me, but I met him with the cross.

Like when I did this with the first vampire in Underground Atlanta, there was that same momentary clash of wills before my current attacker shrieked and retreated back into the mists.

In fact, the mist itself retreated. It made sense, it was made of atomized vampire. Too bad it only pulled back a few feet.

"Guys," I called out into the mist as I drew a stake, "crosses will clear the space! Also, I could really use some help here!"

While my ears still rang, my hearing was good enough to hear hammering footfalls approaching from my right. And my left. And from ahead.

With no sign of the help I'd called for coming, I braced for a fight. I staked the first vampire, then drove back the next with my cross. I wasn't quite as lucky with the four others that swarmed over me.

I lost the cross in the initial struggle but, to my surprise, the vampires didn't beat me like a drum. They only scooped me up like a sack of grain and ran with all their supernatural speed.

I'd barely started to struggle when the vampires stopped as swiftly as they'd started, then hurled me like a rag-doll through the air.

I hit the stone floor hard and rolled to a stop, scraped up, bruised, but remarkably alive.

As I got to my feet, I realized they had taken me far away from the battle, and I had no idea which way they'd gone.

There was no gas or mist here, at least. In fact, it looked like a crude break room, probably set up by some maintenance workers who didn't want slog all the way to the surface each time they wanted to sip a cup of coffee.

"I apologize that the invitation was rough, Doctor Roman," came the cultured, even-toned voice from the shadows, "but it's imperative we meet in person, don't you agree?"

I recognized the voice as I spun to face him. Ian Shane Mackenzie, the man who'd spilled so much blood, stood there casually.

He was dressed head to toe in paramilitary gear, complete with holstered pistol and knife. His graying red hair and bright eyes made him seem more like the kindly, older uncle I didn't have than the terrorist leader he was.

"I'm not sure we have a lot to talk about, Mackenzie." I eased into a fighting stance.

He was untouched, not even a cut from shaving, and I'd just gone through a hike in the sewers, then a fight with vampires. While I was ten years younger than he was, I wasn't sure how much that would matter with his Natural abilities.

"Seriously, Doctor Roman?" Mackenzie shook his head and tutted softly. "Well, maybe we do need to a have a demonstration. Maybe, after that, you'll understand that it's better to talk than posture."

With that, he came at me with the same accelerated speed I myself had.

Chapter 34

"What I'm sure you don't know is that we are as different as they are," Mackenzie calmly said as he threw a right hand at my head.

Slipping under his first punch, I barely saw the second jab blur in, but I still deflected it. Unfortunately, I had to use my right forearm, which reminded me that, while the pain had lessened, it hadn't healed fully.

As close as we were, I retaliated with an unorthodox head butt, looking to clash skulls right at the start.

He must've seen it coming just as I'd seen his own attacks, because he leaned back at the knees, evading the blow.

"Oh really? I know you're crazy and I'm not. There's one difference." My banter might distract him, but I didn't bet on it.

I didn't stop attacking as I spoke. I grabbed the lapels of Mackenzie's camo jacket and pivoted, swinging him with all my might at the metal door of the chamber.

Before I could release, he countered by grabbing my own jacket. In a complete reversal, he swung me into the door instead.

I didn't fully understand how hurt I was until now, but it was way more than I'd thought. Days of heavy action, starting with The '49er, had caught up to me.

All I could do was keep focused and ignore my myriad injuries long enough to take Mackenzie down.

"Don't play the banter game." He smiled as he pinned me against the door with a forearm. "I can think as fast as you can, faster actually."

"Asshole." I brought a knee up hard into his chest.

Even with his FBI training, he was too close to avoid the blow. Mackenzie grunted and bounced back to avoid a follow-up attack from me.

"Oh, my dear, don't be offended in the least. As I said, people like us - Naturals, as you call us, and trust me, there are more than just we two - have different unique qualities. For instance -"

I interrupted his lecture by hurling a stake at him, blunt end first.

He ducked it, but it was only a distraction to cover my kick aimed at Mackenzie's family jewels. Mackenzie barely managed to deflect my kick.

He was right. I was already seeing the differences between us.

Mackenzie was clearly slower than me and not as strong. If I wasn't a walking road map of injuries, I'd probably be winning this handily.

Likewise, he could clearly talk to me and keep focused on the fight. From his movements, he was then using his accelerated thinking to make up for his slower reflexes - putting himself in the right place to block or dodge. His mind had to be faster than mine.

Who knew what other differences there were?

I recovered from my deflected kick and threw a quick jab at Mackenzie's jaw. He blocked that shot easily enough and tried to counterstrike with a cross.

My superior speed let me duck before the hit landed. After his punch whistled over my head, I threw a sharp, short uppercut.

Mackenzie barely pulled his head back in time, but I still scored a hard tap on his chin. I followed up with a kick toward his knees, but he hopped over the sweep.

As he landed, before I caught my balance from the kick, he struck like a snake, stabbing his fingers into the muscles of my side.

Ignoring the register of pain, I pulled away, hoping he'd follow. He was too smart for that and danced back a few steps.

"See? That right there." Mackenzie chuckled, rubbing at the growing bruise on his chin. "That amazing quickness, it's breathtaking. The footage really doesn't do it justice. I hope to see it someday when you are at your best."

He might be stalling, but I'd take advantage of the moments to get myself together.

"Point made. I may not be quite as fast thinking as you, but I'm not stupid."

"I know you aren't. Why do you think I stayed far away until now and observed? I couldn't risk a potential confrontation before I was ready or, more precisely, you were ready."

"What makes tonight so gosh darn special?" I could see the muscles starting to tense in his arms. He was about to move.

Mackenzie rolled his eyes. "Oh please. I'm not one of your silly Push Crooks. The Whiteout hasn't blanked my mind like so many others."

He drew his sidearm in a blur. I guess this was his way of testing how fast I actually was.

I moved with all the speed I had. With two swift steps towards the nearest wall, I dodged out of the way of his first shot. I leaped and kicked off the wall and Mackenzie's second shot struck the stone behind me.

That brought me right into his face. Before Mackenzie could squeeze the trigger again, I smacked the gun out of his hand.

There wasn't a look of surprise on his face, though. He wasn't even trying to shoot.

Instead, he'd spent that last moment drawing an electric stun gun from his belt. I heard the spark but, before I could draw back, he jammed the stun gun into my ribs.

I don't know how many volts of electricity ran through my body. Muscles contracted, nerves fired erratically, and a million danger signs fired off in my brain.

As I fell backward and twitched, I found I was still grimly hanging onto my focus. I tried to will everything in my body to work.

In theory and practice, it was possible. There were trained people who could shrug off a full-powered taser in moments.

As I fought my own body, I heard Mackenzie's footsteps approaching my side. "While you were constantly occupied trying to do what you thought was the right thing, I've been watching, studying, and waiting."

He paused a moment. Every extra second counted as I managed to wrangle my rebelling neurons into their pens.

"Still fighting? I suppose you need another shock or three."

I could feel his presence looming. It was now or never.

The second I heard the faint spark of Mackenzie's stun gun, I forced my arm to swat at it with all the grace of a zombie.

Even Mackenzie hadn't expected me to act so soon, so I was rewarded with the smack of flesh and the clatter of plastic on stone as I hit the stun gun away.

That must've annoyed Mackenzie, because he grabbed my wrist and cranked it back.

The sudden jolt of pain through my focus kicked in the adrenaline and, with a sudden biochemical surge, my entire body was back on board with the brain. Too bad my arm was about to snap like a chicken wing.

"The stun gun would've been more pleasant, Doctor Roman, but if you insist."

Something popped as my elbow hyper-extended, but I ignored it as I'd already written off that joint in my brilliant/insane gambit. I drew my knees up to give me a hint of leverage then yanked with all the strength I could muster with my mangled arm.

Technically, Mackenzie had the win. His technique was flawless and his position perfect, but he hadn't factored in all the possibilities of dealing with Naturals. I didn't have to out-technique his hold if I had enough muscle to lift him clean off the ground.

Mackenzie let out a cry of surprise as I pushed up with all my strength. His feet left the floor with the sudden motion while my shoulder screamed in agony. I definitely tore some important tissues, and my unnatural pain tolerance was topping out.

However, I ended up free from his grip, and Mackenzie hit the stone floor hard.

In a desperate bid to keep him down, I hauled off with the hardest punt kick I could manage straight to his side.

To Mackenzie's credit, he managed to roll with the impact, but I knew I cracked one or two of his ribs. He curled up into a ball as he tumbled away.

The moment he stopped, he madly scrambled to his feet, but I was right on top of him, one arm almost useless and the other still tender from the other day, not that I cared one bit.

I led with a wild swing that he blocked. His immediate answer was a sharp jab to my gut.

Ignoring the instinct to curl up from the hit, I kept charging, slamming my body into his until we crashed into one of the stone walls.

Mackenzie was finally open for that headbutt I so wanted. I drove my forehead into the bridge of his nose and was delighted by the crunch of cartilage as blood poured out his nostrils.

That didn't stop him, just as it wouldn't stop me. Taking advantage of my hurt arms, Mackenzie managed to squirm an arm free and jab his fingers into my newly strained shoulder.

I tried to focus through it, but that was the breaking point after all the brutalization my body had taken. I cried out and staggered back, letting him slip free.

As I tried to get a handle on the pain, Mackenzie went for the smart move and drove a hard punch at my head, probably hoping for a sweet-spot knockout.

I was still retreating, which saved me from his haymaker. Desperate, I threw a wild, low kick that knocked Mackenzie's legs out from under him.

I used the few moments as Mackenzie got to his feet to retreat further and assess things. I had two hurt arms, an aching side, and painfully sore muscles from the stun gun. Mackenzie had taken some hits, but he was still quite fresh.

But that didn't matter, I realized. All it would take was one lucky shot from either of us to injure the other permanently, maybe kill them. We were just too strong and fast, and we didn't have the protection of a Pushed's unnatural shell.

That explained a lot of Mackenzie's tactics. Just as he'd given his vampire lackies rubber bullets and stun grenades, he'd hit me with a stun gun. Mackenzie very much wanted to take me alive.

As if to confirm that, Mackenzie didn't use my moment of weakness to punch or kick my head off. Instead he rushed in to grapple me.

I brushed aside his first attempt and tried to push him off with the sole of my boot.

Instead, Mackenzie caught my extended leg and heaved upward with all his focused strength.

The world spun as I flipped over backward but, by some miracle of agility, I managed to land on my feet.

As impressive as that had to look, I was at a horrible disadvantage, and Mackenzie had no qualms about capitalizing.

He grabbed me by both shoulders, digging his thumbs hard into the joints. I didn't give him the pleasure of crying out, but the surge of pain, only dulled by my focus instead of being locked away, left me open to two swift knees to my gut.

I contemplated throwing up on him out of pure spite, but I pushed against his grip with all my strength.

We both got a demonstration of how much stronger I was than him. The violent push didn't just break Mackenzie's grip, it threw him a half dozen feet away.

Seizing the moment, I rushed him. I saw his counterattack before he threw the punch, and I slipped under it and past him. With his back open, I slammed a fist into his kidney then shoved him hard into the nearest wall.

I knew the kidney punch hurt him bad, but I was even worse off. My vision was turning hazy around the edges, it was getting hard to think straight, and I knew my focus was slipping away fast.

With one last desperate rush of energy, I swung a full-strength haymaker at his exposed back.

But Mackenzie wasn't there. All his experience and extensive training combined with his Natural focus to let him roll before my finishing blow landed.

Instead, I broke my knuckles as my punch shattered a fist-shaped hole in the wall.

A tremendous, stabbing pain exploded in my left shoulder blade. I'd been stabbed enough times over the last six months to know Mackenzie had just shoved his knife down to the bone.

My pain centers overloaded, and I slumped against the wall.

I tried to keep standing, scrabbling for some handhold, but I continued to slide down. Crumpling to the floor, I found that it was damp, cold, and surprisingly soothing.

"Well now," Mackenzie said with a startling level of calm, "that was educational. You really would've beaten me if I hadn't ensured you were properly prepared."

Just how much of the trouble I'd faced over the past few days - the past months - had Mackenzie orchestrated? At the very least, it'd started with The '49er. Mackenzie was now confirmed to be the mysterious man behind The '49er's latest attack.

I grimly pushed up to my hands and knees. Just as I didn't know everything Mackenzie had done to ruin my life, I didn't want to know what he intended to do now.

Despite my valiant effort, I just couldn't force myself back up. I heard the scrape of plastic then his footfalls approaching me.

"Don't worry, Doctor Roman. You won't enjoy this, but you won't be dead." The electric crackle of the stun gun filled my ears. "When you wake up, let's try to have a rational conversation, all right?"

The first shock locked my joints, and I felt my cheek hit the floor. The second one finally shattered my focus completely, and one giant wave, agony, nausea, and fatigue hit at once.

Thank God for the black slate of unconsciousness that followed.

I knew I wasn't dead because I dreamed. Unlike the other lucid dreams I had in the past, this was an incoherent mix of dream and nightmare. No council of Irenes or clear dream vistas, just a wild blur of motion and an overwhelming sense of panic.

I had a strong suspicion I was drugged, which would account for the untamed state of my subconscious mind. Eventually, I came out of the psychedelic haze and dropped into normal sleep.

When I woke up, I was sitting upright in a plush, high-backed chair. The chamber I was in was dimly lit, but there were many subtle clues that I was still in the Atlanta sewer system.

Someone had treated my injuries professionally. In fact, I felt better than I had in weeks, and I now wore white cotton scrubs and what felt like thin sneakers. That meant no communications gear and no GPS tracker.

I wasn't even restrained as far as I could tell. If it weren't for the fact that I was sitting across a table from Ian Mackenzie and had a strange weight around my neck, I'd have been rather happy.

"Ah, right on time," Mackenzie said, certainly not sounding like the madman I knew he was. "Now, Doctor Roman, let's have a chat."

Chapter 35

"I'm sorry that I had to hurt you as badly as I did, but you didn't leave me much choice," Mackenzie began.

Okay, *now* he sounded a little more unhinged.

"I only wish I'd given you no choice at all, and I guess the only reason I have to listen to you now is this thing around my neck?"

"Well, I'm not stupid." He held up a small remote. "That collar is simply a more powerful version of the stun gun I used on you. Most likely it wouldn't kill you, but it would certainly put you down."

I gave him a sharp look, but that was all I could do. So much for my fantasies of leaping across the table and taking him out before escaping. My throat was dry, and so I drank from a glass of water on the table. In fact, it looked like there was a full meal laid out for the two of us.

Mackenzie watched me drink until I emptied the glass. "Aren't you afraid the food or drink is poisoned?"

"If you wanted to kill me, I'd already be dead. Who'd tend to someone's wounds, wakes them up, then poisons them?"

"A Pushed," Mackenzie said without hesitation. "As well as most people under the influence of the Whiteout."

I wondered about that. Yes, the Pushed were melodramatic and strange, but that might be a step too far.

"I know you think I'm a monster, an insane terrorist. All I ask is that you hear me out. Listen to my story and my plans."

"I owe Extinguisher an apology. He pegged you dead on." I rolled my eyes. "Why would I ever think you're a monster? You only murdered your own colleagues, unleashed Reaper, jeopardized the entire nation, and now you're unleashing a vampire Hog plague on Atlanta."

I stopped my rant to grab a bite of chicken off my plate. The hunger inside me was gnawing at my insides and demanded to be sated.

Mackenzie let out a deep sigh. "Fair enough. You must see that those were acts of desperation in fighting an invading army, not random acts of malice."

He must've taken the sight of me eating as time to begin his own meal as he tucked into his food, cutting the meat into small, even squares before eating one bite at a time.

"Invasion? Don't you think that's an extreme stance to take? The Pushed are people, too. You must know that. You must see the same things I see."

"I do and, yes, at an elemental level, they are. I think the problem is that you've blinded yourself to the big picture."

I was about to throw out another retort, but he held a hand up calmly for silence. I decided to give it to him for now.

"Before we get into an actual debate, would you allow me to lay my cards on the table? I think you'd agree that it's poor science to jump to a conclusion without having as much knowledge as possible, right?"

"Fair enough, but remember your observational bias. Try to stick to the facts."

"Duly noted, Doctor."

No matter what kind of crazy tale he spun, I figured that it'd give me time to devise some way out of this mess. I had no idea where I was, what had happened to my friends, or even how long it had been since Mackenzie and I had fought, but none of that changed the fact I had to get out of here.

"I'm sure that Duane and Rachel have told you about my past. Bright-eyed and eager out of high school, I spent six years in the U.S. Army. I had the right stuff to enter military intelligence then, after that, I pursued a career in law enforcement. With my qualifications, I wound up working for the FBI. The precise details are unimportant - it's all very mundane."

He smiled with what seemed like honest pride. "In the Bureau, I became something of a go-to man for unusual cases, a task I relished. I always wanted to believe that there was another layer to human experience right underneath the surface, so looking into cults, unexplained disappearances, bizarre crimes, and all manner of oddities scratched that intellectual and spiritual itch."

"Rachel mentioned something about that. She said that you were very open-minded before the Whiteout."

"True. I still am, if you can believe that. I ask you not to repeat what Duane's said about me. Very colorful, I imagine."

"That's one way to put it."

"I hope to be redeemed in time. To my dismay, I never found any actual evidence of the unnatural. Every once in a while, I thought I may have found something, but it was never concrete. Still, I persisted."

I took this time to keep examining the area. I guessed the thing around my neck was some kind of booby trap, and there was only one metal door leading out of this room. My initial prospects for escape didn't look good.

"When the Whiteout happened and the Pushed appeared," Mackenzie continued, "my qualifications made my superiors assign me to investigate the situation before I could even ask."

"Fortunate for you, unfortunate for everyone else."

"In your point of view, I suppose. Within an hour of the event, NASA had worked out the probable origin of the event here in Atlanta. Before noon of the first day, I'd already sent Rachel and Duane to track down information which, as you already know, led to you."

"Yes, they're good at their jobs."

I continued eating because, if I had any hope of escape, my body needed to be refueled. "And this has been a great trip down memory lane, but it hasn't explained why you decided to go become a terrorist ringleader. You did that within the first day, because you talked to Gerald Schuller, pushed him to become Reaper, *and* started manipulating the Hogs at least a day before the Battle of Washington."

"That's simple, Doctor. Observation and the first interview with Epic made it plain to me what I needed to do. Come on, you know what I'm talking about."

I had some ideas what the madman could be fishing for from me, but I wasn't going to give it to him. Instead, I gestured for him to continue while I worked on a chicken leg.

"Very well. Simply put, the entire human race had been mentally altered against its will and, the same day, a supremely powerful being put himself forward as the first among a new race. Not only that, he promised to protect us poor, pitiful mortals. That doesn't sound like a savior. That sounds like an invader justifying his actions."

"You called it an invasion before. Why do you see it that way?"

"Why don't you?" He sighed. "Very well, I'll spell it out for you. The Pushed don't think or act in a way that aligns with human thought, even human thought influenced by the Whiteout. You've seen that yourself."

"I think you're overstating it, but carry on."

"Am I? More than half of the Pushed population believes in taking over the world, either in mock beneficence or honest subjugation. They have more in common with a hypothetical alien invasion than the normal human condition."

In some ways, he wasn't wrong. Epic and his Crusaders were a real threat to the world, and Push Crooks were their own kind of problem.

And while I wasn't organizing a guerrilla war on the Pushed like Mackenzie, if I succeeded in stopping the Whiteout, it'd get rid of the Pushed all the same.

"Assuming I find any validity in your beliefs, Mackenzie, nothing you've said so far has convinced me your crimes are justified."

"Let me explain, then. During my time investigating bizarre cases, I spoke with many brilliant people, experts in their fields, about the hard realities of the possibilities of aliens. It's universally accepted that any civilization that could devise the means to travel the stars in a reasonable time would be so dramatically advanced over us that we would be ants to them. If they wanted to take over our planet, there would be nothing we could do."

"Just like now, in your eyes."

"Exactly, Doctor Roman. And really, how far from the truth is that?"

He steepled his fingers. "The Battle of Washington changed little except for adding a division in the ranks of the invaders, thanks to you. Governmental regulation can do no more than incite counteraction. No military force can hold a candle to the destructive power of the Pushed, especially if they continue to unite into groups and factions as they're doing now."

"We're holding out just fine in Atlanta," I argued, "and the Pushed I work with aren't like that. There are good people among them. They just need to get organized and unified to counter-balance the bad ones."

"Look. I don't want to burst your bubble, because frankly I'm rather impressed with what you've managed to do so far. There's a reason I haven't overtly interfered in Atlanta until recently, even as you hunted me down like a dog. Let's be realistic, though. You are one woman with a small elite group backing you up."

Mackenzie leaned forward, as if he were a lecturer about to delve into a complex topic. "Let's be generous and say you and your friends are each the equivalent of ten of Epic's so-called heroes. Congratulations, it is now ninety to a thousand odds instead of nine to a thousand. You're going to be crushed all the same."

"Then why haven't we?"

"Please, Doctor." Mackenzie shook his head kindly, like he was my actual professor. "You know the answer, so why don't you tell me?"

Chapter 36

Mackenzie was right. I did know, and I wanted to punch him in the nose for making me say it.

"Epic is still obsessed with me."

"Correct. He's holding back out of 'love' for you. But that won't last forever. In fact, his initiative to move on Atlanta has already begun."

I scoffed. "You can't possibly mean the Argent Archer. Not that he couldn't be dangerous, but he's too, well, good to be some kind of secret saboteur."

"I do mean him. Do you really think Archer was sent to Atlanta to help out of the kindness of Epic's heart? But let me ask you another question first. I'm being so open about myself that I feel it's only fair that you do the same."

Before I could object, he pulled my mask out from under the table and waved it in the air. "Why, Doctor?"

I blinked in surprise, not quite sure what answer he could possibly want.

"You know Indomitable is a lie. You're so elementally different from the Pushed that you're their very antithesis. You can't even touch what they consider to be their real bodies, yet you dress up like them and play the same games they do. Why do you do it?"

I looked down at my empty plate and thought about that question. To be honest, it'd dwelled in the back of my head since I'd talked with Archer and Extinguisher the night before, but things had gotten so frenetic that I hadn't found a real answer.

Rational Irene supplied the factual reasons. At the start of the Whiteout, Indomitable had been a ruse, a disguise, something to let me get close to the Pushed and turn things around, to either stop the Whiteout or influence it.

She also supplied the doubts. I wasn't stopping the Whiteout, and I didn't know if I was changing anything anymore. Did all the speeches, all the rallies, all the hard work really change any hearts or minds? I didn't know.

Whiteout Irene just shook her head. What did it matter if I wasn't succeeding? I was doing the right thing - saving lives, fighting evil, and trying to make life better for everyone I could. A little self-sacrifice was worth it.

I, the central pillar of our trinity, said the only words I could. "It's the only way I can think of to mitigate the damage. I'm partly responsible for this, after all. I'd stop it if I could, but –"

"You feel justifiable guilt, and you have the ability to save lives, so you do that. There are always more lives threatened by the Pushed, so many that you never have time to think about other courses of action. Indomitable, our tireless protector."

He tossed the mask into the center of the table. The rusty red bloodstains stood out on the blue material. That was *my* blood.

"Can't you see how pointless it is? That mask will never solve the real problem."

Mackenzie sighed and now tossed his sidearm into the center of the table. "And neither will that pistol. Both of our chosen methods are dead ends. You'll never change enough hearts and minds to domesticate the Pushed, and all the military might I could muster will never stand against them."

"If your suggestion is that we stay in an underground bunker and wait for the dust to settle, I'm going to have to decline. I just don't think that household will work out."

"Never fear. I vowed not to remarry after my dear Patricia died. No, what I propose is a third option, one that requires us both. It's the option I'm sure you've always thought to pursue but could not, and the option that I always wished for but didn't know was possible. Not until now."

"You want to reverse what Epic did. Stop the Whiteout entirely."

"Close. I want to rewind it. Think of all the lost lives, all the displaced people, all the ravaged minds. We could sweep all that away and place everything neatly back into the natural order."

"And how do you propose we do this?" I knew the only real answer, but I wanted to confirm what all he knew.

"We must recreate the experiment Epic performed. The Whiteout altered the very fiber of reality, which means it can be rewoven. You provide the core knowhow, and I provide the safety and resources. Together, we can accomplish this mission and save the world."

"You said you didn't think this was possible before. What happened to change your mind?"

Mackenzie gave an enigmatic smile. "All I am at liberty to say currently is that certain information has come into my grasp. Now, let's get back to Epic and his Crusaders. I think that topic might help put my offer into better perspective."

"Sure. Now, is Epic scheduled to take over the city before you? Or did you manage to pencil in your name ahead of his on the City Invasion sign-up sheet?"

Mackenzie chuckled. "I'm glad the situation hasn't ruined your sense of humor. No, I want to try to show you the method behind Epic's actions here."

"Carry on then."

"Don't worry, it's rather simple. Let's take a hypothetical situation – a town threatened by an enemy army. They don't know where this army is, precisely, and they know little about the invaders themselves, so the townspeople are ever vigilant for strangers."

I could already spot the parallels, but I wanted to see where Mackenzie was going. I'd already gleaned a lot of insights about his motivations, his abilities, and just how much he really knew about the Whiteout.

"One day, such a stranger comes into town. A diplomat from the opposing army, he impresses the suspicious townspeople by being a decent human being. They get to know each other, and the townsfolk start to see that this monstrous enemy is, at the end of the day, just like them.

"Meanwhile, the stranger experiences life in the city and learns all about it as the two cultures mingle. After he has done his job as a diplomat, the stranger returns to his people, leaving hope for a peaceful tomorrow."

I finished the story for him. "The diplomat, of course, was a spy, even if he wasn't one knowingly. He's sure to talk to his superiors about the city, its people, and about its defenses. In fact, it'd probably work better if the diplomat wasn't a spy, just in case he's found out. As for the town, who their guard has been lowered as their defenses are given away to their enemy."

"You're so good at this, Doctor. Your Argent Archer is that diplomat. I'm sure he has no idea what his true purpose here is, but do you doubt that once he returns to Epic, he won't recount every single thing he saw, heard, or said?"

"I can't say that you're wrong." I didn't ask what Mackenzie's suggested course of action was. It would undoubtedly be imprison or kill Archer. "But the good citizens of Atlanta shouldn't worry about your vampire army, right?"

Mackenzie retrieved his gun. "I won't lie to you. It hasn't been easy dealing with something so...Pushed-adjacent. Especially something so horrific. However, until recently, I've been thinking purely in terms of how to stymie the Pushed through warfare. If I could find a way to manufacture an army of Naturals like us, I would've taken that option."

"But you'll take the plague of walking corpses instead?" I snarled. "You realize that makes you seem as mad as any other comic book mastermind. Do you want me to start plucking examples to compare you to? I could do it all day."

"I'm afraid that the specifics of my strategy might be lost on you, not for lack of intelligence, but lack of military experience."

He raised a finger. "Let's not forget that you're still an enemy agent. I'm not a villain out of a comic book. I'm not going to spout off my entire plan and organization to you here and now just because I have you 'in my clutches,' as I'm sure you'd say."

As Mackenzie continued, I finally finished all the food left on the table and a man, completely human, dressed in paramilitary fatigues, came in and gathered up the empty plates. There were some human Hogs left, after all.

"Now, let me make this plain. You have a simple choice." Mackenzie put one hand palm-up on the table as the Hog attendant slipped out. "You can join forces with me. Between the information I have and your knowledge of the Whiteout's origins, we can rebuild reality and fix everything."

He then put his other hand palm-down on the table. "Or you can choose to keep going as you already have been. How long do you think you will last before your body or your heart gives out? Frankly, the scars and injuries I saw while treating you don't paint a pretty picture of your future."

"How many of those are you responsible for, Mackenzie? A week's worth? A month's worth?"

"I had no real choice." Mackenzie sounded neither happy nor sad - his voice was perfectly even. "If I'd approached you, there would have been violence before discussion. Completely understandable, but I couldn't have you taking me into custody or, worse, killing me before that point. That was a very real, very likely possibility given what we know of our respective capabilities."

"How many innocent people were hurt or killed so you could soften me up for our talk? Let's not even discuss how much pain and suffering I've gone through because an e-mail just couldn't do." I didn't try to mask my anger and pain.

Mackenzie frowned slightly. "I'm not happy that happened, Irene, but you see now that this is a war. Winning a war requires sacrifice and, sometimes, that sacrifice comes from the innocent."

"Even if I take you at your word that you have some vital piece of information and are willing to devote everything you have to fix this, what gives us the right to do this?"

Now I decided to argue with morality and ethics, not cold logic, and those were weapons I knew how to wield. "If it was wrong for Epic to change the world, what makes us different from him?"

"I hate to put it this way, but who cares, Irene?" Mackenzie was still ice cold. "Don't you see? All my crimes, all your mistakes, all the blood and death will get wiped away. Clean slate. Full reboot."

"You make it sound so simple and, in a way, it is. Maybe you're right, that we can reboot the Whiteout and rewind time itself. With the power to alter reality, what's impossible?"

Mackenzie seemed pleased by that, but I wasn't done yet.

"The problem is that I've seen firsthand that this power has limits. You have to know about Epic's parents, or else you'd never have known to look for Gerald Schuller. If Epic couldn't bring back them back, it's likely his reality-warping machine can't, either."

"Likely isn't impossible," Mackenzie countered. "It's clear to me that Epic doesn't have the full power of the Whiteout at his fingertips. If he did, we Naturals wouldn't exist, and he'd have already conquered the world."

"And that should be further evidence that it's not as easy as simply rebuilding Epic's machine and strapping your brain to it. Do you really think Epic, a genius physicist and avid comic book aficionado, fueled by the pure motives of making a better world protected by superheroes, would make *this* reality?"

"No, of course not. Epic's world is flawed because the man himself was flawed, traumatized, and using a rather poor template for a sustainable future."

Mackenzie laughed. "What kind of utopia allows a hero to monologue dramatically as a civilian bleeds to death in front of him? Or force people to fight with horrific consequences simply because reality picked one to be good and the other evil?"

"Then what makes you think the world we would create would be any better? I can tell you there's plenty of demons in my mind, Mackenzie. The question you need to ask yourself is what traumas are hidden in yours?"

Mackenzie was silent for a few long moments. Hopefully, that super-charged Natural brain of his was putting together my words and realizing I was right.

None of us were free of flaws and trauma, so any reality we created would be warped from our intentions.

"Everything you've said is correct, Doctor, but there is something new to add to this equation." Mackenzie tapped his forehead. "This."

"I know you're a genius yourself, but do you really think you're smarter than Epic is?"

"That's the wrong question. The real question you need to ask is if I'm smarter *now* than Eric Beck *was* when he generated the Whiteout."

I saw exactly what he was saying now. "You think going into full focus mode to accelerate your brain is going to let you map out every thought and emotion better than Epic did with his then-unenhanced brain."

"Precisely, Doctor Roman." Mackenzie's wristwatch pinged softly. "While I've enjoyed our little discussion, your time is up, and I'm afraid that I need your answer now. Where is your loyalty? With me and mankind, or with your friends and the chaos out there?"

I needed more time. I needed to think this through. Fortunately, I had a way to squeeze a few more moments of thought out of my brain. I slipped into focus, and my mind sped up with it.

Maybe I wasn't as mentally swift as Mackenzie, but it would do.

So, what is it going to be? Whiteout Irene echoed in my head. *Partner with a man ruthless enough to kill whoever he needed to in his course of saving the world or die for your principles? I know what I'd do.*

It's not that simple, Rational Irene chimed in, *and you know it. All refusing does now is get you shocked, then two bullets in the back of your head.*

Traitor! You can't seriously mean for me to work with this monster!

I butted in then. *Calm down. Even if she's the calculating one, she's a part of me. She's got morals, just like you.*

Thank you, Rational Irene said. *Mackenzie himself gave us the right course of action when he revealed Epic's plans for Archer.*

I knew then exactly what Rational Irene was proposing, and it sounded like Whiteout Irene wasn't far behind. *Oh, we're going undercover. Why didn't you lead with that?*

Sounds like we're in agreement, and it looks like Mackenzie is getting ready to press his shock button. I pulled out of focus to conserve energy and looked Mackenzie eye-to-eye.

"After everything you've revealed to me, there's really only one way I can answer - I'm siding with humanity."

Chapter 37

Mackenzie looked honestly surprised, and I took a little pleasure in the fact I'd finally said something that took him off-guard.

"I'd hoped you'd see reason, but I didn't think you'd do so. Not that I don't think you're intelligent but, before now, you've always chosen morality over rationality."

"This is the point where morality and rationality cross over. You're right – both of our methods have failed, just like Epic failed."

Acknowledging Mackenzie's intelligence seemed a good way to stroke his ego and bring his defenses down more.

"But I think I know why. We all took on the burden of change alone. Epic didn't bring me into his trust and ask for my help to craft the reality-warping device – he stole my invention from me."

"While I'm opening the door to collaboration fully and equally. I can see why that would appeal to you, Doctor, after what Epic put you through."

I hadn't learned the lesson of cooperation from Epic – I'd learned it from my friends in the Foundation. But Mackenzie was right about the appeal of working together. That appeal helped to make my lies more believable.

"So, how did you get the vampires?"

"Doctor Roman, you can't expect me –"

"Not every detail, of course. I don't expect you to trust me immediately after the fight we had, but I can't help if I don't at least know part of it."

My hunger still wasn't fully sated, and I knew I needed to be as prepared as possible. "And, a smaller request – any chance I could have some more food? You know how much I've had to call on my focus lately *and* how many calories that consumes."

"A good point. You do need a little more information to go on. Apologies, there's not very many people I've been able to trust since the Whiteout, you must understand. Leonard?"

At Mackenzie's call, the same Hog as before stepped back through the door. I didn't know if Mackenzie had the room wired with microphones or if Leonard was hovering outside the door the whole time. Probably both.

Leonard saluted crisply. "Yes, sir?"

"Get our new ally here some more food and water, please."

"Yes, sir. I'll be back shortly." Leonard left again, and Mackenzie smiled at me.

"Leonard is my aide, the only one of my human associates I feel I can trust, so don't worry. We can speak freely around him when he returns."

I nodded. If Mackenzie didn't reveal much, Leonard could be easier to interrogate. "So, back to the vampires."

"It's simple, really, once you know one fact – this hasn't been the first Whiteout or similar event."

Epic had told me that supernatural creatures had existed in the past. But knowing there had been large, sweeping changes instead of small, incremental shifts in consensual reality made me wonder.

Could one of these supernatural creatures have persisted through the ages, sustained by fringe belief, pop culture interest, and enduring folklore?

If any creature could, vampires were near the top of the list.

"So, you're telling me you found a vampire from one of these previous Whiteouts?" I asked. "Something our new Whiteout woke up?"

"Yes, correct. I assume there may be other such entities out there, but vampires suited my particular needs. Powerful, able to reproduce swiftly, immune to many conventional and Pushed forms of attack, and, most importantly, intelligent."

I tried not to shudder at what all could still be out there, and I kept my conjecturing as to what famous vampire from the past he was working with. It had to be someone famous in history or legend - the notoriety would generate more belief to sustain them.

"How are you intending to use the vampires you have left?"

"A good question, and the part of the plan I feel you need to know the most about."

"Agreed. I already said how strange it is to see you working with Pushed and Pushed-adjacent things, so this is of particular interest to me. Especially how these things threaten innocent lives."

"Good. You're not leaving your morals behind. While they do complicate our budding partnership, they also show you remain true to your principles. It means you'll remain truthful and loyal in our dealings."

"Of course. You have my word."

That seemed to satisfy Mackenzie. "After today, we won't need the vampires or their leader anymore but, for now, they serve as a final diversion to keep your friends and allies occupied while I and a small unit of agents finish the heist."

That confirmed my suspicions about a master vampire working with Mackenzie, as opposed to him having full control of all the vampires.

"Will that be a sufficient diversion, though? It's going to take a lot of vampires to keep the Five occupied, especially since Facet has to be back in town. You can't have that many left, not with the amount of blood it has to take to sustain large numbers."

"Excellent points, but I've already planned around them. The answer is simple, of course - most of my vampire army aren't vampires...yet."

Leonard came in then and began laying out another almost identical meal out before me. I used the break in the conversation to absorb what Mackenize had told me.

As Leonard finished, Mackenize smiled at him. "Considering we're all friends now, I'd like you to stay, Leonard. Please, take a seat."

Leonard looked a little surprised at the request, but he relaxed almost immediately. "Of course, sir. Thank you."

That made me nervous. Mackenzie didn't do anything without a reason, so what was the reason to bring his trusted aide into the room now, and put him at risk in case I was about to betray them?

I tried to mask my nerves by eating.

"So, back to our planning, Doctor Roman," Mackenzie began. "Human agents are easier to maintain and lack any kind of Pulse, so they've been gathered in one central location. When the signal is made, they'll all be turned in one go, creating an instant vampire army."

Leonard shifted a bit uncomfortably in his seat. Some potential dissension in the ranks?

"The transformation can be that fast? I saw one of the vampire's victims transform, and it seemed like a slow process, one that required the victim to die first."

"I can see why you'd think that, but you have a very limited sample size to observe. Trust me, when a normal human directly consumes blood from the mother vampire, the transformation from living to undead happens in seconds."

I took the time while he answered to get some more chicken in me. He specifically said "mother," so that at least gave me a little bit of information about the leader of the vampires. If my theory that she had to be a major figure from pop culture, folklore, or history, it narrowed the list of suspects.

The other revelation, that Mackenzie could create vampires almost instantly, was bone-chilling. I washed down the food with a whole glass of water.

"But when we get the reality-warping device and calibrate our new reality together, we're getting rid of the vampires, right? We're bringing everyone back to life and fixing all the damage?"

Mackenize nodded. "I want my hands washed clean of blood as much as you do, Doctor." He glanced at my nearly empty plate. "Now that you're finishing up, it's time we seal our little partnership in a way that will assure me of your trustworthiness."

I willed myself to be calm and cool. "Thank goodness. As informative as you've been, I'm a little sick of dancing around the specifics. If this will make you trust me fully, let's do it."

Mackenzie smiled as he raised the remote to the shock collar. I was about to make a move for it when he pressed a button on it - but instead of countless volts running through me, the door locked with a loud click.

"Apologies for the theatrics. I couldn't help myself. Now, we won't be disturbed."

My heart was still pounding as I nodded. "If I didn't know better, I'd think the Whiteout was getting to you."

"No chance of that, Doctor. Now, what I require of you is simple." Mackenzie drew his pistol again, but he didn't point it at me. Instead, he tossed it across to the table, right next to my plate. "Shoot Leonard with my pistol."

"What?" Leonard shouted as he leaped out of his chair. "But I've been nothing but loyal, sir!"

I grabbed the pistol. It was definitely loaded, and the safety was off. "I'm going to have to echo his question, Mackenzie. Why waste the life of a loyal soldier? Isn't offing your underlings a bit supervillain of you?"

Mackenzie's expression was cold as ice. "Leonard has been loyal until now, but we're entering the most fragile moment of our plan. If your friends get even a hint of his existence, nothing will stop Mind's Eye from plucking every bit of information from his head psychically."

"I'd kill myself first, sir," Leonard pledged as he cowered against the door, and he was deadly serious. "The monsters would never get anything from me."

"I know you believe that, my friend, but we all know the only minds proof from the Pushed are mine and Doctor Roman's." Mackenzie turned from Leonard to me. "What harm is it? We'll bring him back soon, without even a bad dream about his demise."

I knew then he wasn't going to listen. Armed with the excuse that everything would be fixed, Mackenzie gave himself license to do anything, no matter how much it harmed others, right up to cold-blooded murder.

So, I had no choice. I raised the pistol, aimed at Leonard, then dropped into focus.

Mackenzie thought faster than I did, but I moved faster, especially now that I'd healed so much. I shifted my aim to Mackenzie before he could even flinch and pulled the trigger.

The pistol roared in my hands, and my aim was dead-on. But Mackenzie didn't fall. He didn't even recoil as if I'd hit him in an armored location. He didn't even flinch.

"Come now, Doctor Roman. Did you think I'd ever give you a gun loaded with live ammunition?"

I didn't answer – I pounced.

But Mackenzie was already stabbing the button on the remote as he dodged out of the way. My entire world spiraled into electric spasms as I crashed into the chair he'd been sitting in.

"I must commend you, though. You were clever enough to take the lesson I had taught you about Archer and turn it into a weapon against me."

Despite the incredible pain, I willed myself to rise, just like I had before, but he hit the button again. I collapsed into more convulsions as burning pain broke my focus.

"You even had me going for a few minutes. As you might say, you got me reveal my evil plans to you.

It only took a few moments, despite my best efforts, before convulsions and burning pain led to unconsciousness, a blackness I didn't expect to wake from.

Chapter 38

Much to my surprise, I woke up. My situation was far worse than it had been the last time I awoke in Mackenzie's care.

At least I had clothes on. Unfortunately, it was still the scrubs and thin sneakers instead of my uniform.

I was hanging from manacles around my wrists in a different chamber, but still in the sewers. The manacles' chains ran up a yard or so and looped through the rung of a ladder set in the old brickwork.

That ladder went up to a closed hatch set in the ceiling, and down to a small platform far below. Even further below was the faint reflection of water.

In the process of looking from top to bottom, I realized how big this new chamber was, though the dim lighting made it hard to see the full extent of the room.

The wall behind me was slick with moisture, a few of the ladder rungs pressed painfully into my back, and my feet dangled freely. Evidently, I'd been hanging long enough for the manacle cuffs to cut into my wrists and my arms to start aching.

I brought up my focus, then felt for a ladder rung with my heels. When I got a heel on one of the rungs, I put weight on it slowly. As I did so, I pulled down with my arms, trying to keep the chains taut so I kept my orientation.

"This isn't how I wanted our discussion to end, you know," Mackenzie called out. He was on a small platform to my right with an open vault door, the only significant source of light in the chamber.

I hadn't realized he was there, so I stopped any other movement, just in case.

"I have to say we agree on that point." I tried to sound upbeat. "So how are we going to do this? Mutant sewer gators? Sharks with laser guns in their foreheads? Good old-fashioned piranha?"

"This *is* pretty melodramatic, isn't it? Damn if I don't know why I didn't shoot you in the head, but this is good enough."

Mackenzie gestured at the water below. "This is a central chamber for containing and rerouting sewage. Very soon, this chamber will fill from top to bottom with raw sewage water."

"Oh, lovely."

"Redistribution doesn't start for ten minutes after it fills, possibly longer depending on who throws the switches. You drown, and no one finds your body for days. By then, it's all too late. Pretty basic, really. Now, I have a theft to perform and a city to take over."

He turned for the door. "I'm sorry it didn't work out between us. Thank you for holding off Epic these past few months. I couldn't have done this without you. Goodbye, Doctor Roman."

With that, he closed the hatch. There was the distinct sound of a locking mechanism, and I was alone in the now-complete darkness.

Time to figure out how to get out of this deathtrap.

Despite the pain in my arms from hanging around and my recent bout of electrocution, I felt in pretty good shape. That was concerning in another way - I had no idea how long I'd been unconscious - but, at that moment, it was a good thing.

I had one other advantage - this was a weak deathtrap. I'd been in some real puzzlers over the last six months, but this wasn't unbeatable, so long as I moved deliberately.

That's when it hit me. Mackenzie was a genius, one who clearly prided himself on being a planner. But this deathtrap wasn't part of his plan.

In fact, it was a sign he was giving in to the Whiteout. So Mackenzie had had to slap together this deathtrap in a hurry, especially as he seemed to be on a schedule. Meaning I needed to hurry as well.

With both heels on the same rung and my center of gravity now stabilized, I carefully turned, pulling and relaxing on the chains so I wouldn't fall.

One last shuffle and I was facing the rungs. I leaned my head forward slowly and felt a rung at forehead height. I moved one hand up, and then the other, and held onto this rung tightly.

I lifted my right leg up slowly, hoping my foot would find another rung, but my knee found it first, almost immediately. Thankfully, my knee didn't hit the metal too hard.

Just in time, as I heard the distant grind of valves and the gurgle of water filling pipes.

The real clock had officially started.

Climbing up was scarier than it should have been because of the darkness. However, the rungs were spaced at regular intervals, so I just pretended I was rock climbing and made sure I had a firm foothold before I tried to move my hands and body up.

It seemed like it took forever to reach the rung my chains looped through, but it really didn't take long at all. It was a relief all the same.

I reached up with one arm and found the rung above the chain. Grabbing hold, I climbed up a little more, so that my weight was distributed between my higher arm and the rungs I stood on.

I took a deep breath and ran my free hand over the rung my chains were attached to. I had two options - pull the rung out of the brick or break the rung itself - and which one I would chose depended on the condition of the ladder rung.

I felt a lot of flaking rust on this rung. In fact, one part in the middle of the rung was already warped, as if a great weight had hung on weak metal.

Like my body, for instance. If I'd waited much longer to start climbing, Mackenzie might've had his wish, after all. The rung would've broken, and I'd have died when I hit the platform below.

Ignoring the urge to look down pointlessly, I took advantage of this lucky break. I started to pull on the weak spot with my focused strength.

The torturous creak of rusted metal overpowered the crash of the rising waters below as the rung began to deform. I relaxed for a moment, refocused, then yanked as hard as I could.

The sudden force snapped the weakened metal, and I bent the rung a bit more for good measure. My arm ached from the exertion, but the chain was free. However, I was still manacled to it.

The rising waters sounded far too close for comfort now. I was running out of time, but I couldn't panic. Not now, when I was so close.

With a mix of speed and caution, I maneuvered the chain so that, instead of hanging down from my wrists in front of me and interfering with my legs, it hung down my back. It was still heavy and awkward, but a little less of a hazard.

Then I started climbing. In the inky blackness, I had no idea how close I was coming to my goal or how much time I had before the sewer waters engulfed me. All I could do was concentrate on moving upward, from rung to rung.

If I fell now, I'd be lost in the surging waters, dragged down by all this steel chain, and drown.

It was as much a stroke of luck as it was my physical prowess and focus that got me to the top before the water caught up with me. Thankfully, I felt the hatch with my right hand while searching for the next rung before I knocked my head onto it.

Happily, the hatch was clearly far better maintained than the ladder leading to it. Instead of having to wrench a rusty wheel open, it spun easily.

The sound of metal scraping on metal as I finished spinning the wheel gave me hope the locks had opened. With no idea where the hinges were, I had to press blindly against the hatch.

It took me a couple of pushes to feel the hatch out, and on the third push, it started to open. That was my cue to climb higher.

I wanted to give into panic and rush to get out, but I resisted. I'd die embarrassed if I slipped on this final step and fell into the waters now.

As I rose, I shoved the hatch the rest of the way open. The dim lights in the tunnel above still hurt my eyes, as they'd become adjusted to total darkness, but I kept climbing.

Only when I got into the much drier and far less filthy tunnel did I turn to look down.

The water looked like it was just about to wash over where I'd been hanging. Shuddering, I closed the hatch and quickly re-sealed it.

As I let my focus slip, aches ran through my body. It could've been far worse. With how fast I healed, I just needed a few minutes to recover. I needed to catch my breath, anyway, and it would give me a moment to get my bearings.

That's when I had the terrible realization that I had *no* idea whatsoever where I was other than underground. The lack of raw sewage or gushing water made it feel very un-sewer-like, as did the lights set into the ceiling.

My best guess was that this was part of a proper water treatment facility. It did make sense that Mackenzie had attached his lair to one, for easier and safer access to the surface and various utilities. But I couldn't be sure.

I took a deep breath. This wasn't a big problem. I just had to navigate a labyrinth of unknown tunnels with enough chains and manacles that I felt like Jacob Marley and get out before Mackenzie twisted reality like a pretzel.

At least I knew one thing - out was up. The best way to solve a maze was to pick a wall and follow it, at least until I found a ladder, stairs, or some signs to guide me.

Once again I pulled up my focus, gathered up my chains, picked the left wall, and started to follow it into the unknown.

Chapter 39

The only company I had was the clanking of my chains and my own thoughts as I made my way through the terribly confusing tunnels. I decided to make the best use of my time was to put together all the pieces of Mackenzie's plan that I'd learned.

Mackenzie was certain he could revert the Whiteout, then mentioned a theft he had to commit. That meant he was planning on stealing the neural stimulator I'd invented from the Georgia Tech campus. Either the actual device that could kickstart the Whiteout, the blueprint and research that would let him build one, or both, if he could manage it.

Meanwhile, his vampire master and her brood would sweep across Atlanta in the mother of all diversions. Who knew how many people would die in the process?

I held onto the hope that I wouldn't be too late, a hope sustained purely by the fact that Mackenzie was only now moving to complete his grand theft.

That hope was fading, because I'd passed a lot of hatches leading down and not a single thing going up. I was about to turn a corner, still hugging the left wall, when I heard something from around the bend.

Shuffling steps slowly advanced toward the corner, accompanied by pained wheezes. There was no Pulse coming either, vampiric or Pushed.

While it could be a trap, it was much more likely this was someone in trouble. To be safe, I waited by the corner, as still and silent as I could manage.

A few more steps, a groan of pain, then the source stumbled around the corner.

The high-and-tight hair, the paramilitary garb - this was Leonard, Mackenzie's aide. When I'd last saw him, he was in fear of his life and now, he was worse off.

Leonard was hunched over, one hand trying to cover a nasty wound in his gut with little success as he used the wall for support. There was a lot of blood staining his shirt and pants.

I didn't have to guess what happened - Mackenzie had carried out his own order and shot his loyal henchman. A total Whiteout move, meaning Mackenzie might be more affected by the Whiteout than I thought.

"Leonard -" I said as I took a step toward him.

He let out a shriek of terror and almost fell backward as he tried to retreat. "You're dead! He killed you before he shot me. That can only mean you're a ghost!"

Normally, that would've been a ridiculous notion, but this man had seen his dead comrades rise up as undead vampires. For Leonard, me turning into a vengeful ghost of some kind wasn't a stretch.

"No, I'm not dead." I kept advancing. "And I'm sure as heck not the Ghost of Whiteout Present. Calm down and let me help you."

Leonard shot me a feverish glance, and I thought he was going to bolt. Fortunately for him, he didn't, though he still flinched away from me. "That isn't much better. You're with the aliens invading the world."

"Are you talking about me or Mackenzie? I'll point out that I'm not the one that shot you, if that'll help you figure things out."

"I don't want to admit it, but...you're right." Clarity seemed to settle into his eyes. "Even during the test he had you do, you didn't try to shoot me. Guess you're a good person, even if you're siding with the aliens."

"That's good enough for now. Are you going to let me take a look at that wound now?"

Leonard nodded stiffly and let me approach. It only took me a few moments of examination to see that Leonard had two holes in him - an entry wound in the back and an exit wound through his abdomen.

Mackenzie hadn't just shot him - he'd shot him in the back.

My mind raced, trying to figure out how to save Leonard's life. He needed extensive medical help on the double if he was to have any chance of survival, but we needed to get out of here for that.

For the moment, I could bind his wounds far better than he could on his own. It'd buy him some time.

"I'm going to die, aren't I?" Leonard groaned as I eased him down into a sitting position so I could get to work.

"I'm going to do everything in my power to keep that from happening."

I started tearing up his fatigue shirt and my marginally cleaner scrub top into wound dressing material, leaving us both in tank-top undershirts. "But I need you to stay awake. Tell me what happened."

Leonard nodded weakly. "He shot me. I thought he was just testing you, but after you passed out, he asked me to fetch some chains. When I turned my back to him, he shot me, anyway."

He sobbed. "Why? I was a good solider. Just promise me, if I do die, I won't turn into a vampire."

With the torn-up material, I did what I could to pack and bind the wounds. It wasn't much, but it would stymie the blood loss and apply pressure.

"I promise, Leonard. You're not going to become a vampire. How did he convince your group to agree to this in the first place? Doesn't seem like a very Christian option." I cinched the crude bandage tight, and Leonard gasped. "Sorry."

"It's okay." Leonard thought about the bigger question for a moment. "Mackenzie said they'd be martyrs and would go to heaven. Guess I never believed that." He stared up at me, a haunting look in my eyes. "God doesn't make monsters like that."

"True enough." I gently helped Leonard to his feet and let him lean on me for support. "I want to do what I can to save you *and* your friends. Maybe I can stop this before they change, but to do that, I'll need your help."

"What kind of help can a dying man be?"

"To start with, I'm guessing you know how to get out of here. If we can get to surface, I can call for help, get you to a hospital, and rally my team to stop Mackenzie."

Leonard straightened up a little bit, as if my words had given him a little sliver of hope. "Okay. There's still time, I think." He pointed with his free arm back the way I'd come. "That way."

Of course I'd passed the way out. The way my Whiteout luck went I shouldn't have expected anything else. I nodded and followed Leonard's directions. My burden was heavier now, but I was determined not to falter.

We'd only backtracked a short way and taken a side corridor I'd passed following the left wall when Leonard slumped. He was clearly losing the war with consciousness.

"Come on, Leonard." I shifted more of his weight onto my shoulders so I could hold him up. "Stay with me. We can't save your friends if you don't help me."

He tried to rally, shaking his head to help him stay awake. "I'll try. In case I pass out, though…" His head started to slump again, but he caught himself. "Second left ahead, take it. Ladder there. Goes up to the treatment station proper. Exit signs plenty there."

I nodded and kept us moving. "What about your friends? Where is Mackenzie going to do this mass transformation?"

"Skyway," Leonard gasped out before going completely limp.

I felt numb. I never thought I'd hear that name ever again. Why there? Why the place where Eric's parents had lived and where he'd created the Whiteout? Had Epic left something behind that Mackenzie needed?

But that was impossible. I was there. Epic had taken away all the equipment with which he'd sullied his parents' apartment.

I snapped out of my numbness. Leonard was still dying, and the clock was still ticking - there was still time before Mackenzie enacted his master plan.

With Leonard unconscious, the only sensible thing to do was to move him into a fireman's carry over my shoulders. Extinguisher had taught the entire Foundation team basic rescue techniques, and we'd learned this one on day one.

Now, it was time to really get moving. With my enhanced strength and speed, the corridors flew by us. It only took me a few minutes to follow Leonard's directions, which led me right to a ladder clearly marked with an up arrow and the text "To Main Facility."

"Hold on, Leonard." I shifted my grip on him to prepare to climb.

Getting an unconscious victim up and down ladders had been on day five of Extinguisher's rescue class, but I'd gotten far too much practice in it.

With a man Leonard's size and a vertical rung ladder, it'd have been almost impossible, even with the right technique. But I had the advantage of my focused strength to give me enough power to manage.

It wasn't a smooth ride for Leonard, as I had to position him across my front, one arm under his armpit and the other looped through his crotch. I tried not to bump him too hard into anything, but the fact he let out a groan of pain halfway up told me I was only partly successful.

Still, I got us up and into drier air. This looked like a proper industrial facility, with decent lights and plenty of signage.

I set Leonard down for a moment so I could carry him again properly. He let out another wheeze, and I could see that he was clutching both hands over his gut wound.

I couldn't help but feel sympathy for the man. No matter the horrible things he'd done before, death was never the right solution to the problem. Dead people couldn't make amends for the past. They could only rot.

I clutched Leonard's trembling hands, trying to be soothing. "We'll get you out of this, I promise."

Despite my promise, I had to be realistic. No matter how hard I tried, the chances that this man would live were next to none.

I closed my eyes, to center myself and push on.

As I opened my eyes, I heard strange scraping and the crunch of debris under a boot sole from down the hallway to my right. In my gut, the faint twist of on-coming Pulses hit, and I was pretty sure these weren't vampire Pulses.

I wanted to call out as I opened my eyes. The only Pushed I thought would be down in the sewers were my friends, but caution took over. I didn't know who these Pushed were, and I had a charge to protect.

I pulled Leonard to the side of the hall, behind the ladder so he had a minimal amount of cover, and waited.

The boots sounded ever closer, and the scrapes now sounded like stone skidding across stone. I held my breath, ready to talk, fight, or flee depending on who turned the corner.

Two figured turned the corner, and I almost jumped for joy at the sight of them.

"Indy?" Facet's double voice - one the air, twinkling notes of her crystal lungs and the other the voice of the adopted little sister I'd known for years, pierced the silence. "Is that you?"

Relief poured into my heart as I basked in the rainbow radiance coming off Facet's body.

Once a shy, retiring electrical engineer, she was now a confident, forceful, superstrong being made of living crystal, and it felt so good to see her.

My joy redoubled at the fact Extinguisher was with her.

"Irene, thank God, you're safe." He tried to say more, but he didn't get the chance.

I crossed the distance to them in a split second, gave Facet a fierce hug, then grabbed hold of Extinguisher by the lapels of his fireman's jacket.

His eyes went wide in surprise, then melted in happiness when I greeted him properly with a deep kiss. He didn't hesitate to return the gesture, moment for moment, movement for movement.

Facet let out a chiming giggle, but I didn't care. I only cared about seeing the man I loved again.

It hit me there was something critical that'd been left unsaid for far too long. As Extinguisher and I broke our kiss, I stared deeply into his frosty blue eyes.

"I love you, Will."
"And I love you, too, Irene."

Chapter 40

Extinguisher's ice slide was crowded with four bodies, but things got easier after we delivered Leonard to Grady Memorial on our way to the Foundation building. To my surprise and relief, he was somehow clinging to life, though his prognosis still wasn't good.

The nurses on duty at the ER almost dragged me in, too, certain I was a victim in need of care, but Facet and Extinguisher cleared that up quickly.

It was still daytime as we raced toward the Foundation building, though clouds were starting to gather. Fall thunderstorms weren't uncommon in Atlanta, but these couldn't be coming at the worst time.

"How long have I been gone," I finally asked, "and what happened after the vampires snatched me?"

"Three days," Extinguisher said over his shoulder. "When you disappeared, the remaining vampires vanished into the sewers. We tracked them down, hoping they'd lead us to you, but with their mist transformation, we lost them."

"What about the vampire blood pumping? From what I got out of Mackenzie, he can transform people into vampires instantly with the right kind of blood."

"Not a drop in the pumps. It'd all been a diversion."

"Just like everything else these past few days," Facet chimed in from behind me. "When Ken and I made it back from LaGrange, everyone was frantic to find you. We pitched in immediately and, since then, we've all been dancing around, chasing leads, both to find Mackenzie and you. The Hogs have been setting off bombs across Atlanta, and little clusters of vampires have surfaced to cause havoc."

"I know you all did everything you could. Don't worry, though. Between what Mackenize told me and Leonard's help, I think I can clear it all up."

I squeezed Extinguisher's shoulder. "Ask someone to get me a uniform and have it waiting in the meeting room. I'll run everything down there as I get suited up."

"Your wish is my command, Indy."

While Extinguisher sent that message forward, I glanced back at Facet. Out in the sun, the light radiated through her body in a rainbow glow. "I know this reunion is rushed, but I'm so happy to see you again. We need you and Ken, more than you can imagine."

"Considering the mess you guys made while we were gone," she teased, "I thought that was obvious. But seriously, I've already seen what I can do to vampires by channeling sunlight."

"That's not all. Mackenzie knows about the neural stimulator."

Facet looked as if a monster from the past had risen from the grave, because it had. "Oh no. We'll stop him."

"We have to, or else these past six months have been meaningless."

I thought that statement would put me into a grim mood, but I was more resolute than worried. Yes, the stakes were high, but I wasn't alone to face them.

In fact, the whole gang was back together, including a guest star from out of town. We saved the country and probably the world once already - we could do this.

Extinguisher started to descend toward the Foundation building. His course would take us around the back of the Foundation building to enter through the all-too-familiar loading dock.

That's when I saw that there was media circling the building, including a bunch camped out in the alley now. Before Extinguisher got too low, I tugged on his jacket to get his attention.

"Don't go down. Land us on the roof. We need to take the stairs down into the Foundation proper to avoid the press."

He pulled up to stop our descent and circled over the roof. "Why? I was going to blow past them, anyway."

"Mackenzie thinks I'm dead, so let's keep it that way."

"Indy's got a good point," Facet chimed in. "Let's keep our ace in the hole in the hole for as long as we can."

Extinguisher nodded, then adjusted his course to go right for the roof access.

All the flights of stairs down made for great cardio, though Extinguisher cheated by ice sliding down most of the way. Facet and I toughed it out, though.

Honestly, it served as a reminder of how much I'd healed and rested over the past days of forced inactivity. Part of me wondered if Mackenzie had given me any pain meds, especially the ones to which I was addicted.

I'd worry about that later.

Once we exited the stairwell on the first floor, we headed straight for the meeting room.

We entered to a packed house. The rest of the Atlanta Five were there, impatient for my return. Archer was mingling with them, not secluded to his own little corner of the room any longer.

Brooks, Choi, and Ken - another sight for sore eyes - were in the midst of the huddle, comparing notes.

Everyone was working together like a well-oiled machine. All eyes turned to me and a cacophony of joyous words filled the room.

I drank in the cheers, the welcomes, the shouts for a moment, then raised my hands. "I love you all, too, and I'm glad you're all safe. I feared the worst, probably as much as you did."

"Just remember, next time you let the bad guys snatch you," Brooks said, "drop us a note so we know not to worry too much."

"What he means is that it's nice to see you safe, Indy," Choi added.

A few of the more exuberant people here, namely Tank, Ken, and Hexagon, took their chances to get in and get hugs.

By the time I disentangled myself from them, Medusa was there, holding up a bundle of leathers, boots, gloves, and underwear from my apartment. Unsurprisingly, there was a bandolier filled with sharpened stakes atop it all.

"You need these, *chica*." Her unblinking eyes were watery with happy tears. "I'm glad you're back with us."

"Thanks, Meds." I gave her a warm smile, then got serious. "Ex and Facet got me up to speed on the slide over, so let's get down to it. There's no time to beat around the bush."

I took the bundle and set it on the edge of the meeting table. "It also means there's no time to worry about personal shame. If any of you have a well-developed sense of propriety, look away."

I paused and glanced between Mind's Eye and Tank. "Maybe you better cover Tank's eyes."

Tank blushed at that, while Mind's Eye laughed. "I believe we can trust our young friend not to violate anyone's privacy. Yes, Tank?"

I laughed myself, and it felt good to know that, even with how bad things were, I could still find some humor.

As for Tank, he nodded and diligently rotated on his treads to look away, but he wasn't alone. Archer, Hexagon, and Ken all discretely looked away.

"Right, folks." I peeled off my scrubs and started to get suited up. I'd have given a lot to have the time to take a long, hot, scouring shower and get every last bit of sewer smell off me, but we didn't have it. "Let's get everyone up to speed."

It took a surprisingly brief amount of time to recount what had happened to me under Mackenzie's care. The one thing I left out entirely was Mackenzie's theory about Archer's presence.

Not because I thought Mackenzie was wrong, but because it didn't matter at this moment. Archer was on our side right now, and stirring ill will was stupid when we had the hardest fight of our lives ahead.

Outside of a few questions to clarify my story, the team listened quietly as they absorbed the details. By the time I'd finished, I's managed not only to get fully suited up, but I'd also consumed a protein bar and a couple of bottles of water.

The fuel was necessary, and it felt shockingly good to be in uniform again.

"See?" Medusa said. "You should listen to us when we say you need to get your rest."

It was half-joke and half-rebuke, but it made me chuckle. "For that, I sincerely apologize, so let's focus on the big picture."

I felt strangely clear-headed. Was it simply the forced rest or something else? I flexed my aching hand, and a distant echo in my head wondered if I wouldn't be that much more clear-headed if I took something for the lingering pain.

It took some real willpower to silence that echo.

"Skyway," Ex muttered, rubbing his chin. "We haven't heard that name since you first told us the full story about Epic and the Whiteout."

"If it's connected to Lord Epic, it must be a place of utmost importance." Archer's voice was thick with curiosity. "I can't say why, though."

"Indy, perhaps you should bring Archer up to speed," Choi suggested. "You were there, after all."

"Skyway Apartments is where the Whiteout started. Eric Beck, the man you know as Epic, jumpstarted the process there after stealing my technology to make it happen. I was there that night to confront him and try to stop him."

"Epic betrayed a lot of us that night," Ken growled. "The woman he loved," he gestured to me, "his best friend," he tapped his chest, "and his adopted little sister." Ken nodded to Facet.

"And now it's gotten worse." Anger roiled in Facet's voice like a thunderstorm. "His meddling with reality has brought back worse monsters, past monsters, like the vampires now living in his parents' home."

I couldn't see Archer's face behind his helmet, so I don't know how he reacted to these revelations. One thing I knew is that he didn't offer a defense of Epic or the Crusaders. He simply nodded slowly.

"But Skyway isn't the only problem," I reminded everyone. "I need to get to Georgia Tech and try to intercept Mackenzie himself."

Ken moved up next to Facet. "What about us? We know almost as much about the neural stimulator and where the archives are as you. We should come with you, at least."

"As much as I'd love that, you'd be best staying with Rachel and Duane to coordinate everything from here, and Facet is our ultimate anti-vampire weapon. You guys will need that firepower at Skyway, in case you don't make it in time."

"We can handle vamps either way, I'm sure." I could see the concern on Extinguisher's face. "I'm just worried about you solo against Mackenzie. The last time you two fought, he almost killed you."

"I understand, Ex, but this is different. That last fight went the way it did because Mackenzie set up everything to give him the advantage. This time, he thinks both Leonard and I are dead. He thinks no one in the world knows his plans."

I clenched my fists. "Most importantly, I'm ready. I hate to sound clichéd, but I'm chomping at the bit for a rematch."

Murmurs rippled through the team, but Facet spoke first. "I'd hate to be Mackenzie when you catch up to him. Give him an extra kick in the teeth for trying to corrupt our work."

"Indy's got this, Ex," Medusa added as she clapped me on the shoulder. "We'll take care of the vampires, don't you worry."

Extinguisher locked eyes with me. I gave him a little nod of reassurance, and he seemed to accept that. "Okay. Then that's the play. Rachel, Duane, and Ken, we're depending on you to keep us coordinated and ready to switch targets."

"Smart play," Brooks replied. "Ian was already sharp, and it sounds like he's even sharper now. This Skyway nest could be another diversion."

Choi nodded. "While you all were discussing, I pulled the financial records on Skyway Apartments. Quite a few of the recent tenants have suspected affiliations with the

Humans for God and other racist groups. Whether a diversion or not, there are Hogs to root out there."

"I'll put a call through to PART," Ken added. "They need to be ready to move if things go south, and you guys could use backup at Skyway."

"Then let's get moving, people," Extinguisher commanded. "I want us out of here ASAP." He turned to me. "Irene –"

I took his hands in mine. "Don't say good luck or goodbye. Good luck sounds like we're leaving this to chance and goodbye sounds too final."

"It's a good thing I wasn't going to say either of those things, huh?" He squeezed my hands and pulled me in for a kiss.

It's not like anyone other than Archer didn't know before now, and even he'd had an idea from what he'd said during our one-on-one talk. Besides, I didn't care anymore.

As we broke apart, we shared a brief smile. "I'm happy to be wrong this time."

Chapter 41

My new motorcycle, courtesy of the Foundation, roaring through the Georgia Tech campus caused a bit of stir, but I didn't care.

The time for stealth had passed now that I was on campus - speed was of the essence. I raced down familiar roads, then cut through pedestrian walkways and staircases.

As I'd done six months ago when the Whiteout had first hit, I didn't bother with a parking lot. I just pulled up in front of the building, parked on the sidewalk, and dashed inside the Administration building.

When I stepped into Dean Reginald Tyson's office, it felt like I'd stepped back in time. In a sense, this was where the countdown to the Whiteout had started, when Reggie had authorized the final test of the neural stimulator and I'd gotten my first hint of just what Epic had done.

I brushed the nostalgia aside as I stepped past Reggie's secretary to get through the door.

"I tried to stop her, Dean Tyson, but –" the secretary sputtered, but Reggie waved her off.

"It's fine. I don't know why Indomitable's here, but I think I can make time for the woman that saved our nation."

The secretary retreated and closed the door behind her.

Reggie focused on me now. For a split-second, I wondered if he could see past the mask and uniform to see the woman underneath. "What can the College of Sciences do for you, Indomitable?"

The power of the Whiteout was going strong, but I didn't have time to be bitter about it. "Reggie, let's cut the formality. It's me. It's Irene." I gestured at my face. "I'd take the mask off to prove it, but it's a whole production and we don't have time for it."

Reggie blinked a few times in disbelief. I almost thought the Whiteout was going to step in and fire off a wave of intrusive thoughts to knock him right down to ignorance again, but his eyes went wide.

"Oh God," he gasped as he rose from his chair. "It really *is* you. *You're* Indomitable?"

"It explains the indefinite sabbatical, you have to admit."

"Indeed it does. Do I even want to ask about Doctor Beck, or Mister Louis, or Miss Guiterrez?"

"Depending on what happens, I might not have a choice but to tell you. But let's focus. Time is short, and I'm racing against a madman to try to save the world."

"Just like something out of those comics you and Eric enjoyed so much," Reggie muttered. "Then I suppose we've rounded back to the start. What can I do to help you?"

"A very bad guy is after my research. Epic –" I didn't catch myself in time, but pressed on. "Eric's research, too, if I'm any kind of guesser. I'm hoping that you can get me access to the schematics for my old prototype and data for the neural stimulator faster than he can steal it."

"As you likely suspect, we moved both your research and Doctor Beck's to the archives. It's all under lock and key, but I'm sure that's not going to stop whoever this madman is."

He rummaged through his top desk drawer and grabbed his keys and ID card from the same place as always. "While I do love proper procedure, let's skip all that."

"Thanks, Reggie."

"You're welcome, Irene." He stopped himself. "Or is it best I call you Indomitable now? We've been very busy studying the Pushed phenomenon, but only the biological aspects, not the cultural, so if I've been addressing you incorrectly, let me know."

I chuckled despite the dire situation we were all in. "Indomitable or Indy is fine in public. By the way, if we find that our villain is currently breaking into the archives when we get there, I want you to hide and stay safe. Now, let's go."

"One last thing before we start rushing around, Indomitable." I saw an almost paternal smile on my old dean's face.

"As much as I'd prefer for you to be safe and sound, pursuing your research here at the Institute, I want to say how proud I am of you and what you've done. I knew when we first met that you'd go on to do great things - I just thought they'd be in science."

Two feelings struck me hard at the same time - joy at Reggie's warm feelings and guilt. Guilt for not letting Reggie know what I was doing sooner. And, right after that guilt, the reminder that I'd left my mother mostly in the dark crept up.

"Thank you, Reggie, I really appreciate it." I opened the door for him and stepped aside. "You've reminded me of something critical I need to do, but I can do it on the way. Lead on."

I kept enough attention on Reggie as he headed out of the administration offices to follow closely. The rest I put towards grabbing the cellphone out of my utility bag. Every time I lost or destroyed one in the line of duty, Choi would have another one waiting for me, programmed with the few phone numbers I needed.

I really wanted to call her but, at any minute, we could run afoul of Mackenzie and his goons. So I fired off yet another text instead.

> Hey, Mom. Sorry, this is brief. You know why. Sorry I haven't called more. I want to say I was busy, which I was, but that's no excuse. Let a lot of important things get away from me. Sorry for all that, but not sorry to be your daughter. Got to save the world again. If I make it through, I'll introduce you to the new boyfriend. Love you, hope to talk to you soon.

It looked far too close to some of the rambling texts I'd sent her as a teenager. Considering my life right now was ten times more turbulent than back then, this made a lot of sense.

The storm clouds were thick overhead as we rushed across campus, but the rain hadn't started yet. Some shafts of the afternoon sun still pierced the clouds, but nightfall would come soon and vampires with it.

We stepped through the doors to the College of Science's archive building. My presence alone caught the attention of the attendants on duty and, when they saw Reggie, they practically sat up at attention.

"Dean Tyson, is that Indomitable?" the head attendant asked, glancing over at me.

"Yes, it is," I answered. "The dean and I need your help, as fast as you can manage it."

"Yes, speed is crucial," Reggie agreed. "We need to be shown to the archives where Doctor Irene Roman's research and prototypes are being stored during her sabbatical."

The head attendant ran a quick search on his computer, then leaped up. "Follow me."

I sincerely hoped we weren't too late. Mackenzie had to be ahead of me by now, but I did my best to tamp down on that fear. By thinking.

If I'd learned anything about him, it was that Mackenzie was meticulous in his plans, but he was also incredibly *careful*. The fact that we couldn't find him until he was ready to find *me* was significant.

He considered himself humanity's last hope and, while he fully believed that salvation required sacrifice, he wasn't going to be said sacrifice.

That made Mackenzie move slower than other masterminds. Meaning we might still had a chance to cut him off.

We moved quickly down the halls, past numerous doors behind which were various archives, until the attendant finally stopped in front of the door marked Physiology.

"This is it." He unlocked the door, a process that involved his key, his thumbprint, and a scan of his ID. He was about to open it wide and step through, when I stopped him.

"Stay here, okay? Just in case." I looked at Reggie. "You, too."

The attendant seemed eager to follow my orders, but Reggie shook his head. "I want to see what's happened with my own eyes. I promise, if there's the least hint of trouble, I'll get right back out."

Reggie was a stubborn mule. Not that I could complain - I was just as stubborn. "Alright, fine." I nodded to the attendant. "Open it up."

He swung the door wide, staying behind it the whole way.

Not that he needed to do so. No gunfire, grenades, or hissing vampires flew out of the room. Either we'd beat Mackenzie to the punch or we were too late.

Like the majority of the archive rooms, this one was filled with long units of shelves. They were arranged alphabetically, so we moved quickly down the rows until we hit the Rs.

Again, no violence awaited us and there wasn't the least hint of anything out of the ordinary. At least there wasn't until we reached the section of shelf that should've been dedicated to Dr. Irene Roman.

That shelf was entirely empty. Not a single scrap of paper, hard drive, USB stick, or old prototype pieces remained, though I immediately saw the outlines in the dust where they'd once sat.

"Oh no." Reggie sighed. "It's like a ghost came in and spirited it all away. If we head back to the front, we can ask them to bring up the security cameras –"

"No need. I'm pretty sure I know what happened, so that'd only waste time."

All it would take is one vaporized vampire to ghost in here in the middle of the night, materialize and grab everything, then walk out the door.

"Then what do we do? I'm certain if we check Doctor Beck's archives, we'll find the same thing."

Reggie was right. I frowned, desperate to salvage anything from this situation.

"I feel like I'm missing something," I said. "This madman, Mackenzie, doesn't do anything without a purpose, and that includes luring me into this position."

"It's clearly not to spring a trap, but what if this is just part of the lure? Perhaps he did leave something behind we haven't found yet that's meant to lead you further."

Of course. I was still crediting Mackenzie with thinking like someone free of the Whiteout's influence.

"Maybe not for me. He thinks I'm dead." Reggie opened his mouth to ask a question, but I raised a hand.

"Long story. But he would want people to know what he did here."

"Then let's begin." Reggie started examining the entire shelf, but I had another idea. Or better to say Whiteout Irene had another idea.

Mackenzie is turning into your typical egotistical evil genius. He'd either leave a calling card right here, out in the open at the scene of the crime, or in a place that could be associated with him.

I only had to consider for a moment before I had a hunch. We were in an archive room, with everything sorted by the name of the scientist who invented it. Why wouldn't Mackenzie want to enshrine his own genius here?

"I'm going to check on a hunch, Reggie."

He nodded absently, his attention still on his part of the hunt.

I found the M aisle and an empty space caught my eye immediately. It was exactly where the name Mackenzie would've been filed.

But it wasn't quite empty. A folded piece of paper with "Irene" written on it in neat handwriting.

A sickening sense of déjà vu fell over me. This was the evening of the Whiteout all over again, when Epic had left a note for me after stealing the neural stimulator.

I forced the feeling out of my mind, took a deep breath, and opened the note.

Chapter 42

Irene,

If you're reading this, you've somehow survived the predicament I left you in. I thought you might, so just in case, I prepared this for you. Just so you know I still care.

I can imagine what you're feeling right now. You're shocked, hurt, angry. You can't believe this is even happening. But let me assure you, it is. I'm sure you figured out how I stole your research, but the truly important question to ask yourself is when.

I was being honest when I asked for your help with the neural stimulator, but I didn't need your help to access it or Epic's research. That's where I did lie to you – I wasn't off to some heist. I'd already committed it.

It's too hard to explain the intricacies of my plans and I'm running out of space, so I'll get to the point.

If you still hold the self-righteous need to stop me from saving the world, you'll know where to find me by the time the storm clouds blot out the sun. I won't be alone, of course. I have a member of vampiric royalty to entertain.

So please. Come to me and bring your friends. If you live long enough, we'll have a chance to see whose beliefs win out. After all, we know that belief is power, don't we?

Ian

A mixture of shock, fury, and frustration welled up inside me. Mackenzie wasn't just one step ahead of us - he was playing an entirely different game.

But something else disturbed me.

Did Mackenzie know what had happened between me and Epic that fateful night? He must have, because he'd recreated it in eerie ways, right down to some of the phrasing of this note. But how was that possible?

I knew I was starting to spiral, so I counted back from ten slowly. By the time I was done, I'd regained a bit of self-control and much needed clarity.

Intentional or not, Mackenzie had made this so personal for me that I was getting lost in my emotions. I needed to concentrate.

First things first. I needed to contact the Skyway team. It looked like Skyway was a diversion, but a very different kind of diversion than what Mackenzie had told me.

I had to make sure they were safe.

"Choi, Brooks, Ken," I called over the comms, "talk to me."

"I'm here, Indy," Ken replied. "We were just about to call you."

"Let me guess, things didn't go as we expected?"

"You could say that. Everyone's safe, though, before you ask. How's your end of things going?"

"Other than a reunion with Reggie, it's gone terribly, but we might still have a chance to save the day."

"Damn."

"You can say that again. Patch me into the team channel so we can figure this out."

"Roger that." There was a click and I was thrust into the swirling conversation of the full team's chatter.

I was met with a volley of greetings and questions, but Extinguisher got things under control fast. "People, we're short on time and answers. Let me update Indy quickly, and she'll get us up to speed on her end."

"Literally, I cannot wait."

"When we arrived at Skyway, it was filled with Hogs but they'd been vampires for a while. Any civilians had already been used as vampire chow and turned into more vampires."

"Gag."

"I know. But, in a way, this made our assault easier, because we had no innocents to worry about. And because the sun chose to peek out occasionally, Facet was able to unleash her full power and she made short work of the vampires."

"I enjoyed it," Facet said. "A lot."

"That's my girl."

"Yeah. Irene…there's more." Facet's tone told me that I wasn't going to enjoy the next part.

"Facet led us to Epic's parents former apartment," Extinguisher said. "We figured we'd look for clues there."

"And you found?"

"A note."

"Addressed to whom?"

"To the Atlanta Five."

"Oh. Goody. And it said?"

Extinguisher cleared his throat. "This was the test run. Looking forward to seeing you for the real show soon."

We were all quiet for a few moments. "Well, that tracks. Let me share the fun I've been having." I launched into my own update.

As much as I tried to keep my update like an academic report, I couldn't help but let some emotion out as I read over Mackenzie's taunting note.

"What a jerk," Tank said before anyone else. "When we catch up to him, we're going to give him what for and what five, too, because it really sounds like he's trying to taunt you and make you feel stupid but you're not, even though we've basically all been running around like crazy, and it feels like we're back at square one."

"Thanks, but you're right," I replied. "He's outthought, out-planned, and outplayed us."

"But we're not licked yet," Facet said. "Mackenzie clearly couldn't help himself, because he let some important information slip in that note."

"Facet's right," Ken agreed. "Maybe you're too close to it, Indy, but think about what he actually stole."

Those words finally broke through the emotional clouds. Of course, they would be the ones to see it, being the other two who'd been involved since the beginning.

"Of course. Mackenzie doesn't have the complete neural stimulator, because that was destroyed when Epic started the Whiteout. And he doesn't have Epic's equipment either, as it was all gone when I woke up after the flash."

"Exactly," Facet said triumphantly. "He's got all the early notes, the research, pieces of old prototypes. Whatever he's put together, because we must assume he accomplished something or else he wouldn't be acting now, it can't be a full-on God machine like Epic made."

"Thank goodness." Relief filled Extinguisher's voice. "That means we've still got a chance here."

"That's why he was trying to recruit you, Irene," Medusa hissed softly. "He needed your expertise to bring his machine to full power."

"All well and good, but we are as yet without a true inkling of his masterplan, nor where he has concealed himself," Archer pointed out.

"Maybe the bit about vampire royalty might help?" Mind's Eye asked. "It may both be a clue about the identity of this vampire mother you told us of, Indy, and about where such entertaining might take place."

"I'd guess Count Dracula," Brooks grumbled, "but he's already disqualified. Assuming anything Ian said was the truth."

"Now that I'm thinking straight, I feel I have this figured out."

That statement of mine got a lot of excited chatter from Tank, Alma, and Ken. "Go ahead, Irene," Extinguisher said once he got them calmed down.

"Considering the smaller number of famous female vampires, I've already narrowed my list down to two - Camilla, a famous literary character and the real start of the lesbian vampire trope, and the woman more like Count Dracula than most know."

"Well, a literary character couldn't be the one, right?" Ken asked, sounding unsure.

"With the Whiteout, who knows? But I'm pretty sure that Mackenzie has found Countess Elizabeth Báthory."

"Wait, do you mean the serial killer who bathed in the blood of virgins?" Mind's Eye asked. "Or are you referring to the victim of a terrible slander campaign targeting a powerful woman?

"Both."

"I can see it, so to speak," Mind's Eye said with a dry chuckle. "Countess Elizabeth Báthory was warped by folklore and horror novels into one of the most famous historical vampires."

"That holds with all the evidence we have so far," Choi said. "Again, this assumes anything Ian has said is true."

"I think they must," Mind's Eye said thoughtfully. "The best and most believable lies are grown from kernels of truth, and Mackenzie has proven a very proficient liar."

"Then perhaps, continuing the logic of the note, Mackenzie would entertain an illustrious foreign noble in a diplomatic fashion," Archer suggested. "An embassy, perhaps, or a seat of government."

"The State Capitol, maybe?" It felt right as I said it. "We have to assume that Mackenize has Epic factored into this plot, as well. He wanted my help, and he fears Epic is about to go on the warpath with his Crusaders. So a big, public move to take over the city would attract Epic's attention and force him to act."

"It's not about the city." Medusa sounded utterly confident.

"She's right," Facet said, and my mind was already snapping back to my conversation with Mackenzie as Extinguisher said what everyone was already thinking.

"It's about you, Irene. Mackenzie intends to use you as bait to bring Epic here."

My fists clenched involuntarily. I was sick of being used and manipulated by arrogant men who thought they were smarter than me, knew what was best for me. Mackenzie was no better than Epic, at this point.

"Then let's get moving. Mackenzie said I'd know what he was doing by the time the storm clouds blot out the sun."

"Hate to break it to you, Indy," Hexagon cut in, "but it's near pitch black out here."

"Reggie, I'm going!" I shouted. "Take cover and find all the silver crosses you can!"

I broke into a run. Whatever Mackenzie intended to do, it was going down, and we all knew it.

Extinguisher was calling out orders to the team, while Choi, Brooks, and Ken went into action themselves, checking in with PART and emergency services.

However, it was Mind's Eye's sudden cry of pain over the comms that confirmed the worst.

"What happened?" I asked as I ran for my motorcycle. "Are you okay?"

"I will be," she replied, but the pain lingered in her voice. "Atlanta, however, is in dire peril. A sudden wave of anguish rose up just now, the cries of thousands of minds all dying at once, and now, there is only the blank darkness the vampires leave behind in their place."

My heart sank. "He said Skyway was a test run. What he told Leonard and me wasn't fully a lie. He *does* have a way to turn people into vampires almost instantly."

"He simply lied about the location to us," Mind's Eye said. "Truly, a diversion, but of an entirely different sort than we believed."

I burst out of the archive building to see the sky filled with ominous black thunderclouds. It might as well have been nighttime, which I was sure suited the vampires just fine.

"This changes nothing," Extinguisher said with his usual firm confidence. "One vampire or a million, we still have a city to save."

He was right, of course, and I'd made it this far through the insanity of the Whiteout by never giving up. It was, I realized, my real superpower.

"And we're going to do just that," I matched his confidence with my own. "I'll see you all at the Capitol."

Chapter 43

Rain started to fall as I raced towards the location for Mackenzie's grandstand.

He'd picked the time for this attack well, because it was now smack dab in the middle of evening rush hour. Atlanta traffic was infamous before the Whiteout, and it'd only become more awful since then.

That wouldn't stop me. I dropped into focus, ready to break a ton of traffic laws, since I'd need my heightened senses and reflexes not to kill myself or anyone else.

I used my motorcycle's agility to weave in between vehicles as I tried to maintain a high speed.

That got me, the Nationally Acclaimed Superhero, an assortment of screams, shouts, honking horns, and obscene gestures. Some things never changed, no matter how Epic tried to twist reality.

"My ETA is ten minutes tops," I reported over the comms.

"We're trying to match that," Extinguisher replied. There was the sound of battle over his comms. "But we've got vamps trying to chow down on the passengers of a MARTA bus and every pedestrian nearby."

I couldn't blame my friends for intervening. They were superheroes, after all. "Understood. If I get there first, I'll do what I can."

"I don't want to make the situation sound worse," Choi said, "but we're already getting reports of unnatural intruders in the Capitol building. Ex, can you divert some of the team to go straight to the Capitol to protect the Governor and other state officials?"

"Roger that. I'll send Mind's Eye and Tank ahead."

I gave my motorcycle all the gas I could. "I'll meet them there."

The situation degenerated fast as I approached the State Capitol. It was clear this was where Mackenize had unleashed the majority of his vampiric forces, and havoc ran rampant in the streets.

Hasty barricades set up by the Atlanta Police and PART were in various states of disarray as vampires swarmed through the streets and over the grounds of the Capitol.

Most of those posts were abandoned, though I saw a small group making a stand at the main entrance. I hoped this meant that Mind's Eye and Tank were already inside.

The groans of the dead and dying mingled with the bursts of gunfire and the whine of unleashed superhuman energies. The collective Pulses, both Pushed and vampiric, almost overwhelmed me, but I kept it together.

I drove up onto the main walkway, heading for the steps of the Capitol. In the process, I ran over two vampires and even got in a drive-by staking.

I was about to head right up the steps to join the remaining defenders when a woman conjured herself out of the swirling fog of war around me.

She stood between me and the front steps. Before I could even decide if I was going to run her down or swerve aside, she moved forward with inhuman speed. She swiped her hand like a claw across the front end of my motorcycle and sliced it into ribbons.

I leaped off the bike before she tore through the rest of it and got to me. I tumbled hard on the stone walkway, protected by my helmet and motorcycle armor, and came up in a crouch to face the woman.

To call her a woman didn't begin to describe what was before me. She was so unreal, so inhuman, that I thought my eyes would burst just trying to force the two images to coexist.

One was of a woman of noble bearing, looking as if she'd stepped out of a medieval portrait, but dressed in modern elegance. The other was a pulsing, flowing pile of ashes and decayed dust underneath the shell of unreality.

There was none of the vampiric Pulse I'd grown accustomed to coming from her.

Instead, the aura that filled the air was some darker, primal drumbeat that shuddered through my soul, an ancient thing that was only a distant cousin to the Whiteout I'd become familiar with over the last six months.

This had to be the master vampire, the mother, as Mackenzie had called her. Also, as we'd deduced from his clues, I knew exactly who she was.

"Countess Elizabeth Báthory, I presume?" I asked, trying to process both the unreality of her form and the fear beating in my heart.

Báthory didn't deign to speak as she moved to grab my throat. Still in full focus from the race to get here, I avoided her hand and tried to meet her lunge with a stake drawn from my bandolier.

She swatted the stake out of my hand like candy from a misbehaving child, then followed that with a dismissive backhand.

It was so fast that all I could do was roll with the hit. I must've still had some degree of resistance to whatever ancient Whiteout powered Báthory, but that strike hurt more than any hit I'd taken from a Pushed.

The impact sent me hurtling backwards. I hit the Capitol lawn and kept going, tearing a line through the greenery until I finally came to a rest.

"What disgusts me more than the transformation that centuries of lies and slander caused in me is the lack of respect the people of this horrid age pay to their betters," Báthory snarled in accented English.

"Imagine my surprise when one of you had the decency to present an option that didn't involve stakes, crosses, or accusing priests."

I scrambled to my feet as she glided closer. "Mackenzie, I presume? You can't believe him, Countess."

"Why can't I? I have all the advantages. If he dares move against me or my brood, I'll simply snuff him out like a candle."

She tried to look into my eyes, but I'd read up on my vampire folklore. I avoided her gaze, just in case she could hypnotize me.

"If Sir Mackenzie requires an army to fight his age's brand of hero, so be it. It's not like I haven't played out this tale before."

Báthory blurred forward again, but I was prepared this time. I knew I couldn't grab or hurt a body made of ash, but I could use her true form to my advantage.

I didn't dodge away, but dove *through* the cloud of ashes.

To her surprise, and a little of my own, I burst out her back, rolling to my feet as soon as I hit the ground.

This situation was spiraling out of control fast, especially as a good number of the vampire Hogs gathered into a mob in the streets below us. My only chance was to keep trying to negotiate with Báthory until the rest of the team got here.

"Things have changed since you two made your agreement." The fact that Báthory was now patiently listening to me made me even more uneasy.

I kept talking anyway. "Mackenzie used you to get a hold of something more powerful to do his work for him. He told me himself he's going to get rid of you and your vampires the second he has the power to do so."

"Intriguing, but any desperate ploy on his part is sheer folly, my dear."

Báthory smiled, showing her fangs as she stalked slowly in my direction. "If you haven't felt it in the marrow of your bones yet, let me assure you that I'm unlike anything your low-minded future can comprehend. I was forged from the dreams and nightmares of an age of true faith and every time I've awoken since I've only grown stronger."

She let out a short, derisive laugh. "If you represent the best hopes and dreams of this modern age, humanity has lost its capacity to imagine. You might, however, be worthwhile to keep alive for some time to hang on my torture rack and entertain me."

The creeping black terror she exuded threw off the aim of my first stake, but damn if I didn't throw it despite that. The shaft sank into her undead flesh and tickled the ashes underneath.

Báthory let out a cry of surprise and pain as she gripped the stake in her left shoulder and ripped it free. I think she so believed in the terror she invoked that she didn't think it was possible for me to attack her.

That's why the second stake really surprised her. Still, after my first attack, Báthory's instincts were sharp enough that she threw her forearm in the way.

If I was going to get killed by a relic of mankind's dark past, I was going to die standing on my two feet, not broken on her or anyone else's torture rack.

"Very well, peasant," Báthory snarled as she pulled the stake out of her arm. "I'll leave you to be scraps for my dogs." She snapped a finger, and the pack of vampires idling at the base of the steps charged.

"We've got your back, Indy," Extinguisher called over the comms.

A wall of solid ice sprung up in the vampires' path, curved slightly to keep them contained. The was immediately followed by a chorus of inhuman shrieks and I saw the wooden points of crossbow bolts come through the ice. Nice to see Extinguisher and Archer teamed up.

"And the sad thing is that still puts you one up in the save column on me, Indy," Extinguisher called out as he streaked overhead on his ice slide.

To say that he was unhurt would be a lie. His coat was ragged with tears and holes and the blood on his uniform wasn't entirely the vampires'.

Still, to see him up and fighting gave me a spark of hope to hold on to.

"Fear not, Indomitable, the others are close behind us." Archer hopped over the ice wall with a burst of his jet pack and leveled his crossbow at Báthory. "Now please, with all due respect, Your Ladyship, I request you stand down, or I will be forced to fire."

Báthory smiled slowly at the two Push Heroes. "Ah, so these are the true heroes of your age." She glanced back at me. "You're but a normal girl playing at being more than you are. That explains everything."

Báthory turned to Archer then. "Unfortunately, good sir knight, I would request that you stand down instead. I could use a noble warrior like you in my court and would not wish to slay you where you stand."

She cast a glance at Extinguisher as he spiraled down for another pass. "The same offer stands for your occult friend, as well."

"I must respectfully decline, Your Ladyship." Archer fired his bow with a loud twang as Extinguisher unleashed a spray of frost to hold Báthory in place.

I sprang into action, too. I certainly wasn't going to let some reawakened corpse from hundreds of years ago ignore me.

My accelerated mind could barely keep up with the sudden burst of speed Báthory put on. Archer's bolt landed nowhere near close to her, while Extinguisher's blast of frost was even farther off target.

I was the closest, but my fingers only barely touched the edge of her ashen form before she slipped away.

Before I could turn to follow her movement, I heard the crunch of metal as Báthory held Archer aloft, her white claw of a hand slowly crushing his neck guard.

Another second or so and Báthory would pop off Archer's head like a cork, no matter how much he struggled and kicked.

Extinguisher swept past me on his ice slide. We didn't need comms or words or even a gesture to fall into rhythm. I knew exactly what he was planning as I jumped on behind him, grabbing hold as he accelerated.

The plan was simple - he'd accelerate as fast as possible so I could get Archer free.

I wasn't sure we would be there in time to save him, even with teaming up, but we weren't the only ones making the save.

I don't know how Medusa silently slithered close to the action, but she did. She sprang up behind Báthory and grappled with her.

As the struggle began, Medusa's snakes plunged their fangs into the vampire's dead flesh in a dozen locations.

"Let him go and let's talk," she hissed, a depth of rage I'd never heard before dripping from her words. "One mythological monster to another, *sí*?"

Báthory let out a slight gasp as Medusa's venom fought with infernal regeneration, and each bite wound started to turn to stone. Báthory dropped Archer to the ground and twisted to pry Medusa off her.

The two struggled and finally locked eyes. As Extinguisher and I swept past, I pulled the ailing Archer onto the slide and free of the clash of unnatural forces - vampiric hypnosis versus gorgon petrification.

"Get ready to drop Robin Hood off before we go in again," Extinguisher called back to me.

I grunted an acknowledgment, and we dropped Archer off behind the still-intact police barricade at the entrance to the Capitol.

The remaining police and PART officers fired into the masses of vampires. They weren't effective at all, but they provided some cover for Archer, at least.

Extinguisher and I sliced our path hard and away, back toward where Medusa and Báthory fought.

"Got a plan, Ex? The only idea I've got is to get Facet here and get her some sunlight."

"That'd be great," he admitted as he picked a good path of attack. "If you know a weather manipulator around, you call them in, too, assuming night hasn't already fallen."

That reminded me of another rare bit of vampiric lore – in some myths, the most powerful vampires could control the weather.

"Those clouds won't disappear until Báthory's down, but I don't plan to give up. How about you, sugar?"

"I'm raring and ready for round two."

A smile crossed my lips as I squeezed Extinguisher's shoulder. "Let's go get her."

Chapter 44

The struggle between the two creatures of legend was ongoing as Extinguisher and I swooped down to them.

Medusa's sinewy muscles were tensed as she tried to fight the hypnotic sway of Báthory's vampiric gaze. Meanwhile, Báthory's regenerative powers tried to overcome the creeping petrification from Medusa's supernatural vision.

As Extinguisher brought us within safe jumping range, Báthory snarled and narrowed her gaze. Medusa made a strangled cry as her gaze abruptly swept up at us.

Extinguisher pulled up hard, saving us from a future as garden statuary, but the weird energies of Medusa's gaze turned the ice slide under our feet into a solid hunk of stone.

Gravity instantly grabbed a hold of the rock and threw it - and us - towards the earth. My reflexes kicked in as I grabbed Extinguisher and jumped free.

I didn't need to ask for the snowbank Extinguisher conjured up to break our fall. As we fell into fluffy coolness, I was already prepared to get going.

If Báthory had all the powers a vampire of folklore had, it was only moments before Báthory commanded her new Medusa puppet to sweep her gaze across the final line of human defenders in the Capitol.

I rolled out of the snowbank, intent on stopping that. I was halfway across the yard to where Báthory and Medusa stood when Medusa grasped her head and dropped to her knees.

Báthory turned from Medusa, but the smug smile on her lips turned to shock when she saw me. "Get up, beast, and do my bidding!"

Quarter-way there.

"You vile monster," Mind's Eye's voice called out from the Capitol building floating in the air over the lines of defense, "how dare you try to twist my friend's mind?"

She floated over the barricade at the entrance to the Capitol. She snapped her fingers, and Medusa shook her head, looking dazed.

Báthory bared her fangs at Mind's Eye as ripples of mental force cascaded out from the psychic, lifting two wrecked police cruisers into the air.

Right behind Mind's Eye, the Human Tank roared up, taking aim as both of his arms glowed with a building charge of energy.

"Go back from where you came from and disturb the living no more," Mind's Eye roared.

That was plenty enough warning for me of what was about to come. Just before all hell broke loose, while Báthory was still focused on Mind's Eye, I snatched Medusa and got us out of the blast radius.

A split second later, the air burned with Tank's plasma discharge, just as Mind's Eye sent both cars hurtling at Báthory. There was a burst of superheated flames, followed by a cloud of shrapnel and debris as the cars smashed into pieces.

Medusa and I turned to look at the results of the carnage as clouds gathered overhead.

Rain began to drizzle down as a pall hung over the battlefield. Extinguisher rose out of the snowbank on a fresh ice slide while Medusa and I kept backing from the growing conflagration.

Hexagon bounded over the Capitol's gold dome with a very tired-looking Facet in his six arms. He landed beside

Archer, still recovering from his throttling at Báthory's hands, and set Facet on her own two feet.

The gang was all here, but it seemed as if the fight might be over.

"There," Mind's Eye said confidently as she dusted off her hands. "Now let us find Mackenzie and end this farce."

Tank was about to say something, but a loud rumble of thunder interrupted the young cyborg. Nothing stirred from the wreckage, but something wasn't right.

That ancient primal energy wasn't gone. Not by a long shot.

"Wait, it's not over," I shouted, but it was too late.

A tremendous lightning bolt blasted down from the roiling clouds and struck Tank dead center, ignoring every lighting rod on the Capitol roof, every porch, and every other metal object.

For a moment, the electricity danced over his protective shields before they violently collapsed from the strain. When the lightning faded, Tank was sizzling and smoking. If I hadn't seen his chest heave, I'd have assumed he was dead.

Mind's Eye's blind gaze widened in shock as Báthory suddenly materialized out of the growing fog. Before Mind's Eye could defend herself, Báthory grabbed the psychic by her sash and slammed her into the hard stone floor.

The impact was sickening as thunder rumbled ominously overhead.

"I need Archer," Choi cut in over the comms. "Can you spare him?"

"If it'll save our lives, he's all yours," I answered as I pulled Medusa up to her feet.

"By your leave then." Archer retreated behind the barriers while the others still up sprang into action.

Hexagon rushed forward, Facet moved to the nearest light source - one of the still functional streetlamps, and Extinguisher flew on an approach to flank Báthory.

"C'mon, Meds." I kept Medusa steady as she tried to her bearings. "We're not done yet."

"Her mind is so old, so twisted, so powerful. What can we possibly do to stop her?"

"We'll do whatever we can. We're heroes, after all." I forced myself to smile, which seemed to help Medusa focus.

While I was rousing Medusa, Hexagon was unleashing a barrage of inhumanly strong blows at Báthory while cagily staying under cover of the Capitol overhang.

He didn't have had any luck laying a glove on the insanely fast vampire, but every time it looked like she'd go on the attack, Facet sent a pulse of focused light from the streetlamp through her body that drove Báthory back.

Between the two working together, Báthory seemed to be held at bay.

Extinguisher took that as a chance to grab Mind's Eye and pull her to safety. Meanwhile, Medusa ran past me to check on Tank.

I looked for an opening to strike. Maybe if Hexagon could lay his hands on Báthory, he could hold her just long enough for me to stake her.

I drew my last stake. For a moment, I wondered where Mackenzie was, and what he was up to. There was no way he didn't have a hand in this battle. But how?

I didn't know, but the fact he hadn't struck yet was starting to make me paranoid.

Hexagon swung a wall of backhands at Báthory. She had to turn to mist to avoid the attack. But as she reformed behind him to strike, his other three arms pivoted back and hit her full force.

Báthory rocketed through the air from the tremendous blows, hitting and shattering through one of the porch's pillars.

Her flight didn't stop until she hit the Capitol lawn and dug a deep furrow in the earth. Only then did she finally come to a rest.

That was my opening. I sprinted down the muddy lawn to build speed and pulled my crucifix from my neck with my free hand. I only had one shot at this, so I had to make it count.

Using all my speed, I leaped over the edge of the furrow Báthory's body had dug. She was still sprawled out there but already starting to stir. As I plummeted towards her, I presented the crucifix forward and instantly felt a tremendous pressure in what I could only call my soul.

Two unidentifiable but tangible forces clashed as I landed knees-first on top of Báthory. My cross-wielding arm wavered as that dark, primal evil pushed deeper and deeper.

A faint voice echoed in my head, the same voice that had urged me on in my addiction. This time, though, it urged me to surrender. After all, wouldn't it be easier to just give up? There wasn't anything someone like me could do to stand up to so much darkness.

I gritted my teeth and focused. I didn't give up when the Whiteout happened. I didn't give up when I was tied up to a tent pole in Washington. I didn't stop when Epic and Reaper were tearing apart an entire city.

I kept going even when my body was failing and addiction chewed at my mind.

I sure as hell wouldn't give up now.

Báthory and I locked gazes then. For the first time, I felt an outside psychic presence in my mind, but my Natural defenses still filtered it. Her twisted, ancient mind was indistinct through all the mental static, but Medusa was right. It was horrifying on a level I couldn't put into words.

But I didn't have to, I just had to win. And what had been a contest of faith with the crucifix now turned into a battle of willpower. It was the one arena where I might reign supreme, and I wasn't going to let fear spell the end of me, the man I loved, the friends who cared for me, and the city I was born in.

Slowly, relentlessly, I brought the stake down into position over Báthory's heart.

I was so focused on the battle of wills that I didn't hear the fresh wave of vampires running over the Capitol lawn. I didn't hear the desperate stand my friends were making around me. I only noticed the vampire Hogs when they grabbed me by both arms and pulled me away.

Suddenly, the pressure on my soul was gone, and I was struggling in the grasp of two beefy vampires.

I let out a primal yell and pulled hard on my captors' arms, tearing decaying flesh clean from the sockets. I instinctively lashed out, staking one before smashing the other upside the head with the undead arm now in my grasp.

Things had just gone from bad to worse as I turned towards where Báthory had been. She was gone.

Not for long, though, as Báthory materialized like a cheap jump scare in front of me. Before I could react, her eerie, unbreakable grip, composed of writhing ashes, curled around my neck.

"You insufferable brat of a woman," Báthory roared as she hoisted me into the air. "How dare you resist me? For that sole offense, I'm going to drain every drop of life from your body and use your own strength to murder your friends."

She reared back, and her jaws unhinged like a monstrous snake.

I snarled in defiance and threw a few hard kicks at her body, but the impacts didn't disrupt her ashen form enough to free me.

It looked like I'd cheated Death one time too many, and he was finally going to collect.

Before Báthory could make good on her threat, though, the sky lit up with an all-too-familiar white flash. Before my eyes could clear, I heard a booming voice.

"I think not, monstrosity," Epic's voice bellowed. My eyes cleared as Báthory dropped me and turned to her new aggressor. "Her life and the lives of all who dwell in this city are now under Epic's protection!"

That must have been what Choi needed Archer for – to call in the big guns.

As I looked up to see Epic flanked by a half-dozen Crusaders descending through the rain like the Second Coming, I wasn't sure if I preferred being saved by him over becoming vampire food.

Chapter 45

I rolled away from Báthory's feet. Knowing Epic's usual tactics, the immediate area around her was going to be very unsafe, even to me.

True to form, before Báthory could say a word in response to Epic, a barrage of pure white beams from his hand filled the air.

When the barrage cleared, the ground was mulched and cratered, but the vampire remained, smoking but still standing.

Epic's six Crusaders arced out over the battlefield away from their leader. My best guess was that they were heading to clusters of vampiric activity to throw back Báthory's army.

I could recognize most of them from the files Choi and Brooks had collected - Battalion, the one-man army, Fray Justicia, a Mexican priest turned holy masked *luchador*, Wavelength, the living rainbow, and Gaslight, steampunk inventor extraordinaire. A couple I didn't know and, frankly, I didn't much care who they were.

I flipped up to my feet as Archer landed beside me in one jet-assisted bound.

"Indomitable –" he started to say as Báthory moved to meet Epic head-on. Lightning cascaded down from the unnatural storm overhead, but it did nothing to slow the nigh-invincible Push Hero.

Unfortunately, it did do quite a number on the Capitol building.

"Not now," I told Archer. "We need to regroup."

He nodded curtly and grabbed me under my arms. His jets flared, and I braced for the inevitable acceleration as we took to the air. There were times like this when I wished that Pushtech worked for me – a suit of armor and a jet pack would make this hero gig a lot easier.

We landed on the far side of the Capitol lawn, away from the raging fight. We were safe for a few moments, but not for long. The battle between Báthory and Epic was intensifying.

What was surprising was that it wasn't over already. Epic could do almost anything, after all, so dealing with a vampire, even an ancient one like Báthory should've been easy.

I chewed on that as the rest of the team gathered around us. Everyone was in various states of disrepair.

Extinguisher, battered and bloody, supported Mind's Eye as she swayed unsteadily on her feet, holding onto her lower back.

The Human Tank's cybernetic parts were still sparking and spasming, making him seem more like a broken appliance than anything else, but he managed to move.

Now that I was up close to Facet, I could see that parts of her crystalline skin were smoky and cracked, as if they'd been overloaded.

Hexagon was the most unhurt of us, kneeling beside Medusa as she clutched her head. Having felt a little touch of Báthory's mind myself, I could only imagine how much it hurt Medusa to feel the vampire's full power.

"Good work, team." I tried to sound upbeat. "We're all still alive."

"This won't last if we don't think of a real plan soon," Mind's Eye muttered between groans.

"That's why I summoned forth a contingent of Crusaders," Archer said. "Dame Choi insisted I do so. She said it was your plan, actually, one you entrusted with Sir Brooks."

That made me remember my conversation with Brooks before we entered the sewers. "Of course. She wants to light Báthory up with sunlight."

"It should work," Facet said, "just like when I channeled sunlight through Skyway." She rubbed one of her cloudy facets. "Might've overdone it, though."

"I do regret summoning my lord." Archer sounded genuinely concerned. Maybe he was starting to realize Epic might be up to no good. "If there were any other way –"

"Don't worry about it none," Hexagon reassured him. "We need the help. This ain't just a Push Battle, this is a fight for our city. One we were losing, I might add."

"Maybe, but we won't let the Crusaders have all the fun, will we?" Medusa was starting to sound a bit like her usual self as she pushed up to her feet. Both Archer and Hexagon gave her a hand-up, then shot each other a brief glance.

While the others were talking, I was thinking. As Choi and Archer had brought Epic in specifically with my plan in mind, why hadn't he already started with a portal to the sun?

That's when Mackenzie wormed his way back into my mind. I'd been wondering what he was doing to influence this battle, and I had a terrible realization as to how.

"We have a larger problem, one that I think is stopping Epic from doing we need him to do." I scanned the area. "We don't know how long Mackenzie has had the neural feedback or reality machine research."

Facet's crystalline form couldn't pale, but her true form underneath could. "Do you think he actually created a working device of some kind?"

"Does that mean he can change the world or some junk, but no, if he could do that wouldn't he have already ended this with him winning and stuff?" Despite the damage to his systems, it was refreshing to see that Tank still had the gift of gab.

"He clearly doesn't have a fully powered device. The thing Epic used filled half an apartment. However, I think Mackenzie has something like a prototype. Something that he's using to influence reality subtly."

"Like dampening Epic's powers?" Ken asked over the comms. "From what you told us about how this works, if he even got the neural stimulator working and calibrated, it sounds possible."

"Then whatever doodad Mackenzie has is our goal," Brooks said.

"Doodad?" Tank cut in. "Is that the scientific term?"

"In truth, 'doodad' is used quite commonly by the scientifically inclined," Archer replied.

"Focus up," Ken, of all people, called over the comms. "Quips are great, but there's vampires eating people across town, so we need to beat this lady fast."

"Copy that, Ken," I replied, a little proud of him. He'd come a long way since the Whiteout.

I took a look at the battle. Epic landed a good uppercut into Báthory's chin that sent her flying into the sky, then unleashed a column of energy into her.

I understood that vampires were supposedly almost immortal, but that much pure energy should have atomized anything physical.

It had very little effect on Báthory. She slammed into the ground, but as Epic sped toward her, she was already on her feet, fully regenerated.

"We need to find Mackenzie and take him out. Epic plus Facet is how we win this." I glanced at Extinguisher, a little gesture to ask if he wanted to take the lead or let me.

He gave me a small nod - it was all me this time.

That was for the best. I knew the weapon involved, I knew Mackenzie pretty well at this point, and I was comfortable in my own mask.

"Okay, team, here's the plan." I gestured toward the raging battle. "I need to talk to Epic. He's the only person more knowledgeable about whatever device Mackenzie has than me. Support him and divert Báthory, except for you, Tank."

Tank had been trying his best to look ready for action, but I didn't need to be a robotics engineer to know he was badly damaged. "But, Indy –"

"But nothing. You need to hang back for now and engage your self-repair circuits." That was the Pushtech way Tank regenerated like the rest of the Five. "We're not going to have anyone die today."

"Listen to her, please," Mind's Eye said. "For me, if nothing else."

Tank hung his head. "Okay, Miss Eye, I promise I won't do anything stupid, and I'll try to fix myself up as fast as I can, then I'll try to help, and even so, I can help keep an eye out for Mackenize, right?"

I nodded. "If you lay eyes on Mackenzie, let me know, but I doubt he'll show his face unless he has to."

"I'd assume that by 'has to' you mean when we're about to undo his plans with Báthory," Mind's Eye said.

"Yes, but I also hope Mackenzie will realize Epic and I are conspiring. That should get him worried. We're the two biggest dangers to his plans, after all."

"Alright, you heard the lady," Extinguisher said with all his usual confidence. "Let's go get that monster."

Despite injury, pain, and mental anguish, everyone who could still fight turned towards the clash of titans not a hundred yards distant and headed once more into the fray.

Chapter 46

I sprinted toward the battle but, as we got close, I cut to the left, towards the fringe of the lawn. I only hoped Epic would listen to reason and follow the plan.

"Mockery of life, I will bring you to heel," Epic bellowed as he slammed his hands together, creating a tremendous pressure wave that would've blown Báthory away if she hadn't turned to mist once more.

It still scattered her gaseous form, but not for long.

Archer's message must've reached Epic then, and he began to float back from the melee. Though he wasn't looking at me, he was clearly moving so that our paths would intersect.

As mist-form Báthory began to flow after him, an invisible wall of telekinetic force cut her off, followed immediately by a giant slab of ice dropping down on the mist.

Unified by the field of unreality around her, Báthory was forcefully ejected out one side. Off-balance, the vampire took her physical form once more, right in front of a waiting Hexagon.

"Eric, we have a problem."

The demigod arched an eyebrow at the use of his real name. Under the larger-than-life shell, I could see that Eric himself seemed drawn, almost prematurely aged.

"I thought that name was dead to you, Indomitable. Why do you wish this parlay when there is evil to be destroyed?"

He was correct. I'd said that the last time we'd a peaceful conversation, and I'd meant it. But the crisis at hand didn't need Epic, at least not at this moment.

"The real threat isn't that walking corpse. The real threat is Ian Mackenzie using the technology Eric Beck and Irene Roman invented."

That got Epic's attention as, across the field, Hexagon unleashed a bruising series of punches against Báthory, driving her against the block of ice Extinguisher conjured behind her.

"Impossible."

"Not if he's working off old notes, old theories, and old prototypes. However he's doing it, he's managed something - not quite what you did, but close enough to be a big problem. So stop with any kind of impossible and let's focus on reality."

Out of the corner of my eye, I saw Báthory gaze at the big six-armed powerhouse. Hexagon began to succumb to her hypnotic glare, but not before Archer unleashed a warhead-tipped bolt that exploded into a barrage of wooden splinters a few feet from Báthory.

That caused her to howl in pain, but no lasting harm.

"I assume then he has the neural stimulator as well?" Epic asked, his voice and the demeanor were more and more that of the brilliant scientist I'd once known.

"All the notes and blueprints, but not the actual device. Not that he probably hasn't rebuilt it, or at least an earlier prototype, already. The important thing is that he's here, watching, using whatever tech he cobbled together against us."

"That explains why my vast powers feel constrained. I attempted to rip open a hole to the sun, a simple task usually, but I couldn't."

"Right, that's what I thought." I looked Eric, not Epic, in the eyes. "I know he's immune to your omnipresence, the same as me, but can you find him with, I don't know, x-ray vision and ultra hearing? He's not invisible."

Epic looked away from me and swept his eyes over the battlefield. After a moment, he looked back at me, frustration knitting his bow. "My supreme senses feel as limited as my powers. More of Mackenzie's foul work, no doubt."

"Then how do we counter this tech?"

"I don't have an answer. The effects of any God machine based on my work can only be counteracted by an equal application of God particles. If it were a simple contest of, say, you versus Mackenzie, your will would crush his, no doubt. But, without the brainwave amplification loop from the stimulator, it would take thousands of believers all focused on counteracting his desires to stop him."

"What about power concerns? I know you had a lot of conduits in Skyway routing power to the God machine to make the Whiteout."

Thunder echoed in my ears as an enraged Báthory called down a barrage of lightning on Archer. He would've been fried if he hadn't already been jetting away.

Medusa took the opening to pounce, injecting Báthory with a full dose of her petrifying venom before collecting a swift backhand for her efforts.

Slowed as parts of her body turned to stone and instantly regenerated, Báthory found herself suddenly enclosed in a solid block of ice by a wave of Extinguisher's hand.

Medusa wiped blood from her mouth and nose as she stared hard at the ice. The block instantly turned to stone.

"The lack of electrical power to the device limits its effect and range," Epic continued, "but we can't know its full capabilities otherwise. If he can channel even a small mass of

God particles all tuned to a specific fervent belief, he can do almost anything in a very small space. Nothing can stand up to the power of raw reality."

"That can't be true." I grabbed Epic by the shoulders, his real shoulders. "I resisted the Whiteout, so did Mackenzie. It can't be impossible to resist this."

"Then I think that the person you need to ask for help isn't Eric Beck or even Epic. You should instead speak to Irene Roman. Only she might know how she resisted the God machine."

Epic shrugged out of my grasp as a glowing white aura gathered around him. "Act swiftly, my love. I fear Mackenzie's influence over our reality will only grow the longer he uses the device."

He jetted forward, leaving a shockwave in his wake.

I was confused for a split-second, then realized Epic knew the answer, but expected me to figure it out for myself.

I didn't need to ask myself how I'd resisted the Whiteout. I didn't need to ask myself how I wasn't being affected by whatever Mackenzie was doing. I was just confident that I *was* immune to whatever power Mackenzie had found for himself.

He certainly hadn't dampened my abilities or granted Báthory the strength to take over my mind. I was, as I'd reminded myself only a couple of hours ago, a stubborn mule. I didn't believe in the Whiteout because I actively *chose* not to believe.

That meant Epic wasn't the real threat to Mackenzie – *I* was. And Mackenzie was using what he knew of my character to distract me now. He knew I wouldn't be able to turn away from this no-win battle as long as my friends and the man I loved were in danger.

But the only way to win was not to play Mackenzie's game. Just like the test with Leonard, Mackenize would always cheat.

I *could* break the rules, though. If I could find him, I could break Mackenzie's machine without fear he'd Thanos-snap me out of existence.

None of this stopped the battle swirling before me, though. Báthory was still encased in her new tomb, and the rest of the team was gathering to try to end this.

"All together now," Extinguisher shouted over the roaring winds and thunder.

Hexagon hefted a car over his head. Archer loaded one more bolt as he helped Medusa to her feet with his free hand. Mind's Eye telekinetically gathered a bevy of wooden debris into a cloud of projectiles around her.

Tank must have prioritized repairing his weapon systems first, because he managed to charge his plasma blast. He aimed at a waiting Facet, her arms pointed to amplify and channel the blast at Báthory.

Extinguisher spiraled up over the shuddering block of stone, hands rimmed in a blue corona as Epic sped in with startling speed.

Just as the stone block exploded into fragments, everyone attacked in rapid succession. The air seemed to tear asunder from the violence of their collective onslaught.

Dust and debris swirled through the air as my eyes cleared. I couldn't make out what the end result of the assault was until Epic emerged from the cloud, violently ejected by some tremendous, unseen force.

Hexagon was the next thrown aside like a rag doll.

There was no way to defeat Báthory like this. I just had to hope everyone could stay alive long enough for me to stop Mackenzie.

I cleared my head and concentrated. Just like I'd embraced my role in this new reality, Mackenzie had as well, whether he admitted it or not. He'd slipped into the Whiteout's thinking several times already – trying to kill a loyal henchman, putting me in a deathtrap, and leaving a taunting message that gave away vital clues.

Where would a master planner, the villain who always struck from the shadows, hide himself where he could watch his enemies be destroyed? He'd find a way to hide in plain sight, as a personal testament to his guile and cunning.

I stopped myself, trying not to listen to the sounds of pain and fury of battle as my team, my family, fought for their lives. My enhanced senses scanned the area, and I focused on every out-of-the-way vantage.

That's when it struck me. I'd tuned it out before, but there was a rooftop barricade on the Capitol, right by the golden dome. A few remaining police officers remained ensconced behind it, seemingly untouched.

The squad captain had a very bulky backpack on, and his helmet sat awkwardly on his head.

Without a second thought, I hopped on top of the remains of a broken pillar, using that as a boost to launch myself up to the top of the Capitol's porch.

I got a closer look at the captain. His half-smirk, the sheer look of concentration on his face confirmed it. That man was Mackenzie.

That meant the other police were more of his Hog flunkies in uniform. Despite my speed, one managed to spot me and shouted an alarm, but it was too late – I was already rushing the barricade.

I'd make Mackenzie pay for his arrogance or die trying.

Chapter 47

I kicked two Hogs-in-police-clothing in mid-leap. There was a satisfying crunch as both dropped like rocks.

My presence finally registered with the rest of the Hogs, but they were moving in slow motion compared to my focused speed.

Mackenzie, however, reacted instantly, retreating out of my immediate grasp as he drew an automatic pistol.

I kept moving so he couldn't draw a bead on me. I grabbed another goon by his jacket and spun him fully around, just as Mackenzie pulled the trigger. The goon's bullet-proof vest took two shots for me.

"Stop her!" Mackenzie barked, sounding like he'd lost his cool. "She's just a normal woman!" He didn't believe that for a moment, but I supposed he had to tell his minions something to keep them from cutting and running.

I shoved my current dance partner hard in the back, sending him barreling into another of his buddies.

Unlike some Hogs, this batch was smart enough not to fire into a brawl. The two closest to me dropped their rifles and rushed me unarmed, while another stowed her rifle and drew a police baton.

I didn't have time for this - Mackenzie and his device were the real goal. I ducked down and slammed my shoulder into the gut of the faster of my two attackers. When I straightened up, I threw him over my body and into the other goon.

The two crashed hard onto the rooftop, and I turned on the baton wielder. Two steps forward and a knee lift to the chin got her out of my way.

No doubt Mackenzie had stressed the importance of his machine, because the remaining three Hogs formed a defensive line around their leader. Before I could get them, they opened up with a spray of suppressing fire.

Instinct and adrenaline took over as I ran, tumbled, and leaped ahead of their aim. Bullets flew and bounced all around me. A particularly close shot gave me a flesh wound on my left shoulder, but I instantly shut off the pain.

I was aiming for the nearest intact barricade so I could take cover and reassess my approach, and I was almost there.

One of the Hogs must've anticipated that, too, because just as I tumbled behind cover, the familiar shape of a stun grenade dropped behind the barricade with me.

But, after the battle in the sewers, I was ready for something like this. I immediately scooped the grenade up and tossed it right back into the Hogs.

The shouts of alarm were music to my ears as I dropped behind the barricade. The brilliant flash of magnesium lit up the rooftop, and the thunderous concussion from the explosion drowned out the battle below for a moment.

While I couldn't be sure, the screams of pain told me at least some of the Hogs didn't make it behind cover. Mackenzie must've been in focus, just like me, so I couldn't assume he was blinded or stunned.

Whatever their condition, the Hogs didn't let that stop them from spraying and praying. Bullets ricocheted off the barricade and surrounding rooftop, and quite a few cut the air overhead.

Between the wild gunfire and Mackenzie waiting for his own shot, I was still pinned down. I needed to do something and fast.

A crazy idea struck.

My uniform wasn't bullet-proof, no matter how tough it was. Few things were. But the armored barricade I leaned against was plenty bullet-proof. As it was meant to be broken down and set up quickly by a squad, it even had handles mounted on the side.

If Mackenzie wouldn't come to the mountain, I'd take the mountain to Mackenzie.

I grabbed hold of the barricade and began to lift. This would normally be a four-man job, but I trusted in my enhanced strength. My muscles strained almost to their limit.

Almost.

With a cry of effort, I lifted the barricade off the ground and held it in front of me like an oversized shield.

"That's no normal woman," one of the remaining Hogs muttered.

On that note, I charged. Bullets slammed into the barricade as I charged right into the Hogs. The sudden impact of bodies against my shield and the resultant cries of pain on the other side told me I'd plowed through their frontlines.

Just to be sure I tossed the barricade down, right on top of them. The remaining Hogs were either unconscious from the impact or pinned by the barricade, but I was now mere feet from Mackenzie.

He had his gun aimed unwaveringly at my head. I could see cords coming out of the backpack he was wearing, going up into his helmet. "You're not going to stop this, Doctor Roman."

I stared defiantly down the barrel, watching for any twitch of his trigger finger. "Are you so sure of that, Mackenzie?"

A flare of light shone from behind me as the team was shouting over the comms.

"Get Báthory off Epic and Facet, team," Extinguisher ordered. "If we can't keep them safe, it's game over. Indy just needs a little more time."

"Those Crusaders are letting too many vampires through," Medusa hissed.

"I'm out of bolts, friends, my apologies," Archer reported. "But I'll fight with my bare hands, until my last breath."

Mind's Eye sounded like she was panicking, something she'd never done in my presence. "I don't know how, but my telekinetic shields are fading. I can't keep them away from Tank anymore!"

I growled. It wasn't Elizabeth Báthory that was killing my friends - it was Ian Mackenzie.

"Enough of the heroic bravado." Mackenzie tried to sound calm and collected again, but his voice trembled. "I'll give you one last chance - help me fix all this. Your friends dying down there? Never happened. All the people I killed to get here? Alive once more. It's so simple. Please."

In his eyes, I could see that, somewhere deep down, there was a man who wanted to make it all better, just like Epic did when he changed the world.

Too bad I'd seen Mackenzie's arrogance and ruthlessness, as well.

No matter how smart he was, I didn't think it'd be enough to filter the trauma out of his thoughts. If Mackenzie ever had his chance to remake the world, he'd create something just as bad as Epic's world. Maybe worse.

My answer wasn't words, but action. I ducked low and to one side as I lunged like greased lightning at Mackenzie.

Though I was faster than he was, Mackenzie's reflexes were still remarkable. He pulled the trigger, but my movement threw off his aim.

Instead of blowing my head off, his shot grazed my ear.

Before Mackenzie got another shot, I swatted at the gun with enough force to break his wrist.

As the gun skittered uselessly away, the resolve in Mackenzie's eyes flickered for the first time. White motes gathered around him, and the storm overhead faded in direct proportion.

"Next time, Indomitable."

I didn't know what he was doing, and I didn't care. I threw all my strength into a haymaker aimed at his face. In a last-ditch effort to save himself, Mackenzie turned away from the blow.

My punch missed his face, but it slammed into the backpack presumably containing the God machine instead of his head. A crunch of metal and a spray of sparks erupted from the pack.

A look of existential horror crossed Mackenzie's face as the white motes suddenly exploded around him with blinding light.

When my vision cleared, Mackenzie was gone, leaving behind only a smoking helmet filled with electrodes and a charred mark on the Capitol's roof.

"What the hell just happened?" Brooks shouted over the comms. "That storm's just disappearing."

"Wow, I feel like a million bucks," Hexagon hooted.

"Irene did it, guys," Extinguisher called out, pride and relief in his voice. "Let's wrap this up double-time. Mind's Eye, Tank, Hex, sweep the minions back. Meds, try to petrify

Báthory again – you might have better luck this time. I'll cover Facet and Epic. Do it!"

I smiled and walked to the edge of the roof, my hand pressed to my hurt shoulder.

As Brooks had reported, the storm clouds overhead were rapidly fading away as moonlight began to shine down on the battle-torn streets below me.

At the center of the lawn, Epic concentrated, and a white circular portal opened, cascading pure, warm sunlight out of it. Facet stood, stance wide and feet planted, in the path of that light.

As she bathed in it, the Sun's rays reflected, intensified, and refracted through the millions of facets that comprised her body.

The weakest of the vampiric hordes began to run at the first sign of daylight. Báthory, stubborn to the end, lunged at the threat, despite being half-stone.

But Mind's Eye shoved the vampire countess back with an invisible telekinetic wave, then Extinguisher froze Báthory's legs to the ground. Seeing their chance, Hexagon and Medusa each grabbed one of Báthory's flailing arms while Tank brandished a glittering Star of David in her face.

My entire world lit up, like it had six months prior. But, instead of the blank void of the Whiteout, I was surrounded by warm, radiant sunlight, bright but not blinding.

The light projected out in all directions from Facet's living crystal body, from the cut angles of her muscles to the tiny planes of her eyes.

Once more, the air was filled with screams, but they weren't the screams of my friends or the innocents they protected. They were the unholy death throes of the undead.

Whenever the sunlight struck one of the vampires, said vampire swelled like an overdone hot dog and exploded into a messy spray of rotting tissue and stolen blood.

Countess Elizabeth Báthory didn't explode like the others. Instead, the rays of sunlight pierced her ashen form like arrows. Each shaft obliterated more and more of the stain of evil from the Earth.

She didn't scream as she was destroyed. Instead, she looked up, straight into my eyes.

I couldn't tell if it was some shred of humanity that thanked me for her reprieve or the darkest depths of the ancient evil inside her that cursed my soul.

Either way, a shudder ran through my spine as she blew away.

Ashes to ashes, dust to dust.

We'd done it. We'd saved our city. I could barely believe it.

It wasn't all sunshine and rainbows, though. How many policemen, firefighters, and average citizens had died from Mackenzie's insane scheme?

But I took heart knowing that we'd avenged the deaths, and this city would, indeed, see a brighter dawn in the morning.

As Extinguisher raced up on his ice slide, worry in his eyes, I could only smile.

Chapter 48

Extinguisher's coat was in tatters and he had more than a few slowly bleeding wounds, as well as a swollen ear. How nice, we'd match.

"Irene, are you –"

"Okay? I'm doing great. Just a couple of flesh wounds." I pointed to my arm and ear, then glanced down from the porch of the Capitol building. "Give a girl a lift?"

"My pleasure." Extinguisher offered me a hand which I gladly took.

"How bad off are we?" I asked as we spiraled back down to where the others, my friends as well as Epic and his Crusaders, were gathering.

Almost as if decreed by natural forces, the two groups had separated and now stared at each other across an invisible divide.

"No one on our team's dead, if that's what you're asking. We're a lot worse off than the Crusaders, though."

"Then let's be gracious hosts and not pick a fight," I broadcast across the team's comms.

That got noises of assent in general, but Ken spoke up the loudest and the angriest. "Tank, can you put us here at the Foundation on speaker? I want a word with my *old friend*, and Rachel wants to say her piece, too."

"Sure, those are one of the few things I got that're still working, and I want you to tell Epic off for real," Tank replied with relative brevity.

As we landed, I took the seemingly open spot in our line-up opposite Epic. I'm sure I wasn't the only one who noticed that Archer still stood at the fringes of our group, checking on Medusa's wounds instead of falling in step with his Lord Epic.

"It would appear that we've won the day," Epic offered. "What has become of the terrorist Ian Mackenzie?"

The wounds the demigod had suffered were already healed, and Extinguisher's assessment of the other Crusaders was correct. They were barely scratched up.

I stood up straight, trying to look as strong as possible. "He tried to use his God machine when he realized I was about to take him out, but I hit the machine itself. I think something went very wrong, and he poofed."

I shrugged. "I don't know if he survived or was blown to atoms or erased from reality or what."

"Unfortunate," Epic rumbled. "I would've preferred to see him face Crusader justice. He has committed great crimes against the Pushed."

"And a lot more crimes against normal folks," Hexagon pointed out. "So, if anybody deserves to get custody of Mackenzie, it's us. That way, the courts would decide his fate."

"As if we could ever trust human governance to make the right decision. Seeing as Reaper still lives, slumbering in their prison like a dog waiting to be unleashed. We should search now and find Mackenzie before –"

"It's a moot point," Choi said through Tank's speakers, surprising every Pushed on both sides. "He escaped, so no one is taking him for anything. There are more important matters to deal with."

Even I was a bit shocked. It took something special for a normal human to speak up to any Pushed, let alone interrupt the most powerful one on the planet.

"Rachel is absolutely correct," I said. "We have loads of casualties, a ravaged city center, and who knows how much property damage. We can't even be sure that we kept the vampires from killing any of the city government."

"Yeah, man." Ken didn't even try to hide his anger. "Do the right thing, Eric, and help set things right before you start throwing your weight around."

Epic's godly form looked cross, but there was still a twinge of hurt in real Eric's face underneath. "Kenneth, this is neither the time nor the place for mortals to in interfere in the affairs of gods."

"Us interfere in *your* affairs? You're the one that interfered in *everyone's* affairs. If you hadn't, *none of this* would've happened. That makes you responsible for *all* this, so the least thing you can do is to fix some of it. It'll never make up for how you betrayed us, but it's a start."

Epic paused for a shocked moment, but the surprises were still coming as Archer, of all people, stepped up to Epic.

"Dame Choi, Sir Louis, and Indomitable present a fair point. After all, don't we have a duty to the normal as well as to the Pushed? We can get the wounded medical attention and lend a hand in the rebuilding, at the very least."

A few of the other Crusaders nodded in agreement, Fray Justicia in particular. "*Señor* Archer speaks the truth, Epic," the masked man said. "It is a blessed thing to give comfort to the needy."

"Of course, my Crusaders." Epic's tone was parental and almost condescending. "It's always been our way to protect all people, Pushed or normal."

Epic turned to me. "Indomitable, we'll shelve the matter of Mackenzie's fate for now and carry on with our most vital of duties."

He smiled, then. I didn't like that smile, not one bit. "Before we begin, however, I'd ask your permission to use the full extent of my powers. We've had conflict before, and

I wouldn't wish to have it again, so soon after we've come together to defeat a common foe."

I could feel Extinguisher bristle beside me. I figured he was getting the same bad feeling I was.

The problem was that we didn't have a choice. It was more important to help the people of Atlanta than ask the Crusaders to leave the city. All we could do was prepare for the inevitable double-cross.

"Considering it'd be one of the few good causes you've put all that power behind," I said, "sure, be my guest. With you lending a hand, we can at least fix most of the damage and attend to the wounded."

Epic nodded and turned swiftly in mid-air, his crimson half-cape billowing around him. "Come, my Crusaders, to work!"

With that command, they broke off in different directions, each apparently well-drilled in the part they were meant to play.

Archer lingered behind for a moment, glancing at me and Extinguisher. Extinguisher gave Archer a brief nod, releasing him to his own teammates.

"Anyone feel in good enough shape to spread out, help out, and keep an eye on those guys?" Extinguisher asked as soon as the Crusaders had taken off. "Outside of Archer, I don't trust them farther than I can throw them. If you need to be patched up, though, don't play hero and sit your ass down, okay?"

He was looking at me when he said that, but I didn't put up a fuss. I just sat down on a flat chunk of rubble.

At least the bullet wounds were grazes. My ear had already stopped bleeding, and my shoulder would be fine between some first aid and my own fast healing.

"I can go because –" Tank began, but Mind's Eye, Extinguisher, and I all turned as one.

"No," we said in unison.

"Oh, uh, okay, I guess I'll sit here and do more self-repairs and let Ex look over me just in case, huh?"

Mind's Eye put a hand on Tank's shoulder and favored him with a thin smile. "That's good. Besides, you can keep me company while I rest."

Hexagon saluted. "Don't worry none, Ex. I'm already healing up, so I'll keep an eye on our guests."

Like any good Boy Scout or rescue worker, Extinguisher always had a medical kit in his own utility bag. That plus supplies scavenged from the area around us let him set up a triage station.

To the credit of the citizenry, now that calm had come to pass, the survivors came out from their shelters to begin to care for those who hadn't been so lucky.

The thing was that, as far as I could tell from Hexagon's reports, the Crusaders were doing what we ourselves would do if most of us weren't about to keel over. Saving lives, helping ambulances get through the wreckage, shoring up crumbling infrastructure – the real meat and potatoes of heroism.

I never imagined they didn't do these things, but when faced with a foe in a perpetual conflict, the human mind tended to dehumanize their adversary.

In fact, I couldn't stop hearing Mackenzie's theory about Archer in my ear. Was this just one more step in that campaign to humanize the Crusaders and make us drop our guard?

Facet and Medusa joined Hexagon, while Mind's Eye used her psychic powers as she rested physically.

But would that be enough? Even if we got whiff of foul play on Epic's part, could we stop him before he summoned up the hundreds of Crusaders at his beck and call?

I had a sinking feeling.

Still, despite my paranoia, the next hours passed with no conflict. There were even a few moments of cooperation between the Five and Crusaders along the way.

As much as I hated to admit it, having someone with Epic's nigh-infinite power on hand for this kind of clean-up made a tremendous difference.

While there was still a considerable bit of work left to do, the amount that the Crusaders had managed to fix in that short space of time was admirable.

Choi was the one who called for a pause in our collective efforts.

While we'd been busy licking our wounds and dealing with the aftermath, she'd managed to get through to the city and state government, as well as Captain Braxton.

She then transmitted Braxton's request that we gather, Foundation and Crusader alike, at the crumbling front steps of the Capitol building.

Fortunately, Extinguisher had finished patching us up to the best of his ability by then, and Tank's self-repairs got him mostly operational. We were still rough, but in surprisingly good shape from the battle we'd been through.

"I - well, I don't mean to hold up the fine work all your people are, well, doing for our fair city," Braxton said nervously, "but the Mayor and the Governor both wanted me to personally, uh, extend their gratitude to both of your groups for, well, saving the city."

Epic smiled like a kindly god. "Though the Mayor has remained distant from my overtures to her in the past, I'm very pleased to see that she's now realized what an asset our kind can be to the city."

"Well now, I wouldn't, uh, put it quite like that, Mister Epic. While she's, uh, appreciative of this, the Mayor is still pretty set that she doesn't want the Crusaders as a fixture of, uh, the city." He glanced at us, then back at the Crusaders.

Was the Mayor trying to start *The Battle of Washington Episode Two – The Crusaders Strike Back* right now? I glanced at my friends, then across the divide at Archer. We were all tense in anticipation, and Archer seemed especially uncomfortable.

"I see." Epic was silent for a few moments. "I'd hoped that, in light of all that had transpired, she'd see the error of that judgment." He took a deep breath and let it out in a slow sigh. "If that is her wish, we will abide by it."

"Please don't attack –" Braxton began to plead. "Wait, what did you say?"

I had to admit, I wasn't sure I'd heard Epic correctly either.

"There's no need for additional bloodshed today," Epic reiterated.

I was more wary now than I'd been, but everyone else seemed greatly relieved. Epic turned away from Braxton and began to hover down towards the street. The rest of the Crusaders fell in line, save for Archer.

He seemed frozen, as if his armor had locked up, but I didn't think that was the case. He turned his visor towards us, as if he wanted to speak.

"Archer." Epic's voice was deep, resonant, commanding. "It is time to go."

"No." Archer turned back to his lord. "You don't mean to go. I cannot be a party to this cowardly act."

Epic blew Archer off his feet with a single, intense blast of white energy. He tumbled hard and smashed against the wall of the Capitol building.

"You forced me to act before my plan came to fruition. For that, you can join your new friends in the dust of history."

I didn't wait for the rest of the incoming monologue as I moved. Everyone else would gape and listen, making it the perfect time to strike.

Even so, by the time I'd crossed the space between Epic and myself, a dozen glowing portals opened. Epic had decided that he preferred the way of the conqueror more than the way of the diplomat as a dozen Crusaders poured out.

"I declare that this city is under the domain of the Crusaders!"

Chapter 49

I had the distinct satisfaction of driving a stiff uppercut right into Epic's smug mouth right after he said that. I gritted my teeth as his invulnerable shell sent vibrations up my arm but, unlike every other time I'd hit Epic, I knew what I was doing now.

Instead of breaking my bones then passing through, the discomfort faded fast before I pushed hard, busting Epic's lip and sending his head rocketing back.

He might've summoned enough Crusaders to take the city twice over, with more on the way, but I'd be damned if he was going to get away with it without paying a price.

Wavelength, as fast in action as the light she manipulated, let loose a rainbow wave of energy in defense of her leader. The blast of multicolored light accomplished nothing but giving me mild sunburn.

She wasn't alone in closing ranks. Battalion, apparently all too eager to start the invasion, swung the two massive Pushtech rifles he wielded in my direction, only to be flash-frozen in a slab of ice.

"Keep them off Indy," Extinguisher called out over the com as he sent a spray of jagged ice shards into the bulk of the Crusaders. "She takes out Epic, and it's game over for them, no matter how many of us fall in the process."

It didn't surprise me that the only response to that suicidal order was for each and every one of my friends to call out targets.

It gave me all the more reason to take out six months of pent-up aggression on the man that caused all of this.

Covering his bleeding mouth with one hand, Epic swatted at me with his insane might. It was a crude swing that would've been a joke if not for the man throwing it.

I bobbed under the blow, my hair flying from the tremendous wind it left in its wake.

The problem with fighting a flying opponent was their three-dimensional movement. Epic knew that and started to fly up and away from me.

Before he could pick up speed, I threw myself at him. All I needed was to get a solid hold on the real Eric underneath.

Epic put on a burst of speed, but I managed to get a grip on his left ankle. That's when he blasted straight up. Whatever physics-defying means Epic used to fly seemed to protect me from the wind to a degree, but I was still jerked painfully.

Every joint screamed in pain, and there were only moments before I'd slip free and fall.

I screamed and pulled, finding the strength to throw my dangling legs up at Epic's ascending body. When taking on a god, I figured it's okay to fight dirty, so I smashed my boots into Epic's crotch.

Unfortunately, I couldn't properly slow then push the strike through his invulnerable skin. The backlash rattled my body and shook my injured right arm free.

The good news was that the low blow arrested Epic's ascent before we reached the airless void that would kill me instantly. The bad news is that I was only holding on with one weakening hand.

"Irene," Epic shouted above the roaring winds. "You can't stop this!" The strain in his voice gave me a grim smile. "Now, take my hand and end this foolishness. I want you by my side, not under my heel."

He bent over in mid-hover, as one Herculean hand stretched out to me.

It wasn't every day the bastard that betrayed your love and stole your life's work offered you one of his limbs. I took his hand, and Epic's strong grip made it easy to pull myself up close enough to drill another punch into his face.

"You *will* end it, Epic!" I screamed with all my fury. His head rocked back before coming up, only to meet my fist again. "You're the one attacking my home. You're the one who betrayed my trust. Alma's trust. Ken's trust." I punctuated every sentence with another punch. "You're the cause of this."

No matter how powerful Epic was, Eric was a mortal man, and those punches rattled him, busting his lip and his nose in the process. His grip on me lessened, and we both started to fall through space.

I didn't care, not one bit. Grabbing the collar of Epic's stupid toga, I twisted us in mid-fall so he'd hit first, one fist cocked back ready to punch him again. "Answer me, you bastard - why are you invading Atlanta now?"

"You proved you can't protect this city yourself. What else would you have me do? Can you not see your own failure?"

I growled and let my fist fly, but there was a pulse of white light, and he was gone. Teleported away, the coward.

That left me with a very real problem. The Earth was rushing up to greet me at an alarming rate, and one of the few things I didn't have in my utility bag was a parachute.

I had a brief flash of regret when Epic materialized right next to me. Not regret for beating him up, but regret that plowing into the Earth at terminal velocity would be less painful than what he was about to do to me.

Epic rocketed into me from the side. There was no way to dodge, and no amount of twisting in the air could help. All I could do was curl up into a ball and pray I didn't go splat when he hit.

Pain rocketed through my body as he plowed into me. If I'd been a normal human, I'd have exploded into chunky salsa. Even with my Natural defenses, I was lucky that nothing was broken.

Just after the impact, another white flash signaled another teleport before I could retaliate in any fashion.

As I tumbled through the sky, now hurtling both down and sideways, I tried to focus past the churning in my stomach to find him before he could strike again.

I could've called on my friends to help but, from the sounds on my comms, they were barely staying alive themselves.

Epic appeared in a blink of an eye, one hand shooting out at inhuman speed. Before I could block him, his hand was snug around my throat. My stomach took another wild tumble as my momentum instantly dissipated, leaving me hanging as his hand tightened ever so slightly.

"This is the end of your games, Indomitable." His voice was cold, hard now. There was no Eric there, only Epic. "I do love you. I want to share the utopia I'm creating with you."

He squeezed ever so much harder, Eric's real fingers around my throat now, and I grabbed his wrist to relieve some of the pressure.

"At the same time, I have a greater duty to create that utopia. Your defiance can no longer be tolerated." His gaze narrowed, filled with blinding white light. "Will you stand down. or will I snap your neck? Healthy or crippled, you *will* sit by my side."

This was the sign that there was nothing of the Eric Beck I'd loved within Epic. Maybe there never had been.

Before Epic decided to make that snap, I swung my legs up, scissoring his arm as I squeezed the real Eric's wrist with all my enhanced strength. I was nowhere near as strong as a superstrong Pushed, but I was more than strong enough to break Eric's normal human bones.

Epic's grip went limp as he roared with pain.

"There's my answer, Epic. You take us down to the ground, or I'll snap the rest of your bones, one by one."

It was no mock threat, and Epic knew it. Fear flashed in the real eyes behind the god-like mask.

Just to speed the process along, I started to apply pressure on his elbow. I only hoped that I was so closely grappled with him that he couldn't teleport without taking me along for the ride.

"Very well, woman." Our speed and course angled downward. "I'd be careful what you wish for, though. Your allies are dangerous, but there's a reason why I've amassed such a large following."

"Spare me. Seeing you like this should give the Crusaders a sobering look at their overall chances."

Epic scowled, trying to process a witty comeback through the pain. But he didn't have my Natural abilities, nor did he undergo six months of hardship and pain to toughen him up.

Still, he wasn't entirely wrong. Unless the Crusaders instantly rolled over, there was no way we could hold out much longer.

We landed on top of an office building a good distance from the Capitol.

"This isn't the ground," I snarled.

"I know." Epic snapped his fingers and glowing portals shimmered in the air all around us. I could hear hurtling metal in the distance, like a train hurtling down the tracks of multiple tunnels. "I truly apologize for this, Indomitable. I wish there'd been another way."

There was no time to snap his arm. I kicked off and madly scrambled away as six sedans, no doubt pulled from places all over the planet, hurtled out of the portals and smashed down where Epic was standing.

The tremendous impact sent a shockwave across the roof of the building. The blast caught me in the back and threw me perilously close to the ledge.

Debris and wreckage shot out at every angle. A muffler, of all things, slammed into the back of my head.

My perception spun as my head shot forward from the impact. If I wasn't immediately concussed, it was a miracle. I tried to stop myself, but I continued to lurch forward.

Only the fact I couldn't keep my balance saved me from a fall over the edge. Instead, I flopped over a few feet short.

I rolled and sat up to see Epic shoving the crumpled remains of the cars aside. He emerged from the twisted wreckage unscathed.

"The mistake I've made in dealing with you before is that I've attacked you too directly. You can injure me with shocking ease, but my energy projections are mostly ineffectual against you. While I may be able to hurt you with a punch or a kick, you've grown far more skilled in hand-to-hand combat than I have."

I took advantage of his monologuing to will the world to stop spinning.

"What I can do is throw the world you consider to be real at you." Epic absently picked up the crumpled rear end of one of the cars in his good arm, like it was a piece of fluff. "Like this."

He lobbed the entire rear end like a softball in my general direction. I barely rolled out of the way as the mass of metal tore off a man-sized chunk of the roof.

"The whole world is my weapon, and you can't dodge it forever." To back up his threat, Epic gestured grandly, and every piece of wreckage hovered up, surrounded by white light.

I could only curse under my breath and start running.

Chapter 50

Twisted metal and shards of glass cut the air around me as I ran, tumbled, and dodged. The only hope in hell I had now was that Epic, in his infinite arrogance, would toy with me for a while and make a stupid mistake.

There was no escape. The roof access was wrecked in the initial crash, and jumping off the roof was a no-go. There was nothing close enough in height to make that survivable.

I skidded to a halt as a car hood spiraled like a pizza cutter right in front of me, gouging up the roof. That was far too close for comfort.

"What shall I use next? I could use this building. I could use the people in it. I could rip the sun asunder if I so wished - I've already summoned its power as a weapon today. I'd do it all for Utopia."

White energy engulfed the air conditioning equipment and the satellite dishes before they ripped free of their moorings

"Utopia?" I turned on him. Let him shred me to pieces - I'd get my final say.

"Do you even know what that means? The future you've talked about for the past six months isn't safe. It isn't secure."

I pointed out across the sea of buildings, at the masses of people in them. "You may have all the power in the universe to keep them under your thumb, but what does that make you, Epic? Their tyrant, that's what. Do you really think, Whiteout or not, they will accept that?"

"What do you know, Indomitable? Many places have opened their arms, happily I may add, to me and my

Crusaders. So many people live in fear and, to allay that fear, they want strength."

He pointed at me accusatorily. "You haven't provided that, so they continue to flock to me. I am no tyrant - I am a savior."

"I think if you used that massive power of yours to read their minds and peek into their hearts, you'd find that their fear hasn't disappeared. It's shifted to fear of you and what your wrath might bring if they disobey."

"You'd be disappointed. Not surprising, as you don't get it. *You* are the one that is an outlier, that refuses to accept the inevitability of reality. A dinosaur from a past age, like the vampires we laid to rest."

Epic gestured widely around him. "This is my world, Indomitable. I made it with my mind and soul. It may not be the perfect world I envisioned, but it *is* mine. I made a place in it for you, but you refuse it."

He opened his arms to me. "Please, I beg you, take your place by my side and end this mad conflict now."

To be technically accurate, he was right. I *was* the dinosaur, the base creature that refused to evolve. Would the Whiteout have progressed better if I'd never questioned Epic? If I'd just done what he'd asked from the beginning?

No. Because he was wrong, in a way he'd never realized.

He thought I'd refused the place he made for me in this madcap comic book reality. To be fair to him, I'd done exactly that for months.

But now I'd opened my eyes and realized the truth. I'd embraced my role in the world, a role Epic didn't even understand. I was here to be the other side of Epic's coin.

He'd wanted a sidekick - a lesser but linked superheroine to work by his side and sing his praises.

That wasn't me, though. Instead of Jimmy Olsen, I was Wonder Woman with a liberal splash of Batman. I didn't bow to him. I challenged him, questioned him, and when he committed evil, I fought him to uphold a higher principle.

I started to approach him, then. Though Epic watched me, he must have assumed I was coming to embrace him. He made no defensive moves as I broke into a run.

Only at the last moment did he realize I'd clenched my fists, far too late to stop me from punching him hard in the stomach.

Shock and surprise were etched on Epic's face as he folded like a house of cards.

"Maybe you're right," I growled as I grabbed him by the hair to drive his face into my knee. "Maybe I am the hold-out."

Left and right, I snapped off two kicks aimed at his kidneys. "But you're wrong."

He clutched his sides, howling in pain. Epic's outer shell cushioned the blows somewhat, but they all struck the human inside.

I spun once - very risky, but I had the advantage now - and landed a spinning back-fist right across his jaw. I felt something crack as blood and a tooth flew out of Eric's mouth.

"Even if the entire world tells you something wrong is right, you put your foot down and stand against it."

Epic spun with the momentum of the impact before he collapsed on his hands and knees. He finally was experiencing some fraction of the pain his Whiteout had caused me and countless others, and it didn't look like he was handling it well.

I stood over him, looking down with a strange mixture of triumph and pity. "Your world is wrong, Epic, and I'll always stand against it."

Epic looked up, trying to rally himself, but his godly features were already diminished. His confidence had finally shattered, and his powers faded with it.

"Now, stand down and help me fix it."

For a moment, I thought I'd won but, more importantly, that *the world* had won. Epic was about to crack, and I could convince him to work with me and properly fix this.

Not some heavy-handed solution like Mackenzie wanted, more like a tune-up. No one would have to suffer, and no one would forget the bloody lessons we'd witnessed.

It was a glorious thought. Too bad it fell apart when I realized that we weren't alone anymore.

"Step away from him, Indomitable, and surrender!"

At a quick count, there were at least a dozen Crusaders arrayed around me, looking all too eager to rip me to pieces.

I sucked in a tight breath as I considered my options. Had Epic gated in these Crusaders when I wasn't looking? No, they must've come after the initial wave of invaders, those that could get to Atlanta under their own power.

I had to know a few things before I decided how to answer the Crusaders' demand.

Epic was still bowed and broken at my feet when I glanced at one of the nearby Crusaders. Twister, I thought his name was, probably because he was sitting suspended by a spinning cyclone.

From the drooping moustache to the Wild West inspired get-up, he looked the part of a superhero sheriff, and he was clearly the spokesman of this particular bunch.

"Where are my friends?" I demanded. "If you've killed any of them…" I raised my boot above Epic's head.

"No, of course not," Twister replied in a Texas drawl. "We're not the bad guys here, Miss Indy."

"That's rich. You're the ones that attacked us."

There was an uncomfortable murmur among the Crusaders. Epic seemed to be slowly recovering, but I knew for a fact that he'd never gotten the crap kicked out of him before. It would be a while before he got to his feet.

"I'm sorry about that, but it was necessary." Twister didn't sound entirely convinced, but he stuck to his guns. At least he was loyal. "The Atlanta Five, Facet, and Argent Archer are in custody but safe. Now, are you going to make us fight you, or are you going to give up?"

I contemplated what to do. I could finish it now, deprive the Crusaders of their leader and maybe provide hope for everyone else fighting against them.

Of course, that would turn me into a murderer. That wasn't the woman I was or the woman I wanted to be. But maybe it'd be worth it.

Those thoughts were interrupted by a crackle in my earpiece. "Irene, give up," Choi whispered harshly. I could only guess she'd escaped, hopefully with Brooks and Ken. "I've got a plan. You must trust me, or we have no chance."

Part of me wanted to ignore the buzzing in my ear, just like a part of me wanted to stomp Epic's head into a bloody pulp.

However, my trust in Choi was far stronger than those violent whispers. As much as I hated the idea, I raised my hands over my head.

"Fine. I surrender." As Twister and another Crusader came up to me with some rather massive manacles, I smiled.

"Just remember what you saw here. Remember who was kneeling before whom."

With absolute confidence, I held out my hands so they could clap those heavy chains on. "I'm going with you to ensure my friends' safety, not because I can't beat every single one of you."

Given the careful gazes and wide berth the other Crusaders gave me as they moved to collect their beaten god, I think they believed me.

I smiled brightly as Twister and another flying Crusader scooped me up under the arms to fly me away. That smile only unnerved them more, as if they didn't understand what was going on.

In their eyes, we'd lost.

But that wasn't true. Sure, this was a setback, but we'd saved the people of Atlanta, cleansed the world of an ancient evil, and I'd personally shown the Crusaders that they couldn't beat me, no matter what they threw at me.

Most importantly, like Epic, the Crusaders didn't understand who Indomitable really was.

No matter where they imprisoned me, no matter how thick the shackles or how strong the guards, I'd find a way to break out and escape. I'd come back fighting harder than ever, the proverbial phoenix from the ashes.

Why did I believe that?

Because I was Indomitable. My superpower was that I never gave up, and now that I'd embraced that, there was nothing the Crusaders could do to stop me.

I had to hand it to the Crusaders. They'd really thought out how to imprison me. No "throw her in a prison cell with one guard" nonsense that I'd immediately escape from. I rated far more extreme measures.

After all, I was the woman who'd beaten Epic, the most powerful Pushed on the planet in one-on-one combat, the superhero who'd saved the world from the brink of war among the Pushed. I'd stopped the worst Push Crooks the twisted altered reality of the Whiteout had conjured.

I'd also helped stop a plague of vampires from an earlier age and taken down a madman with abilities like my own before he made things any worse.

Epic's lapdogs, following his warped sense of justice, were intent on breaking me, but they forgot who I was.

I was Irene Roman, ex-scientist, but pretty much the rest of the world knew me as Indomitable, the hero who never gives up. And, as I'd sworn to myself when the Crusaders dragged me to this place weeks ago, I wasn't going to start now.

That was why I was about to start Escape Attempt Nine.

I had a good feeling about the number nine. It was almost ten, which one would anticipate would make for a great break point. So, if this attempt worked, that'd make it a bit of surprise, and one thing the comic book melodrama that was the Whiteout loved was surprises.

I just had to wait a little longer to make my move. Currently, six heavily armed normal humans without a scrap of Pushtech on them - that policy went into effect after Escape Attempt Two - marched me at gunpoint to the Rehabilitation Center. That was the word my personal jailer, Twister, called it, but I preferred the Indoctrination and Torture Room.

Oh, how far the "virtuous and just" Crusaders had fallen after conquering Atlanta.

But the guards weren't the biggest obstacle to my escape, not by far. I'd fought against worse odds, even if my Natural immunity to Pushed powers didn't apply to bullets. The heavy shackles that could hold an elephant were up there in the rankings - they were reinforced after Escape Attempt Three - but still not at the tippity-top.

The overarching problem was how the Crusaders had built this prison, something I got to take in during this little stroll outside my cell.

The drab, slate grey walls were solid concrete, probably reinforced with rebar. I had no idea how thick they were, though I guessed half a yard minimum. While they'd been shaped by Pushed powers, the walls themselves were very, very real.

I could break through a lot of things in my focused state, when my mind and body moved as one and everything was jacked to human perfection and beyond. But these walls and the equally sturdy doors were far too strong for me to overcome with brute force, a fact I'd proven to myself during Escape Attempt One.

"What are we watching today, folks?"

Trying to engage the guards in banter was the usual for me. Not only did it help me stay grounded in my humanity, it annoyed them and distracted them in equal measure. I wanted them good and upset for Attempt Nine.

"Is it going to be *Epic - Savior of the Pushed*? Or maybe *Bow Down to the Crusaders - A Human's Guide to Sucking Up to Tyrants*? I really love that one."

A growl rose up from the guard behind me, the usual preamble to one of my beloved captors trying to hit me, but someone interrupted the fun and games.

"Don't let Miss Indy get to y'all," came Twister's familiar Texas drawl from the door to Rehab. "She's just trying to get you riled."

One of the Crusaders that'd I'd surrendered to after I beat down Epic, the former lawman had air manipulation powers, usually manifesting in cyclones and such. He also had a penchant for dressing like he'd stepped out of a Wild West movie.

"Come on, I was just trying to keep my social skills sharp for my eventual release. But, if you'd prefer, we can start a sports team. I hear full-contact rugby is a great way to blow off steam and build character."

Twister sighed hard enough to make his handlebar mustache flutter. "Guess nothing's changed since yesterday's session. Well, Gaslight and Doc Bio have got a new program ready for you today."

Gaslight and Doc Bio were two members of Epic's inner circle.

Gaslight was a steampunk-style inventor of bizarre but effective Pushtech. Doc Bio had one of the most dangerous and helpful powers one could imagine - biokinesis, the ability to manipulate anything biological, living or dead, down to the cellular level, with only his mind.

That also made me think of my imprisoned friends - the Atlanta Five, Facet, and the Argent Archer - and, most importantly, the leader of the Atlanta Five, the man I loved.

Focusing on any one of them was a shot of motivation to get free and help them, but thinking about Extinguisher - Will - would keep me going no matter what happened.

"Hopefully, this'll do it. Then we won't have to do this anymore. I do respect you, Miss Indy, and I hate that it's going down like this."

The guards marched me up to the door, where only one guard stood between me and Twister. Escape Attempt Eight had started here, and I'd knocked Twister clean out on that one. While it was tempting to kick things off the same way, I knew he'd be ready for it.

"Sure, sure." I shrugged as best I could with thick metal cuffs around my throat, waist, wrists, and ankles. "No hard feelings from me. You're just doing your job. Following orders. I'm sure when they put you and the rest of the Crusaders on trial, that'll exonerate you."

My façade of casualness dropped as I shot him a furious look. "It always works for fascists and tyrants like you. Just ask the Nazis."

That earned me a crack with a rifle butt in the back of my head or, at least, an attempt to do so. Even encumbered as I was, my reflexes were as sharp as ever, and I'd been ready for a reaction.

Moving my head to dodge the oncoming blow, I didn't look away from the now fuming Twister.

"And my daily dose of police brutality to top it off. Oh, that's right. You're not police. You're Epic's personal Gestapo. Might as well trade out that tin star on your jacket for a swastika, Twister."

I was in rare form today. Not that I was telling any lies.

From what had trickled through to me during my time here, the Crusaders had taken over Atlanta in what would be an ideal Push Crook move and somehow kept it apart from the rest of the United States.

Epic wasn't holding any elections, I'd bet my life on it.

My cheekiness served a purpose, though, and it was all to get my captors ready for Escape Attempt Nine.

"Ignore her," Twister barked, just as all the guards started to turn towards me. "She doesn't get it yet, and she's lashing out." While he was clearly trying to sound calm and collected, I could tell I'd gotten deep under his skin this time.

"Maybe you're right." I nodded my head toward the door to Rehab with a clatter of chains. "Let's give it the old college try and see if it all makes sense today, huh?"

Twister narrowed his eyes at me suspiciously. For a moment, I wondered if I'd pushed too hard and he'd bypass my daily indoctrination and move straight to "enhanced interrogation" i.e. torture, but he took in a deep breath.

The normally still air in the prison hallway stirred up with his breathing, then calmed as he let it out slowly. "As much as I'd prefer otherwise, it's my duty to keep at this, so let's get her moving, men."

Twister tapped the plain gold band around his right wrist to the panel beside the door, and it slid open with a hiss. I'd pegged that as a master ID and door key - like a less fun version of an old Disney FastPass.

The guards had similar ones, but in silver, which I guessed meant lower clearances.

The problem I'd discovered on Attempt Eight was that the wristband didn't unlock my manacles. There wasn't even a keyhole in any of the bands. Normally, Twister and the guards called some central security station to get them open and closed again.

I'd hoped that the bands would do it, too, in case of emergencies, but that was a no-go.

As with every other time, Attempt Eight had been a learning experience. That was another reason why I thought Lucky Number Nine was my ticket to freedom.

I played along as the guards ushered me into the room. Like the rest of the prison, the walls, floors, and ceilings were the same featureless grey, save for one wall dominated by a large flatscreen monitor set inside.

Normally, the only furniture was the heavily reinforced chair welded to an anchor I suspected was embedded deep into the floor.

But today must've been special, because the Crusaders had installed a new piece of equipment, no doubt courtesy of the two mad scientists Twister had mentioned.

The chair was already set up with all manner of restraints, a substitute for my manacles which were always removed for time here in Rehab. The chains restricted my movement too much for some of the more violent methods used, and the cuffs covered ideal places for drug injection.

Considering my addiction to painkillers, I really hated the drug parts. A little part of me craved the moments they jabbed the needles into my veins or forced the pills down my throat. The rest of me, with Rational and Whiteout Irene - the other fragments of my subconscious self - helping, kept the addiction at bay, but every day was a struggle.

That never stopped the Crusaders from trying a new drug cocktail. If not for my uncanny healing abilities, I'd probably be in a perpetual drug-induced haze.

This new apparatus was something straight out of the movies. Not just euphemistically either.

The welded-on rig that extended from the headrest was clearly a reinforced version of the equipment for the Ludovico technique from *A Clockwork Orange*.

Strips of metal curved out of the headrest in such a way that they'd wrap around my head all the way to my eyes. At the end of the strips were little clamps, the kind used to hold someone's eyelids open forcefully.

Just perfect to force me to watch whatever mind-control Twister would attempt today.

I couldn't help but notice the injection needles, too. Those weren't in the movie, but they were mounted so that they'd plunge right into the blood vessels of my neck. The whisper of addiction in my head wondered just how much of a high I'd get from that.

Escape Plan Nine had to work, because this might be the step that broke me.

I took a deep breath as the guards maneuvered me towards the chair, Twister keeping in step beside us.

"This won't be comfortable at all, Miss Indy. Just know it's for your own good and the good of the city. We need you on our side, or else all the work we've done to save Atlanta is going to fall apart."

There was a note of real regret there. I didn't think Twister liked his job, but he was still doing it. That made him an enemy.

I shuffled up close to the chair, following the usual procedure. Escape Attempt Four had happened on the first day Twister had me escorted to Rehab and, in desperation, I'd tried to fight my way out before I got too close.

"I've heard it all before. If you're not going to reconsider being Epic's stooge, I'd prefer we save the breath and get this over with."

With that, I held out my wrists and looked up at the ceiling. There were no cameras I could see, but I knew they had to be there.

"Now, are you going to unlock these or what?"

Twister grumbled and, as he moved forward to get ready to lock me down once I'd been released, I brought myself into focus.

A cocktail of adrenaline, endorphins, and other biochemicals flooded my system. My mind and senses sharpened as the world seemed to slow down around me, and fresh strength flooded my muscles.

The real trick was not letting on that I'd done this. It was an act of bodily control I must've managed, because Twister didn't seem to notice as he tapped his earbud.

"Control, open Indomitable's cuffs for Rehab."

While the prison walls themselves were the ultimate hurdle I had to overcome, the manacles and cuffs needed to be dealt with.

They were so rarely removed. The guards didn't even have them removed for eating, showering, or other normal life functions.

Rehab was one of the very few times - the only one I could plan around - but I only had a split-second, because they'd shut as fast as one of the guards could call for it.

I'd held off on making an escape attempt with this loophole so far. I used other attempts to learn the rest of what I needed but, as I said, I liked Lucky Number Nine.

As the cuffs opened, I moved with all the speed and power I could muster. My hands lunged for the cuff around my waist, the central point of connection, and pulled it away from me. The speed at which I moved my arms flung those two cuffs off.

Twister was the first to catch up, his reflexes and instincts honed from his former profession as a police officer. "Close 'em! Close 'em *now*!"

If the last cuffs closed as I tried to remove them, they could break my ankles or crush my throat. I ignored that fear as I flung the waist cuff as hard as I could at the cluster of guards.

The chains and manacles went with the waist cuff. The edges of the closing manacles scraped the sides of my ankles, even drew blood at the sides of my neck, but they were away before they closed completely.

The starfish of chains and cuffs clattered into two of the guards, hitting them hard enough to send them sprawling.

Twister's eyes went wide, the guards scrambled to ready their weapons, but I was already on the attack.

Oh, yeah, I was feeling *really* good about Escape Attempt Nine.

Acknowledgements

First, thanks to my brother, David, who handed me my first comic books to read. Who knew that would spawn a writing career?

Next, thanks to Kate, whose critiques in the past paved the way for my writing to improve in the future.

Many thanks to Jeanne and Steve, whose support and hospitality let me stay happy and writing when things were dark and lonely.

Love and thanks to Dave and Reyn, who were always there for me throughout the years - here's to the future.

As always, the biggest thanks to the amazing editors, artists, and staff of Ginger Blue Publishing. Without them, this book wouldn't have been possible in any way.

About the Author

Talented topflight author and editor Jamie Beth "J. B." Garner has written over twenty novels across multiple genres and edited hundreds more.

J.B.'s been and done many things in her life. She's worked at a haunted attraction, at a diaper factory, and in a candy warehouse, where she swears she only sampled a little of the merchandise. Additionally, she sold Honeybaked Hams over the phone. Yes, really. She was also in a cult, but got better.

In addition to doing so many fascinating things, she's lived in the wonderful cities of Baltimore, Atlanta, and Pensacola, before landing in the beautiful city of Chicago.

She's an avid gamer, particularly Pathfinder and Final Fantasy XIV, an enjoyer of comic books, anime, and movies of all stripes.

She guests, exhibits, and panels at cons across the US, large and small, fueled by a love of fandoms and the desire to connect with readers and fans. Through it all, her true passion has always been the written word.

She writes urban fantasy, sci-fi, and pro-wrestling epics, among other things, and is always out to entertain and amaze.

GINI KOCH

The Alien/Katherine "Kitty" Katt Series

Join Katherine "Kitty" Katt as she helps the gorgeous aliens from Alpha Centauri save the world, solar system, galaxy, and multiverse using her knowledge of pop culture, comics, hairspray, and rock 'n' roll...not necessarily in that order.

(*coming soon*)
TOUCHED BY AN ALIEN
ALIEN TANGO
ALIEN IN THE FAMILY
ALIEN PROLIFERATION
ALIEN DIPLOMACY
ALIEN VS. ALIEN
ALIEN IN THE HOUSE
ALIEN RESEARCH
ALIEN COLLECTIVE
UNIVERSAL ALIEN
ALIEN SEPARATION
ALIEN IN CHIEF
CAMP ALIEN
ALIEN NATION
ALIEN EDUCATION
ALIENS ABROAD

GINGER BLUE

J.B. GARNER

The Push Chronicles

The world changes overnight, superheroes and supervillains are everywhere, causing destruction in their wake. But who protects the regular people now? Indomitable does. This high-octane series is an exciting and thoughtful cross between *Wonder Woman* and *The Boys*.

INDOMITABLE
INJUSTICE

GINGER BLUE

TEMPLE HART

Unnatural Powers

Snappy sapphic superheroes solving secret crimes. Say that five times fast. Or, better yet, just grab this fun series and enjoy the ride while our heroines save the day while trying to bring down a worldwide conspiracy.

THE POWERS THAT BE

(*coming soon*)
FIGHT THE POWERS

GINGER BLUE

GINI KOCH & BEBE BAYLISS

The Fall's Girl Mysteries

Stuntwoman Stacey Weir doesn't mean to be an amateur sleuth - she's just got a natural talent for solving crimes, which is good, because crimes happen around her all the time.

FALL'S GIRL
DECK THE FALLS

The Santa Paloma Mysteries

Sleepy little Santa Paloma is a lovely area filled with retirees and, unfortunately, murder. Fortunately, the Gramma Posse and Samantha, their official and unofficial granddaughter, are there to help the police, whether the police want their help or not.

SOMETHING WICKED

(*coming soon*)
SOMETHING FISHY

GINGER BLUE

GINI KOCH

The Martian Alliance Chronicles

Come fly with the crew of the *Hummingbird* as they take on the galaxy's most awful crime family, one con, caper, and rescue at a time!

THE ROYAL SCAM
THREE CARD MONTE
A BUG'S LIFE

GINGER BLUE

EMELIA QUANTRILLE

Tales of the Walled City

There are a million stories in the architectural marvel that is the Walled City...these are some of them. Epic fantasy meets noir in this compelling series.

SONGS & SORCERY

(*coming soon*)
CONSPIRACIES & CONJURATIONS

GINGER BLUE

GINI KOCH

PLUSH LIFE

Friends to lovers Tom and Meggie are in the middle of the biggest business deal of their lives. But when Meggie's life and sanity are put in jeopardy, only Tom, a street thief, and the Voodoo Queen of New Orleans are going to be able to save Meggie from the devil himself.

GINGER BLUE

GINI KOCH

Collections

MEDIA & ME
MY LOVE/HATE RELATIONSHIP WITH HOLLYWOOD

Reading reviews has never been so fun, or so funny!

RANDOM MUSINGS FROM THE FUNNY GIRL
OR HOW TO MAKE THE MOST OF MULTIPLE PERSONALITY DISORDER

Want to know the untold story of Gini Koch? Is it fact or fiction? You decide.

HAPPY ACRES HOTEL FOR ACTIVE SENIORS
AND OTHER STORIES

This collection brings together some of Gini's best-loved science fiction, fantasy, and paranormal short stories for the first time. Be prepared - laughter is definitely on the horizon.

writing as JEMMA CHASE

THE DISCIPLE AND OTHER STORIES
OF THE PARANORMAL

Get a taste of blood and chocolate and enjoy your journey into the worlds of Jemma Chase. Just remember to bring a map to lead you back to your normal world, because the writer's web is like a maze, and not all mazes have exits.

GINGER BLUE

A.E. STANTON

The Legend of Belladonna

The true story of the West's most notorious female outlaw, the men who love her, hate her, and help her, and why she won't stop until the most evil man alive is in prison...or dead.

NATURAL BORN OUTLAWS

(*coming soon*)
ALWAYS OUTNUMBERED, NEVER OUTGUNNED

The New West

The Old West was hard on woman and horses. The New West is hard on everyone...

THE DAWNING OF THE NEW WEST

(*coming soon*)
RIVERWORLD

GINGER BLUE

JEAN MARIE WARD

Sorcerer vs. Sorcerer

A fun and funny series that's a cross between *Dumb and Dumber* and *Spy vs. Spy*. You'll root for someone...we're just not sure who.

BURNING DOWN THE HOUSE

(*coming soon*)
GLASS TRANSIT

Collections

DRAGONS, CATS, & FORMIDABLE FEMMES

This witty, gritty, and whimsical collection brings together a plethora of offbeat and unexpected tales to entertain and amuse.

GINGER BLUE

Made in the USA
Middletown, DE
06 May 2025

75181147R10219